Freedom's Price

Path to Freedom - Book One

Pegg Thomas

Spinner of Yarns Publishing

S PINNER OF YARNS PUBLISHING
Ossineke, Michigan

Praise For Freedom's Price

Appealing characters and their heart-wrenching dilemmas quickly drew me into Pegg Thomas's latest release, *Freedom's Price*. As always, Thomas portrays the historical setting with vivid, accurate strokes and develops the characters in an engaging way that brings them to life on the page. Gwen Morgan's precarious situation as an indentured servant particularly affected me. The Baldwins, an older couple facing a dangerous migration to a slave-free territory with their Quaker settlement, also captured my heart, as did Micah Pike, whose believably rendered struggle with love and forgiveness deeply resonated. I loved the theme of how God places his children in families and was convicted by the vivid reminder that lies, no matter how justified they may appear, inevitably bring destructive consequences. *Freedom's Price* is a compelling and uplifting story, and I highly recommend it to readers!

—J. M. Hochstetler
Author of the *American Patriot Series*

A secret, an oath, and a bid for freedom—these are the things that send Gwen Morgan from the wealthy North Carolina family who held her indenture on a journey with the Quakers to the Northwest Territory. Much more than a romance—and it's a compelling one—*Freedom's Price* takes readers on Gwen's emotional journey as well, from innocence to maturity, from loneliness to the heart of family, and from fear and bondage to faith. Stirring historical fiction from Pegg Thomas!

—Denise Weimer, multi-published author of

the *Scouts of the Georgia Frontier Series, Bent Tree Bride,* & *The Witness Tree*

Pegg Thomas has written a heartwarming, authentically researched story in *Freedom's Price*. When indentured servant Gwen is offered her freedom by the powerful man who owns her, she has to vow to keep a family secret to avoid scandal. Because she longs to be free and wants to find her sister who is also indentured, she agrees to go along on a wagon train west with a group of Quakers wanting to find a better life. But as Gwen grows close to the kind couple who took her, her secret begins to weigh her down. Then she meets a man who has his own past hurts and begins to think she could be happy with the Quakers. But danger is at every turn and as Gwen grows stronger, she begins to open up to her new family. When her secret is threatened unless she does something immoral, will she tell those she's come to love the truth and risk losing her freedom and her happiness? What price will she pay to be forever free?

—Lenora Worth NY Times, USA Today, and PW bestselling author of *The Forgiving Quilt* & *The Memory Quilt*

Join Pegg's Newsletter

writing updates – sneak peeks – fiber
arts updates – personal content
https://www.subscribepage.com/Pegg
Thomas

DEDICATION

Dedicated to the men and women who came to these American shores—some of their own will and some not—who fought to build and keep a country that would one day include freedom for all.

AUTHOR'S FORENOTE

The Quaker use of thee is not the same grammatically as the Old English use. The Quakers did not use thou, only thee and thy, a variation that they considered more plain.

Acknowledgements

Oh, my... how do I start with the acknowledgments for a book that took twelve years to see print? It started with the germ of an idea to showcase a Welsh immigrant because my father's family immigrated from Wales, while also showcasing the Quaker heritage from my mother's side and honoring the Quakers' dedication to oppose slavery long before that opinion became popular. It also followed my path from writing newbie to published author, trailing in my wake like the proverbial redheaded stepchild.

First to see the early chapters were the good people of the American Christian Fiction Writers Scribes group. Many of them helped me poke and prod the opening of this book into shape.

Realizing I needed something more organized and personal than Scribes if I was going to be serious about writing, I approached Robin Patchen about starting our own critique group, which we dubbed the Quid Pro Quills. All these years later, together with Jericha Kingston, Kara R. Hunt, Candice Patterson, and Susan Crawford, we're still together—all published authors now—and helping each other put out the best books we can.

Then in 2014, I met with literary agent Linda S. Glaz at a writers' conference, and she signed me on as a client based on this story. After shopping it to publishing houses for a couple of years—including numerous requests for the full manuscript—it still hadn't found a home. It doesn't fit the typical romance formula, and that hurt its chances of publication, even though we got many sincere compliments on both the story and my writing. It was frustrating!

It also pushed me into learning formulaic romance and writing it. I'm not complaining, because as soon as I did, I signed three contracts in a year! But my heart hurt for *Freedom's Price* because I knew the story was worthy of print.

Finally, in 2021, when I was pushed kicking and screaming into indie publishing *(thank you, Robin Patchen, you were right all along!)*, I had the option to put *Freedom's Price* out myself. So I re-read the manuscript and cringed throughout the whole process. While the story was solid, my writing had evolved to a much higher level. So I put it away again and focused on my *Forts of Refuge* and *A More Perfect Union* series.

Yet, Gwen's story still spoke to me. So I battled through that initial manuscript and did my level best to bring it up to the standard I'd reached in the twelve years of growth in my writing. The Quid Pro Quills were instrumental in my accomplishing it! My proofreader, Jenny Leo, deserves credit for putting the polishing touches where they needed to be. And my cover artist, Hannah Linder, once again crafted a beautiful, eye-catching cover.

But in the end, I need to acknowledge the One who makes all things possible, Jesus Christ. Without Him, none of this would have happened. He is the true Creator, the Maker of everything, the Inspiration for everything. Forever and ever, amen.

Chapter 1

November 1798

A DOOR HINGE SQUEAKED, and light spilled into the second-story hallway. Gwen Morgan darted behind the brocade drapes drawn across an alcove. She held her breath, ribs tight against her stays, heartbeat pounding in her ears.

Heavy footsteps thumped along the hallway.

Gwen's skin crawled at the memory of the last time he'd caught her alone in the hall. She suppressed a shudder at the thought of his hands tightening on her shoulders, his hot breath in her ear. If Cook hadn't arrived in time—

A floorboard creaked in front of her. With the edge of the tea tray digging into her waist, Gwen pressed deeper into the shadowy alcove. She winced as the molding bit into the flesh between her shoulders. She pinched her eyes shut.

"Jonas!" Frustration vibrated through Daniel Whiteford's bellow. "Where are you?"

Gwen jerked and popped open her eyes. The teacup rattled on its saucer before her trembling hands could secure it.

"Coming, Father." Jonas Whiteford paused in front of the drapes, a moment of silence that shot a ripple of fear through Gwen's belly before his footsteps faded down the hall.

She waited until his boot heels thumped down the front staircase before she slipped from behind the drapes and hurried to Miss Constance's door. She tapped on the thick wood.

"Enter."

Gwen cringed at the imperial tone of her mistress's voice but schooled her features into a servant's expressionless façade before she slipped inside the room.

Miss Constance's mouth pulled into a pout, eyebrows meeting above the arch of her nose. "Where have you been?"

"I'm here now, Miss Constance." Gwen bobbed a curtsy and kept her eyes lowered to the tray in her hands.

"'Tis about time. Put that tray on the dresser and fetch my day gown, the rose linen. 'Twill bring out the color in my cheeks quite nicely, I think."

"Yes, miss." Gwen hustled to do her mistress's bidding. She opened the towering oak armoire which matched the room's honey-hued paneling. Removing the gown, she let her fingers linger over its softness. Her own gray dress was burlap in comparison. Her breath escaped in a wispy sigh. She wouldn't be a servant forever. When her indenture was met, she would own a gown like this. Perhaps one even finer.

"Quit dawdling. I'm waiting."

Gwen fitted Miss Constance's stays over her shift, then tied on the petticoat before slipping the gown over her head and pinning the stiffened stomacher in place. She arranged the skirt to prevent wrinkles as her mistress sat in front of the mirrored dresser.

Her mistress was pale again that morning, but Gwen knew better than to mention it. She hoped Miss Constance wasn't coming down with an illness. As bad as her disposition was on a normal day, it worsened tenfold when she fell ill.

Gwen grabbed a brush off the dresser and set to work on the long locks in front of her. Soon, she had the golden tresses twisted and pinned in place.

"Is that the best you can do with my hair?" Miss Constance leaned forward and frowned into the oval looking glass. "I'm to meet Stanley's mother today. I must make the best impression. If all goes well, I will soon be Mrs. Stanley Landon." Miss Constance examined her reflection, turning from side to side.

Gwen's mistress had pinned her hopes on wedding Stanley Landon. His loose lips, bulbous nose, and paunchy waist repelled Gwen like a spider in her tea. Miss Constance seemed willing to tolerate these things in her desire to be the mistress of his plantation, Bridgewater.

"I could twist and tuck a few tresses higher if it pleases you, miss."

"I have no time for that now. You have dawdled overlong already." Her customary pout returned and marred Miss Constance's otherwise flawless complexion. "This will have to do. Fetch my wrap. You remembered to have that wretched stable boy hitch the horses, I trust?"

"Yes, miss."

"Good. Run and tell Arthur to bring them around."

Gwen drew in a breath at the door and glanced both ways before dashing for the back staircase. Her feet barely landed on each step. At the bottom, the warmth of the kitchen enveloped her with its lingering scents of fresh yeasty bread and spicy sausage. The kitchen was her sanctuary in the house. Mr. Jonas would never enter there.

Cook straightened from the hearth and brushed off her apron. "Perfect timing again this morning, lass?"

"Nay. He opened his door as I reached the hallway. I fear he discovered my hiding spot."

Cook *tsked* and shook her head, tendrils of curly gray hair swinging from each side of her mobcap. She drew a hand across her forehead, leaving behind a faint smear of ashes.

"I heard the master say Mr. Jonas will be leaving in a couple of days for the coast. Mayhap we can devise a better plan to keep you safe by the time he returns."

"I hope so. I must fetch Arthur and the carriage before Miss Constance comes downstairs."

"Hurry, lass, hurry." Cook flapped a towel in her direction.

Gwen scooted out the door. Chickens scattered before her as she trotted to the two-story stable behind the three-story house of matching Flemish bond bricks.

Mark Allen Teed, the Whitefords' stable boy, held the bridles of a matched pair of dapple-gray horses. His slender form dwarfed by the tall animals, he turned as she approached. The morning light sparkled off his hazel eyes.

A grin tugged at the corners of Gwen's mouth.

"A good day to you," he said. "Is Miss High and Mighty ready for the carriage?"

"You mustn't speak that way." But Gwen's voice lacked any sternness, and her grin lingered. "Miss Constance requests Arthur to receive her at the front door."

Mark Allen jerked his head toward the stable. "Be right out, he will. I shall tell him to hurry around front."

"Much obliged." Gwen turned to leave, but he touched her arm.

"When Cook has no more chores for you, might you slip away for a walk?"

She looked into his eyes and gave a quick nod before tucking her chin and hurrying back to the kitchen. At the door, she turned. He still watched her as he calmed the large beasts in his charge.

Mark Allen was the only servant near her age at the Whitefords'. Also indentured, he would be free in a little more than two years, while she had five left to serve. She hated to think about those final years without him there. Loneliness tightened her throat. If only Mr. Whiteford had purchased Faye's indenture along with hers. Her heart twisted at the thought of the sister she hadn't seen in over two years.

"Do not stand there all day. Do you suppose there's someone else to finish your chores?"

Gwen jumped at Cook's voice. She hurried through the kitchen and above stairs to tidy her mistress's bedroom. Neither Mr. Jonas nor Miss Constance would return until supper. The rest of the day she'd be busy but not harassed.

And a walk with Mark Allen would be a nice finish to a fine day.

"When do thee expect them to return?" Betsy Baldwin asked Thomas as she placed a wooden bowl filled with steaming soup, rich with the scents of onions and turnips, on the table in front of her husband.

"I know not. I reckoned they would have by now." He dropped his battered felt hat on the bench beside him.

Betsy eased onto the bench opposite, and they lowered their heads in a moment of silent prayer. She thanked God for the food before them and asked His blessing on the decision to be made when the men returned, a decision that would affect their Society of Friends community, known by most as the Quakers.

Thomas cleared his throat, marking the end of their prayer time.

"The nights are so cold. I hope they make it back before the snow flies." Betsy broke a small loaf of bread and handed half to Thomas. His cold fingers brushed hers.

"Surely they will. So much hinges on the news they bring to us." Thomas dipped his bread in the thick soup. He sank his teeth into the first bite and gave Betsy an approving nod. "Nothing like hot soup on a cold day."

"We are feeling the cold more in our old age, husband."

"True, true, but God is faithful, and He has provided well for our winter months again this year."

"I wonder." Betsy set her spoon down. "Will next year find us so well-stocked? Or will we Friends be traveling to a new home instead of harvesting and storing?"

"'Tis in the Lord's hands. If He leads us, we will follow." Thomas sopped up more soup. "'Tis getting harder and harder to stay here. Just today I watched a man. . ." He shook his head, his bushy gray eyebrows gathered above his eyes. "I cannot tell thee what I saw. The things one man will do to another based upon the color of his skin. It may not be a crime, but I cannot witness much more lest my heart break for sure."

"Thee has witnessed too much sorrow by the docks."

"Which is why I forbid thee from attending there."

"I know." Betsy had no desire to see such atrocities herself.

These past three years, since the legislature had deemed it an unlawful offense to free a Negro slave, Thomas was driven to find their group a new place to live. Her husband carried much responsibility among the Friends in North Carolina. A hardworking wheelwright, he had been elected as part of the group of leaders charged with finding them a new place to live. It was no longer enough to stay outside the city in their own settlement. Their desire was to relocate into the newly acquired Northwest Territory, deemed a free territory where the institution of slavery was banished.

Moving such a multitude of people took careful planning and resources. While Thomas didn't think of himself as a modern-day Moses,

Betsy sometimes pondered the similarities.

She smiled at her husband with a heavy heart. She supported his decision to move, but it came at a cost. Their humble cabin had been their home for more than twenty years. Their children had been born there. Her only remaining connection with their son and two daughters was her weekly walk through the burial plot behind the meetinghouse.

To lose that small comfort tore at her heart.

She turned her face and wiped away a tear before Thomas could see it. He had more than enough worry without her adding more.

Thomas lifted his bowl and rubbed a piece of bread around the inside, collecting the last drop of soup. He'd just returned the bowl to the table when boot heels thumped on the porch. Rapid pounding followed. He raised a brow at Betsy and popped the bread into his mouth.

She rose and hurried to the door.

"We greet thee, Mistress Baldwin. Is thy husband home?" Joseph, Borden, and Amos, faces unkempt, grinned at her. They stood in their grimy travel clothing, hats dangling from their fingers, and dried mud to the tops of their boots. She clasped one hand to her chest and pulled the door open wider with the other.

"Thomas, they have returned." She ushered them inside. Amos ducked under the lintel. The two shorter men stepped in. Betsy sent a silent prayer of thanksgiving for their safe return as Thomas greeted the men with handshakes and back-thumping.

"Welcome! Welcome! Did thee, indeed, find land for us? Is it well placed? Close to water? Is the soil good for farming?"

"Husband, let us offer these men a bit of soup and bread. 'Tis past midday, and they appear to have ridden straight to our door."

"Forgive me, please." Thomas motioned for them to sit at the table. "In my haste, I have neglected to see to thy comforts as my good wife says."

Only after the men were seated with hot soup and bread before them did they tell their story. Betsy listened while she opened apple preserves and pickled beets for the hungry travelers. They wove a tale of adventure and risk, of dodging Indians and surviving a rockslide, before finding what they described as the promised land.

Thomas sat on the edge of his bench, one elbow on the table. He shifted and leaned toward each man as they took turns telling the story. He interrupted with questions often, probing every detail. He nodded and smiled more than he grimaced and shook his head.

It was going to happen. They were going to pack and move the whole settlement.

She paused by the window and cast a lingering glance at the meetinghouse, just visible through the trees. The burial ground lay beyond.

She squared her shoulders and plucked one more crock of preserves off the shelf. God would see them through and give them strength. He always had.

Betsy was going to need it in the coming move more than ever before.

Chapter 2

G WEN SLIPPED PAST THE kitchen door and into the warmth of the midday sun. She twirled, face to the sky, arms outstretched, glorying in a free afternoon. Seldom did she have an hour to herself, much less an entire afternoon. Her days started in the kitchen helping Cook before dawn, and she wasn't allowed to seek her pallet under the eaves until Miss Constance retired for the night. In between, she was fetching and cleaning and dodging Mr. Jonas.

Mark Allen's laughter stopped her mid-spin. Gwen caught her balance and cocked her head. With a snap, she flipped her plain wool shawl around her shoulders. "'Tis not gentlemanly to spy."

"'Tis hardly spying when you cavort in the open with the whole world as witness."

Gwen looked around, her cheeks warming from more than the sun. Relieved that no one else was about, she laughed. "I suppose you are correct. But the afternoon is so fine, and I'm free to enjoy it. I cannot help but let my good fortune show."

"You shall hear no complaint of mine." He tipped his head and examined her from head to heels. "I say it shows beautifully."

The warmth of her cheeks spread into a fiery blast. "You mustn't say such things." Gwen peeked over her shoulder and caught a glimpse of Cook's white cap in the window.

"'Tis only the truth. Come." He crooked an arm toward her. "Let us not waste a moment of the afternoon."

She rested her fingertips at his elbow, careful not to touch his side. He tossed a satchel over his other shoulder, and they strolled away from the house. She cast another glance back. Cook's white cap bobbed once, twice, and then disappeared.

The Whiteford estate bordered the growing town of Greenesville, North Carolina. The front opened onto a residential street while the forest pushed against the pasture behind the stable.

Mark Allen led Gwen along the fence row to the towering trees beyond. They stopped beneath a large maple, aflame in its fall glory. He opened the satchel, withdrew a rough blanket, and spread it on the ground.

"Cook prepared this as a surprise." He fished out a wedge of cheese, a round loaf of bread, and an earthenware jug. "Arthur and I pressed the cider yesterday, and the bread is still warm from the oven."

Gwen sank onto the blanket and nestled her shoulders against the deep ripples of the old maple's bark. A cool breeze swirled by, and she hitched her shawl tighter. Winter approached with the stealth of a bobcat. As if nature illustrated her thought, a maple leaf landed on the edge of her mobcap and hung in front of her eyes. She laughed and swatted it away.

"'Twill be the last picnic of the year." Mark Allen sprawled beside, retrieved the colorful leaf and twirled it between his fingers.

"No doubt, but 'twill be a fine day. One we can remember in the months ahead."

"I wish..." Lines marred the smoothness of his forehead.

"What do you wish?"

"I wish we were closer to our freedom."

"As do I." She was sixteen years old and bound to serve Mr. Whiteford until she reached her majority at twenty-one. "But we cannot change what is." No matter how desperately she wished she could.

Mark Allen plucked her hand from the blanket.

Strange flutterings in her ribcage made drawing a full breath difficult. His strong fingers held hers in a warm grip that didn't frighten her, not the way Mr. Jonas's touch did. He leaned over and kissed the back of her hand.

Gwen gasped and snatched it away. Her heart tripped and stammered. The intensity of his gaze unnerved her, but not the way Mr. Jonas did.

"I wish I could change many things." His eyes sparkled.

"M-my father used to say, 'If wishes were fishes, we'd all be throwing nets.'" Her voice was nearly breathless.

"Your father was a wise man. I wish I might have known him."

She let the silence stretch between them. Toward the stables, three of the riding horses cropped grass in the pasture, their serene rhythmic movements a stark contrast to the fierce longing inside Gwen. The loss of her family lay ever heavy against her heart. Tears blurred the edge of her vision.

"Forgive me. I did not mean to unsettle you."

"'Tis only that I miss him so. And Faye." She gripped the edge of her shawl. "My dearest wish is to gain my freedom and find my sister. She is my last living relative. If only we had been older when we arrived on these shores from Wales. If only..."

"If only Mr. Whiteford would have purchased her the same day he did you and me."

"Aye." The memory of her sister's face, twisted in anguish, as they were wrenched apart and sold to different masters haunted Gwen. They were separated, bound by their indentures until they reached the age of twenty-one. And she had no idea where her sister was.

"You know I shall help find her as soon as I'm free."

"We know not who has purchased her."

"There must be a way to find out. I shall start my search back in New Bern. Surely they keep records there of whom they sold to whom. Perhaps Mrs. Whiteford will take me along as coachman next time she travels to her sister's house. I could find a way to visit the docks there and see what I could learn."

Gwen couldn't meet his earnest face. "Mrs. Whiteford will never take you for a coachman. She only trusts Arthur to drive her and Miss Constance."

Mark Allen clenched his fists. His slender frame lacked the flabbiness of Mr. Jonas's. The bones of his shoulders pushed against his coat, hinting at a breadth and strength to come. His rough hands were tanned and callused.

She shivered, remembering Mr. Jonas's hands on her shoulders, their clamminess seeping through the fabric of her dress.

"Does the cold trouble you?" He started to remove his coat, but she raised a hand to stop him.

"Nay, I'm warm enough. 'Twas only a stray thought."

"Jonas, no doubt." He scowled. "If he touches you again, inform me, and I shall handle it."

"There is naught you can do."

"Do not be so sure." He flexed his hands, finger joints popping.

"You mustn't lay a finger on the master's son." Gwen placed her hands over the top of his, stilling them. "If you should, you would be flogged and sold away. I would have no friend here then. Please, promise me you will never do such a thing."

"I cannot stand by while that milksop paws at you. Your friendship is sweet, Gwen, but you know I long for more."

She never should have confided in Mark Allen about Mr. Jonas. She hadn't at first, but in the past few months—since her sixteenth birthday—Mr. Jonas's attentions had become more numerous and more disturbing.

She should have limited her confidences to Cook, who had taken stock of the situation and moved Gwen's sleeping pallet into her own cramped room on the third floor. Cook's snoring proved far more tolerable than worrying about who crept up the stairs at night.

"Cook is watching over me. Alice seems to understand the situation as well." Mrs. Whiteford's housekeeper wouldn't waste time showing an underling like Gwen kindness, but neither would she tolerate anything that might disrupt her precision-run household.

Mark Allen shot her a sideways glance, eyes wide and framed by thick lashes. "I could approach the master about seeking your hand in marriage."

Gwen sucked in her breath and looked away. She was very fond of Mark Allen. Being near him did strange things to her, but the idea of marriage unsettled her. Indentured servants could marry if they received their master's permission, but they would still have to finish their terms of service. Mark Allen would be free more than three years before she was. How could they be married with him free and her not? She shook her head.

"Do you not love me, then?" he asked in a hoarse whisper.

Her heart squeezed into a knot. Given the choice to stay with Mark Allen or leave to find Faye, she would leave. She might love Mark Allen in some fashion, but she loved her sister more.

"Everyone I have ever loved has been ripped away from me. Do not wish for my love. 'Tis a burdensome thing."

"No. 'Tis a wondrous thing and what I greatly desire. If your father lived, I would approach him this instant."

"If my father lived, I would not owe this indenture that must be repaid."

With the tip of his finger, he lifted her face toward him. "I can wait for your love. I will wait for it. You shall see."

Gwen shivered again, perhaps from the wind, or perhaps from his words. She snatched the cooled bread and the cheese from the blanket, broke them, and passed him half. The tightness around his eyes caused her a pang of guilt.

But she couldn't tell him what he wished most to hear.

Moonlight flooded through the open windows on the late November evening. Packed with people, the Quaker meetinghouse needed no fires in the great open hearths at both ends. Betsy sat near a window and listened to the conversations around her. She knew in her heart that the decision had already been made. They would journey to the Northwest Territory in the spring, to a place called Ohio.

The countryside beyond the window was bathed by a full moon casting shadows on the frostbitten ground. Beneath it lay the bodies of her children. She closed her eyes to better remember their faces.

Timothy had been their firstborn, with his shaggy straw-colored hair and serious blue eyes so like his father's. Abigail came along two years later, the happy child, always ready to laugh. Her graceful figure danced across Betsy's memories. Losing them both to an outbreak of measles when they were ten and eight years old had devastated her and Thomas. The pain of that loss was never far from her.

Ten years later, after all hope had fled, God granted them little Hannah. Such a delight that child had been. Apple-cheeked with reddish hair, she brought a smile to Betsy's lips. Her mischievous, adventuresome daughter succumbed to an infection of the blood after breaking her leg in a fall from the barn loft when she was seven years old.

So much sorrow lingered in New Bern. Why should Betsy be reluctant to leave? The children weren't really there. Their heavenly Father had collected them at the moment of their deaths. She rested fully in that assurance. But their sweet memories lingered strongest in the home where they lived and across the countryside they had walked together.

The new place, Ohio, would have no reminders of Timothy, Abigail, or Hannah.

Betsy bowed her head and asked God to give her the strength she needed to move on. She asked for peace of mind and a quiet spirit for the journey. She pushed aside the loneliness that threatened to overwhelm her.

The move was the right thing to do. The Society of Friends could not tolerate the enslavement of fellow human beings any longer. With the new, rigid laws in place, several Friends had been arrested—even jailed—for their acts of Christian kindness toward the Negroes. For purchasing and freeing them.

Betsy turned her face away from the window and the moonlit graves. The right thing to do, as happened so often in life, was not the easy path to take.

Chapter 3

"STOP THAT." MISS CONSTANCE shoved Gwen away. "You are pulling out more hair than brushing. You cannot even do this adequately. I have a mind to tell Father to sell you for a field hand. You are useless to me."

Gwen backed against the wall with her head bowed. Time had taught her that this was the best reaction to Miss Constance's temper tantrums. The threat, often repeated, was empty, but her stomach twisted anyway.

Few plantation owners wanted indentured servants anymore. Slaves were plentiful and indentured servants had to be freed at the end of their terms, while the Negroes remained in bondage for life. It made them a better investment.

"Remove yourself from my sight." Miss Constance jabbed her finger toward the door.

Gwen wasted no time slipping past it. She ran above stairs to the third floor and didn't stop until she closed Cook's door behind her.

"Miss Constance is in a fine high temper tonight," Cook said from her bed.

Miss Constance had a voice that defied the confinement of horse-hair plaster and lath, so the whole household heard it.

"She ordered me to leave." Gwen sank onto her pallet, the corn-husks crinkling beneath her.

"'Tis one order you were happy enough to fulfill, I vow."

Gwen nodded and leaned against the rough board wall of the servants' quarters.

"I suppose things did not go favorably when she met Mrs. Landon." Cook gave a firm shake of her head. "Mrs. Whiteford was in quite a taking when they arrived home, or so Alice told me. I heard the doors banging from my kitchen."

"Perhaps Mrs. Landon had word of Miss Constance sneaking out to meet with Hector Rawlings."

"No, child. If she had, she would not have invited them to tea in the first place. Hector Rawlings has no proper family, no connections. Why, he is little better than a pirate."

"But he works for Mr. Whiteford. Surely the master would not hire a pirate."

Cook snorted and hiked herself up on one elbow. "He may keep himself out of trouble while in port, but 'tis a sure thing he did not come by the money he flings around ferrying freight at what the master pays his ship captains."

"Why does Miss Constance risk all to see him, then?"

"Land sakes, child. Have you not looked at the man? Handsome enough to charm a fox vixen from her hole, that one is, and silver-tongued as well. Oh, I have heard him speak, I have." Cook fanned herself with one hand. "If I were thirty years younger, I would not mind sneaking out to meet him myself."

Gwen giggled and rose. She pulled her nightgown off the peg on the back of the door. Fingering the worn wool, she tried to imagine Cook chasing after a man. Impossible. Wasn't it? But Cook hadn't always been old.

"Why do some men cause your heart to beat faster and you enjoy it, while others cause it to beat faster, and you dread it?"

"Ah, the picnic with Mark Allen went well, did it now?" Cook leaned forward from the edge of her bed. "You could do a lot worse than our stable boy. There now, I mustn't be calling him a boy any longer. He is a man full grown, or close enough."

"He will be eighteen after the first of the year."

"Aye, and more than old enough to know his own mind." Cook winked at her. "And heart."

"He wants to ask the master for permission to marry."

Cook's eyebrows disappeared beneath her nightcap. "And how do you feel about that?"

"I know not." Gwen untied her apron and pulled off her gown. "Part of me wants to love him. But another part"—she pulled the nightgown over her head—"wants to wait out my indenture and find my sister."

"Child, the likelihood of finding your sister in this big country..." Cook wagged her head, sad eyes fastened on Gwen. "'Tis slim at best. 'Twould be easier to find a fish market free of stray cats."

"But I must try. You understand, aye? She is the last of my family. Everyone else—" Gwen swallowed the lump in her throat. "Everyone else is gone."

"Perhaps 'tis time to be thinking of starting a new family. Mark Allen would father some handsome children, I daresay."

Gwen sank onto her pallet against the wall opposite Cook's bed. She pulled the tattered blanket around her. She'd never considered starting a family apart from finding Faye. How could she? Wouldn't that mean abandoning one for the other?

Cook blew out the candle. Her rope bed squeaked in protest as she settled herself for the night. "Aye, you could do a lot worse."

But Faye needed her. Of that, Gwen was certain.

Gwen arrived at Miss Constance's door the next morning without encountering Mr. Jonas. She tapped on the polished wood. Perhaps her mistress would be in a better temper. At the muffled "enter," Gwen opened the door and slipped inside.

"Here you go, Miss Constance." Gwen placed the tea tray on the carved stand beside the bed. Her mistress struggled to sit upright, her face as white as flour paste.

"Are you ailing, miss?" Gwen pulled the pillows up against the tall headboard.

"I feel awful. Dreadful. I think, I think—" Constance's eyes flew open, and she pitched forward, hands grasping at her middle. She spewed her stomach's contents over the bedclothes and down the front of Gwen's apron and dress. Gwen stepped back, arms out at her sides, looking at her soiled garments.

"Do not just stand there—help me out of this mess." Miss Constance moaned. Gwen gathered the soiled bedclothes, wiping her dress and apron on them as best she could in the process, and then helped her mistress to the chair in front of her dresser.

"Bring me a bath and—ugh." Her mistress shoved Gwen away. "Go change first. The smell of your clothing will make me sick again." Miss Constance's face twisted.

Gwen snagged the chamber pot and plopped it on her mistress's lap. Thank heavens it was empty.

With a grimace, Constance waved a hand at Gwen. "Go change. I cannot abide the stench."

"I shall take the bedclothes with me." Gwen grabbed the bundle of soiled bedding.

"Hurry and leave."

Gwen rushed down the hallway to the servant's staircase. She skidded around the corner and ran smack into Mr. Jonas. She gasped and grabbed for the handrail to keep from falling. The bedding tumbled from her arms and tangled at their feet.

His eyes narrowed in satisfaction as he slipped his arms around her and crushed her against his chest.

Mouth open and heart pounding, her voice abandoned her.

"Just who I have been waiting for." His nose wrinkled. "What is that odor?" He pushed her away and glared at his clothes and the tangle of fabric on the floor. "You—wench. Look at the mess you have made of my shirt."

Gwen took advantage of his tirade to leap over the pile of bedding, lift her dress and apron, and run for the kitchen. She skidded to a stop in front of Cook, who stepped back, eyes wide.

"Whatever has happened, child?"

"Miss Constance spewed this morning. She needs a bath, and I need to change, but Mr. Jonas—" Gwen pointed at the staircase behind her. "He was waiting for me by the staircase." One hand on her chest, Gwen caught her breath in ragged gasps. "He grabbed me."

Cook tipped back her head and laughed, hands splayed across her jiggling middle.

Mouth agape, Gwen glanced toward the staircase, hoping nobody else heard.

Cook's mirth wound down until she mopped her eyes with her apron and straightened her cap.

"Go along then and change your dress. Worry not, Mr. Jonas will not bother you again. He is likely already in his room bellowing for Silas to bring him a bath and clean clothes." Cook made a shooing motion with her hands. "Go on with you. I shall fill all the kettles and get the water heating."

Gwen's heart pounded louder than her feet on the stairs. She leaped over the soiled bedding still lying in the upstairs hall and ran the last flight to Cook's room. She peeled off the offensive clothing and pulled on her only other dress and apron.

It served Mr. Jonas right for grabbing as he had. A grin tugged at her cheeks. Maybe Jonas *would* think twice before trying it again. She wadded the soiled garments into a bundle and took them to the kitchen, scooping up the dirty bedding on the way. She'd have to scrub them all later.

Gwen whisked a pair of thick cotton cloths off the table and grabbed two steaming kettles. She moved carefully up the stairs, placing her feet so as not to spill the hot liquid. If Mr. Jonas grabbed her this time, he would get a scalding for his trouble.

Setting the kettles on the floor, she tapped on Miss Constance's door before opening it and levering them inside.

Her mistress raised her head off her crossed arms on the dresser's top, hair hanging in strings around her face.

"What took you so long?"

"I have your hot water, Miss Constance. I shall pull the tub out and fill it. Are you feeling any better?"

"Do I look as if I feel any better? Pour the water. Then leave me alone." She stood and poked a finger in Gwen's face. "And do not be talking about me in the kitchen, do you hear? Nobody needs to know I was indisposed this morning."

"But miss, Mrs. Whiteford will wish to summon the doctor."

"My mother has no need to learn of this. I'm fine. It was just something I ate last evening."

Then she'd been eating the same something for a fortnight or better, although it was the first time she'd spewed, but Gwen was in no position to mention it. After pouring water into the copper tub, Gwen cast a searching glance at her mistress. She did seem to have a bit more color in her cheeks. Gwen gathered the now-cold tea tray and paused at the side of the bed.

"Do you need anything else, miss?"

"When I do, I shall ring for you. Take that tea away. I cannot abide the thought of it." She grimaced and turned her face away.

Gwen bobbed a quick curtsy before heading to the kitchen. The rest of her morning would be spent doing laundry. At least she could scrub her own clothes with the bedding. A door banged from the direction of Mr. Jonas's room. She was out of soiled clothing and scalding water, so she scurried as fast as she could without slopping the tea down her front.

Standing on tiptoe, Gwen pinned the last sheet to the line behind the house. The crunch of wagon wheels on the gravel drive drew her attention.

Phineas Browne pulled his sturdy workhorses to a halt beside the stable and waved at her. His monthly delivery of grain for Mr. White-ford's horses weighed down the back of his wagon.

"Good morning, Gwen."

"Good morning, Mr. Browne."

"'Tis a brisk morning to be hanging out the wash."

"Aye, 'tis, but this fresh breeze will see it dry shortly."

"It must be my day for encountering pretty girls on my route." He gave her a friendly wink as he hefted the first sack off the wagon. "I saw another beauty with curly hair as black as yours and skin almost as fair."

Gwen took one faltering step and then hurried after him as he disappeared into the stable. "Where, Mr. Browne?"

"Where what?"

"Where did you see such a girl? Was she near my age? Do you have her name?"

He pushed his hat back and scratched his forehead. "She was hanging wash, same as you, on the other side of town round back of Lily's Boardinghouse. I did not ask her name, but she looked to be about your age. Do you know her?"

"I. . . mayhap. . . good day to you, Mr. Browne." Gwen whirled and raced for the kitchen door. She burst through and almost collided with Cook.

"There now. What is this all about? Would you take the very legs out from under me then?" Cook huffed and crossed her meaty arms.

"There is a girl across town who looks like me."

"So you say, and is that your excuse for nearly running me down?"

Gwen drew in a steadying breath. "It might be her."

"Who might be her? Make sense, child. I have the supper to finish, and cannot spend my time solving riddles."

"Mr. Browne said he saw another girl with hair like mine and fair skin, hanging wash behind Lily's Boardinghouse." She bounced on her toes, unable to stand still. "I must go and see. It might be Faye."

"Slow down, now." Cook took her by the shoulders and gave a gentle shake. "You will be going nowhere without the master's permission."

"But surely he will give it."

"He may, but he is not in the house and will not return until nightfall. You cannot ask him until then."

Gwen's stomach fell to her toes. "She may be gone by then."

"Nonsense, child. If she was hanging wash, then she most likely works for the lady who owns the boardinghouse. She shall be there tomorrow, and the tomorrow after that."

Gwen caught her bottom lip between her teeth and glanced out the door. She wanted to run and beg Mr. Browne to take her to the boardinghouse, but he knew she couldn't leave without the master's permission. Her lip wobbled despite her teeth.

"There now, chin up, 'tis not as bad as all that." Cook patted her shoulder. "At least you have a place to start looking. That is more than you had this morning. Best you see to Miss Constance now. She has yet to ring, but she should have. Go on and see if she wants a bit of breakfast yet or a fresh cup of tea."

Gwen's shoulders slumped, and she trudged up the stairs. The burden of her indenture added lead to each step. She would speak to Mr. Whiteford that evening. Sunshine filtered through a window above. She willed the bright orb to hasten on its journey.

Was Faye across town that very minute? Could they have been so close the past two years and not even known it?

Chapter 4

G WEN PACED THE DARK paneled foyer with its imposing double
doors. Shadows danced on the wall from the lone lamp on the
narrow table. Feeble moonlight outlined the two long windows on
either side of the door. She paused from time to time to peek at the
stately clock in the parlor. Surely Mr. Whiteford should've been home
long since.

Miss Constance and Mrs. Whiteford worked on their needlepoint in
the sitting room. Their conversation drifted down the hallway occa-
sionally, but Gwen didn't bother to listen. She hoped they would stay
occupied for some time yet. She desperately needed to be in the foyer
to see Mr. Whiteford. If called upstairs to attend Miss Constance when
he arrived, she'd have to wait until the following day to speak with him.
She turned again and continued her pacing.

Sweat dampened her temples in spite of the drafts sneaking around
the door. She twisted her wrinkled apron in her hands when the
unmistakable clatter of carriage wheels approached and stopped out
front. She peered from one of the windows. The lanterns on the
carriage threw enough light to see a man walking up the steps. She

scurried back against the far wall and tucked a few loose curls under her cap. She patted futilely at her apron to straighten it.

Silas appeared and frowned at her before opening the door.

"Good evening, sir," the butler said.

"Frigid is more like it. We'll have frost half an inch thick by morning."

"Yes, sir." Silas eased the great coat off his master's shoulders. He tucked it over his arm and reached for the muffler and hat.

"Have the ladies retired for the evening?"

"They await you in the sitting room."

"And Jonas?"

"Mr. Jonas has yet to return."

"Very well. Bring a glass of port to the sitting room." Mr. Whiteford took one step before Gwen cleared her throat. She squirmed under the disapproving stares of master and butler.

"Excuse me, Master." Gwen bobbed a curtsy, fingers laced together in front of her, knuckles tight.

"What is it?"

"Sir, I have received word that someone who resembles my sister was seen today working at Lily's Boardinghouse. May I..." Gwen swallowed, trying not to gulp. "May I have a half day of leave tomorrow to investigate?"

"Leave the house? I think not." He strode down the foyer, where she had paced moments before, his boot heels striking like a judge's gavel.

Gwen reached toward his retreating back.

Silas sniffed and shook his head.

Her master disappeared into the parlor, and her hopes dried in his wake.

Then, she hiked the hem of her dress and fled to the kitchen, raced up the servants' staircase to the third floor, and threw herself onto her pallet. Sobs shook her, muffled by the wadded blanket she pressed against her face. The unfairness of her situation pushed against her heart with every beat. She'd been unjustly forced into bondage with no way out until she was twenty-one years old.

Five long years would pass before she could find her sister.

Gwen poured the contents of the chamber pot into the privy.

At least Constance had made it to the pot in time before spewing that morning. Gwen rubbed at the crease on her forehead as she glanced at the second-story window. The drapes were still drawn against the morning sun. She hoped that whatever ailed her mistress wasn't catching. Gwen rinsed the pot with fresh water and left it setting in the sun to dry. She returned the water bucket to the pump beside the stable.

"I thought I saw you out back." Mark Allen's crooked grin lifted her spirits.

"Miss Constance spewed again this morning." Gwen slapped her hand over her mouth. "I should not have told you that. She forbade me to speak of it."

"Be at ease. All the servants know. Your encounter with Jonas was the talk at supper last evening. We missed you. Are you feeling well yourself?"

"I'm not ailing."

Mark Allen's brows gathered, and his hazel eyes glittered. "He got better than he deserved with just a shirt full of slop. I would like to give him a thrashing for touching you."

Gwen placed her hand on his arm and shook her head. "You mustn't. For striking the master's son, you would be sold away from here. I would lose you, too."

He turned his face away. "I shan't always be in bondage. The day I'm free, that man better not cross my path."

"I dream of little else than being free." Gwen sighed and leaned against the stable wall. "Mr. Browne told me of a girl who looks like me across town working at Lily's Boardinghouse. Last night I asked the master for leave to go and see if it might be Faye." She wiped a smear of dampness from her cheek. "He refused me."

Mark Allen ran his hand along his jawline, then cocked an eyebrow. "Then we shall find a way to sneak out after they retire some evening."

"We?" Gwen pushed away from the stable wall. "You would help me?"

"I would do anything for you. You must know that." His expression softened.

"If we should be discovered—"

"We shan't. I—"

Cook's voice rang across the yard, calling her back to her duties.

"Coming!" Gwen started that way, but Mark Allen held her gaze—and winked.

"I shall arrange it. As soon as possible."

The promise in his eyes strengthened her for the day ahead and planted hope deep in her heart.

"What ails you now?" Constance's shrill voice cut through Gwen's daydream.

"I'm sorry, miss. I'm distracted today."

"What could there be to distract someone like you?" Constance looked down her nose at Gwen, as one would view a distasteful insect. "Fetch my green gown, the one with pearl buttons. And mind you don't wrinkle it."

Gwen pulled the garment from the wardrobe. "You look lovely in this gown. Mrs. Landon is sure to be impressed."

"Mrs. Landon is a crabby old harridan in expensive clothing."

Gwen fumbled the gown, grabbing it back before it touched the floor.

"I see I have shocked you but 'tis only the truth. I shan't spend another minute in her company until I am married to Stanley. And then I shall see her removed into the far wing of Bridgewater as soon as possible."

Mrs. Landon might not be so quick to give up her role as mistress of Bridgewater Plantation just because her son brought home a bride. But as always, Gwen kept such thoughts to herself.

"I am meeting Hector today if you must know. He and I, well... we understand each other." Miss Constance preened in front of the looking glass.

Gwen cocked her head and waited, but Miss Constance said no more. Perhaps they were friends like her friendship with Mark Allen. She let her hands grow still again at their task.

Had he devised a plan yet? She ached to hear from him, but he'd gone with the master on business and wouldn't return for several days.

Constance's elbow caught Gwen in the ribs and she stumbled backward. She grasped her side, mouth open but without sound.

"Finish buttoning my gown. I'm sick unto death of your dawdling. I shall speak to Father about this." Constance's face was nothing short of a thundercloud ready to toss lightning bolts.

"I'm so sorry, miss. Forgive me." Gwen's fingers flew over the buttons. She wrenched her mind away from the pain in her ribs and Mark Allen.

She even tried not to worry over Faye.

Cook whacked a wooden spoon on the table.

Gwen jumped, one hand clasped to her chest to keep her heart from bursting forth.

"Wake up, child." Cook wagged her head, eyes half shut, and huffed out a deep breath. "What can be done with you? Your head is in the clouds while the work lies before you on the table."

Gwen slumped on her stool, apple in one hand, knife in the other. Her face burned. The bowl of apples mocked her puny efforts to peel them.

"I can think of nothing but Faye, perhaps on the other side of this very city, perhaps peeling apples and thinking of me." She sniffed and pushed her mobcap up with the back of her wrist. "The master's refusal of my leave request has caused me to grieve her loss all over again."

"Getting yourself sold off as a malingerer won't help you find your sister. Your lot would only become more difficult." The harsh lines melted from Cook's face. Her lips lifted in a sad sort of smile. "Each day has enough worries of its own. Worry today about readying those apples and worry another day about finding your sister."

"Aye, Cook." Gwen concentrated on paring the apple in her hand. One at a time, apple after apple, she kept at her task until the bowl emptied.

"Toss those peelings to the chickens now," Cook said. "We shall have sweet eggs for breakfast."

Gwen lifted the bucket at her feet and left through the kitchen door. A colorful assortment of chickens ran towards her in their jerky gait.

She tossed the apple peels and cores, while they squabbled over the choicest portions. She flung the last handful as the buggy approached. Her heart lurched, not unlike the chicken's jerky motion, at the sight of Mark Allen holding the reins. She waved. At his nod, she raced to the stable to meet him.

"You return early." She bounced on her toes until he hopped off the high seat.

"Mr. Whiteford wrapped up his business, and we made good time on the roads."

"Did you...that is...did time allow for you to think about. . ."

"I thought of little else." He grinned before turning to unhitch the lathered horse. "I shall linger in the kitchen this evening after supper. If you can slip away, we might take an evening stroll. I could tell you of my plan then. I have to see to the mare now, and Cook is frowning at us through the window."

Gwen took a step back and glanced over her shoulder to see Cook shaking her head. "Until this evening then." Gwen picked up the hem of her dress and dashed for the door.

The day suddenly seemed brighter.

Miss Constance stormed down the hall. Jaw tight and eyes like brittle ice, she marched to her room and slammed the door.

Gwen scurried after her, working hard to keep focused on the tasks at hand. Cook's warning of being sold as a malingerer burned in her mind. As bad as things could be at the Whitefords' estate, that threat sent a cold stab of fear through her. She only had to get through the day, and then tonight she'd hear Mark Allen's plan.

When Constance announced she had a headache and would retire early, Gwen schooled her face to blankness. Inside, she wanted to twirl and laugh. She'd have plenty of time to meet with Mark Allen.

Gwen took extra care to comb and braid her mistress's hair and fluff her pillows, earning not so much as a grunt of satisfaction from Constance. Once dismissed, she closed the door and crept down the steps until she arrived, breathless, in the kitchen.

Mark Allen waited for her.

She barely noticed Cook brush past her on her way up the stairs or Arthur's nod as he ambled out the door.

Mark Allen rose and crooked an elbow for her. She grabbed a heavy shawl off the back of the door and wound it around herself before slipping her hand under his arm. Once outside, they walked through a low mist that curled and eddied around their legs.

When they reached the edge of the pasture, Gwen could hold back no longer. "Tell me what plan you have devised."

"'Tis a simple plan, really. Next month, Mr. Whiteford is sending me to collect a wagonload of freight and deliver it to the docks at New Bern. 'Tis part of the deal he worked out on our journey. I am to leave several hours before daylight and travel straight through to reach New Bern before sunset. The load I'm to pick up is not far from Lily's Boardinghouse. I could drop you off there and return for you after the freight is loaded, then circle back and let you off a couple of blocks from the house. You could sneak back in before anyone would know you had been missing."

"But you must reach New Bern before sunset. Would you have time?"

"With Master Whiteford's fine horses? I will make it and with time to spare."

Gwen grasped his sleeve and pulled him around to face her.

"Truly? This can happen as you say?"

"Truly. And no one the wiser. You shall learn if that girl is Faye."

Gwen stared at him in the evening darkness, her heart so light she feared it might float from her chest.

The moonlight flashed in his eyes before he lowered his head.

She sucked in a quick breath before the warm press of his lips caressed hers. She stumbled back, crossed her arms, and lowered her chin.

"Gwen." He reached toward her.

She shook her head, "Nay. We mustn't." What would Cook say if she'd seen?

"You tug at me so. I could not help myself."

Gwen squeezed her eyes shut. The thought of finding Faye, even if they couldn't be together for a few years, filled her with hope to the point of almost physical pain. But the touch of Mark Allen's lips unsettled her in ways she didn't understand. There was nothing repulsive about his touch. Or his kiss—her very first. In fact, both made her stomach skitter and twitch in a way not at all displeasing. She pressed two fingers against her lips.

"I know not what to think. I'm not free to give my heart away. I'm little better than a slave. I cannot even go looking for my sister without doing so in secret. If Mr. Whiteford ever saw you kissing me..." She cast a glance at the candlelit windows of the house. Did a curtain move on the second floor? A shiver spider-walked the length of her back.

"'Tis worth the risk. You are worth any risk to me."

"Nay. You say that now, but you could be sold as a malingerer. And so could I." She pulled the heavy shawl tighter. He moved closer. Although tempted to lean into his protective presence, she knew better. She wasn't ignorant of the ways between a man and a woman.

He raised his hand as if to touch her and then let it drop to his side.

"W-will you still help me find Faye?" She couldn't control the tremor in her voice. She couldn't meet his eyes, either.

He touched her then. Fingers under her chin, he lifted her face toward him.

"I will."

She nodded and then fled to the house, the confusing and exciting emotions creating a tangle inside of her.

Chapter 5

December 1798

"FETCH THE DOCTOR. TELL him to hurry. I will know what is ailing my daughter."

Gwen stopped in the hallway at Mrs. Whiteford's commands, a scrub bucket and brush to clean yet another morning mess dangling from her hands. When Alice glared at her through the open door to Constance's room, Gwen scurried inside and knelt on the floor.

"You there."

Gwen tried not to cringe at Mrs. Whiteford's strident voice. She stood and curtsied in Mrs. Whiteford's direction.

"Why was I not summoned at once?" the woman demanded.

"'Twas Miss Constance's wishes."

"What nonsense." Mrs. Whiteford stood and thrust her shoulders back. She resembled an elegantly dressed scarecrow, all sharp edges and angles. "My daughter would never hide an illness from her mother."

"Aye, Mrs. Whiteford." Gwen bobbed another curtsy. "I shall see to the cleaning up now."

"You do that." Mrs. Whiteford flicked a hand at Gwen as one would shoo away a bothersome fly, turning to Alice. "See that you alert me immediately when the doctor arrives. I will not be kept in the dark about the goings-on in my own house." She shot a withering glare at Gwen before sailing from the room with the frowning Alice in her wake.

Gwen dropped to her knees. She pulled several old rags from her waistband and set about mopping the floor.

"Is she gone?" The feeble voice from the bed summoned a twinge of sympathy in Gwen's heart.

"Aye, miss."

A groan answered her. Gwen whisked the brush over the wood, scrubbing and dunking it in the bucket over and over again. She worked her way back to the door. Finished, she stood, grabbed the bucket, and then closed the door behind her.

But when she turned, Jonas stood between her and the servants' staircase.

She gasped, the water sloshing in her bucket.

His lips twisted in more of a sneer than a smile. He took two steps and stopped so close she could smell last night's whiskey on his breath.

Gwen's stomach threatened to do the same as Miss Constance's.

"Cleaning up after my sister again, are you? At least you are not coated in it this time." He pressed even closer, crowding her back against the door frame. "You certainly smell better than when last we met."

She moved a step to the side, and he moved with her. He fingered the wayward curls that escaped her mobcap. She flinched away and took another step. He followed in a sinister type of dance.

"I know about you, little Gwen." He chuckled, but it wasn't a pleasant sound.

Beads of perspiration dampened her brow. She wished Alice hadn't left with Mrs. Whiteford, or that Cook would come upstairs. The urge to empty her stomach almost overpowered her.

"I saw you with him in the moonlight. You play the innocent with me, but now I know better. I shall show you what a man can do." He ran the back of his fingers down her cheek. "You have no need to run to that stable boy ever again."

He clamped his hand around her jaw and forced her head back.

Without thinking, she dumped the bucket of dirty water down the front of his breeches. He gasped and flung himself backward. Before he could recover his balance, Gwen dropped the bucket and fled down the staircase to the kitchen.

Cook and Silas stood by the large brick hearth when Gwen skittered to a halt halfway across the room, holding her dripping apron away from her dress.

Cook's mouth fell open. She surveyed Gwen from head to toe. Then her lips twitched, and her belly jiggled. She poked Silas on the arm.

"You best be tending to Mr. Jonas. I would wager my last coin he needs a dry change of clothing."

Silas huffed and shot a frown at Gwen.

Cook poked him again and scowled. "'Tis not the lass's fault, as well you know."

Silas squared his shoulders before he pivoted and left the room without a word.

"Stuffy old curmudgeon anyway," Cook muttered. "So, child, Mr. Jonas accosted you again, did he?" She tapped her fingers on her chin. "I daresay you shall quench his ardor if you keep dousing him with slops."

"He said he saw Mark Allen and me in the moonlight. H-he made it sound like I... like Mark Allen and I... like we..."

"What is this? When did this happen?" Cook's smile evaporated, and she arched one eyebrow. "Speak up, child. I shall know the truth of it. Now, if you please."

"'Twas nothing untoward. We took a stroll out back, to talk, and h-he kissed me once, only the briefest kiss." Gwen hung her head. "I know 'twas wrong. He never did it before, and 'twill not happen again."

At Cook's *harrumph*, Gwen snapped up her head.

"Mark Allen may feel differently." Cook released another *harrumph*, and heat broke over Gwen's face. "'Tis all water under the bridge now. You'd best clean up the mess you left and change your apron. When the doctor arrives, I have a feeling we are in for a rough go of it."

"Why do you think so?"

"The truth will be out soon enough. Now, do as I say."

Gwen removed her soaked apron, grabbed a stack of clean rags, and headed upstairs. She'd get nothing more from Cook about her thoughts on the matter, but maybe they'd have answers by noontime.

Then Gwen could concentrate on more important matters... like Mark Allen's plan for her to visit Lily's Boardinghouse.

Pregnant.

Gwen's mind reeled at the thought of Miss Constance being with child. The doctor had come and gone, but the turmoil had just begun.

Mrs. Whiteford, after fainting dead away at the news, had been given a draught by the doctor and sent to bed.

Mr. Jonas pounded down the street soon after, flailing his poor horse with a riding crop.

Constance, her face a puffy mask, still sobbed uncontrollably into her pillow while Alice and Silas crept around on silent feet. Gusts of wind shook the rafters as if the house itself trembled in anticipation of the master's return from his office at the docks.

Gwen shivered with each chilly blast.

The front door crashed open. A torrent of wind dashed through the foyer and along the wide hallway, slamming several doors along its path.

Gwen winced and ducked behind one of the alcove drapes at the end of the second-story hallway. She had no desire to encounter either of the Misters Whiteford. The pounding of boot heels on the stairs forced her back tighter against the paneling. A wrenching sound, like someone trying to tear a door from its hinges, made her cringe.

"I shall have Stanley Landon here within the hour. This matter will be settled tonight." Mr. Whiteford's voice reverberated down the hallway and back. "He must cover for your disgrace to this family. This is intolerable."

A muffled reply came from Constance. It might have been words or simply whimpers. Gwen couldn't hear enough to tell the difference.

"What do you mean it was not Landon!" Mr. Whiteford's shout threatened to loosen the shingles on the roof.

A scuffling of slippers heralded Mrs. Whiteford's arrival. "Daniel, oh Daniel. You've heard."

"Jonas found me. But your daughter says the blackguard is not Landon."

"Whatever shall we do?" Hysteria quivered in the older woman's voice. "We are ruined."

"What can one do with a harlot?"

Miss Constance's wail roused sympathy in Gwen, but not enough to draw her from her hiding place and expose her to the master's anger.

"Daniel! That is not true. It cannot be. Our daughter was taken advantage of, duped into believing..." Mrs. Whiteford's voice trailed off followed by a rustling and a soft thump.

"Now see what you have done to your mother, girl. Where is Alice? Alice!"

Gwen peeked from behind the drapes as Mr. Whiteford carried his wife to her bedroom. With no one else left in the hallway, she dashed to Cook's room.

It seemed the safest place to be.

Cook found Gwen there an hour later. "The master will see us all in his study after supper." Her usually cheery mouth pulled into a grim line.

"What will he do?"

"We shall find out after supper. Come now, I require your help in the kitchen. You cannot hide up here. The servants must be fed at least. I doubt any of the family will eat this evening."

As Cook predicted, the ladies refused food, Jonas still hadn't returned, and Mr. Whiteford remained in his study calling only for a bottle. Cook paced between the table and workbench. Silas, Arthur, and Mark Allen ate in silence while Gwen pushed the thick pork stew around her bowl. Alice remained upstairs with Mrs. Whiteford, who had not risen from her bed.

Silas stood and straightened his jacket. Arthur washed down the last of his supper with a long drink of buttermilk, wiped his mouth, and rose. Cook nodded and dried her hands one more time on her apron. She followed the men out the door.

The time had come.

Mark Allen reached toward Gwen. She blushed but took the offered hand, dropping it when she stood. They left the kitchen a few steps behind the others. Alice descended the stairs. She must have been waiting for them while keeping an ear open in case her mistress needed her.

Silas hurried to the broad oak door of the master's study. He knocked and eased it open. Standing at attention, he let the others enter first, then followed and closed the door behind him with a soft click.

Light from a single oil lamp illuminated Daniel Whiteford's presence in the leather chair by the bay window, the room filled with the acrid odors of alcohol and cigar smoke.

Gwen huddled with the rest of the servants in a loose knot and waited in silence.

Finally, Daniel Whiteford jerked his head in their direction and lurched to his feet. He kept one hand on the back of his chair.

"You all know what happened here this day." His words slurred together. "You all know that my daughter is a... she is a disgrace to this family." He sucked in a loud breath and pointed a shaky finger in their direction. "But that knowledge shall never leave the walls of this house. Do I make myself understood?" His voice rose, and he levered himself into a more upright position, waiting for their nods of agreement. "At the first whisper of scandal—the very first, mind you—I shall sack every free person without a reference and sell off the indentured. Am I fully understood?"

Gwen swallowed even though her throat had dried to a husk. Sold off. Miss Constance's dire threat might yet come true.

"Arrangements will be made after Christmas for my daughter to wait out her confinement elsewhere. You shall know more when the time arrives and be given the appropriate story to spread concerning her whereabouts." He weaved on his feet, glaring at them. "Leave me now." He thrust an unsteady hand in the general direction of the door before collapsing back into his chair. Everyone filed out except Silas, who advanced into the room to remove the empty bottle from the table beside Mr. Whiteford's chair.

"Is that all? We just keep our mouths shut?" Mark Allen asked when they all arrived in the kitchen.

"It shan't be as easy as you think," Cook said. "'Tis more than us keeping mum. Other tongues will wag. We must be sure and silence them before they can spark a rumor."

"Cook speaks the truth," Arthur said. "Keeping a secret is no small task. We shall be asked sly questions by the servants of other houses, mark my words. Their mistresses will send them to ferret out information. We shall have to be on constant guard."

"Why would they?" Gwen asked.

"Because nobody feels so grand as one who can put another down." Cook huffed and shook out the skirt of her apron. "Mark my words, the other young mistresses and their mommas will smell blood in the water over this for sure."

There was a moment of shuffled feet and cleared throats.

"Would he really do it?" Gwen scanned the somber faces of her fellow servants. "Would he sack and sell us?"

"Aye, and some of us be not young enough to start over." Alice glared at Gwen and Mark Allen. "You mind your tongues, the both of you." She gave a sharp nod and then turned on her heel before marching out the door.

"'Tisn't our fault Miss Constance got herself in the family way," Mark Allen said.

Arthur clamped a hand on the stable boy's shoulder. "Neither is it any of our business." He ushered Mark Allen out of the kitchen.

"Cook?" Gwen turned to the older woman for some sort of reassurance.

Cook shook her head and piled the wooden bowls in the wash basin. Gwen grabbed a rag and cleaned away the remnants of their supper from the table. They worked in silence. Half-formed questions plagued Gwen, most of them beginning with *what if.* When the dishes were cleaned and put away, Cook jerked her head toward the staircase.

"You best be seeing to Miss Constance."

Gwen looked up the staircase and back toward Cook. At the older woman's nod, she lowered her head and climbed, feeling as a convicted felon must when he approached the gallows. Miss Constance would surely blame her for word of her illness getting to Mrs. Whiteford.

She peeked into the hallway first, out of habit, but Mr. Jonas had not yet returned that evening. One small blessing in a day of disasters. On cat's feet, she approached Constance's door, hoping her mistress had already fallen asleep. She heard nothing, so she tapped with one fingertip. At the muffled response, she squeezed her eyes shut and drew in a long breath, then opened the door.

Constance sat in the middle of her bed, her hair in wild disarray as if she'd been pulling on it. She turned her swollen face toward Gwen and bared her teeth.

"Come to see the harlot at last?"

"Miss Constance." Gwen closed the door behind her. "Let me get you into your nightgown." She reached to help her mistress off the bed, half expecting a stinging slap. But Constance sagged in on herself, shoulders drooping and chin against her chest. Gwen took her arm and helped her to her feet. After the gown was unbuttoned and eased off, Gwen unlaced the corset. Constance took a deep breath, and Gwen slid the nightgown over her head. Then she helped her mistress into the chair by her dressing table and brushed the blond strands, artfully untangling the damaged locks.

Tears slipped down her mistress's cheeks, revealed in the oval looking glass in front of them.

"It wasn't Stanley, you know." Miss Constance spoke in a monotone, as if she had no more emotion to give that day. "Hector Rawlings and I..." Miss Constance met Gwen's gaze in the looking glass. In spite of the puffiness and tears, there was more than a glimmer of defiance and pride in that look. "I'm not a harlot. He loves me. Father would never abide a marriage between us. We both knew that. All that left to us..." She slapped the dressing table with her palm. "I know not why I'm telling you any of this." She clamped her lips tight and turned her face away from the looking glass.

Indeed, why would Miss Constance tell her such things? Gwen smoothed the golden locks into a long braid and helped her mistress back onto the bed. Once Gwen escaped to her pallet under the eaves, she lay for a long time listening to Cook's soft snores and pondered life and men.

But before she drifted into sleep, it was Faye's blue eyes and ebony curls that filled her mind's eye.

The weeks leading up to Christmas held none of the festive spirit Gwen remembered from her previous two years at the estate. Mrs. Whiteford still ordered the house decorated with evergreen boughs, mistletoe, and bright red bows, but Alice and Gwen placed each adornment with silent, somber precision. The vivid green and red trimmings mocked the oppressive mood of the household. The family barely spoke to each other. The servants remained tight-lipped, casting nervous glances over their shoulders at odd times of the day.

Miss Constance rarely left her room now, which was a blessing. Her manner changed like quicksilver from ranting to weeping. Each summons from her mistress was cause for dread. Gwen escaped to the kitchen as often as she could, but even Cook lacked her usual positive outlook and jolly wit.

Gwen yearned for Christmas to be over. Mark Allen's delivery was scheduled for three days after. Gwen counted off each day, marking time until she and Mark Allen would steal away to find Faye.

Christmas Eve arrived, and the servants enjoyed their special holiday meal as best they could. Mr. Whiteford himself came to hand out the gift packages wrapped in white paper. He gave each one a tight-lipped smile, but shadows lay in dark circles beneath his eyes. After wishing them all Merry Christmas, he asked Gwen to follow him into his study.

She glanced around the table, but there was no means of escape. Cook nodded to the door, and Gwen forced herself to rise. She trotted down the hall to catch up with Mr. Whiteford before he reached the study door.

"I know you wonder why I have singled you out." The master closed the door and sank into his chair behind the massive mahogany desk.

Gwen managed a slight nod.

"Miss Constance will be leaving here the day after tomorrow and spending her confinement with her Aunt Matilda in New Bern. You will, of course, accompany her to Mrs. Cummings' residence and remain with her throughout her confinement."

Gwen's heart dropped, and tears gathered behind her eyelids. She twisted her fingers together so tightly they hurt.

"I know things have been difficult these past two weeks, but I assure you, they will get better. This is the right and proper thing to do." He drummed his fingers on the desk. "You will be charged with the same responsibilities you perform here. Chief among them is to keep the situation in complete confidence. Miss Constance will not be leaving the house once she arrives, which will make it easier. Only

Matilda's slaves will be privy to the situation, and she insists they can be trusted." He grimaced. "When the time comes, a suitable midwife will be engaged who will be handsomely reimbursed for her silence."

Gwen's legs wobbled beneath her. Her breath came in soft gasps. Her heart breaking. All chance of finding Faye slipping from her fingers.

Mr. Whiteford leaned forward. "Are you ailing?"

"Nay, sir, just... surprised."

"And a little frightened perhaps." He settled back into his chair. "Have no fear. Matilda isn't as harsh as some say, and you do, after all, belong to me and not to her. I will make it plain that your duties are first and foremost with Miss Constance. You will assist the Cummings staff only when your primary duties are completed." He picked up an envelope from his desk, and Gwen was dismissed.

She stumbled into the hallway. Not seeing anyone about, she dashed for the servants' staircase and arrived at Cook's room out of breath, where she collapsed onto her pallet. Arms wrapped around her knees, she rocked and sobbed. The day after Christmas, two days before Mark Allen's delivery, two days before she may have found her sister. Heartache washed down her cheeks and dripped off her chin.

Cook's voice roused her a short time later. "Pull yourself together, child. 'Tis not as bad as all that. Miss Constance's confinement will end in the spring. You shall be back with us before the lilacs wither, or I miss my guess." A gentle hand patted her hair, Gwen's mobcap having come off at some point in her misery.

"Nay, you do not understand." Gwen swiveled on her rump, eye to eye with the kneeling older woman. "We had plans, Mark Allen and I." Her sniff became a hiccup.

"Tush, tush, child. That one will wait for you. Have I not seen him making eyes at you myself?"

"Nay. He is to make a delivery three days after Christmas, in the dark of night and traveling directly past the boardinghouse where my sister might be."

"And you thought to stow away with him?" Cook rocked back on her heels. She shook her head. "'Tis a good thing for you not to be here then. If the master ever found out..." Her face pulled into somber lines.

"I must try. I must know."

Cook rubbed her chin between her thumb and finger for a moment.

"Arthur will be driving you to New Bern. I see no reason he could not drive by the boardinghouse on the way."

Gwen held her breath.

"Mind now, 'tis no guarantee the girl will be in sight when you get there. Still, I shall speak to him. I'm afraid 'tis the best that can be done."

Gwen launched herself into Cook's arms, forcing a grunt as the older woman balanced them both. "Lord love you, child. Let not your hopes get too high."

She was try to heed her friend's warning, but what else did Gwen have but hope?

Chapter 6

W HILE THE FAMILY CELEBRATED Christmas the next evening, with guests coming and going and the whole house smelling of pine, cinnamon, bayberry candles, and spiced cider, Gwen folded Miss Constance's clothing. Her only chance to speak with Mark Allen came when he hauled the empty trunks to Constance's room. He snatched off his battered hat. The grooves on each side of his face deepened. His attention fastened on his fingers as they fiddled with the hat.

"Your leaving lays heavy on my heart. I wish I could write to you, but..."

She swallowed against the lump in her throat. Her own sparse education left her able for little more than scrawling her name.

"I shall be waiting for you." He looked into her eyes, and his breath quickened.

"I know." She scanned the hallway, then leaned forward and kissed him on the cheek. "If I do not see you again..." Mr. Whiteford might decide his secret was safer without a young maid who knew too much coming back to the estate.

He mashed the hat on his head. Understanding glowed in his hazel eyes. They remained suspended in that moment of shared grief until he pivoted and stormed out the door.

Gwen's breath left in a rush.

She would miss Mark Allen, but not in the way he wished she would.

The clock downstairs chimed nine times. Gwen hurried to finish packing. At least she didn't have to pack Miss Constance's ballgowns. Alice had given her strict instructions on the type of clothing to take, right down to which gown Miss Constance would wear home in the spring.

Gwen paused. What about the babe?

He or she would need wrappings and gowns. She hadn't considered that before. What plans did Mr. Whiteford have for his grandchild? Remembering the night he called his daughter a harlot, Gwen shivered. Surely he wouldn't... he couldn't plan to sell the child or give it away.

His own grandchild.

She rubbed her hands against the goosebumps covering her arms.

Mrs. Whiteford stood ramrod straight atop the stair by the front door. She offered no smile nor did she lift a hand in farewell.

Miss Constance turned her face away and stepped into the carriage. Gwen fussed with her mistress's gown, and then tucked the heavy lap robe over her legs.

Gwen sat opposite Miss Constance and sighed. Memories of her own mother faded with each passing year. What she remembered most was being loved. Her father had loved her, but in a different way. Even in his own grief and despair, she had known his love. To witness the coldness between Miss Constance and Mrs. Whiteford, along with Mr. Whiteford's absence at his daughter's departure, tugged on a string of sympathy within her.

Arthur closed the door. The carriage rocked as he climbed onto the driver's seat. It swayed a few times as he rechecked the luggage and settled in.

"A moment." Cook's voice cut across the frosty morning.

Gwen peeked between the window coverings as Cook trotted toward the carriage, waving one hand at Arthur, the other clutching a small crockery pot.

"If you would, drop this crock of preserves off at Lily's Boardinghouse for me," Cook announced in a loud voice. "A late Christmas gift."

Gwen couldn't understand Arthur's grumbled response.

"And why would I send Mark Allen with you driving right by?" Cook turned on her heel, her hands empty. Gwen covered the grin that tugged at her mouth. Bless Cook, she had found a way for Arthur to stop at the boardinghouse.

Hope soared within Gwen.

She sneaked a glance at Miss Constance, who lay propped against the corner of the carriage with her eyes shut. Sympathy nudged her again. The morning sickness had passed, but the trip would still prove tiresome for one in her condition.

The carriage lurched forward, and Gwen steadied herself against the cushioned seat. She wadded and wadded again the edge of the blanket she'd drawn over her lap. She had no idea how far away the boardinghouse was, but she counted each turn. After the seventh, the carriage rocked to a halt. She held her breath.

"You there, girl." Arthur called down.

Miss Constance lifted her head and jerked her chin towards the door.

Gwen scampered out.

"Take this crock through that door yonder," Arthur said. "See they know it comes from Cook. Be quick now."

Gwen almost dropped the crock at his exaggerated wink. Gathering her wits, she scurried to the door and knocked. A lanky, elderly woman answered and looked her up and down. Gwen thrust the crock at her.

"From Cook at the Whitefords', ma'am."

The woman took it and blinked in confusion.

"Do you have a girl here, under indenture, by the name of Faye Morgan?" Gwen asked in a flurry of words.

"Nay, I know of no such girl nor any cook at the Whitefords' either." With the crock tucked under her arm, the woman frowned and shut the door.

Gwen stared at the door, then at the carriage.

Arthur beckoned, and she stumbled back on numb legs. Tears threatened when she met Arthur's sad-eyed look, but she gathered her bottom lip between her teeth and climbed into the carriage. Miss Constance ignoring her, Gwen pressed her hands to her eyes and willed herself not to cry. She'd shed too many tears these past weeks. She would shed no more today.

The carriage carried her toward a bleak future.

The trip from Greenesville to New Bern could be made in a long day, but out of compassion for Miss Constance's condition, they broke the journey midafternoon at a dusty inn along the road. Her mistress complained of the lumpy bed, the overcooked chicken, the uncouth staff, and Gwen's complete incompetence before finally falling asleep.

Gwen wrapped herself in a thin but reasonably clean blanket and curled into a ball on the floor near her mistress's bed. She lay awake long after Miss Constance slept, her mind going back again and again to the lanky woman's frown as she shut the door. She wanted to believe the woman lied, that her sister resided somewhere in that house, but she couldn't. Faye was as lost to her as ever.

Was it really just two nights ago that Mr. Whiteford had called her into his study? So much had changed since then. Her dashed hopes of finding Faye had occupied her mind the entire trip, but there was more to consider. In New Bern, she wouldn't be forced to spend her days dodging Mr. Jonas. She breathed a bit easier at that thought. Mark Allen came to her sleep-fogged thoughts and the tiny flicker of relief at their separation surprised her.

Sleep claimed her before she could ponder what that meant.

The landscape rolled past the carriage window. In the two years since the ship carrying Gwen and Faye across the ocean had landed at New Bern, the city had sprawled into the surrounding countryside. Everywhere she looked, new buildings stood in varying degrees of completion.

She remembered little of the city from her brief stay before. The riverboat captain who had purchased her and her sister's indentures from Captain Reynolds kept them on the boat until their sale. Under guard and afraid of the riverboat crew, she and Faye had stayed in their corner below deck, huddled together against the damp and cold.

Gwen squeezed her eyes shut at another memory of clinging to Faye. They stood in a high-sided chute with other frightened men and women, mostly Negroes. Many, like themselves, were little more than children. Two foul-smelling men wrenched her sister from her arms before pushing Gwen onto the platform in front of the auctioneer. She had fallen on her knees and cried out, reaching back for Faye, who had screamed her name.

"What do you have to whimper about?" Miss Constance's voice sliced through the pain of her thoughts.

Gwen hadn't meant to make that sound.

"I was remembering the last time I was in New Bern, miss."

"And a lucky day that was for you. You could have done far worse than my father for a master. If he had not taken pity on you, you might be toiling away in a field with the darkies. You should be grateful for the easy lot you drew."

"Aye, miss." Gwen bowed her head and studied the blanket on her lap. Grateful. Grateful that her father died aboard ship, leaving her and Faye orphans? Grateful to Captain Reynolds for keeping Father's money and selling them into bondage for more? Grateful to be ripped away from her only living relative?

She'd like to see Miss Constance survive half so much and feel grateful.

Resentment smoldered within her, turning her stomach sour.

When the carriage bumped to a halt, Miss Constance swept aside the curtain beside her. "'Tis about time." She let the cloth fall back into place.

Arthur opened the door and helped Miss Constance from the carriage.

Gwen tumbled out in her wake. An imposing brick structure towered three stories above them.

A black man in livery waited beside an elaborately carved door.

Gwen followed her mistress up the wide stone steps, where the servant bowed and opened the door, ushering them into a wide hallway. He closed the door behind them, shuttering the hallway in darkness.

Shadows clung to the dark paneling. Instead of the smell of beeswax polish that lingered in the Whitefords' foyer, it smelled of age and disuse.

Gwen pulled her shawl closer.

"My name is Jonathan," the liveried man said. He stood perfectly straight, which seemed at odds with the deep grooves of his face under his salt-and-pepper hair. "This is Ruth." He waved his hand in the direction of a tall black woman with piercing eyes and hair the color of cold hearth ashes.

"Follow me." Ruth's dry, cold voice sent a shiver along Gwen's spine. "I is to show you to your room, Miss Constance. Mrs. Cummings will greet you in the parlor before supper this evening. Your maid can settle your belongings." Nearly black eyes raked Gwen from head to toe. By the disdainful arch of an ebony eyebrow, she'd been found wanting.

"Very good." Miss Constance held her head high as she gathered her skirt and climbed the staircase a step ahead of Ruth. "I shall need time to rest and refresh myself after that loathsome journey."

"Of course, miss." Ruth inclined her head in a graceful gesture that Miss Constance didn't see.

Gwen's heart dropped as she followed Ruth. She hoped all the servants didn't prove to be as austere as the two she'd met so far.

The door of the bedroom clicked shut at Ruth's departure. "Aunt Matilda did not even greet me." Constance threw her reticule against the back of the door. "I have half a mind to tell Arthur to leave my trunks on the carriage and return home on the morrow. Can you imagine?" Miss Constance's voice rose in pitch and volume with each word.

Gwen cast a glance at the closed door. Likely everyone in the house could imagine it.

"Please reconsider, Miss Constance. Your father—"

"My father never liked Aunt Matilda. And for very good reasons. He would understand my not abiding this unforgiveable rudeness from her."

"But where else would you go until—?"

"Any place would be preferable." Miss Constance turned her back on Gwen and strode to the window that overlooked the back of the house. Head held high, nevertheless, a tremor shook her shoulders and a stifled sob followed.

"Allow me to assist you out of those travel clothes, miss. You rest in this fine bed until supper." Gwen stood with her hands folded in front of her. Her earlier resentment warred against the persistent stab of sympathy for her mistress. Miss Constance's situation may be entirely the result of her own actions—unlike Gwen's—but she had been separated from her family too.

"I believe I will lie down until supper. I am sorely fatigued from that insufferable journey."

A tap on the door drew a frown from her mistress as Gwen scooped up the reticule before opening the door a crack.

Two burly lads in street clothes stood in the hallway, each shouldering a heavy trunk. Gwen showed them where to set them and asked that they leave the remaining cases in the hallway as her mistress wished to rest. Once Miss Constance was undressed and tucked in, Gwen went in search of the servant staircase and followed her nose to the kitchen below.

"Ah, and who might you be? The maid to the young mistress?" A wizened face peered at Gwen from around a stack of barrels.

"Yes, ma'am." Gwen bobbed a curtsy.

"Never do that." The woman walked toward Gwen and shook a bony finger at her. "Doan be treating me like a white woman."

Gwen took a step in retreat.

"You calls me Evie. Everyone does." Evie was scarecrow-thin and years older than Cook, with warm brown eyes that twinkled in the glow from the fireplace.

"Sit yourself down, chil'. I reckon you could put away a cup of tea and a biscuit with jam."

Gwen sank onto a bench beside the kitchen table as Evie put the tea together.

"The young mistress is settled?"

"She is resting."

"*Tsk-tsk-tsk.* I doan know what that girl expects, but the missus ain't none too happy to have her here." Evie slid a plate of golden biscuits and a pot of jam in front of Gwen, returning a moment later with the chipped teapot and two mismatched cups. She sat on the bench opposite Gwen.

"Why is she not happy?"

Evie looked at her, planted one elbow on the table, and dropped her chin onto her hand. The mystery of the ages might have lived in the depths of her eyes. "You doan know?"

Gwen shook her head.

"The missus got no use for Mr. Whiteford, nor his daughter neither."

"Then why did she allow Miss Constance to come and stay?"

"Money. Her daddy be paying plenty to keep that girl here until that babe be born. Enough to pay off the gambling debts Mr. Cummings left when he up and died."

"Do you know... have you heard... what will happen to the babe?"

"I doan know." Evie shook her head. The already deep wrinkles pulled tighter, and the twinkle faded from her eyes. "I doan know."

The biscuit crumbs dried in Gwen's mouth.

Chapter 7

E VIE AND SAPPHIRA, ANOTHER of Mrs. Cummings' elderly slaves, served the evening meal downstairs while Gwen unpacked her mistress's trunks. She was kneeling in front of the dressing table drawer and tucking in the last pressed handkerchief when the bedroom door burst open.

Gwen jumped to her feet with a half-gasp, half-squeak.

"That woman. That insufferable—woman." Miss Constance drew herself to her full height in the open doorway. Her chin thrust out, she advanced into the room. Gwen backed up until the dressing table bit into her thighs. "She had the nerve to call me a—" She sliced the air with one hand. "Never mind. She said it in front of those darkies."

"I'm sorry, Miss Constance."

"Fetch paper and ink. I shall write my father. Arthur will carry the letter back with him. I cannot abide here until the spring." Tears shimmered in Miss Constance's eyes. They could have been from indignation or self-pity. Or quite possibly both.

Gwen gathered the writing supplies and placed them on the desk by the window. She bobbed a curtsy.

"May I be excused, miss?"

"Be back in an hour to deliver this letter."

Gwen slipped down the servants' stairs to the kitchen, where the three house servants and the aged cook sat at the table eating from shallow wooden bowls. Four sets of dark eyes rested upon her. Only one face offered a smile.

"Join us, chil'." Evie stood and ladled another portion of the fragrant stew into a bowl. She set it beside her own and motioned Gwen over. "Sit right here beside me."

Gwen sank onto the bench. Across the table, Ruth glowered at her. Gwen dropped her gaze and lifted the spoon. Barely tasting the sweet onions and tender pork, she focused on emptying her bowl. Several minutes passed in silence. The others had stopped eating. Maybe she should take her meals somewhere else. But where?

"Things is gonna be uneasy for the next few months." Gwen jumped at Jonathan's voice.

Evie patted her leg under the table, and when Gwen risked a glance at her, the kind woman smiled and winked.

"I 'spect we'll all get used to things," the tiny cook said. "So, chil', you haven't told us your name."

"G-gwen," she stammered. She bent her head back over her bowl. The thick stew cooled and solidified around the spoon.

"The missus say you an indentured servant. How much longer 'til you free?" Ruth demanded.

Gwen glanced up at the emphasis Ruth put on the last word. "Five years."

Evie hummed and rocked on the bench. "Not long at all, chil'. Not long at all. I got aprons older than that."

"I got handkerchiefs older than that," Sapphira said.

"Me, I got heartburn older than that." Jonathan slapped the table with his open hand and laughed.

Ruth's frown encompassed them all.

"Must seem like forever to a young thing like you. How old is you?" Evie spooned up another mouthful of stew.

"Sixteen."

Evie swallowed and hummed. "Sixteen. I think I got aprons older than that too." The others laughed again, except for Ruth, who didn't appear to have any laugh lines among the wrinkles on her face.

Gwen turned back to Evie. "How... how old are you?" That loosened more mirth around the table.

Evie patted her hand. "Oh, chil', they ain't no use countin' after fifty. And I was fifty a long time ago."

More than fifty years with no hope of freedom. She cast another glance at Ruth. Maybe her lack of humor made more sense than the laughter of the other three.

Gwen picked up her spoon and concentrated on finishing her stew. The others continued their discussion of the changes Miss Constance's arrival brought to the house.

When they all stood, Gwen took her bowl to the sink and pushed up her sleeves. An approving nod from Sapphira lifted her spirits a bit as she plunged her hands into the soapy water and started washing.

Evie hummed a tune while she cleaned the table and Sapphira dried the dishes. Jonathan and Ruth left to attend to the missus. It wasn't so different from the kitchen at the Whitefords'.

If one overlooked the skin color of those working.

After delivering Constance's letter to Arthur and wishing him a safe journey for the following day, Gwen retraced her steps to her mistress's room. Constance would spend most of her time for the next four or five months in that room. Mr. Whiteford would not send Arthur back for them until after the babe's birth. All the pleading in the world wouldn't change his mind.

Not that Constance's letter was apt to be pleading. Demanding would be more like her.

The servants' talk made it quite plain Mrs. Cummings was not happy to have a pregnant niece in her house. That small tug of sympathy nipped at Gwen again. She couldn't imagine her father treating her so harshly, but then, she couldn't imagine bringing such shame to him either.

She tapped on the door and eased it open.

Miss Constance slouched in a large chair by the window, gazing out into the darkness. A book rested unopened on her lap.

Gwen tended the fire and turned down the bed before clearing her throat.

"Would you like me to help you change, miss, and brush out your hair?"

"No. Just leave me alone."

"Miss Constance?"

Her mistress ignored her.

"Miss Constance, I know not where I am to sleep."

"Neither do I, nor do I care. Go ask that sour-faced darkie."

Gwen retrieved her carpetbag from Miss Constance's trunk and shut the bedroom door behind her. She looked both ways down the hall, but Mr. Jonas was back in Greenesville. According to Arthur, that was forty-five miles away. Her step was lighter as she skipped down the dark staircase to the kitchen.

"Back so soon?" Evie rocked in a chair by the huge hearth.

"I know not where to put my things."

"I shall show you to your bunk. Sapphira got it ready for you." Evie's joints creaked and popped as she rose from the chair.

"If you but tell me—"

"Nonsense, chil'. 'Tis time for me to go up too. Jonathan will bank the fire before he goes to sleep. He always do." She took a tin candleholder from the table and hobbled up the stairs to the third floor. Several low doors opened off a narrow hallway. Evie opened the third one.

"You be in here." Evie lit a candle stub off the one she carried. "Doan let it burn too long. The missus be mighty stingy with candles. You won't get another till Sunday. Rest well."

Gwen nodded, and Evie closed the door behind her, shutting out any warmth. The room was small and stark, but it had a real bed mounted against the wall. Gwen poked the mattress. It rustled with fresh straw, and the blanket was clean and heavy.

Shivering, Gwen pulled her nightgown from the carpetbag. She changed as quickly as she could and blew out the candle before sliding beneath the wool blanket. She drew her knees close to her body and the blanket over her head.

Sleep claimed her before she could begin to grieve over Faye.

For the first week, her mistress paced the floor and demanded Gwen investigate every carriage she thought she heard stop in front of the manor. Each day that passed with no sign of Arthur, Miss Constance grew more peevish.

Gwen's day brightened whenever she was dismissed and could escape to help Evie in the kitchen. She rarely glimpsed Mrs. Cummings and did her best to stay out of the lady's way.

The New Year came and went with little fuss. The Cummings's household, quiet compared to the Whitefords', offered Gwen a new kind of freedom. Without the daily worry of Jonas lurking around each corner, she gradually relaxed. Miss Constance didn't require her attention in the middle of the day, with no parties to attend or people to entertain. So Gwen spent her extra hours with Evie, learning to cook and bake. While she'd stirred pots and mixed batters for Cook, there hadn't been time to learn much about what she was doing. Under Evie's gentle guidance, Gwen discovered she enjoyed working in the kitchen.

One blustery evening in late January, a commotion drew Gwen and Evie's attention from the kitchen while they prepared to serve the evening's dessert. They exchanged glances and Evie nodded toward the door.

Gwen trotted down the hallway to the dining room where Miss Constance's voice issued forth in shrill agitation. She hurried behind her mistress's chair and lowered her eyes as she'd been instructed.

"And that is another thing." Mrs. Cummings tipped her head back as though looking at something distasteful. "I shall never understand my brother-in-law's aversion to the use of slaves. They are much less flighty and, to my mind, make far better servants. Those with an indenture to fulfill think too highly of themselves. A proper slave knows her place and is happy in it."

Gwen flicked a look at Sapphira, who stood behind Mrs. Cumming's chair and stared at the floor. There was nothing happy about the curve of the slave woman's shoulders or the lifeless expression on her face.

"There. Did you see that?" Mrs. Cummings poked a fork in Gwen's direction. "She proves my point. She does not know her place." And with that, she skewered a morsel of beef as if it had offered her a moral offense.

"Gwen suits me fine." Miss Constance's carefully spaced words shocked Gwen, but she kept herself from gaping. Never had she heard such praise from her mistress.

"I'm glad to hear you are satisfied with her. You shall soon be retired upstairs until your time comes. Her company will be the only you will have."

"What? Am I to be banished to my room?" Miss Constance half rose out of her chair.

"Sit. Down." Mrs. Cummings bit off each word. "First of all, 'tis not your room. You are here only at my benevolence. Of course you will be retired upstairs once the situation begins to present itself. Any decent woman of breeding in your situation would not let herself be seen. As for you, well, we cannot risk one of my friends spotting you looking like"—she waved a forkful of beef at Miss Constance's belly—"that." Then she popped the meat in her mouth and chewed.

Miss Constance pushed her chair back, and Gwen took a hasty step out of the way.

"In that case, *dear* Aunt Matilda." Miss Constance slapped her napkin on her plate, splashing gravy onto the snowy-white tablecloth. "I shall bid you farewell here and now. If our paths do not cross again before my departure, all the better." She pivoted and strode out the door.

Gwen scurried to catch up, fearing the blowout that would follow in the bedroom.

"Fetch me paper and ink." Miss Constance cried as soon as they entered her room.

Gwen did so, fully aware of the futility of her efforts.

"When my father hears of this latest indignity heaped upon me, he will fetch me home with all due haste. I can be sequestered in the comfort of my own room." She tore the paper from Gwen's hand, her voice rising to a shriek. "I will not be subjected to such *benevolence* any longer."

Soon, Miss Constance was scribbling fiercely, quill flying over the sheet, oblivious to the ink that splattered between pot and paper.

Gwen ducked out of the room and hurried to the kitchen. The four slaves looked up from their supper as Gwen entered.

"Was it as bad as it sounded?" Evie asked.

"'Twas, aye." Gwen helped herself to a bowl of stew and slid onto the bench next to Evie.

"There be no peace in this house till that girl be gone." Jonathan shook his head.

"She wants to be gone. She is writing her father even now." Gwen shrugged. "Again."

Jonathan snorted.

"You sure he won't come after her this time?" Sapphira asked.

"Aye. She is here until the babe comes."

"Another four or five months." Ruth heaved a sigh and rose. "Peace or no peace, we just do what we always do. Doan matter much to us, anyway." She left, Jonathan following her.

"A baby comin' should be a happy time." Evie hummed and rocked on the bench for a moment. "Should be."

Sapphira stood and collected the empty bowls. "But this ain't as it should be."

Gwen swallowed a mouthful of stew and put down her spoon. Four or five more months of Miss Constance's ill temper and tantrums and then—what? What would happen to the child?

What would happen to Gwen?

Betsy walked into the shipping office with Thomas. Three other couples followed them through the door. They were the people selected to organize the migration—for Betsy could think of no better word to describe it—of the Quakers. The entire population of their Society of Friends, those who lived in and around New Bern, had agreed to join the move northwest. And it wasn't just them. Thomas had received word of several more settlements in the outlying areas who were also organizing to leave the slave-holding states.

The drumbeat for freedom sounded loudly among the quiet people of the Quakers.

Pride rose in Betsy's breast, but she silently berated herself. Pride had no place in this. Doing what was right and good, what the Lord had placed upon their hearts, should be an everyday part of their lives. Not something special to take pride in.

The men would work out the route to take, the most effective way to move hundreds of people to the new land. The women would calculate the needs of each family to supply itself in the new settlement as well as provisions for the journey.

Because the whole settlement was leaving, they would be traveling with many specialists in various crafts. Thomas was the best wheelwright in the area. They'd need his experience once they reached the rough wilderness trails that could reduce a wagon wheel to kindling. They'd also have plenty of carpenters to repair the wagons, a cooper to repair barrels, and several blacksmiths.

One thing niggled at Betsy. They didn't have a doctor in their group. A number of the women were skilled with the uses of herbs and poultices, and Zachary Brown could set a broken bone or pull a tooth, but if a sickness went through the wagons, they'd have to trust God for that. But trusting or not, she was honest enough to admit she'd feel better if they could recruit a doctor before they left.

Thomas and the other men stepped away from their discussion with the clerk at the counter and joined their wives, who had waited near the door. After stepping out into the brisk winter wind, Thomas waved them all into a group.

"We have secured a ship to sail from New Bern to Alexandria, Virginia."

"The ship can carry us all? Our wagons and livestock?" Betsy asked.

"We must purchase new wagons when we arrive. But I suggest we write to the businesses in Alexandria and let them know we are coming and what we shall require when we arrive."

"Will it be expensive?" another wife asked.

"Aye, but 'twill take weeks off our travel, and few of us own wagons fit to go the whole distance anyway." Thomas shrugged. "We could spend money here to refit our existing wagons, and still spend too much time repairing them along the way."

"From Alexandria, where will we go?" Betsy asked.

"We plan to follow Braddock's Road." Amos nodded to the two other men who had accompanied him on the initial exploration trip. "We have been on it. 'Tis rough, but passable."

"What is this Braddock's Road?" another woman asked.

"'Twas the route taken by General Braddock when the British fought the French and Indians at the Battle of the Monongahela." Amos said. "They cut their way through the wilderness and left a good trail."

"Did they not lose that battle?" one of the men asked.

"Indeed. But they won in the long run." Amos shrugged. "Not that it matters one way or the other to us."

Indeed, Betsy agreed silently. Quakers did not fight. Most of them, anyway. The Fighting Quaker, Nathaniel Greene, for whom the nearby town of Greenesville was named. He'd played a major part in the Revolutionary War that had separated the American colonies from the British. He had also been expelled from the Society of Friends for that reason. The Quakers were pacifists, and Betsy believed it was for the best.

She snugged her wool shawl tighter around her shoulders as the women left for the mercantile. They needed to make their plans.

The men followed them into the store and made a beeline for the pot-bellied stove at the center. They'd talk among themselves there while the women pored over catalogs and calculated weights and measures of food staples.

Nobody mentioned it, but an island of space formed around their group. Hostile stares followed them around the store. It was time to leave the place where man enslaved his fellow man on the basis of his skin. Where people who didn't agree with slavery were disliked and distrusted.

New Bern was making it clear that Thomas's decision was sound.

Chapter 8

February 1799

G WEN ADJUSTED THE BASKET in her arms while keeping her cloak pulled tight around her against the mid-February chill. She hurried to catch up with Sapphira, almost bumping into the older woman, who had stopped in the middle of the boardwalk. Gwen craned her neck over Sapphira's shoulder to see what held her attention. A group of strangely dressed people walked by on the other side of the street.

"Who are they?"

"They is Quakers." Sapphira's tone was hushed, reverent.

"What are Quakers?"

Sapphira craned her neck around and gave Gwen a hard stare. "Where you been all your life?" She nodded at the group now entering one of the shipping offices. "They is saints, is what they is."

"Saints?" Gwen stood on tiptoe for a better look as the last one closed the door. "I thought saints were all dead people."

Sapphira snorted. "Quakers is Christians that doan believe in slavery. They used to buy slaves and set 'em free before the state wrote a law makin' it illegal."

"Do they buy indentures and set them free?"

The stark disapproval on Sapphira's face made Gwen wish for her hasty words back. The slaves all treated Gwen kindly, but they never seemed to forget that one day she'd be free—and they never would.

Gwen cleared her throat and changed the subject. "Why do they dress like that?"

"They calls it 'plain.' It means they doan put no importance on how a body looks, sayin' what counts is what is in your heart." Sapphira clasped a fist to her chest. "Doan matter what color your skin is to Quakers."

Gwen was ready for Sapphira to move on. Quakers or no Quakers, the groceries grew heavier by the minute, and they had six more blocks to walk against the biting wind. Finally, the older woman trudged forward, a smile tugging at the corners of her mouth.

Mrs. Cummings had said slaves were happy in their place. If they were so happy, why did those Quakers bring a smile to Sapphira's face?

Gwen lugged the groceries into the kitchen and stayed to help Evie. The old woman hummed as she opened and refilled the various crocks and jars.

"What do you know of Quakers?" Gwen asked.

Evie stopped with her hand mid-reach for another jar. She looked at Gwen, her brow furrowed deeper than normal.

"Why you askin' me that, chil'?"

"Sapphira and I saw some in town today. She said they are saints, but I do not understand. I thought all saints were dead people."

Evie chuckled and pointed to the bench. "Sit and let me tell you some things." They settled across the table from each other, and Evie took one of Gwen's hands in both of hers. "There is saints that is dead and buried. They be watchin' over us all the time, right beside the angels. Then there is saints who walk beside us. Quakers be that type of saints. They love people no matter what, and they help whoever have need." She patted Gwen's hand. "Saints on earth, 'tis a fact."

"My father did not believe in any saints, alive or dead. At least, not after my mother died."

Evie *tsk-tsked* and wagged her head. "We should not be blaming the Good Lord for all the troubles of this ol' world. He created man, but it was man who done the sinnin'. And we's had a heap of troubles ever since." She shook a bony finger at Gwen. "But you mark my words, chil'. Those Quakers is as close to gettin' it right as any people has ever lived."

"Getting what right?"

"Life lived as the Good Lord intended." She stood and patted Gwen's shoulder. "Now you best get yourself upstairs and see to your mistress before she sets up a holler."

Gwen climbed the stairs and thought about what Evie and Sapphira had said as she tapped on the door and pushed it open.

Miss Constance lay propped up in bed, one hand holding a book and the other splayed over her rounding middle, her eyes wide. Gwen hurried to her side.

"Are you ailing, Miss Constance?"

"No, not ailing, 'tis the babe. The movements are stronger now." She looked at Gwen, a slight smile parting her lips. "I felt a kick, not just a flutter, but a real kick."

"That is good, miss. It means your babe is healthy and strong."

Constance's eyes narrowed. She snatched her hand away from her belly. "'Tis not my babe. I want no part of it. Once 'tis born, my father will find a place for it, and I'll be able to go home to my old life."

Gwen shivered.

She remembered the joy in Father's eyes after Mother brought forth her younger brothers. And she remembered the soul-piercing sorrow Father endured when his wife died, unable to give birth to their fifth child.

Only eight years old, Gwen had stepped into the role of raising her younger sister and two brothers. Within a year, the fever had taken both boys. Her father had never truly recovered. Their flight from Wales had been more about escaping the past—and the pain—than hoping for a better future in a new country.

Maybe Miss Constance was right. Maybe children brought more pain than blessings to their parents. Even so, no babe deserved to be born unloved from the start. A wave of protectiveness toward the unborn child washed over her.

What would Mr. Whiteford do?

April 1799

Winter faded and spring settled softly upon the land. The first tentative pale sprouts gave way to a lush shade of green that tangled around Gwen's legs as she attacked the herb garden behind the kitchen. The damp soil released its fresh scent with each swipe of the hoe. Loosened dirt, cool and soft, shifted under her bare feet.

Gwen straightened her back and wiped the sweat from her forehead with the back of her hand. The tang of the sea carried on the wind. She breathed deeply. Their time here was coming to an end. Miss Constance was as big as a rain barrel and less graceful. At last, her mistress was content to remain in her room and await the birth of the unwanted babe.

How could anyone go through these months of waiting and not want the babe who would come? That question kept Gwen awake more often as the day of its birth approached. She didn't understand the eagerness to get rid of something so wonderful. She shoved the hoe into the dirt and leaned against it.

What would it be like to have a babe of her own? Heat crept up her neck and washed across her cheeks. She knew how babes came to be. That wasn't what interested her. But to have one of her own to love, someone of her very own. Not to replace Faye—nobody could ever replace her—but to have a child would be to have a family again. The ever-present ache of loneliness tightened beneath her ribs.

"Is you hoeing that garden or holdin' it down?" Evie called from the kitchen doorway.

Gwen jumped with a squeak, dropping the hoe.

Evie laughed and waved before disappearing back inside.

Gwen got back to work. It was silly wasting her time thinking about a babe. First she'd need to be free, and then she'd need a husband. Miss Constance hadn't waited for the husband, and look where that had gotten her.

Gwen intended to do things proper.

A bell clanged from the open bedroom window above.

Gwen dropped the hoe and ran for the back door, wiping her hands on her apron as she went. It wouldn't do for the neighbors to hear Miss Constance's voice, so Mrs. Cummings had given her that bell to summon Gwen.

By the frantic tenor of its chime... she'd better hurry.

Gwen scurried to do the midwife's bidding. All through the night and into the early hours of that rainy April morning, she did as directed. She cast another anxious glance at her mistress's face. Pale and exhausted, Miss Constance moaned and thrashed her head on the pillows. Gwen's memories of her mother dying, unable to bring forth her last child, haunted her throughout the night.

"Won't be long now," the midwife said with a satisfied nod. "You have done right well, mistress, and your wee one will be here with another push or two."

Miss Constance struggled to lift her head but let it fall back against the pillows. Gwen wiped her brow with a cool, damp cloth, but she groaned when another contraction gripped her. She grabbed Gwen's hands, squeezing hard, sweat making them slippery.

"Sit up some if it helps. Gwen, assist her." The midwife coached them. "This is it now. You have to do your best work here, a big push then, mistress."

Miss Constance bore down, and Gwen leaned into the back of her, helping her bend forward. The groan rose to a screech that curled Gwen's toes.

"Here we are!" The midwife lifted the child up in the receiving blanket. "A right handsome lad he is."

Gwen held her breath and looked between the still child and midwife. The midwife turned the babe upside-down and delivered a firm whack in the middle of his back. The resulting cry brought Gwen's gasp of relief. She squeezed her mistress's shoulders before easing her onto the pillows.

Miss Constance squeezed her eyes shut and turned her face away.

"Gwen, hold the lad while I tie his cord, and then I shall finish here with the mistress."

Gwen took the squalling infant in her arms and looked into his wet, red face. She shifted her weight from one foot to the other, humming under her breath. The child relaxed and quieted until the midwife snipped the cord.

"You are a natural, Gwen. You shall make a fine mother yourself someday, the Good Lord willing," the midwife said.

Gwen flushed and hurried to wash the babe in the water she had prepared and left before the fireplace. She cleaned him from head to toe, marveling at the miracle of birth. She dried him with a soft cloth, and his hand wrapped around her finger. She stared at that tiny hand, so small and so perfect, holding on to her. She pulled him snug against her body, and he burrowed closer in response.

Rising from the floor with her burden, she looked at the bed. Constance still lay with her face turned away.

"Miss Constance?"

"Take it away."

"Oh, but—

"I said take it away."

Gwen took a faltering step toward the door, and then looked at the midwife, uncertain what to do.

"I shall meet you in the kitchen when I'm done here." A frown marred the midwife's brow.

As soon as Gwen entered the kitchen with her precious bundle, Evie rose from her rocking chair, her hands outstretched to take the babe. Gwen handed him over with a wistful sigh.

"I won't keep him long, chil'. I just needs to hold a babe one more time." Evie's eyes misted over. "'Tis been so long, so very long." She sank into the rocker and hummed. Tears flowed freely across the folds and valleys of her cheeks.

"Do you have children?" Gwen kept her voice quiet. She was reluctant to intrude but curious about Evie's tears.

"I guess I do. I ain't seen a one of them in more than twenty years."

"Where are they?"

"Only the Lord knows. They was all sold off when they was old enough to work the fields. Four boys, all strong and tall like they daddy. I miss my babies, and I miss my man as well, him dead these past fifteen years. It does my heart a heap of good to hold this little one."

"A boy."

"Mm-hm. Did she name him?"

"I think she will not."

"What gonna become of him then?"

"I know not. She said her father will find a place for him. Until then, I suppose he is ours to look after." The light in Evie's eyes must have reflected in her own.

"Doan get too attached, chil'." Evie shook her head, her bottom lip thrust out. "It hurts when they take them away. Doan hold on too tight."

"I shan't," Gwen said. But she feared the warning had arrived too late.

Betsy slung the wet blanket over a rope Thomas had stretched between the porch and a nearby tree. Even as low as he'd hung it, the strain of lifting the heavy fabric pulled at her shoulder. She finished smoothing out the dripping blanket and then rubbed her aching muscles. She wasn't spry anymore, but she wasn't packing dirty blankets and linens for their journey.

She paused, her attention once again drifting toward the meeting-house and the burial plot beyond. If her daughters had lived, they would be helping her with the preparations for the move. Betsy blew out a long breath. There was plenty more work to do. Wishing for what she didn't have wouldn't get it done any faster.

The laundry kettle held one last blanket. She lifted it with a long wooden paddle and let the scalding water stream from it. Steam billowed into the crisp spring air. When it was cooled enough, she wrung out as much water as she could, and then slung the blanket onto the rope beside the others. She was smoothing out the ends when the jangle of harness and clip-clop of hooves announced Thomas's return. He was back early.

He stopped the team in front of the barn, climbed down, and stretched. His joints weren't any more limber than hers. Were they crazy to think they could make this trip and start over again at their age?

Did they really have a choice?

Betsy crossed the yard and looked into the wagon. "Did thee purchase all we shall need?"

"Nay. Not today. But his clerk said that Daniel Whiteford himself has ships coming into port weekly and will be in town day after tomorrow. I shall speak with him then."

"'Tis the fabric, mostly, that concerns the women."

"Indeed. 'Tis ever that way with the women." Thomas's eyes twinkled.

Betsy planted her hands on her hips. "Thee knows many of the women have only recently adopted dressing plain. They wish to spend much of the journey sewing for their families."

"Surely there will be fabric to purchase in Alexandria."

"Calicos and brocades, to be sure. But good solid broadcloth, linen, and wool? Enough to outfit the new settlement? 'Tis not likely."

"Alexandria is much larger than New Bern."

"Even so. 'Tis only prudent to start out with an ample supply. 'Twill take some time to be able to produce our own."

"Indeed. I'm sure Daniel Whiteford will be able to meet our needs."

Betsy smiled. Thomas might tease her, but he would do all he could to please her as well. She reached up to loosen Lad's harness, but pain stabbed. She let her arm drop and rubbed her shoulder.

"What is this?" Thomas's eyebrows flattened into a hairy line.

"'Tis nothing, just a twinge."

Thomas looked at the dripping wash and back to her. "Did I set the rope too high?"

"Nay. Any lower and the blankets would trail in the dust. 'Tis just the stiffness of my aging bones."

He put his hands on her shoulders and rubbed. "Then take thy aging bones to thy rocking chair and rest. After I unhitch, I shall join thee."

"Thee fusses too much." But how nice his hands felt.

"Thee are working too hard. Perhaps thee could ask one of the other women—"

Betsy held up a hand to cut him off. "Nay. All are busy preparing for our departure."

"Most have plenty of hands to help." Thomas raised his head and looked toward the meetinghouse. "Surely someone could spare a day?"

Betsy shook her head. "There's not much left to do."

Thomas snorted, raising one eyebrow. "Thee would tell me that, I think, even if 'twere not so."

Betsy's cheeks warmed. She turned and started for the house. "Perhaps I shall rest a few moments, as thee suggested," she said over her shoulder. Sure his gaze bored into her, she kept her back straight. If she slouched, he'd worry about her, and heaven knew he had enough to worry about without her adding to his burden.

She lowered herself into the rocking chair on the porch and released a long sigh. More than help, companionship would be welcome. Loneliness lay like a weight against her spirit some days.

She closed her eyes and prayed for contentment.

Gwen dipped the twisted bit of muslin into the bowl of goat's milk and popped it into the babe's gaping mouth. In no time he sucked it dry. He was perfection, from his tuft of white-blond hair to his pudgy pink toes. She leaned down and let the fine hairs of his head tickle her nose while breathing in his fresh scent. He mewed, and she re-soaked the bit of rag and popped it back into his mouth. Once the babe was satisfied, his little eyelids drooping, she set aside the rag and rocked the old chair beside the kitchen hearth. If only he were her child. She drew him tighter to her chest. If only—

The kitchen door was snatched open, and Sapphira stepped through. She closed the door behind her, leaning back against it. "He come." Her face might have been carved from dark marble, and her somber tone required no further explanation.

Evie set her sewing on the table, her face almost as unreadable as Sapphira's.

It was the moment they'd been dreading.

Just six days after the child's birth, Mr. Whiteford had arrived.

Gwen's heartbeat quickened, and she struggled to pull in a steady breath. He couldn't take the child away. Her arms tightened until the babe squirmed in protest. In spite of Evie's repeated warnings, love for the child had taken root in her heart.

Far too soon, Mr. Whiteford entered the kitchen.

Gwen stood, clutching the babe to her breast.

The master halted and remained one step inside the doorway. He stared at her and the wrapped bundle she held. She took a tentative step toward him, but he raised a hand to halt her.

She glanced at Evie who only shrugged.

"Do you not wish to see him, Mr. Whiteford?"

"Never." He looked out the kitchen window into the gloom of twilight beyond. "I understand Constance has followed my suggestion to not see him either. Is that correct?"

"Aye, sir."

He faced her again, assessing. His glance scanning her head to toe, then cupped his chin with one hand. Gwen resisted the urge to squirm.

"How old are you?"

"Soon to be seventeen, sir."

"Jonas tells me you've been keeping company with my stable boy, is that correct?"

Gwen sucked in a short breath, her jaw fell open, but she found no words.

"Never mind." He waved a hand before she could form an answer. "The child could be yours, which is all that matters."

Gwen gasped and took a step backward. She bumped into the rocker.

Evie reached out and steadied her.

"Follow me." He said over his shoulder, "Leave the child here."

She handled her precious bundle to the wide-eyed Evie and followed him down the hall to the library.

He sat in a wingback chair and motioned to the one opposite. "Sit."

She perched on the edge of its plush seat, heart hammering. Never had she pictured herself sitting—being allowed to sit—in the presence of Mr. Whiteford.

"I have spoken with a man who is sailing next week with a group of Quakers to settle in the Northwest Territory. He would not take an infant." His mouth twisted, and he looked out the window before turning his attention to her again.

Her back stiffened another notch.

"He will, however, take in a mother and child. I will write you a release from your indenture this very evening, give you your freedom, if you sign an oath to never reveal the child's true parentage. You must accept him and claim him as your own blood son."

Freedom.

She had never swooned in her life, but the room tilted under her feet. If she hadn't been seated, she would have collapsed. He offered her freedom in return for the oath.

And the babe.

Her sister might be lost to her forever, but Gwen could keep the babe. She wouldn't be alone in the world anymore.

There was no trace of guile in Mr. Whiteford's face, and in spite of everything, she couldn't remember a single time when he had ever been less than straightforward with her.

He meant it. He was offering her everything she craved.

Speechless, Gwen nodded.

"Hear me well." He pointed at her. "I will hold you to this oath for the rest of my life. The child will be yours. You will acknowledge yourself as an unwed mother. If ever I hear that you have told a living soul who the child's true mother is, I will come after you. The oath you sign will explicitly state that betrayal of my trust will result in you not only finishing your years of indenture but will multiply them tenfold. Have I made myself clear?"

A chill filled her.

Freedom could be hers—at a price. What would people think of her, a young unmarried woman with a babe? Did it matter, compared to her freedom? Compared to her keeping the babe? The scent of his downy hair still lingered in her nose. Mouth too dry to speak, she nodded again.

"Good. I will draw up the papers this evening. You—and the child—will be collected at the kitchen door tomorrow before noon. You will be given the necessary provisions for the child as well as a goat to provide milk."

"Thank you, Mr. Whiteford." She managed to force the words past her stiff lips.

"Thank me only by keeping your oath." His face softened for such a brief moment she would have missed it had she blinked. "And take care of the boy."

"I will, sir."

And with those words, her life was forever changed.

The enormity of her oath lay heavy on Gwen's chest that night. Stretched on her bed, the babe nestled in his box within reach, she contemplated the paper she had signed. She had listened to every word Mr. Whiteford read to her. Her release. Her freedom. At what price had she purchased it?

The babe sighed and rustled in his blankets, yawning but not waking.

She rose on one elbow and peeked at him.

Her son. For him, the price was worth it.

What about Faye? She flopped onto her back. How could she find her sister when she was moving to the wilderness? Was Faye forever lost to her now? The babe flailed an arm in his dreams, and Gwen's lips curved of their own volition. Heart divided, she settled to her side and pillowed her head on her hands. Sleep danced at the boundaries of her reach until the wee hours.

In the morning, she would meet the couple taking her and her son into the wilderness.

Quakers.

Saints.

And she must convince them to believe her lie.

Chapter 9

"ARE THEE CERTAIN THIS is the will of God?" Betsy asked. Her emotions had swung from one extreme to the next since her husband's abrupt announcement upon his return from town. She wasn't sure if she was more hopeful or apprehensive.

"As best I can tell." Thomas spread his hands. "When Daniel White-ford first approached me on the subject, he asked if I would take on a child, a newborn no less. I said nay. But then he assured me he meant the babe and the mother, an indentured servant of his. 'Twould seem she is quite young and alone in the world." He pushed his hat back and scratched at the tuft of gray hair above his brow. "'Twas decidedly odd how he worded it."

"And yet thee accepted." An unwed mother. What sort of young woman was Thomas about to bring into their midst?

"Hmm, 'tis difficult to put into words." He looked bemused. "'Twas on my tongue to refuse, but surely the Lord changed my mind. I told Daniel we would accept the young mother and her babe."

Betsy picked her knitting off her lap. There was nobody she trusted more in such matters. If her husband felt led by the Spirit, that was good enough for her. "The girl will join us tomorrow?"

"We are to collect her in the forenoon from his wife's sister's house in town." His eyes, often creased at the corners with humor, regarded her with a solemn earnestness now. "Thee are agreeable to this? 'Tis no small thing to take in a young woman and a newborn babe with the journey we are about to embark upon."

"The poor dear has likely been through much. Indentured servants are little better than slaves. Surely, we will help her." Betsy paused. "Did he tell thee who the father is?"

"Nay. But I have my suspicions." At her raised eyebrows he shook his head. "Those are best left unspoken as they are no better than gossip."

Betsy laid her knitting needles in her lap again, unable to concentrate on the simple task. "Not himself, surely?"

"I do not believe that to be the case. I have known Daniel Whiteford to be an honorable man. One well regarded by many. We have done much business these past years." Thomas shook his head. "I cannot believe that of him."

"What of the girl's family?"

"Daniel says she has none. 'Tis how she came to be indentured in the first place."

"But she is free now?"

"Aye, and not quite seventeen. He promised to give her written release from her indenture. He offered to transfer it to me, but I told him we could not abide to keep another in bondage. She will, of course, be our moral obligation until she comes of age. And we must see to the care and needs of her child."

"A boy or a girl?"

"I know not."

Betsy picked up her knitting, the rhythmic clicking of the bone needles a soft cadence against the sporadic chorus of frogs. Both calmed her as she considered the additions to their household.

Thomas's eyelids drooped and on occasion, his head bobbed against the chair's high back.

A smile ticked at the corners of Betsy's mouth. The rocker creaked against the boards of the wide porch, the pungent scents of the earth waking from winter to spring rising around her. A time of new life. She gazed above her knitting at the meetinghouse in the distance.

"Thee are happy, I see." His voice startled her.

"I thought thee dozing."

"I did some." He stretched without leaving the chair. "This arrangement, it pleases thee?"

"To have a girl in our home again? And a babe, thee did say a newborn? I think 'twill please me indeed."

"Does thee think this may fill a spot long empty?"

"I fear to hope."

Thomas nodded and turned toward the meetinghouse while emotions played across his face in the waning light. He combed his fingers through the gray curls of his beard, his bottom lip protruding as it always did when he pondered. The lines of his forehead relaxed, and he gave a shallow nod. It warmed her heart that he echoed her longings.

Betsy closed her eyes and prayed for the Lord's will in the situation, asking for His blessing on the girl and babe, and for strength for herself and Thomas.

It would not be an easy thing if they were to be disappointed again.

"No, chil', not like that. Let me shows you again." Evie twisted the wrapping with a flash of her leathery hands and had it snug in place around the babe's bottom.

Gwen groaned.

"You be learnin', doan you worry. Just takes practice. You be gettin' plenty soon enough. This little boy be keepin' you hoppin' before you know it."

"I know not how to be a mother. Evie, what if I... fail?"

"Lord, chil', you ain't gonna fail. You said you done raised your sister and brothers."

"But they weren't newly born."

Evie took hold of Gwen's shoulders and gave her a gentle shake. "No woman on earth is born knowin' how to be a momma. We all gots to learn it."

"My mother is gone. I have no one to teach me."

"You gots me and Sapphira right here, and soon that Quaker family come for you."

Gwen's stomach wobbled. The last time she'd been hauled off by a stranger, he had taken her into a life of servitude. Would this be any different? The two slave women seemed to think so.

"How can you be so sure they will help me?"

"They is Quakers. They help everybody. They believe God created all people equal. They believe in helping others. 'Tis what makes them so special. They doan hurt nobody, and they doan look down on nobody."

"They are very religious, then?"

"Lord, chil', I should say so."

"They will think I am... that my son is..." Gwen whispered the words, even though the slaves all knew about her agreement with Mr. Whiteford. Voices carried in the house, but apparently nobody cared if the slaves overheard. Not even Mr. Whiteford, for all his threats should she tell anyone of her oath.

"They already agreed to accept you, even with a babe born on the wrong side of the blanket." Evie's eyes bored into Gwen's. "What you doin' be savin' him from who knows what sort of a life. But people will see him as a bastard chil'. You best get used to hearin' it. The Quakers might not say it out loud, but others will. And when they do, you raise your head and look them in the eye. He your son. You be proud of him! You know you done nothin' wrong, but you ain't never to tell nobody else. So you be proud of him, you hear me?"

Gwen nodded, the fierceness of Evie's words searing into her mind.

Evie and Sapphira waited in the kitchen with Gwen, taking turns holding her son. *Her son.* Gwen's heart both stumbled and sang as she paced from one end of the room to the other.

Packed in a new carpetbag were the provisions Mr. Whiteford had promised. It held plenty of cloth and sewing supplies to keep the boy clothed, along with cakes of soap and several small feeding cups. The goat, a scraggly white creature with a full udder, browsed what she could reach while tethered to the hitching post outside.

Her release from indenture lay wrapped in an oilskin at the bottom of her own worn carpetbag. Nestled beside it was one of Mr. Whiteford's embroidered handkerchiefs, knotted around three silver coins. She would never forget the look in his eyes when he pressed that into her hand and then left without a word.

Money had not been part of their agreement. Perhaps, deep in his heart, he harbored a love for the babe he refused to look upon. His first grandchild.

The rattle of a wagon drifted through the open window. The three women paused and looked at each other. Nothing stirred in the kitchen for a long moment.

Evie broke the stillness when she clutched the babe and peeked around the curtain. "Bless the Lord."

"It be them?" Sapphira pressed close to the glass.

"Quakers."

The reverence in the old cook's voice sent a shiver down Gwen's spine. The two slave women smiled and hugged each other, the babe secure between them.

Gwen stepped back into the shadows of the kitchen. She pressed both hands to her stomach. Her father's deep distrust of religion painted a jarring contrast to the hope and reverence she read on the dark faces of Evie and Sapphira.

Sapphira hurried to the door and jerked it open at the first knock. She curtsied low and moved to allow the Quakers to enter before curtsying again.

"Bow not before us, friend," the man said. "Such deference we are not worthy of."

Sapphira pressed the back of her fingers to her mouth, her eyes so wide the whites gleamed in the kitchen's low light. To be spoken to with such kindness and called "friend" had clearly unsettled her.

The Quaker woman's eyes sought Gwen. Silver wisps of hair framed in front of a black bonnet. A wide white cloth wrapped her neck and shoulders, covering the bodice of her gown. Her gown and petticoats, in a soft shade of gray, were devoid of any lace or trim and brushed the tops of her buttoned black shoes. She reached only to the man's chin, even though he held no claim to height.

The lower half of the man's face was hidden behind a curly gray beard. From the upper half, his eyes peered at her from behind round, gold-rimmed spectacles. His black felt hat needed reblocking, and he did not remove it upon entering the kitchen as was the custom. His coat and breeches were of the same soft gray as the woman's clothing, his hose a few shades darker. His neck cloth was white but free of any lace trim. Sapphira called their way of dressing "plain." Up close, Gwen could see why.

"Thee are Gwen Morgan?" the man asked in the same warm voice he'd used to address Sapphira.

"I am." She bobbed a curtsy.

"Thee owes us no such deference either." He spread his hands. "We are all equal before the Lord."

Gwen stood mute, her tongue stilled by the strangeness of this couple, her stomach aflutter with uncertainty. What sort of future would she and the babe have with these people?

The silence stretched until Evie presented the babe. The Quaker woman stepped forward and placed her hand on the old cook's shoulder. Evie straightened her back, lifted her chin. She gracefully handed over the bundled child.

The Quaker woman snuggled him in the crook of her arm.

"Look, Thomas. 'Tis truly a beautiful babe." She traced the babe's cheek with her finger. "Boy or girl?" She looked at Gwen, her smile deepening lines well used to that action.

"A b-boy," Gwen said.

"What has thee named him?" the Quaker woman asked.

Gwen shot a panicked glance at Evie who closed her eyes and nodded. Evie trusted these Quakers. Gwen pulled in a long breath, fortifying herself with the old cook's trust.

"He has not yet been named," Gwen said.

"There is plenty of time." The Quaker woman's eyes shone with kindness. "Oh my. Pardon our manners. We have yet to introduce ourselves. I am Betsy and this is my husband, Thomas Baldwin. 'Tis our understanding that thee wishes to join us in our journey to the Northwest Territory."

Gwen nodded. She looked from wife to husband and back again. Did they know she had no choice? That wasn't true. She'd had a choice, and she'd made it. She took a step forward.

"Daniel Whiteford advised me he would write thee a release of indenture," the man said. "Has he done so?"

Gwen reached for her carpetbag, but Thomas raised a hand. "I need not witness it, only to know it has been done." At her nod, he continued. "Then we can be on our way." Thomas lifted the two carpetbags from the table and stepped outside.

"The Lord bless you and the boy." Evie's watery eyes looked into hers.

Gwen hugged her tightly while a bony hand patted her back. Evie's hope-filled words whispered against Gwen's cheek. "You will do fine, I knows you will. You be in good hands with them Quakers."

Sapphira, her bottom lip trembling, stood behind Evie. Gwen reached out and hugged her goodbye. The woman's stiff body relaxed, and she stroked Gwen's back before stepping away.

Betsy smiled at the trio before she carried the babe outside.

Gwen paused in the doorway, one hand on the worn doorpost. "I shall never forget you," she whispered, then fled out the door and hurried after Betsy.

Thomas helped Gwen onto the wagon seat. She settled her skirt before Betsy handed her the babe.

"We mustn't forget the goat," Gwen asked.

"Goat?" Thomas looked at the white creature who belched up a cud to chew. He turned to Gwen. "Thee has a goat?"

"For the milk. For the babe." Gwen lowered her chin, resting it over the babe's head on her chest. She peeked at Thomas's bewildered expression.

Betsy and Thomas exchanged a quick look before he untied the goat and hoisted it onto the wagon bed. He tethered it to the back of the seat and then helped Betsy settle beside Gwen. He walked around the wagon and sat on Gwen's other side. When the horses started forward with a jerk, Gwen tightened her hold on her son. She turned as much as she could, sandwiched as she was on the bench seat. Two faces pressed against the pane of the kitchen window.

Betsy patted her knee. "We are happy thee has come to us."

Gwen looked into Betsy's eyes, and then dropped her own to her son. The goat pushed against her back, and she gasped.

Betsy leaned close to Gwen. "I have known several women who had need of a milk goat when they could not produce enough on their own. There is no shame in such." She spoke in a voice low enough that Thomas would not overhear.

Betsy accepted the child as hers.

Gwen breathed a sweet sigh of relief. But what if they discovered the truth? Cook's warning months ago concerning the difficulty of keeping a secret rode on her shoulders like an itch she couldn't scratch. She gathered her bottom lip between her teeth and breathed in, the muscles in her stomach twitched.

She would see this through. She had to.

She'd made her choice.

The babe stretched and yawned. His face turned toward her even though his eyes remained closed. He needed her to keep her oath. He needed her as no one else ever had.

Not even Faye.

Emotions, so powerful her skin seemed to expand to contain them, welled within her. Love, pride, joy... she struggled to name them all.

Gwen lifted her chin and looked forward, to the future and whatever it held for both of them.

Chapter 10

W HATEVER GWEN HAD EXPECTED, this wasn't it. The dim interior
of the cabin closed around her as she followed Betsy inside.
Everything was neat, tidy, and... plain. Unlike anything she had seen
before. The rounded logs created uneven walls, the only plaster in
sight chinking them together. Two small windows with straight white
curtains let in enough light to prevent her from stumbling into the few
pieces of furniture before her eyes adjusted to the gloom.

The stark room tucked under the eaves at the Cummings house
looked frilly in comparison. And yet the warmth of home permeated
the space in a way never known in that cramped upstairs room. A
pottery crock on the table held wildflowers, and a rocking chair with a
shawl draped over its back stood beside the hearth. Shelves of dishes
and cooking pots lined one wall. Two doors opened off the back of
the room, opposite the windows, and a ladder disappeared into a loft
above.

The babe fussed in her arms. Evie and Sapphira had done so much
to help these past few days. For the first time, the duty of motherhood
weighed solely on Gwen's shoulders. She tried to soothe the child

while her mind raced in three different directions. Would Mr. Baldwin bring in her carpetbags with the nursing cloths? Where had he taken the goat? What would she do with the babe while she milked the creature?

"May I hold him?" Betsy asked.

The calm in the older woman's eyes helped slow Gwen's breathing. "Yes, Mrs.—"

"Call me Betsy, and my husband is Thomas. Our surname is Baldwin, but we are not formal here." She took the babe, who scrunched his face and let out a howl of protest. "He has strong lungs." A smile curved her lips as she pulled the blanket away from his little red face. "Probably hungry. Thee can take a bowl from the shelf and fetch some milk from the goat. Thomas will have it in the barn by now. I shall walk with this wee one for a bit until he settles down."

Gwen grabbed the bowl and fairly flew out the door. Two steps off the porch she collided with Thomas.

"Whoa, there." Thomas steadied Gwen with a hand on her shoulder. In the other, he held her carpetbags.

"Pray, forgive me, sir." Gwen's face flamed hot.

"'Tis not sir, just Thomas, and there is nothing to forgive." He nodded at the bowl in her hands. "Thee will find the goat in the barn." He pointed to a building not much different in structure from the cabin.

"Thank you." She bobbed a curtsy out of habit and scurried past him.

The goat nibbled from a pile of hay when Gwen skidded to a halt beside it. She looked at the bowl and back at the animal. She'd never milked a goat before. Why hadn't she thought to ask Sapphira about that?

"Be easy, goat. I have need of a bit of your milk. For the babe."

The furry creature chewed its hay. Its bottom jaw swung in a lazy rhythm. Gwen stepped closer and ran her hand over its back. It leaned against her. The bony points of the goat's hips pushed into her leg. She knelt and placed the bowl under its udder. The goat pivoted its rear end away from her.

Gwen blinked at the whiskery face.

The goat blinked back.

"This won't do." Gwen picked up the bowl and moved to the goat's side again. The white creature did another pivot and brought her face back to Gwen's. Gwen huffed and sat on her heels. "Now see here, goat. The babe needs your milk."

"Is she giving thee trouble?" Thomas asked.

Gwen jumped to her feet and whirled toward the door, her hand to her chest.

"I did not mean to frighten thee. I thought to show thee where a bit of grain is."

"Grain?"

"Indeed." He moved into the barn and lifted a wooden lid off a large bin. "A bit of grain will do the trick." He scooped a double handful into a shallow trough and set it in front of the goat. She plunged her nose in. "Now thee can milk her without a fuss."

Gwen slid the bowl back in place and reached under the goat.

"'Tis best if thee squeezes at the top, by the bag, then work the milk down with thy fingers." He leaned over and demonstrated the motion.

Gwen did as Thomas instructed, and a creamy blast of milk splattered into the bowl.

"If thee puts one hand on each side and takes turns, thee will have that bowl filled in no time." He nodded and left the barn. Gwen placed her other hand under the goat and squirted another stream of the frothy warm milk. It wasn't difficult. She could do it. She moved into a rhythm of alternating squirts with the rhythmic munching of the goat until the bowl was full.

She stood and scratched the white creature's knobby head. "'Twasn't so bad. Not bad at all." The wail of the babe caught her ear, and she hurried back to the cabin.

It was time to start being the babe's mother in truth—maybe not by blood, but by love and labor. She would be his mother in all ways that mattered. It was the oath she swore to herself as she dashed back to the cabin.

"She is so unsure of herself," Betsy said. "The poor girl. So young to be a mother and with no mother of her own or family to help her."

"Indeed. Perhaps that is why the Good Lord placed her here with us."

"And this little one." Betsy stared into the murky blue eyes of the babe. "Oh, husband, I cannot tell thee..."

His hand cupped her shoulder as he leaned over and peered at the child. His eyes grew misty. So many years they had been husband and wife. She knew his thoughts well.

"Leaving our own behind, well, 'twill make it just a wee bit easier, I think." She looked out the window toward the meetinghouse and the burial ground beyond. "New life, new hope, surely God has given us a gift."

"'Twould seem so." Thomas's voice was a rough whisper.

Betsy's heart swelled to an almost painful fullness. She shifted the babe to one arm and carried the carpetbags into the small pantry they had hastily converted for Gwen's use, thinking it easier than climbing the ladder to the loft with the babe in her arms. Betsy opened the newer bag first and found the babe's supplies in there. After changing him, during which he wailed his protest, she returned to the cabin's main room and settled in the rocking chair. He quieted and snuggled against her.

The precious bundle lay against her heart in every way.

Gwen rushed through the door without slopping milk from the wooden bowl.

"No need to hurry. We are fine here." Betsy held the babe close while she rocked. "I have changed him, and he has settled. How have thee been feeding him?"

Gwen looked around for her bags. "Muslin cloths. I dip a twist of muslin in the milk and let him suck it dry." She sat the bowl on the table. "What I need is in the carpetbag."

"Your bags are in that room." Betsy nodded to the narrow door behind the table. "'Twill be thy room until the journey."

Gwen hurried in and dug out a hemmed square of muslin. Evie had packed a large stack of them, each one folded and smoothed by her dark hands. Gwen approached Betsy, unsure how to ask for the child, unsure about so many things.

Betsy stood and offered her the babe. Their hands touched as Gwen studied the older woman's face. So serene. So comforting.

"He is a fine boy. That bit of hair is so fair. He must resemble his father." A deep blush stained Betsy's cheeks. She touched Gwen's elbow. "Forgive me. That was thoughtless."

Gwen swallowed and looked away. The babe fussed again, and she patted his back. She cast around for something to look at other than Betsy. Her heart raced like a bird caught in a snare.

"Sit thee down and feed him." Betsy's hand on Gwen's elbow guided her to the bench at the table near the bowl of milk.

Gwen twisted the muslin and dipped it into the warm milk before popping it into her son's open mouth. His slurping and sucking noises filled the awkward silence.

"I'm sorry to cause thee any distress." Betsy twisted her white apron in her hands. "'Twas a thoughtless thing to blurt out that way."

Gwen cast a quick peek at Betsy before she dipped the cloth in milk again. The older woman's face was drawn into sorrowful lines. Gwen pulled in a long, shaky breath. "'Tis fine... Betsy. You meant no harm."

"Thee are gracious." Relief colored her words. "Know this, if thee ever needs to discuss... anything... I would be honored to listen and hold thy confidences in my heart, even as thy own mother would."

Gwen gasped softly.

Mrs. Whiteford had stood in the doorway of the manor house before the carriage pulled away for New Bern. Constance's mother had not held her daughter's confidences close. But then, Betsy was a world away from Mrs. Whiteford.

"Thee are safe here, Gwen Morgan. Fear not." Betsy ran her fingers down Gwen's long, dark curls that had escaped her bonnet. "Thee has been through much, but thee are no longer alone."

Tears gathered on Gwen's lashes and may have spilled had not the babe released another howl.

"Feed thy son now. I should not prattle on when he needs thee."

Gwen did so as Betsy moved around the cabin preparing the evening meal. Betsy resembled neither rotund, jolly Cook nor thin, wise Evie. Even so, watching the Quaker woman brought a sense of calm such as Gwen had only known in the company of those two women.

Muscle by muscle, she relaxed. The smells, the sounds, the peace of the humble cabin lulled her into a feeling of... she couldn't put a name to it.

She only knew she wanted it to last.

After the meal, they sat on the porch, listening to the night insects and frogs awaken. Betsy's knitting needles clicked, Thomas's head nodded, and Gwen rocked the babe in the only rocking chair on the porch. She felt sure one of them customarily sat in the rocker on such an evening, but both had insisted she take it with the babe.

He shifted in her arms. His tiny lips puckered and slacked as he dreamed. Could she ever tire of watching him?

"The feeling is amazing, is it not?" Betsy's soft voice blended with the evening air. "The love that comes over thee when gazing at the child of thy making."

"Aye." Gwen breathed in the babe's unique scent. Surely she couldn't love him more if he were of her own making.

"What thoughts have thee regarding his name?" Betsy asked.

Gwen's chair rocked to a halt. She wasn't worthy to bestow a name on him, not being his real mother, but she couldn't explain why without divulging her secret, without breaking her sworn and signed oath. The memory of her hand upon the Bible, swearing to Mr. Whiteford, and signing a document to seal it, would be forever pressed upon her heart.

"'Tis a custom among the Friends to name the first son after the mother's father." Thomas's mellow voice ended in a yawn. His eyes remained closed.

"'Tis true," Betsy said. "But 'tisn't always done that way. What was thy father's name?"

"Owen."

The babe waved a tiny fist in the air as she spoke, as if he approved of the name.

Gwen met Betsy's smile. "Owen. I think..." Tears filled her eyes and clogged her throat.

"'Tis a fine, strong name," Thomas said. "I'm sure the Friends will agree to it."

"Agree to it?"

"Another custom among the Friends is that the name of a babe be found accepted at meeting." Betsy waved her hand in the air. "They always are, worry not about that, 'tis only a custom."

"Who are these—friends?" Gwen couldn't control the tremble on the last word.

"'Tis how we Quakers refer to each other." Betsy set her knitting aside and leaned forward in her chair. "We know little about thee, Gwen, but 'tis our hope thee will come to join us in spirit as well as body."

Gwen looked between a fully alert Thomas and Betsy.

"She means, we hope thee will become a Friend, a part of our group of Quakers."

She pulled Owen closer to her chest, ignoring his soft gurgle of protest.

"I see this unsettles thee." Betsy's voice softened. "But my prayer will be that thee will come to know us and love us enough to want to join with us. Thee has been through much, but thee are not alone anymore. No harm will befall thee here in our care."

The sympathy in their eyes tugged at something inside Gwen. Betsy's repeated reassurances of safety comforted and confounded her. No longer alone. No harm would come to her. Her face burned, and she turned away as much as she could in the rocking chair. They believed the babe to be hers, and as an indentured servant, they would naturally assume she had been violated.

Betsy resumed her knitting. "Will thee share with us about thy family?" The needles clicked away.

Thomas gave a grunt that might have been agreement or might have been encouragement as he gave a sleepy nod.

She rubbed the back of her hand over her heated cheeks. "There is only my sister and me now." The silence lengthened until she took a deep breath. "We came from Wales, over two years ago, on a ship with our father. But he died on the journey." She watched the face of little Owen, who though no blood kin, would carry on her father's name. "Father paid our way across, but because we were underage and without a guardian, Captain Reynolds sold us both into bondage to a riverboat captain, who then sold us in New Bern."

"Where is thy sister now?"

"I know not. We were separated."

Betsy's needles ceased clicking as she glanced toward her husband. "Thomas, could thee check the records in New Bern before we sail?"

Gwen's heart leapt, and she lifted her fingers to her lips. Was it possible?

"I can try. Do thee know the date of the sale?"

"'Twas in the fall, two years past." Gwen squinted, dredging up memories she'd worked hard to bury. "Most of the leaves were off the trees, and the roads were deep with mud."

Thomas nodded, combing his fingers through his beard. "Sometime in November most likely. Thy sister's name?"

"Faye. Faye Morgan."

"How old was she then?"

"Just turned thirteen."

Betsy clucked her tongue and set her needles clicking in a sharper cadence. "And thee could not have been more than fourteen."

Gwen nodded.

"I will see what I can find out." Thomas rose and stretched. "'Tis time to retire for the night."

Betsy set aside her knitting and joined him by the door. "Enjoy the evening as long as thee likes." She stroked Owen's cheek. "God bless thee both with pleasant dreams."

Gwen remained on the porch listening to the chorus of frogs. A wild desire to hope warred with her fear of disappointment.

Owen yawned, and his eyelids flickered open. His face puckered and reddened before the first cry. She welcomed the need to attend him. It distracted her from the painfully hopeful thoughts of being reunited with Faye.

Chapter 11

OWEN'S CRY FROM THE wooden crate Betsy had left beside the bed woke Gwen the next morning. Not for the first time. She'd risen and fed him twice during the night. She gathered the infant and soothed him for several moments before changing his wrapping, then pulled on her dress while he cooed at her from the bed. It was topped with a straw tick supported by ropes strung through a wooden frame, like Cook's bed.

Gwen paused. What would Cook think of her now, posing as Owen's mother? Gwen twisted her hair into a knot and pinned it place before covering it with her mobcap. It didn't matter what Cook or anyone else thought. She'd pledged to be the child's mother.

With Owen cuddled in her arms, she entered the main room, where Betsy poked at the hearth fire.

Thomas entered from outside and stamped his boots on the faded rug.

"I thought young Owen would be wanting his breakfast." He held up a small bucket.

"Thank you." Gwen pulled a clean muslin cloth from her pocket and fed her son while Betsy prepared a simple meal of porridge. When the babe refused more milk, Betsy placed steaming bowls on the table. After Thomas joined them, the married couple bowed their heads in silent prayer, as they'd done the evening before.

Gwen bowed her head, although she didn't pray. Who would she pray to? The God her father ranted against, or the God of this Quaker couple? Were they even the same? She waited until she heard Thomas clear his throat before raising her head.

Owen squirmed and mewed as she tried to hold him with one arm and eat with the other.

"Hand that lad over to me." Thomas reached for the boy.

Gwen glanced at Betsy, who nodded, before she lifted the wiggling bundle over the table into Thomas's strong hands. He tucked the infant in the crook on his arm and made faces that quieted the boy.

Gwen watched, her porridge forgotten. Had her father ever done such a thing with her brothers? Not that she could remember.

"Thee should eat while he is suitably entertained." Betsy dragged Gwen's attention back to her meal. She popped in a spoonful of porridge just as Owen released a resounding belch. She clamped her hand over her mouth.

Thomas tossed back his head and laughed. "Owen's praise of the goat's offering."

Gwen's lips twitched in a timid smile before she took another spoonful of porridge.

The bearded man juggled both babe and spoon as he ate his breakfast. He appeared comfortable with the situation, neither clumsy nor unsure.

Gwen finished her porridge and reached for her son, but Thomas shook his head.

"Help Betsy with the dishes. Owen and I will take a little walk outside."

"Wrap him in that shawl on the rocker," Betsy said.

Thomas grunted and raised an eyebrow at his wife before pulling the shawl off the chair. He spoke to Owen as they left the cabin, but Gwen couldn't make out the words.

When they were gone, Betsy faced Gwen. "Thee seems vexed."

"Aye."

"Does it concern thee that Thomas has taken Owen out?"

"Nay. 'Tis only... my father... he would never..."

"We Friends put great value on children. Men and women both help in the raising and training of them. 'Tis my understanding this is not how others raise children."

"Our father loved us, but 'twas Mother who cared for us. When she died 'twas left to me to look after my sister and brothers."

"Brothers?"

Gwen bowed her head. "Two. Younger than Faye. The fever took them not a year after our mother died."

"Thee has indeed suffered much heartache."

Gwen gathered the dishes. The burning compassion on the older woman's face brought a lump to her throat that choked off any more conversation.

That tentative smile of Gwen's at the table had lifted Betsy's spirits. She prayed it was just the first crack in the solemn shell surrounding the girl. She needed them. Of that, Betsy was sure.

Her footsteps whispered in the lush spring grass as she walked behind the meetinghouse through the burial ground. Next week they sailed, and much remained to be done, but she couldn't stay away with time so short. The graves of her children pulled at her that morning. She didn't linger, simply walked by and let her thoughts touch on each of them for a few moments before turning back.

Thoughts of another young woman intermingled with her children's remembered faces. Gwen's sad eyes tugged at Betsy's heart even as she passed the graves of her own dear loved ones. The loss of each child had dealt an almost crippling blow. But her Thomas and the Good Lord had remained steadfast beside her.

At such a tender age, Gwen had suffered grievous loss and been thrust into great responsibility, perhaps—almost certainly—against her will. Indentured women, especially the young comely ones, often fell victim to those with power over them. The thought raised goose-flesh on her arms.

When would the world acknowledge the great wrong of one person owning another—for a time or for a lifetime?

As she returned to the cabin, Betsy prayed for the Lord to give her wisdom and a love for Gwen. Then she lifted her face to the sky, realizing that love had blossomed from the moment she'd seen the frightened girl lurking in the shadows of the kitchen.

She puzzled over the hesitant way Gwen responded to and handled Owen. Was it because she was so young? Hardly more than a child herself, with no mother to train her, and yet she had tended her younger siblings.

Betsy stopped when a troubling thought hit her. Was it the child himself? Did he remind her of what she wished to forget? She pushed the dark thought away and summoned a smile as she joined Gwen on the porch.

"I am unsure what you would have me do," Gwen said.

"We sail in five days. I think 'twould be easier for thee to have some plain clothes for the journey, to help thee blend in among the Friends."

Gwen looked at her clothing, a pink stain rising to her cheeks. It was clear to see that the dress had been sewn for her when she was younger and smaller. Of course, motherhood may have accounted for the tightness of the bodice, even if she couldn't nurse the child, but not the shortness at the hem or the faded thinness of the fabric. The poor girl likely only owned another dress or two, and Betsy assumed they were in no better condition.

"We could have three dresses sewn in time if we work together."

Gwen shrugged. "I have no cloth but that for Owen's needs."

"The trunk under the window is full of cloth. If we need aught else, we'll ask Thomas to fetch it from town tomorrow."

"Will he search the records tomorrow, then?" The dresses apparently forgotten, the girl's dark blue eyes sparkled with hope.

"I expect he will." Her words reaped another fleeting smile that further opened Betsy's lonely heart.

Gwen bent over the soft gray fabric, loading her needle with tiny stitches before drawing the thread through. The sun beat down on the roof, but the shade and the breeze made the porch a pleasant place to be in the afternoon. Owen slept at her feet. A gauzy layer of cheesecloth draped over the box kept insects away.

"Thee sews a fine seam."

Gwen jerked, so intent on her work she hadn't heard Betsy approach.

"I thought a refreshment might be welcome." She handed Gwen a cup filled with water.

"Thank you." Gwen took a sip and then a longer drink. She hadn't realized how thirsty she was. The afternoon shadows were lengthening. "Should I stop and assist with supper?"

"There is no need." Betsy waved her hand. "Thee have plenty to do with the sewing."

Gwen drained the mug. Having someone cook for her and bring her drinks made her uncomfortable. At the same time, gratitude filled her like a gentle tide.

Ever since her mother's death, serving was all she'd known, first her family and then her mistress.

In the doorway, the short, stout woman with iron-gray hair tucked beneath her bonnet looked nothing like Gwen's mother, who'd had raven-black hair piled atop her head and pert little hats she pinned on top. Her mother had been thin and much taller than Betsy, but Gwen remembered most the love that had shone from her mother's eyes. She saw an echo of that love in Betsy's.

Like the acts of service, it made her uncomfortable even while she longed for it.

She knew better than to long for such things. Betsy Baldwin was a religious woman. Gwen was, by her own deceitful admission, an unwed mother. What religious woman would love someone like her?

Gwen set the cup aside, gathered her sewing, and loaded the needle again before pulling the thread through.

Betsy's quiet sigh, and the rustle of the older woman's skirts as she walked into the cabin, let Gwen relax a bit.

She let her sewing settle to her lap, then lifted the cheesecloth and gazed at Owen. His lips puckered in his sleep, one tiny hand curled over his ear. Accepting him as her own brought a great joy and an uneasy fear. Love for him overpowered her at times, clogging her throat and filling her heart. 'Twould be no easy thing for him to grow up without a father.

If she dwelt on that thought too long, the fear built to a painful pitch.

Why had Betsy and Thomas accepted her and Owen into their lives? Was it as Evie said? Were they saints?

She returned to her sewing. Saints or not, the dresses wouldn't sew themselves.

Thrust onto a completely new and foreign road, her life was changing faster than she could adjust. Sewing was something Gwen was good at. The familiar poke and pull of the needle and thread comforted her. She concentrated on the stitches in her hands until mewling from the box caught her attention. She moved her sewing aside and pushed back the cheesecloth. Owen blinked at her like a baby owl at daybreak. He stretched his chubby legs.

She reached for him and drew him close.

"Are you hungry?"

"That is good," Betsy said from the doorway.

"What is good?"

"Talking to him. A babe should hear his mother's voice. It helps him feel loved and cared for."

"I do love him." Gwen lifted her chin and met Betsy's eyes.

"It fairly shines from thy face when thee looks at him. 'Tis such a wondrous thing, the love of a mother for her child."

"Have you and Thomas any children?"

Betsy's smile faltered. "We did. We had a boy and a girl in the early years of our marriage, both lost to the measles. For many years we grieved until God sent us another girl. Hannah was a special gift. She would have turned seventeen this summer, the same as thee." Betsy's gaze drifted toward the meetinghouse. "We lost her almost nine years ago. An infection."

"Almost nine years ago... that was shortly before my mother died."

"And now God has sent us thee and little Owen." Betsy's smile brightened again when Owen let out a lusty bawl. "A hungry little Owen."

Gwen set about feeding her son. Her mind whirled with the thought that God had sent her and Owen to the Baldwins. She didn't even know if she believed in God. But Betsy and Thomas did. They believed enough to take her and Owen into their home.

Wasn't that all that mattered?

Betsy took her walk through the burial ground late the next morning, hoping to catch sight of Thomas on his return from town. He'd left before first light.

Gwen had pricked herself with her needle no less than a dozen times that morning. Too often the girl stopped sewing to gaze into the distance. Betsy feared what hearing any disappointing news regarding her sister might do to their charge. There was something fragile about her, although not physically, to be sure.

Numerous times over the past two days Betsy had squelched the urge to wrap the young woman in her arms. The need for love radiated from Gwen's every timid glance and startled reaction. Yet Betsy found herself held back. She believed the Holy Spirit placed the restraint upon her, and so she would abide by it, no matter how difficult.

She'd just started a second turn around the grounds when the rattle of a wagon caught her ear. Moments later Lad and Lonny, their sturdy horses, trotted through the stand of shagbark hickory trees with the wagon and Thomas behind. She waved to catch her husband's attention.

"Whoa." Thomas pulled the horses to a halt. He leaned over, his hand outstretched to Betsy, who grabbed it with one hand and her skirts with the other to climb up beside him.

"What are thee doing out here this time of day?"

"Waiting for thee."

"I presume this concerns what news I bring of a certain Faye Morgan." The sparkle in his eyes boded well.

Betsy smiled. "Thee does know me well, husband."

"And how thee worries for the young woman in our charge."

"Surely thee understand why?"

"Indeed. I bring her good news, after a fashion."

"After a fashion? What did thee learn?"

He gathered the reins and slapped them on the team's haunches. "Thee shall have to wait. 'Tis only right that Gwen hears my news first. Concerns her most, after all."

Betsy relaxed next to her husband for the short journey to the cabin. He was correct that it was Gwen's news to hear and not her own. His assurance that he brought good news lightened her heart.

Thomas halted the wagon beside the porch.

Gwen rose from her chair, one hand clasped to her breast and the other holding her sewing at her side. Haunted eyes looked out from her pale face beneath the plain bonnet she now wore in place of the mobcap.

Betsy climbed down and hurried to her side. She took the forgotten sewing from Gwen's fingers and put it aside.

Gwen said not a word as she studied Thomas's face.

He came forward, a smile parting his beard. "I found your sister's name in the records at the auction house."

Gwen swayed and Betsy grabbed her around the waist. She eased the girl into the rocking chair and held her upright when she would have slumped forward.

The smile slipped from Thomas's face. He looked to his wife, his hands spread palms up.

"'Tis only the shock," Betsy said. "Pray, do go on."

Gwen bobbed a weak nod.

Betsy knelt beside her chair, keeping a hand on the girl's trembling arm.

"She was sold, as thee knew, into an indenture the same day as thee. She was purchased by an agent of one Mistress Martha McClure."

Gwen pushed wayward black curls under her bonnet with one trembling hand while clasping Betsy's hand with the other.

Betsy once more restrained the urge to gather Gwen into her arms.

"D-do you know where she is?" The hopeful shine in Gwen's eyes pinched Betsy's heart, especially when Thomas wagged his head in response. Gwen's chin trembled, and she bowed her head.

"It seems that Mistress McClure never lived here. The best I could ascertain, thy sister was put back aboard a ship and sent north to Alexandria."

"Alexandria?" Betsy squeezed Gwen's hand. "Is that not the very place we will make port on our journey?"

"Indeed."

Gwen raised her face, her gaze sweeping from Betsy to Thomas and back again. When Owen began to fuss in his box, the sound eased the tension from the air around them.

"I shall tend to him." Betsy pushed herself to her feet.

"We will arrive in Alexandria in a week's time," Thomas said. "I shall make more inquiries there. 'Tis a large city, but someone will know the name of Mistress McClure. I shall do my best to find her." He grabbed Lonny's bridle and led the team toward the barn.

Tears washed Gwen's cheeks, and Betsy forced her feet to take her into the cabin to give the girl some privacy. Tears helped the healing. Heaven knew that young woman needed a lot of healing. As she changed the babe, Betsy's heart begged the Lord for guidance and His mercy toward Gwen.

Chapter 12

May 1799

G WEN FINGERED THE WHITE fabric across her chest. Standing on the deck of the ship in a crowd of women dressed much the same gave her an uneasy sense of belonging. Or at least blending in. Betsy stood beside her, unshed tears shimmering in the older woman's eyes. What must it be like for Betsy and Thomas, who left their much-loved home and the graves of their children behind? Gwen glanced back to watch the shore slip out of sight but felt no longing for what she left. She'd left no family behind, nobody she'd miss other than Faye, whom they might find in Alexandria.

Mark Allen's face flitted across her mind's eye along with a slight twinge of... regret? Relief? She couldn't be sure. She would always think of him as her friend during her indenture. But in the upheaval of her life these last weeks, she had not considered him once. Her rising hope of finding Faye had occupied her thoughts between tending Owen's needs, sewing, and preparing for their trek into the Northwest Territory.

The wind picked up. Gwen turned to protect Owen from its force.

"Come. We will go below and take the babe out of this wind." Betsy guided her to the stairs, where several women and children waited in a line to descend. The men gathered near the front of the vessel. Many of the younger ones hung over the edge just like she and Faye had done when leaving Wales, so eager to find a new place to call home. Never guessing that instead of a happy home in the new land, their lives would be ripped apart.

Gwen shivered despite the heat of the day.

"'Tis but a short voyage. We will arrive in two or three days." Betsy's uncanny ability to read Gwen's thoughts both reassured and unnerved her at times. "'Twill be nothing like what thee endured crossing the ocean."

Gwen picked her way down the steep stairs, little more than a slanted ladder, to the dank, dimly lit cavern. Thomas had stored their belongings at the far end. Watching Betsy winnow out her household into what would fit in their four trunks had saddened Gwen. The plain people didn't have much to begin with. Seeing things lovingly set aside had caused her heart to twist. She'd never had much of her own, aside from a change of clothing. She couldn't imagine abandoning treasured belongings.

Yet it had fascinated her to watch the preparations for the long, difficult trip which would begin in earnest when they left Alexandria in the new wagons. Each decision, whether to bring that pot or leave that bucket behind, was justified by what they could replace and what they could not.

And what they could live without.

Thomas had presented Gwen with a trunk of her own. It held only her two carpetbags and the plain clothing she'd made over the past week. She'd offered to add some of Betsy's things, but the older woman had refused, saying Gwen would need that space later.

The larger trunks doubling as their chairs aboard ship for the short journey, they settled in. Owen succumbed to sleep, the gentle motion of the ship replacing the rocking chair abandoned on the cabin porch.

A young woman approached with a babe in her arms and a toddler clutching her skirt from behind.

"Greetings, Betsy," the woman said.

"Greetings, Faith. Will thee join us?" Betsy motioned to an empty trunk. "Thee has not yet met Gwen Morgan and her son, Owen."

"Pleased to meet thee."

"Pleased to meet you," Gwen said.

Faith's brows rose at the last word. The Quakers used *thee* in place of *you*, but Gwen didn't feel the need to mimic them. She wasn't a Quaker, after all.

"Gwen and her son have newly come to live with Thomas and me."

Faith put a hand on her little girl's head. "This is Mary and my babe is William. I fear his father will only call him Will." Faith giggled, and Gwen's lips twitched in a tentative response. "'Tis the way of things between a father and a son. Does thy husband fuss over his boy as well?"

Gwen's tongue clung to the roof of her mouth. Blood pounded in her ears. Sweat gathered across the back of her neck. She should have been prepared for the question, but it caught her off guard. Betsy placed her hand on Gwen's back. The warmth of that touch steadied her.

"Gwen has no husband," Betsy said. "She is newly released from an indenture. God has placed her in our care now. Thomas and I will help her raise Owen."

There. It was out in the open. Betsy's answer drained the tension from Gwen. The Quakers would accept her or reject her—but Gwen would live by the oath she'd sworn.

Emotions flickered across Faith's face. Her mouth opened and closed before she reached across the space between trunks and laid her hand on Gwen's arm. "If thee needs any help, thee must let me know." Faith's smile lacked neither warmth nor sincerity.

"Th-thank you." Relief washed over her. The first hurdle had been met and survived. Gwen wasn't naïve enough to think her story wouldn't spread like wildfire through the crowded ship. But it was a comfort to know at least some would accept her and Owen.

Faith chatted a few more minutes about the upcoming journey before moving on.

"Faith married young and is not so much older than thee, maybe a handful of years. Thee should understand"—Betsy lowered her voice and leaned close to Gwen—"not all will be as accepting of thy circumstance as Faith."

Gwen gazed at the sleeping babe in her arms. Many would look down on her for having a son and no husband. There would be more uncomfortable questions to come, but she wouldn't let one panic her again.

He is your son. You be proud of him! Evie's voice rang in her ears.

"The Friends are a close group, keeping much to ourselves. If thee comes to a decision to join us, thee would find more inclusion."

"And more acceptance of Owen?"

"Very likely."

The prospects of a child born out of wedlock were limited. While many indentured servants had risen from their humble beginnings to prosper in a trade or start a business, the world looked askance at someone born without a last name.

"Would the Friends have me?"

"If thy parents had been Friends, and raised thee up as such, thee would have been brought before the women for discipline. Having a child out of wedlock is a sin to be dealt with. But as this was not the case, thee will not be held to the same standard. If thee comes to a decision to join us, then thee would come under the leadership. We do not—we should not—judge those who walk not in our way."

Gwen didn't understand what Betsy meant but hesitated to ask. Speaking of religious things sprouted an itch between her shoulders. She remembered her father, much the worse for drink, ranting about the church. She had gathered the children, taken them to the small shed behind the house, and kept them there until he'd fallen asleep. After Mother's death, he never stepped inside a church again, nor allowed his children to. She had been too young to understand his reasoning at the time, and they had never spoken of it after.

Had Father been wrong to turn his back on the church?

Owen's cry woke Gwen the next morning. Thomas snorted and rolled to his side, but Betsy rose from their blankets. There were no beds in the cavernous hold they shared.

"I will tend to him while thee milks the goat." Betsy reached for Owen.

"Thank you." Gwen sat up and faced her friend. "I know not what I would do without you and Thomas." Betsy's eyes shone with a peace

Gwen envied—and with something else she couldn't identify.

She grabbed a candleholder and a small bucket and descended the ladder to the belly of the ship, where the livestock was held. The acrid stench of manure mingled with the odor of horses and cattle and the mustiness of the boat. Her goat was tethered at the very end of a long line of milk cows, dwarfed by her bovine companions. Gwen pulled a few corn kernels from her apron pocket and let the goat lick them off her palm.

"You are such a tiny thing compared to all these cows. I think that is what I shall call you. Tiny." She scratched behind the animal's ears before kneeling down to milk. The warm liquid frothed into her bucket. "After I feed Owen, I shall be back to care for you." She stroked the white nose one more time and turned, almost bumping into a man behind her. She gasped, spilling some of the milk before he righted the bucket in her hand.

"Pardon me, miss." His brown eyes crinkled in the corners. A wide smile lined his dark face.

Gwen took a quick step back, bumping into Tiny, who bleated her disapproval.

"'Twas not my intention to startle thee." He picked up a large bucket by his feet. "It looks as though we have come for the same reason. My Bossy is used to an early-morning milking." He patted the large brown cow beside Tiny. His plain clothing, wrinkled as though he'd slept in them, as had they all aboard ship, was of good quality and showed little wear. Although as dark as Evie or Sapphira, his speech sounded more like Thomas's.

"Are you a Quaker?"

"Indeed, I am. My name is Zachary Brown."

He seemed friendly, but he stood between her and the ladder, much as Jonas had often blocked her from the safety of the servants' staircase. The darkness of the ship's hold, the odors, and feeling trapped by this stranger combined to send her heartbeat to a gallop.

"Gwen Morgan." She dipped in a curtsy. "Pardon me, I must hasten back and feed my son."

He stepped aside.

She inched around him, her back brushing the support beam of the ship, and she hurried away. With one hand on the ladder, she peeked over her shoulder.

Zachary remained as she left him, one hand scratching the cow's back, his dark eyes still focused on her.

She scrambled up the ladder and arrived at their trunks out of breath.

Betsy touched her arm. "Are thee well?"

Gwen shook her head and then nodded.

"Did something happen?" A frown marred Betsy's forehead.

"Eh? What is that? What happened?" Thomas sat up from his blankets. He blinked and ran a hand through his hair, leaving tuffs that stuck straight out.

"Nothing happened. I met a man below. He owns the cow tethered next to Tiny."

"Tiny?" Thomas patted the top of the trunk beside him. Betsy reached over and handed him his spectacles.

"The goat."

Thomas chuckled. "She is a bit of a thing next to those milk cows."

"Who did thee meet?" Concern lingered in Betsy's eyes.

"He said his name is Zachary Brown."

"A good man, Zachary." Thomas leaned back against the trunk and adjusted his spectacles.

Betsy took the bucket from Gwen's hand, setting it on the flat top of Gwen's trunk.

Gwen settled beside it and pulled a muslin cloth from her pocket. She dipped it in the warm milk and offered it to Owen, who slurped the milk from the twist of cloth as Gwen dribbled more on top with a spoon, a technique Betsy had taught her that worked well and hastened feeding time.

When the boy was satisfied and resting in the curve of her arm, Gwen squatted beside Betsy's trunk and leaned close. "Betsy."

"Yes?"

"Zachary did not speak like the slaves at Mistress Cummings's house."

"He is not a slave. Not anymore."

"But he is as dark as any slave I have seen."

"Thee are as pale as any woman I have seen. The color of thy skin means nothing to the kingdom of the Lord. It should mean nothing here on earth either."

"But—"

"'Tis this very reason we left North Carolina and all we know behind. The Northwest Territory is a free land. Slavery is not allowed there. Zachary was purchased by a Friend and given his freedom many years ago. Now the Southern states have made it a crime to do thus. 'Tis surely a sin in the eyes of God for one man to claim ownership of another man... or woman."

"Even in indenture?"

"So we believe. That is why Thomas would not buy thy indenture from Daniel Whiteford, but demanded he release thee instead."

Gwen leaned around Betsy to see her husband.

Thomas met her gaze and nodded.

"I will never be able to repay your kindness." She pressed her free hand to her chest while the other clutched Owen tighter. Freeing her had not been Mr. Whiteford's idea at all. He would have sold her—and his own grandson—to be rid of them.

"Thee has no debt to repay, Gwen." Thomas pushed to his feet and laid a hand on her shoulder. "The Lord brought thee into our lives, and thankful we are that He did." He patted her shoulder twice and then craned his neck, looking toward the deck above. "We are still."

"Indeed," Betsy said.

No waves sloshed against the hull of the ship. The floor remained motionless beneath them.

"I will go see." Thomas snatched his hat and shoved it on his head as he strode off, stopping to speak with a tall man who followed him up the narrow staircase.

Mothers hushed their children as more men filed up the ladder.

"I'm sure 'tis nothing of concern," Betsy whispered.

The ship groaned—an ominous note in the silence that had befallen the hold.

What could it mean?

Chapter 13

B ECALMED.

The word floated on whispers that grew as the morning wore on. Although it meant nothing to Gwen, tension built among the other passengers, which settled against her skin like the scum on a vat of salt pork.

Betsy took her around and introduced her to many of the Quaker women. Most reacted much like Faith, but a few raised eyebrows and lifted chins. Some regarded her as if she were a loathsome form of insect. Gwen would have melted beneath such scrutiny if not for Betsy. The short woman stood like a fortress next to Gwen. Her smile never slipped, her tone never changed, her step never hurried, even when Gwen wished to scuttle away to a dark corner.

The ship remained calm on Sunday, its limp ivory sails sagging against the rigging. The Quakers gathered on deck, and Gwen joined them with Owen in her arms. Her early memories of attending church involved a lot of pageantry, dark woodwork with elaborate scrolling, stained glass, a frightening man in a long black robe, and long sermons about things she did not understand.

The Quakers gathered under the glare of the early May sun. They made seats of barrels and crates or sat on the deck itself.

Sweat beaded Gwen's forehead under the shade of her bonnet and more trickled down her spine. Only the occasional call of a gull broke the silence. She shifted her body to shade Owen, who lay on a blanket in front of her on the deck.

Gwen shifted again, trying to ease her back into a more comfortable position. A man stood to her right. She craned her neck to see him but nobody else did, so she looked at the deck near his feet.

After a long moment, he spoke. "Except a man be born again, he cannot see the kingdom of God. This is told to us in the Bible, and it is well we should be reminded of it. God prepared a way for us to spend eternal life with Him. It belongs to each one of us to own to it. Thee must be born again, convinced in thy spirit that Christ is the Savior. The Inner Light of Christ will show thee the way."

The man resumed his seat on an overturned bucket. Gwen pondered his words in the silence that followed. They made no more sense than those of the man in the long black robe back in Wales.

Owen's fingers twitched as he slept. She had witnessed his birth. She understood what that entailed. How could a person be born a second time? Such a thing was surely impossible.

Owen, perhaps feeling her intent focus upon him, fussed himself awake. She shot a look at Betsy, who nodded toward the staircase. Gwen gathered her infant in his blanket and wove between the people on deck to reach it.

Below, Faith was feeding her son. Gwen hurried to her trunk and uncovered the bucket of goat's milk. She searched Owen's carpetbag for a clean piece of muslin. She would have to wash and boil the dirty ones soon.

Faith joined her.

"Owen awoke hungry, too, I see."

"Aye."

"He seems to thrive on goat's milk. My grandmother was a firm believer in the goodness of goat's milk and never owned a cow. When I was a girl, she kept five goats and each one had a name."

"My goat's name is Tiny."

"How came she by such a name?"

"When I went to milk her yesterday and saw her tethered by the cows, I thought how tiny she looked compared to them."

The musical lilt of Faith's quiet laughter echoed in the cavernous room. It tempted Gwen to join in. She couldn't remember the last time she'd laughed. She let her lips twitch into a smile.

"Mary would enjoy meeting Tiny, I think."

Gwen looked around. "Where is she?"

"On the deck with my sister. She is old enough to sit at meeting now while I tend to William." Subtle pride flowed in Faith's voice.

Gwen dribbled more milk from the spoon to the cloth in Owen's mouth. She knew she'd feel the same sort of pride over each of his accomplishments as he grew.

"They grow so quickly, 'tis good to have another before they..." Faith's mouth clicked shut and she flushed.

Gwen squeezed her eyes tight a moment before speaking. "'Tis fine, Faith, truly."

"I spoke in haste." Faith reached a hand toward her. "Forgive my thoughtlessness."

Grasping the offered hand, Gwen nodded. "There is nothing to forgive."

The pounding of feet drew their attention. The meeting had adjourned. Children scrambled down the stairs ahead of the adults, their happy voices filling the dank space with life. Conversations among adults added to the noise in vivid contrast to the silence of moments before.

Betsy joined Gwen and Faith. She smiled at their hands, still linked. Faith squeezed Gwen's hand one last time before she excused herself to see to her family's noon meal.

Thomas arrived soon after. The deep lines of his face held no smile. He tugged on the end of his beard.

"I shall lay out some food for our meal." Betsy dug into the trunk with their provisions.

"Not too much. We must eat sparingly these next few days."

"Oh?" Betsy straightened and faced her husband.

"The sailors fear the wind will not pick up for some time, perhaps several days."

A tendril of fear climbed Gwen's spine. Owen started to fuss, and she put him over her shoulder, patting his back, but her attention remained on Thomas.

"How many days?" Betsy asked.

"Only God knows. But we will ration our food and water, just in case."

"We have enough for more than a week." Betsy lifted a hand toward the trunk and then let it drop again. "Fear thee it might be longer?"

"'Tis possible. I am going to walk among the people and spread the word quietly. Joseph has already started at the other end."

He left them, stopping to talk with the man nearest their trunks, their voices a low murmur amid the hubbub.

"Betsy, what about Tiny? What if we run out of food and water for her?"

"We shan't borrow trouble that is not here yet." Betsy smoothed her tidy apron with fingers that shook. "We shall be fine."

For the first time, Gwen questioned the honesty of Betsy's words.

One week later

"'Tis all I have left." Gwen knelt beside Tiny and pulled a few kernels of corn from her apron pocket. The goat's velvety lips tickled her palm. "Hay runs low as well. But you must not despair, Tiny. The wind will increase again and... and Owen needs you." Her voice wobbled on the last words.

Zachary approached, his brown felt hat just visible over his cow's tall back. He looked nothing like Jonas and acted even less like him. Thomas had called him a good man, but the way he came upon her while she was otherwise alone still unnerved Gwen. She slipped the bucket under Tiny and hid against the goat's soft side.

"Greetings."

She lifted her face enough to nod in acknowledgment, as she had every morning for the past week.

He pushed an armful of hay in front of his cow. Bossy moaned her low greeting and grabbed a mouthful. Her bottom jaw swung as if on a hinge while she worked the dried grasses into her cheeks. Zachary placed the rest in the makeshift manger within reach of both the cow and Tiny.

The white goat stretched her scrawny neck and snitched a much smaller mouthful.

"Tiny, 'tis not yours." Gwen tried to push the hay away from her greedy goat.

"Worry not, Gwen. My Bossy can share." He nodded at the meager handfuls of hay in front of Tiny while he patted the cow's portly side. "She has plenty of extra fat to see her through until we land."

"You are too kind."

He shrugged away her compliment before plopping his bucket underneath Bossy.

Gwen squeezed past him and hurried to feed Owen.

The muslin cloths she used were stiff and discolored from washing in salt water. Owen fussed at first from the strange taste, even though she rinsed the salt out as best she could with a bit of milk first. She wished for a way to boil the cloths, even though she'd have to use salt water, the drinking water being rationed. Evie had warned her to do that frequently to remove any leftover sour milk that could cause Owen a stomachache. But with the lack of wind, every chunk of coal was hoarded for cooking. Several families huddled around each brazier at meal times.

Betsy bundled Owen's soiled clothing to wash on deck.

"I should wash them." Guilt niggled at Gwen. Betsy did so much for her and Owen.

"I have little enough to do while we wait for the wind to strike up. 'Tis best to keep my hands busy."

Gwen understood. Her own lack of activity made her jittery. Tempers had flared between several of the Quakers during the past eight days. The first confrontation had unnerved her and shook her semi-belief that these people might be the saints Evie named them. Betsy explained that people are people first, Friends second, and as susceptible to the sins of human nature as any other. Even so, Gwen could not imagine either Betsy or Thomas ever raising their voices in anger. When she mentioned that to Betsy, the older woman had chuckled and told her that such things were much tempered with age.

Tempered with age or tempers on edge, Gwen would be glad for a bit of wind to drive them on to Alexandria to begin their journey. But first... to find Faye.

Betsy washed out the babe's clothing in a huge bucket a passing sailor had hauled up for her. The hard soap lathered easily in the briny water, but she used as little as possible because it was so hard to rinse out. Even well rinsed, the cloth dried stiff. She worried for Owen's tender skin if they didn't reach land soon.

Her husband stood at the front of the ship near a knot of men. Worry lines pulled at his face. They should have arrived in Alexandria five days past.

The plan had been to arrive on a Monday, secure the needed provisions for the journey by Wednesday, load the new wagons, and be on the trail heading west on Thursday. The Friends who had arranged to meet and join them in Alexandria must be anxious.

Would they give up and start the journey without them?

She was plunging more clothing into the water when laughter erupted from the opening to the hold. Faith climbed from the staircase, her daughter in front of her, and her son in her arms. Gwen followed in their wake. Oh, how Betsy hoped that Faith's friendship would work the healing that girl needed in her life, that Faith's quick smile and easy laughter would coax the same from Gwen. She could think of no better use of the time becalmed at sea.

Betsy wiped sweat from her eyes with the hem of her apron and glanced at the bunched and sagging canvas hanging from the masts. If the wind didn't find them soon, there would be no laughter at all. With no rain to resupply the barrels, the freshwater supply ran dangerously low. She clicked her tongue against the back of her teeth. Thirst would drive people to drink the salty water of the sea. And then they would sicken.

Some could even die.

Sitting on the dank planking in the silence of her second Quaker meeting the following morning, Gwen pressed a hand to her stomach. The odors of unwashed bodies, brine, and the livestock below threatened to undo her meager morning meal. With each drop of fresh water carefully rationed, the Friends met below deck to avoid the drying sun. They exchanged fresh air for the shade and cooler confines below. Gwen chewed on a rough patch on her lower lip. If the wind didn't stir soon...

Her mind recoiled from that thought.

"God and Father of our humble Christ." Gwen startled at the intrusion of a woman's voice from across the hull. "We beseech Thee to send us the wind." Several more people spoke out in agreement, and the silence of the meeting became a disorganized chant of requests to God. Betsy stirred beside Gwen and added her call on the Lord for His mercy and grace upon their ship.

Bewildered by this change from last Sunday's almost complete silence, Gwen shifted and looked around the room. Many faces bowed over clasped hands while others turned upward, eyes closed, some wearing smiles, others frowns.

Then she caught Zachary's eye. He blinked and nodded, as if he could read her thoughts. He shouldn't make her nervous, but he did. She shivered and dropped her head to focus on Owen in her lap until the end of the service was signaled by several men rising and greeting each other.

Coming to her feet, Gwen greeted several women who passed her on their way to their own allotted areas. Betsy's light touch at her elbow guided her back to their trunks.

"Will God send the wind?" Gwen asked when Thomas joined them.

"If it pleases Him," Thomas said. "And often it pleases Him to answer the prayers of the faithful."

"Does He not always answer prayers?"

"I believe He does," Thomas said. "But 'tis not always the answer we seek."

"I do not understand."

"The Lord knows what is best for us. He orders things according to His will and in such a way as will prosper us. Sometimes that means His answer to our prayer is *no* and sometimes it is 'not yet.'"

"'Tis all so confusing." Gwen pressed her hand to her forehead.

"Aye, it can be, but it gets easier with time."

"And it gets easier as thee raises thy children," Betsy said. "When thee tells a child 'no' because it is the best thing for the child, thee begins to understand the role of the Lord as thy Father."

Yesterday Mary had asked Faith for a drink from the washbucket. Mary understood only that she was thirsty and the bucket held water. Faith knew the salty wash water would make Mary sick and prevented her daughter from drinking, even though Mary had whined and pleaded for the drink. That part, at least, made sense.

But it didn't raise the wind.

Betsy and Gwen were cleaning up after a brief noon meal of hard cheese and dry biscuits when a shout from above drew every eye to the staircase. The ship creaked and tilted a tiny bit to the port side.

A cheer erupted from throats below deck. "The wind!"

Gwen laughed, the sound startling her. It had been far too long since she'd laughed.

"Gwen." Betsy pressed her fingers to her lips and smiled. Tears shimmered in her eyes.

Gwen laughed again. It felt foreign in her mouth but delightful as well.

"Praise God." Betsy breathed the words more than spoke them, and her eyes remained on Gwen.

Chapter 14

SIX DAYS LATER THEY stood on the deck as Alexandria emerged on the horizon. The wind they'd prayed for had come in fits and starts. They'd drifted far off course while the wind had refused to lift their sails. Even now, the ship crawled across the flat ocean like a duck dragging its feet. As they neared the shore, the sail high above danced and cracked.

"Now you decide to come to life." Gwen shielded her eyes and gazed into the wind-filled sails.

"God's timing is not our timing, 'tis a fact." Thomas pushed away from the railing beside her. "But we are safely arrived."

"Ten days late. Do thee think the others waited for us?" Betsy stood on her toes and craned her neck for a better view of the shoreline.

"Eleven days," Thomas said. "I doubt they'd venture ahead. They are not many without our number, just a few families from Maryland and Virginia. 'Twill be safer if we travel together."

With the wind cooperating at last, they sailed into Alexandria midafternoon. Unloading their belongings took a long time. Gwen found a shady spot for them to wait and rocked her fussy, sweaty son in her arms. She longed for a bath and clothes that didn't reek of salt and sweat.

Thomas had left as soon as they landed to search for their fellow Quakers in the city. He returned with a line of wagons all driven by men in plain clothing. The Quakers from the ship scurried to load them with trunks, boxes, and furniture. The horses and cattle were brought from the lower hold, gaunt from thirst and blinking in the bright sun.

Betsy joined Gwen. "'Twas by God's grace all the livestock survived."

Zachary waited for Tiny to drink from one of the large troughs at the end of the gangplank, then brought her to Gwen.

"Thank you for helping with Tiny." She took the tether. The man appeared much less threatening in the open sunlight. How could she have ever imagined him anything like Jonas?

"Thee are most welcome." He tied Bossy to one of the wagons before heading back to the ship.

Betsy took Owen and cuddled him to her shoulder. Gwen led the goat toward one of the larger wagons where Thomas spoke to the driver. She passed a wagon with a bull tied to the back, a thick rope secured to a large ring through its nose. The animal pawed the ground and bellowed.

Tiny sprang into the air at the noise.

The tether line slipped from Gwen's hand. She grabbed for it, missed, and Tiny bounded down the line of freight wagons straight for Thomas.

"Catch her!" Gwen grabbed a handful of her skirts and gave chase.

The driver with Thomas leaped from the high wagon seat and hit the ground in front of the runaway goat. He landed with his legs spread and knees bent, his arms flung wide. Tiny skidded to a halt nose-to-nose with him.

Gwen stopped behind Tiny and grabbed the loose tether. She gasped a quick breath before a pair of blue eyes froze it in her throat. A smile slashed across the strong jaw in need of a shave. Brown hair tinged with red poked out from under a dusty black hat. Gwen's heart skittered under her ribs, and she looked away.

Thomas laughed and rested his hand on the driver's shoulder. "Good stop, Micah. Let me introduce thee to the owner of yon feisty creature." He extended a hand toward Gwen. "Micah Pike, meet our Gwen Morgan."

"I am pleased to meet thee, Gwen Morgan."

Gwen sucked in an unsteady breath. "I am pleased to meet you, Micah Pike. And thank you for stopping Tiny."

"'Twas my pleasure to assist." The twinkle in his eyes robbed Gwen of any response.

"Micah will haul our belongings to the camp." Thomas pointed at the wagon, already loaded with their trunks.

"There is plenty of room left for thy goat," Micah said.

He reached for the tether, and Gwen's fingers brushed his. She snatched her hand away, tucking it behind her waist, her cheeks heating.

His eyes crinkled at the corners, and he lifted Tiny as if she weighed nothing and set her behind the seat. Tiny bleated, and Gwen stood on her tiptoes to stroke the goat's soft nose.

Micah tugged on the secured tether. "That should keep her safe until we reach the camp." He winked at Gwen.

Her mouth went dry.

"We shall load the trunks and be on our way shortly, "Thomas said. "Where are Betsy and Owen?"

Gwen pointed to where Betsy spoke with a pair of plain-dressed women. He strode off to meet them. Gwen followed. She cast a peek over her shoulder at Mr. Pike—Micah, because the Quakers shunned the use of honorifics, even the simple ones such as mister and missus. He stood with his arms crossed, leaning against the freight wagon, watching her with those incredible blue eyes. She pressed her hand to her chest and hurried after Thomas.

Gwen caught up with the older couple as they approached Micah's wagon.

"We shall transport our belongings in their wagons, then return to town and purchase our own tomorrow or the next day," Thomas said.

"Where will we stay the night?" asked Betsy.

"There is a large camp set up in a field just outside of town. The women are already rigging some makeshift tents for us to use this evening."

Betsy nodded but Gwen's heart sank. Tents? They were to stay in tents? Her desire for a bath weakened her knees and slowed her steps. She blinked back stinging tears.

"Micah has Gwen's goat loaded along with our trunks," Thomas told

Betsy. "He shall take thee to the camp. I believe I shall stay here and help the others until the wagons return for another load. Our numbers are greater than those already gathered. We cannot fit everything on the wagons at once."

Gwen hung back behind the older couple, keeping them between herself and Micah.

"Micah, 'tis so good to see thee again." Betsy took one of his hands in her free one, the other still holding Owen to her chest. "How is thy dear mother?"

"In fine spirits and more spry than many half her age."

"And thy father and brothers?"

"Much the same, except for Henry, who married last month." The smile slipped away as he said it.

"Thee must join us for supper this evening and tell us everything."

Gwen groaned to herself. The thought of sitting on the wagon with this man, much less sharing supper with him, while she smelled like a fishmonger's cart the day after market... she cringed.

Thomas and Micah checked the heavy trunks to make sure they were securely fastened, along with several other crates from the ship's hull. They tied Lonny and Lad to the back of the wagon. Both horses pranced a bit in their eagerness to leave the ship behind.

Thomas helped Betsy onto the high seat and handed Owen up to her. He helped Gwen next. Gwen smoothed her skirt and took Owen onto her lap once she was settled next to Betsy. The wagon shifted again as Micah climbed up on Betsy's other side. At least Gwen was spared sitting right next to him in her unwashed state.

"I have met Gwen, but who is this little one?" Micah asked as he unwrapped the reins from the wagon's brake.

"Owen is Gwen's son," Betsy said. "They came to live with us shortly before we left New Bern."

Micah nodded and cast a quick glance at Gwen before settling the reins between his gloved fingers. He clicked to the horses and slapped the reins against their broad backs. "Get up, Sassy. Steady on, Hap."

"Wait." Gwen whispered to Betsy and grabbed her sleeve.

"What is it?"

"Faye. We must search for Faye. She may be here in Alexandria."

Betsy patted her hand. "There will be time to search before we leave. Fear not. Thomas has not forgotten."

Gwen blew out a soft sigh and settled back against the seat. Another wait. She was almost used to it. And in truth, she'd rather have the bath and clean clothes before she met her sister again.

Gwen stared in awe at the city that unfolded past the shipyard. Tall brick buildings lined both sides of the street. She had thought New Bern a big city, but Alexandria was far larger. Micah guided the wagon through a maze of streets lined with people, horses, and every shape of buggy, carriage, cart, and wagon. The noise and odors overwhelmed Gwen while the colors and movement fascinated her.

Betsy's brow was creased and the lines around her eyes, that fanned when she smiled, sagged atop her cheeks.

"Is something wrong?" Gwen asked.

"Indeed." Betsy gestured toward the crowds. "So many are held in bondage here."

Gwen looked again and saw what she had missed in the overall busyness of the street. At least half the white people were shadowed by a black slave or two, most carrying packages. Black drivers held the reins from the seats of carriages and wagons. She swiveled around. There were no white drivers other than the Quakers in the wagons following them.

Several women glared at her as they passed. One man spat on the street after looking her in the eye. She scooted closer to Betsy, who put an arm around her.

"Friends are not well regarded here." Micah kept his voice low. "The slave trade flourishes in this city. Any who oppose it are viewed as troublemakers. They have not bothered us and are happy to take our money for supplies, but 'tis best for the women to remain in camp."

The color and movement of the city had gathered a sinister feel. Gwen shivered despite the muggy heat.

Once they left the crowded streets, the road curved through a wooded area thick with brush and biting insects. Gwen covered Owen with his thin blanket. She swatted at the pests in front of her face, thankful for the protection of her deep Quaker bonnet.

Micah chirped to the horses, and they quickened the pace. "We shall be past this swamp soon and leave most of the pests behind."

The trees thinned and the land rose gently until they topped a narrow rise. Below them spread an open field. Wagons and tents dotted its center. A sizeable herd of cattle and sheep grazed to one side, while a long line of tethered horses, mules, and oxen lined the other. Several dogs barked at their approach. A group of barefoot children ran to greet them.

Micah stopped the horses next to a large farm wagon rigged with hoops and canvas that stood on the outskirts of the camp. He jumped off the seat and helped Betsy descend. Gwen handed Owen down first and then took Micah's hand as she climbed from the wagon. His rough leather glove steadied her as his closeness unsettled her. She dropped his hand and reached for Owen as soon as her feet touched the ground. Micah lifted Tiny down last. Gwen made sure their fingers didn't touch, even though he'd donned the gloves, when she accepted the tether from him.

"This is my wagon." He thumped the wooden side. "Thee are welcome to park next to it."

"And thee must take meals with us, Micah." Betsy patted his arm. "Thee are, after all, family."

Micah grinned and tossed a glance at Gwen. He slid the heavy trunks to the ground. "Nothing would please me more." He jumped onto the freight wagon and chirped to the horses, then jogged over to the line of tethered animals to secure Lonny and Lad before returning to the docks for another load.

Gwen turned to Betsy. "He is a relative of yours?"

"Indeed. His mother is my cousin. She and I grew up together." Betsy's eyes took on a faraway look. "Such good times we had then. She was always a lively one. Of all her children, Micah takes after her the most."

"Do they live near here, then?"

"Not even close. Micah traveled quite a distance to meet with us. His family lives near Annapolis in Maryland. They farm the land that once belonged to my great-grandparents."

"Why did he leave?"

"We sent word about the new settlement to many other Quaker meetings. Some have decided to join us. Most are leaving for the same reasons we are."

"Slavery."

"Indeed. I expect we shall see more joining us once the settlement is established. Enough about that." Betsy turned to their trunks. "We must make preparations for the night."

"How?" Gwen's voice came out just short of a wail. Owen answered with a cry of his own.

"First things first. Feed thy babe. I shall see what can be rigged for a shelter. Then I would cherish a wash in fresh water and a change into something that reeks not of that ship."

Gwen nodded her eager agreement before tying Tiny to the handle of the heaviest trunk. The goat plunged her nose into the deep grass and tore off a mouthful. With Owen lying beside her, his fingers grasping and releasing the grass at his sides, she milked enough to feed him. Cuddling him close for feeding, she wrinkled her nose.

Betsy chuckled. "I fear we all retain an odor made more noticeable in this clean, fresh field."

"I fear you are correct." The promise of a wash lifted Gwen's spirits.

Four women joined Betsy and assisted her in turning their supply of blankets and a tarp into a small tent. Three others fetched buckets of water from the stream that bordered the field. Gwen removed Owen's wrappings. She found their shallow washtub and filled it with fresh water. He fussed at the chill, but she scrubbed him clean of salt and sweat and she dressed him in the only gown that hadn't been washed in salt water.

When Betsy finished hanging the tarp, she took Owen and introduced Gwen to the ladies who had come to help. Two were from the same settlement as Micah. Gwen wasn't likely to remember a single name. All she could think about was getting clean. As soon as she could, Gwen excused herself and pulled the wash tub and two buckets of water into the makeshift tent.

She fumbled with her ties and stays in her eagerness to get the smelly clothing off. She poured the first bucket over her head and worked the hard soap into a lather before combing it through her hair with her fingers. Once it hung in a clean, wet curtain down her back, she attacked the rest of her body with a rough square of linen and more soap. Drying and dressing in the confines of the tent posed a challenge, but she managed. She must thank Betsy for insisting she have a spare set of stays for the trip. She bundled her dirty clothes and slipped through the flap of blanket that served as a door.

Betsy sat by herself in the shade of the wagon. She rocked back and forth, humming tunelessly to Owen, who slept in her arms. She looked up when Gwen joined her.

"Thee look refreshed."

"I am. Let me take your clothing with mine to the stream. If I am quick, they should be dry before nightfall."

"Fetch me two buckets of clean water first. Leave Owen with me, and we shall follow when I'm clean."

Gwen tied her damp hair back with a ribbon. She left her bonnet beside the wagon and brought Betsy the buckets, then bundled their dirty clothing and returned to the stream. A shallow area well downstream of the camp looked like the perfect spot. Skirts tied up to keep them dry, she waded in until the water reached halfway to her knees.

After two weeks cooped up in the hull of the ship, she thrilled at the feeling of fresh water rushing around her legs. The scent of wildflowers filled the air. Birdsong kept her company from the trees across the stream. She found a sizable rock and set to work scrubbing the brine from their clothing.

She straightened at the footsteps behind her and turned, expecting Betsy and Owen.

A pair of piercing blue eyes greeted her instead. "Thee have been industrious."

"Aye." Her throat constricted around that single word.

"Betsy asked me to help carry the washing. She is detained by many old friends, or she would have come herself."

"I could have carried them." Gwen waded from the stream and untied her skirt, smoothing it down around her ankles. Her face warmed as he turned his head away.

Micah cleared his throat. "Thy son is the center of much attention at the moment."

Gwen glanced toward the wagon. A flock of plain dresses surrounded it.

"He is in good hands," Micah said.

"Of course. They are kind to look after him."

"'Tis good for Betsy to have a young one around again." His eyes dimmed for a moment. "I know my mother grieved with her when Hannah died." Then he cocked his head and asked, "Are thee planning to stay with Thomas and Betsy then? Will thy husband join thee?"

Gwen looked away, the warmth in her cheeks poured down her neck. "Owen and I plan to stay with them. I h-have no husband." What must he think of her? "'Tis how it is." She scooped her clean laundry into a soggy bundle.

His long fingers brushed hers aside, and he took the heavy load from her. The damp cloth darkened his shirt front.

"Allow me to carry it for thee." His eyes, tinged with sadness, held no censure.

Was he sad for her? The thought both intrigued and angered her, but she didn't have time to sort through her emotions. She trotted to keep up with his long strides.

At the wagon, she melted into the warm greetings of the women around Betsy and moved as far away from the disturbing Micah Pike as the gathering would allow.

Chapter 15

G WEN PUSHED OFF THE blanket and sat up, bumping into a wooden
crate. With a muffled yelp, she clutched her head. Memory
flooded back. She reached, and her fingers brushed the hem of Owen's
gown. He didn't stir in his sleep save for the steady rise and fall of his
breathing. The first gray fingers of pre-dawn seeped through the crack
between the wagon's side and its canvas top.

Micah's wagon.

Thomas and Micah had talked long after sunset about the coming
journey, discussing Braddock's Road and the rough terrain they'd face,
among other things. Gwen had dozed by the fire until Betsy recommended they all retire for the night. Micah had insisted that Gwen
and Owen sleep in his wagon while he slept underneath. Thomas
proclaimed it a wonderful idea, ignoring Gwen as she shook her head.
Betsy had agreed. Before she knew it, Gwen found herself lying atop
a pile of blankets on the floor of the wagon with Owen beside her.

Micah had shuffled under the wagon, preparing his makeshift bed.
Fearing she would never sleep, she'd listened to his breathing become
deep and regular. That was all she could remember before bumping

her head. Gwen curled back into the blankets and closed her eyes. She'd rest a few more moments while her son slept.

Owen's bawl jerked her awake. She pushed up, bumping her head on the same crate. Stifling another yelp, she gathered her crying son to her chest and inched out the back of the wagon. Orange and pink laced the eastern sky while the west still wore its purple cloak. Betsy was stooped by the fire, poking the old coals to life.

"'Tis a fine morning. Did thee sleep well?"

"Better than I expected, and Owen slept the night through."

"Yesterday's excitement wore the poor babe out. He must be half-starved."

"Aye."

"Thomas milked Tiny a few moments ago." Betsy nodded toward the cloth-draped bucket.

"He is too thoughtful."

A slight curl touched the edges of Betsy's lips. "As 'twas thoughtful of Micah to offer thee his wagon."

Gwen wanted to discuss that very issue. But at a shout from below the wagon, Betsy jumped and Gwen spun around.

"Ugh!" Micah crawled backwards, bare feet and muscular legs sticking out from his breeches.

"Is it a snake?" Betsy dropped the stick she poked the fire with and grabbed a nearby shovel.

"Ugh—only if a snake is hairy and white." Micah twisted and sat on the ground. His hair, freed of its leather tie, swirled in all directions. His wrinkled shirt fell in loose folds from his shoulders. He scrunched his nose and wiped the back of his hand across his face. "I have been licked by a goat!"

Gwen covered her mouth. Her shoulders jiggled and breath hissed between her fingers. The first high-pitched giggle that escaped brought an answering snort from Betsy. Tears filled Gwen's eyes, and she leaned forward, bracing herself on one knee for support. She gasped for air and laughter spilled forth. Owen's round eyes fixed on her face, their noses almost touching as she bent over him. That, as well as Micah's glower, set off a second round of hiccupping giggles.

Thomas entered the camp carrying two buckets of water. "What is this?"

"'Twould appear I have entertained the camp this morning." Micah rose and straightened his clothing. He glared at them, then marched off toward the stream, but not before Gwen caught the twinkle of humor in his eyes.

"Thy laughter is as a medicine to my heart," Betsy said. "Now feed Owen before Micah comes back, and then tether thy goat to a tree somewhere. 'Twould be a good idea to keep her at a distance from that young man for a day or two."

Gwen hurried through her chores, then joined Betsy at the fire.

The older woman stirred a pot of porridge over the fire. "He is growing so fast."

Gwen nodded. "Almost a month old already."

"Soon he will be able to take a little thinned porridge."

Betsy's words caught at Gwen's heart. Faith's comment about how fast children grew came back to her, and she breathed a sigh. All things grew and changed, but to hold onto these sweet baby moments a bit longer would be a joy. 'Twould be her only time with one so young.

"'Tis the way of growing things," Betsy said.

"Aye. I was just thinking..." She ran her finger across Owen's downy cheek. "How sad that he will have no brothers or sisters to grow with."

"Best to leave these things in the Lord's hands." Betsy turned back to stir the porridge.

Betsy didn't understand, and Gwen couldn't explain without breaking her oath. In her heart, she knew she could never marry. To do so would expose her lie, at least to her husband. For surely a man would know that her body had never birthed a child. The lie that brought the wonderful babe to her arms also stripped her of the chance to marry and have one of her own.

No. Owen *was* her own, just as Evie had said.

Micah returned and plopped a bucket of water where Tiny could reach it. "Truce, madam goat." The ungrateful animal ignored him as she stripped another mouthful of leaves from a nearby branch. A smile lurked at the corners of Micah's mouth.

Gwen tucked her chin when their eyes met and propped Owen against her shoulder. If she were free to think about a future with anyone—

"Enough of your foolishness." Thomas didn't bother to hide the grin that parted his beard. "We have a good meal before us and a long day ahead of us."

They sat on an assortment of crates and an overturned bucket while Betsy ladled their porridge into bowls. Gwen laid Owen on the grass at her feet, where he entertained himself clutching at the cool stems. After the time of silent prayer, Thomas spoke.

"I shall go into town today to purchase a wagon and gather our food supplies for the trip. Amos has spoken with our guide for the trail and has his recommendations for what we will need. If thee requires anything extra, I can purchase it while in town. I would prefer thee did not return to the city."

"Micah warned us of the attitude in town against the Friends." Betsy set her spoon in her bowl. "Gwen and I only need a few things, mostly cloth for sewing gowns for the babe. Young Owen will grow out of his clothing before we know it."

"He has grown, has he not?" Thomas set aside his empty bowl and reached for the babe.

Gwen's heart lifted as she scooped him up and handed him over. If they never found Faye, at least Owen would have someone as close as family with the Baldwins.

"While you are in town,"—Gwen pushed porridge around her bowl—"you will remember to ask about Faye? And Martha McClure?"

"I shall spread word among the other Friends as well." He patted her shoulder. "If she is here, we will find her."

"Who is this?" Micah asked.

"Faye Morgan is Gwen's sister, a year younger. They were separated when they were sold into indenture."

Micah snapped his glance toward her.

She held her breath. He hadn't known about her indenture. What must he think of her?

He turned to Thomas. "Surely... that is... thee did not..."

"Indeed not." Thomas's voice grew stern. "Gwen is a free woman now. We would never hold another in bondage."

Micah relaxed, but his sharp eyes made her squirm on her crate. "I have a few more things to pick up in town. I shall ride along if it suits thee."

"The others are leaving now." Thomas pointed to a wagon loaded with men.

Gwen turned away as Micah pulled on his stockings and boots. The two men grabbed their hats and joined the others.

"Do you think they might find her?" Gwen asked Betsy.

"I will pray and ask the Lord to direct their path. 'Tis all we can do now."

Betsy tidied the camp, but Gwen stayed and watched until the wagon, with a long string of horse teams tied behind, disappeared over the rise.

Faye was out there somewhere. She had to be. This might be Gwen's last chance to find her.

Thomas pulled the wagon to a stop beside their makeshift tent. He nodded to Betsy before climbing off the high seat.

"Did thee find word of Gwen's sister?"

"Not yet, but many of our men are still in town. All know to ask about her."

He wrapped an arm around her shoulders and swept the other hand in a grand gesture toward the wagon.

"Our home for the next few months."

"It looks new." Betsy ran her fingers over the smooth boards on the side.

"Finished only last week. I was lucky to get it. The town is short of wagons with so many purchasing them." He gestured to the camp. "Several will have to wait for more wagons to be built."

"Will this delay our journey long?"

"Long enough." His voice was a deep grumble. "First, we lose almost two weeks at sea, now this shortage of wagons. We sent word ahead regarding our need of them. I expected they would be ready."

"At least the roads will be dry by the time we set out. I know thee worried about the mud with these heavy wagons."

"Aye, but the snows will come that much sooner. 'Tis a tricky business to move so many through the wilderness." He glanced at the blue sky overhead as if its high clouds might hold snow despite the heat. "I must unhitch the horses and speak with Cobb, our trail guide. That is why I returned before the others. He will not be pleased by this delay." Thomas unhitched the horses and led them away.

Betsy climbed the mounted steps into the back of the wagon. It was fitted with five tall wooden bows covered with sailcloth. Betsy fingered the stiff fabric. It needed to be greased to prevent rain from soaking through. The bows had hooks on the inside for hanging things they needed to reach easily. Two narrow cots met in the middle and took up the front half of the wagon, with boxes and barrels of dried goods already stored underneath. The back of the wagon held coils of rope, a new bucket, a copper kettle, and a crock full of grease.

After climbing out, Betsy walked around the wagon. Two water barrels and two long, front-opening boxes lined the sides. She would keep her cooking wares in the boxes. When open, the front became a bench she could work from. She stepped back for another look. Thomas had chosen well.

Gwen arrived out of breath, Owen's little head bobbing against her shoulder. "Did Thomas return with word of Faye?"

"Nay, but he returned early, and the other men are still in town. Thomas assured me they will continue to make inquiries."

Gwen's shoulders drooped.

A wave of sympathy overcame Betsy. She put her arms around the young mother and child, hugging them tightly. As Gwen relaxed into the embrace, Betsy looked to the heavens, thanking God for His perfect timing.

"Thomas returned with some distressing news. They could not purchase enough wagons. Our journey will be further delayed."

Gwen straightened, a gleam of hope in her eyes. "That will give them more time to search for Faye." She looked toward town.

"It will. And Thomas will do his best. But we have no proof she stayed here in Alexandria."

"I know. I'm afraid to hope, but I must." Gwen's dark blue eyes welled with tears. "She is all I have."

"Not anymore, child." Cupping Gwen's cheek with her hand, Betsy put all the love she could into her next words. "Thee are a part of our family now. Thomas feels the same."

When Gwen wrapped her arm around Betsy, it felt like an answer to prayer.

Gwen stirred Owen's clothing in the new copper kettle Thomas had bought. Sweat dripped from her chin, and she dabbed at it with her sleeve. Between the blazing June sun and the fiery embers under the pot, she might as well have been boiled with the laundry. But it could be her last opportunity to do a proper washing for some time.

It had taken ten additional days for the new wagons to be finished. The men were bringing them to the camp that afternoon. Thomas and Micah worried that the green wood used in some of the wagons would be a problem down the trail, but they had little choice. If they didn't leave soon, they'd never make the new territory before winter.

Gwen dabbed at her forehead again. Faith and her family had one of the green-wood wagons. She hoped Thomas and Micah's worries proved wrong. How could they repair a wagon on the trail in the middle of the wilderness?

With a long wooden paddle, Gwen lifted the laundry, dumping it into the rinse tub to let it cool before she twisted out the water. Pounding hooves drew her attention as she straightened her back and shaded her eyes with one hand.

Micah's red roan horse with the wide blaze thundered toward her. Why was he running the horse in such terrible heat?

Fear cinched her heart.

She snatched up her skirts and ran to the end of the wagon, waiting there until he pulled the horse to a halt and slipped off its back.

"Gwen!" he shouted before his feet hit the ground. "Good news."

She sucked in a breath and pressed both hands over her mouth.

"I heard word of Martha McClure today in town."

"What did you hear?" She grabbed his sleeve with one hand, the other moved to her chest.

"She was in Alexandria a couple of years ago, but she never lived here. Seems she was on an extended visit with a friend. I met a man who works for that lady."

"Where is she now?"

"He said she lives in a place called Pittsburgh in Pennsylvania."

Gwen's heart plummeted. "Is that far from here?"

"Indeed. But 'tis not so far from where we are going to settle."

Gwen's knees wobbled.

Micah grabbed her forearms and steadied her.

"Maybe thee ought to sit down."

"Aye." Gwen sank to the ground. "This man, did he know anything of Faye?"

"Not by name, but he remembered a young woman with curly dark hair and fair skin. He said she arrived by ship with three others the night before Martha McClure returned to Pittsburgh. She was the only one to leave with that woman the next day."

Gwen closed her eyes and bowed her head. She wanted to pray, as the Quakers did, but she didn't know how... or what exactly to pray for.

"What has happened?" Betsy's breathless voice pulled Gwen from her thoughts. The older woman's face was flushed when she stopped beside them, her eyes wide and darting between Gwen and Micah.

"News of Faye, at last." Gwen pushed wayward curls under her bonnet with a shaky hand.

"What news?"

Micah retold what he had learned. Betsy listened and asked the same questions as Gwen. The genuine delight on the older woman's face brought a lump to Gwen's throat. She remembered Betsy's words almost two weeks ago, *Thee are part of our family now*. Tears mingled with the sweat on Gwen's face. Faye wasn't in Alexandria, but they knew where she might be.

And Gwen had people to help find her.

Chapter 16

June 1799

Q UAKERS GATHERED IN A half circle around Thomas, Amos, and
another man who wore a fringed coat and stained buckskin
leggings instead of breeches. They stood on three stumps beside a
large wagon. A huge bonfire cast dancing shadows against the canvas
behind them. Low clouds hung in the twilight sky.

Gwen stayed back with Faith and a few of the younger women.
Swaying side to side, she held her sleeping babe.

"'Tis exciting to know we are on our way tomorrow," Faith said.

"Aye." Gwen smoothed Owen's downy curls.

"Just think. Our children will be raised in a free territory, where no
person is owned by another."

Gwen looked for Zachary. He stood toward the back of the crowd
of men, his arms folded across his chest. He caught her glance and
held it for a second before his smile gleamed in the firelight. Of those
gathered, he understood what freedom meant as much as she did.
Probably more. She recognized his gentle attention toward her now to
be a bond formed of mutual understanding. All fear of him was gone.

She'd been silly for thinking there was anything sinister about Zachary.

Thomas raised his hands until he had everyone's attention. He introduced the buckskin-dressed man as Cobb, their trail guide, and turned the meeting over to him.

Cobb went over a list of rules, which included not falling behind, circling the wagons at the end of the day, and keeping the fires inside the circle. He warned them that they'd push hard every day to make up for the time lost waiting for wagons. Then he stopped and crossed his arms, looking over the heads of the men to the women beyond.

"You have a passel of women and young'uns in this bunch." The guide leaned to the side and spat. "They cain't be wanderin' off. Once we leave the settlements, we will be travelin' through Injun country. Women ain't to be leavin' the wagons. That goes double fer the young'uns. Nothin' an Injun likes better than stealin' a white child to raise fer his own."

Gwen gasped and hugged Owen tighter. A firm touch on her shoulder caused her to jump.

"Worry not, Gwen Morgan. We will watch over thee and young Owen." Micah's voice rumbled in her ear, his warm breath caressing her cheek. The scents of horse and leather clung to him.

Her heart knocked against her ribs. She took a step sideways to face him.

Owen startled awake in her arms. His face scrunched, and he let loose a hearty cry.

"I must go." Gwen scurried back to the Baldwins' wagon. She refused to look back. Even so, there was an itch on the back of her neck that could only be caused by Micah's gazing after her.

Betsy sat on a crate by the fire, her knitting needles clicking. When she saw Gwen, her eyebrows rose.

"What has frightened thee?"

"The trail guide warned of Indians stealing children," Gwen said in a rush.

"He stopped by earlier and spoke with Thomas." Betsy lowered her knitting to her lap. "There will be many dangers along our journey, but God will be with us. Thomas and I both believe that."

"And if He is not?" Gwen leaned against the sturdy wagon, rubbing Owen's back until he quieted. In all her excitement about freedom and finding Faye, she had not considered the physical dangers involved. Putting herself in danger was one thing, but if anything happened to Owen. . . And yet she had no choice. She'd made her decision when she'd signed her oath.

"Thee must learn to trust." Betsy put her half-knitted stocking aside and walked to Gwen. She reached for Owen and smiled when Gwen passed the babe over. "See how easily thee trusts me now? Thee hands over thy son without pause. The Lord is our Father in heaven. He loves thee more than I am able. Thee can trust Him with the welfare of thy son."

"You speak of God in ways I have never heard before. Ways I do not understand."

"Thee are not alone. The Friends started because people realized that the Lord of the Bible is more than what most churches teach. He is an ever-present Friend. In fact, it says in the Bible that He called His disciples friends. 'Twas from that we took our name. 'Twas others who dubbed us Quakers."

"But bad things still happen. Your children..."

"Indeed. And while I cannot fathom why He allowed them only a short time on this earth, I have to trust in Him. He gave me three children to love for a time. And He has brought thee into my life." She glanced at the child in her arms. "And Owen as well."

Gwen's throat clogged at the love in Betsy's voice. The simple beauty of truth on her face. She wanted to believe like Betsy believed, but the things she said were so strange. Gwen left Owen with Betsy and walked to the stream, away from Cobb and the crowd still asking him questions. She needed time alone to think. She sank onto the thick grass by the water's edge.

She couldn't understand Betsy's acceptance of such tragedy. Her father had railed against God and the church for the loss of his wife. When his sons died, he shook his fist at the heavens and cursed. The contrast of his drunken rantings and this woman's quiet acceptance bewildered her. And yet, although it saddened her to think on it, she admired Betsy more. Such disloyal thoughts toward the father she loved scraped her heart raw.

"Such a long face on the eve of our journey." Micah's voice came from beside her.

Gwen pressed a hand to her chest. "You startled me."

"Pardon me. 'Twas never my intent. Thee were much lost in thought."

"I was thinking of all the tragedies that happen, like children stolen or dying of disease. I cannot make sense of it."

He squatted on the grass beside her. "No one can. These things happen, but we should not live in a spirit of fear."

"Because God is in control?"

"Indeed. We could not be in better hands." His eyes held a calm she wished she could feel. At the same time, it irritated her.

"That is precisely what I do not understand." Gwen rose and looked him full in the face, her hands on her hips. "How can God care about us and allow terrible things to happen?"

He tilted his head up at her. "Cobb has truly frightened thee."

Gwen pointed toward the group that still lingered after the man's speech. "He was not trying to scare us, he was trying to warn us. These things have happened. God let them happen."

"Gwen." The warmth of his voice did curious things inside her. He stood and leaned forward. "We cannot blame all the world's ills on the Lord. 'Tis the work of people, not the will of God. He gives us free choice. 'Tis man's shame that too many choose poorly."

Her heart beat faster from Micah's nearness than any thoughts of Indians. He disturbed her as much as Jonas had, although not in the same way. Sleeping in his wagon didn't help. She must convince Betsy to allow her to make a tent from the spare canvas. She shook the grass from her skirt. "I must return to Owen now."

"Betsy has him well in hand."

"Still, I should go." She picked up her skirts and fled.

"Thee are running away," he shouted after her. "Who are thee running from, Gwen Morgan?"

She had no answer for him.

The first bump and jerk of the wagon shot a thrill through Gwen. After weeks of delay and uncertainty, the real journey had begun.

During yesterday's meeting—before Cobb's dire warnings—numerous people had risen to offer praise and prayers. The silence between those offerings fairly vibrated with emotion. Excitement and expectation flowed through the Quaker community.

Gwen spent the night wrestling with the conflicting concepts of a loving Lord and a fearsome God. Her earliest memories of church filled her with awe and trepidation. Gwen remembered one long-faced man in a dark robe who stood and shouted before the people. The Quakers' meetings exuded peace and introspection. They waited in silence for the Lord to speak to one of them. Then that person—man or woman—stood and shared it with the gathering.

Their way seemed more appealing, but there were too many things for one night's grappling to make sense of.

Thomas and Betsy occupied the wagon seat, as close to giddy as Gwen could imagine them. She peered out the back through the opening in the canvas. The team of horses pulling the wagon behind them nodded their heads in plodding agreement. The morning sun broke free of the trees. It would soon be too hot to ride in the mostly enclosed wagon, so Betsy and Gwen planned to take turns walking with Owen throughout the day.

Most of the wagons towed a reluctant cow or an extra saddle horse behind them. The Baldwins' wagon had only Tiny.

Gwen stood and steadied herself to peer over the tailgate at the goat trotting along. With plenty of tether, she grabbed a mouthful of grass as she followed. Gwen smiled, amused that she had grown so fond of a silly goat.

She scooted sideways between the cots and looked between Thomas and Betsy. Micah's wagon, in front of them in the line, swayed when its wheel sank into a hole. Gwen grabbed the back of the wagon seat in preparation for the lurch.

"'Tis truly exciting to be finally on our way." To their final destination and possibly closer to Faye.

"I daresay, we shall all be tired of traveling soon enough," Betsy said. "But thee are right, 'tis exciting today."

"We shall enjoy the forenoon and let the horses grow accustomed to this wagon," Thomas said. "This afternoon, I would like to start teaching thee both to drive."

"Whatever for?" Betsy swiveled to face him, eyebrows shooting up under her bonnet.

"Many things can happen on a trail like this. Should I be unable to drive, someone must take the reins." He glanced at his wife. "Thee have driven a single horse many times. 'Tis not so different with a team."

Betsy nodded. "I expect we shall catch on soon enough, will we not, Gwen?" She patted Thomas's arm. "Thee are a thoughtful man. 'Tis good wisdom in thy thinking too. We should be ready, come what may."

Gwen's high spirits faltered. Cobb's warnings returned, and a shudder raced down her spine. Thomas would prepare for the worst while Betsy relied on God for the best. It was all so confusing.

But somewhere ahead was Faye. That thought revived Gwen's good spirits. She turned to Owen, lying on one cot with his tiny fingers clenching and unclenching a corner of his blanket.

Faye would adore him.

"Look ahead," Thomas said. Their wagon had topped a small rise. Before them stretched a line of wagons snaking through a broad valley below.

"A beautiful sight," Betsy said.

"We have as many wagons after us as before," Thomas said.

Betsy nodded. "More than enough people to start the new community."

"Indeed. With two blacksmiths we may split and form two new communities."

"So many people looking for a land where everyone is free." Betsy sighed.

Gwen sat beside Owen and lifted him to her lap.

A land where everyone was free.

She braced her heels against the rocking of the wagon and smiled at Owen, holding him up and touching noses. Her son would never be owned by another person. Not ever.

"Who be this one?" Cobb lifted a long-whiskered chin in Gwen's direction before he shoveled a huge spoonful of Betsy's thick stew into his mouth. Gravy oozed from the ends of his drooping mustache.

"They are Gwen Morgan and her son, Owen," Thomas said. "They joined our family back in New Bern."

"Her husband?"

Gwen forced herself to meet Cobb's dark stare.

Thomas shifted on his makeshift seat to look Cobb in the eye. "They are under my care."

"Huh." Cobb crammed in another mouthful of stew. His small eyes narrowed beneath squinting lids.

Gwen kept her chin steady and reminded herself to breathe. She refused to look at him again.

"See she stays out of mischief on this train. An unattached female ain't nothin' but trouble." Cobb stood and tossed his empty bowl onto the bench.

Micah rose along with him, straightened to his full height, and curled his hands into fists at his sides.

"Be easy, Micah." Thomas waved him to sit down. "Cobb, my family is none of thy concern. Pray, keep this in mind."

"She will be my concern if she causes trouble among the men." Cobb leaned over and spat.

Betsy planted her hands on her hips.

Micah took a step forward.

Thomas gripped the younger man's arm. "Be easy."

"He has no call to say such things," Micah ground out between his teeth as Cobb sauntered away.

"And what would thee do?" Thomas asked.

Micah clenched and unclenched his hands, his lips a thin slash, his blue eyes cold.

Gwen drew back into the shadow of the Baldwins' wagon, Owen snug in her arms. What Cobb insinuated was horrible, but he wouldn't be the only one to look at her that way. To many, she was nothing but a fallen woman. Being unable to defend herself with the truth added to her hurt. That Micah seemed willing to stand up for her added to her confusion.

"'Tis not for Friends to provoke a fight. 'Tis against all we stand for." Thomas released his hold on Micah. "Thee knows this well."

"'Twas not me provoking it."

Thomas grunted and raised an eyebrow.

Micah released a forceful breath and dropped onto the crate that served as his seat.

Betsy retrieved Cobb's bowl. She held it out between one finger and thumb until she dropped it in the wash bucket, then wiped her hands on her apron. "Perhaps it would be best not to invite Cobb to join us for supper in the future. Come, Gwen. There is no need for thee to retreat from the fire."

Gwen shot a quick glance at Micah, whose eyes met hers, though he didn't smile. She took her seat on an upturned bucket and picked up her bowl of stew. Several flies stuck on the surface of her cooling dinner, and she set it back down. Would Micah have come to blows with Cobb over her? She peeked at him across the bench that served as their table. He finished his stew and left without a word, stalking off in the direction of the horses.

"Cobb is an unpleasant person," Betsy said.

"He knows his business. He should guide us safely through the wilderness. But thee are correct. Most pleasant, he is not."

"Does he truly think I would—"

"He knows thee not." Betsy cut Gwen off. "Would that he knew thee as we have come to, he would not entertain such thoughts."

"Still and all, thee has the right of it, wife. Cobb will receive no more invitations to join us at our fire." Thomas handed over his bowl, rose, then stretched and yawned. "'Twas too much excitement at the end of a long day. I shall check the horses, and then I think it prudent to establish Gwen and Owen in our wagon for the night."

Relief buoyed Gwen's spirits as she splashed water over the bowls in the washtub.

"'Tis for the best." Betsy gathered the spoons. "With the wagons circled for protection, thee would be too far from us now in Micah's wagon."

"With the extra canvas," Gwen said, "I could fashion a suitable tent off the wagon's side." Even with the wagons parked side-by-side at the camp, Gwen had been disturbed by Micah's closeness. Not that she didn't trust him. He was no Jonas. But she wouldn't miss hearing him under the wagon each night as she fell asleep.

Would she?

Betsy straightened and glanced at the wagon. "I think not. 'Twill be safer to have thee in the wagon with me. Thomas will make do on the seat."

"But your wagon seat is too short."

"The floor in front is longer and wider. Indeed. That will do quite nicely."

"But—"

"'Tis settled."

Gwen bent over the washtub and scrubbed the bowls with a square of rough linen. She wanted out of Micah's wagon, but she didn't want to inconvenience Thomas and Betsy. Not that Betsy was giving her much choice.

Would she ever be in a position to make choices for herself? Or would she forever be tumbled about by circumstances beyond her control?

Micah's anger at Cobb picked at her thoughts. Had he risen to her defense? Or was he angry that Cobb would suggest the Baldwins would allow her to make trouble? And why did his nearness fluster her so?

Perhaps it was best if she didn't dwell on that.

Chapter 17

"**G**WEN WAS SO QUIET after supper." Betsy rested her hand in the crook of Thomas's elbow as they strolled around the circle of wagons, nodding greetings to acquaintances and long-time friends.

"That one is always quiet. A less talkative miss I have yet to behold."

"She has been more talkative of late. Has thee not noticed?"

"Perhaps." Thomas stroked his beard. "But I do not see her nattering on as many her age tend to do."

"Indeed. That would not be Gwen. Her thoughts are deep and... sad."

Thomas grunted.

"Young Micah's response was most interesting." Betsy peeked at her husband.

"Indeed."

"Does thee think he might be smitten with our Gwen?"

"Perhaps. But 'tis too soon to contemplate such. They have newly met, and he was recently disappointed by that other young woman."

"I had almost forgotten." Betsy patted her husband's arm. "He wouldn't be with us now if the girl he had hoped to marry had not chosen his brother instead. Sad, that. But perhaps God has other plans for him here among us."

"And whether or not those plans include Gwen 'tis not for us to decide." The quirked eyebrow above his twinkling eyes drew a laugh from her.

"Indeed, husband. It never occurred to me to think otherwise."

Gwen tugged on the tough leather gloves. Far too large for her hands, the fingers stuck out at the tips like heavy sausage casings.

"I might do better without them."

"Thee will raise blisters for sure," Thomas said.

"Better a set of blisters than fumbling the reins, I think."

"Indeed. Perhaps Betsy can fashion gloves that will fit thee."

Gwen shook the gloves off and clambered onto the wagon seat, sliding to the far side to make room for Thomas. A pair of broad caramel-colored backs waited in front of her. Lad and Lonny stood half asleep, heads hanging well below their withers. Sleepy or not, the massive size of them intimidated Gwen. Tiny was the first animal she had ever handled by herself, and the goat only came to the knees of the monsters in front of her.

Thomas pointed to the reins, wrapped around the brake handle. "There they are, grab hold."

Gwen unwrapped the thick leather lines, and the left horse stepped forward. Gwen fumbled and dropped one of the reins.

"Easy, Lad," Thomas crooned to the horse. "Thee must handle the reins lightly, but not so lightly that thee drops them. Each movement is felt by the horse and tells him what thee expects of him."

"Easy, Lad." Gwen's voice trembled. She cleared her throat. "Easy." She glanced at Thomas. "I do not wish to hurt them."

"Thee cannot. Each horse weighs nearly one hundred stone." He cocked his head and eyed her head to feet. "Thee might top eight at best."

Gwen giggled and wiped her damp hands on her lap.

"With just a pair, thee holds two lines in each hand." Thomas put the reins in her hands in the proper position. "The lines in thy right hand are used to turn the horses to the right. One is attached to each horse. Likewise, the lines in thy left hand are used to turn the horses to the left. Keep the lines separated between thy fingers, just so."

Gwen glanced at her hands, clenched the reins, and drew in a deep breath. Mark Allen had driven a coach and four when younger than she. Betsy had managed to drive Lonny and Lad the day before. Surely Gwen could do as well.

Micah's wagon lurched forward in front of them. Straightening her back, she jiggled the lines and shouted in the deepest voice she could muster, "Get up there!" The sturdy pair leaned into their collars. Leather creaked and metal jangled. The wagon moved under her while a sensation of power raced through the lines and into her hands.

"They did it." She turned to Thomas, a grin tugging her lips apart.

"Of course they did. But watch where they go now. Lad likes to drift left and Lonny will wander with him if thee fails to pull them back in line every so often."

Gwen squared herself with the team again and kept her eyes forward.

"A new teamster, Baldwin?" Cobb's voice grated against Gwen's nerves, and she flinched, shooting a glance to her left. He rode beside them on his wiry black horse. His battered hat, decorated with a large feather, shaded his face above the untrimmed beard.

"Indeed. She has the makings of a good one."

"Huh. She might prove useful. Teach her well." Cobb kicked his horse into a lope.

"Worry not." Thomas rested his hand on her shoulder. "We will see thee has as little to do with Cobb as possible."

Lad drifted left. Gwen concentrated on pulling the right rein to correct him.

"Nicely done." Thomas nodded and squeezed her shoulder.

Gwen sat taller on the high wooden seat. She lifted her chin and firmed her grip on the lines. She could do it. She would pull her weight on the journey as much as Lad and Lonny were pulling theirs. Her lips twitched at the comparison, but for the first time she didn't feel like a servant.

She felt like a contributing member of ... of a family.

Gwen squeezed the last of the warm milk into her bucket. Her shoulders ached, and her fingers burned from the leather-chaffed skin. She flexed her hands several times before stroking the white face turned toward her.

Tiny nibbled on her sleeve.

"You have filled out nicely since leaving that awful ship."

"Talking to thy goat this evening?" Humor rippled through Zachary's deep voice.

"You of all people should understand. Have I not heard you speaking to Bossy on many an occasion?"

Zachary's eyebrows shot to the brim of his hat. "Gwen Morgan! That is the most words I have heard thee string together at one time."

Gwen studied the ground by her feet, ashamed of her initial reaction to the gentle man in front of her. All fear of him had fled since they'd left the ship. She shrugged a shoulder and grimaced at the painful movement. "Betsy said much the same thing this morning."

"'Tis good to see thee comfortable among the Friends. Perhaps someday thee will join us in all ways."

"Join the church? I mean, the meeting?"

Zachary nodded.

"I know not." She shifted the bucket in her hands. "There is so much I do not understand."

"Then spend time seeking after the things of God. He who seeks will not be disappointed. We Friends believe that."

"I will think on it."

He nodded and moved on, his bucket swinging in time to the tune he whistled.

Gwen returned to the Baldwins' wagon. Owen's squeal quickened her steps in spite of her protesting muscles. She rushed around the wagon's tailgate to see Thomas, with Owen lifted high, blow noisily on the boy's exposed belly. Owen squealed again and flapped his pudgy arms.

Gwen rocked to a stop on her toes, warm milk washing over her hand before she steadied the bucket.

"Never let it be said my husband was not ready to be a grandfather."

Betsy pointed at the man and child. She pushed a mass of simmering cloth in the washkettle with a long stick. "I have boiled the feeding cloths, but I think 'tis time to try one of those fancy feeding cups packed in the boy's carpetbag."

"So soon?"

"Indeed. Thy son is growing by the day."

The fond gleam in Betsy's eyes could only be described as grandmotherly. Not that Gwen had ever known a grandmother herself, hers having passed on before her birth, but she couldn't want a better one for Owen. Her throat tightened until Thomas's next noisy blow on Owen's belly forced it open with a laugh.

"I shall get the cups and see which one works best," Gwen said.

It took Betsy's more experienced hand, but soon Owen slurped the goat's milk mixed with a bit of cooked porridge from an oblong pewter cup.

Gwen's heart soared—and then sank. There would be no other babies for her. Must he grow and change so fast?

Gwen snugged the lines between her leather-encased fingers. The tanner, a single man among their group of Quakers, had traded the supple leather to Gwen. In return, she mended a basketful of clothing for him while Betsy sewed the gloves. They fit Gwen's slender hands like second skin.

Last evening, Micah and Thomas discussed the need for fresh meat. Cobb pushed the wagons hard to make up for their delayed start, which left no time for hunting. Five days out of Alexandria, they were eager to procure fresh meat for supper. Thomas conceded Micah the better shot, and so they arranged that Gwen would drive the young man's wagon while he hunted.

Gwen looked over the backs of Micah's matching red roans, Sassy and Hap. Three turns at driving the Baldwin team didn't make her an expert, but Micah assured her the team was well-broke and easy to handle. Already an experienced team when he'd left his father's farm, the horses had been driven more than forty miles to Alexandria and were used to his wagon.

The wagon in front of her lumbered into motion. "Get up there!" she shouted to the horses. Sassy and Hap leaned into their collars, and Micah's wagon rolled forward. A sense of pride and accomplishment filled her. And a sense of freedom. For the first time in her life, she commanded control of her circumstances. The powerful animals in front of her moved in accordance with her directions. If only Faye could see her now. Gwen forced herself to sit tall and still on the high seat, though inside she wanted to shout and twirl.

"Feelin' mighty proud of yerself, ain't you, girl?" Cobb's sneering words struck her like the knotted end of a whip.

"I ain't got you figgered yet, but I will. You ain't got me fooled. I ain't no gullible Bible thumper like the others." He leaned sideways in his saddle and spat.

She kept her eyes forward, refusing to acknowledge him.

"Ain't no call to be all high-n-mighty with me, missy. You didn't get that boy at any church social. You know what I'm talkin' about."

Gwen gritted her teeth and ignored him until he slapped Sassy on the rump with a coil of rope. The mare jerked forward, tossing her head and breaking into a canter, pulling Hap along with her. Gwen braced her feet against the kickboard and hauled back on the reins. Sassy settled down after just a few strides, blowing a forceful breath and shaking her mane.

Cobb's nasty chuckle as he rode off lifted the hairs on the back of Gwen's neck.

"Are thee all right?" Thomas's raised voice reached her from behind.

"Aye," she turned and yelled back, his worried face visible through the open ends of the canvas.

After acknowledging Thomas's nod with one of her own, she faced forward again. She raised her chin and drew a deep breath to settle her stomach. Cobb would not intimidate her. She was a free woman under the care of Thomas and Betsy.

She was free—but she was not alone.

Betsy shaded her eyes and squinted down the line of wagons. Micah trotted toward camp on a horse he'd borrowed for the hunt with a deer carcass draped across the front of his saddle. He halted beside the dying noon fire, and Thomas hurried to help remove the deer.

"'Tis not very large, but 'tis the only one I saw this morning."

"A most welcome addition for our supper, all the same." Betsy wiped her hands on her apron. Their fifth day out, and she was already weary of salt pork. Her mouth fairly watered in anticipation of roast venison.

"I will give a haunch to the Smiths for letting me borrow their horse." Micah patted the horse's neck. "He is a good one in dense forest and steady under the gun. 'Twould be nice to borrow him again."

"A fine idea. I know Hazel will be most happy to receive it."

Micah and Thomas cut the meat and tied it to the back of the saddle. Micah was pushing his foot into the stirrup when Gwen came around his wagon leading Sassy and Hap. He brought his foot back to the ground.

"How did thee get along with my horses?"

"They are a fine, steady team, just as you said."

"Until Cobb slapped the mare with his rope." Thomas's frown lines deepened. He shot a glance at Micah.

"What?" Micah spun and stared at the older man.

"'Twas nothing." Gwen patted the chest of the roan mare towering above her. "She spooked for a few steps and then settled back down." The girl's face wore a quiet sort of pride, determination, and spunk. Gwen had come to them a frightened girl and was blossoming into a confident young woman.

The transformation warmed Betsy's heart.

Micah strangled the saddle horse's reins in his hand. His jaw muscles bunched, and he scanned the nearby wagons.

"Gwen is right," Betsy said. "'Twas easily handled. She did a fine job. Go. Return the horse. The call to hitch will come any minute." Betsy laid a hand on Micah's back and gave him a gentle shove toward the waiting horse. "I shall cut some bread and cheese for thee to eat when thee returns. Gwen can drive thy wagon a bit longer so thee can eat."

Micah swung onto the horse and cantered off, still scanning the wagons.

Betsy leaned close to Thomas. "Husband, 'twas it not thee in thy wisdom who proclaimed it the Lord's business whether or not these two young people come together?"

"I believe it was."

"And did I not just hear with my own ears thee mention Cobb's behavior in Micah's presence? Thee knew full well the reaction it would warrant from that young man."

"I have no idea what thee are suggesting." Thomas's mustache twitched as he backed Lonny against the wagon and hitched him.

Betsy turned her head to hide her own smile. As Gwen hitched the roan team to Micah's wagon, her heart swelled with gratitude and praise to God for sending the young woman into their lives. And if it be His will, regardless of the meddling of a childless old couple, she hoped Gwen would find a permanent place with them in the new territory.

And perhaps with Micah.

Chapter 18

WOULD SHE EVER BE dry again? Gwen hunched over Owen, shielding him from the worst of the downpour, and scurried from the back of the wagon to the makeshift shelter. Their largest extra canvas hung from tree branches above the cookfire, angled to release the smoke.

"I had Thomas put a crate down for Owen." Betsy pointed to the wooden box near the fire. "He should stay dry there."

"Will it stop tonight, do you think?" Gwen tugged at her skirt, the damp fabric a heavy drape around her hips. She tucked her wayward hair, which escaped in a riot of damp curls, under her bonnet.

"Only God knows. If it does not, we may be stranded here for a few days. Thomas says some of the wagons cannot make it through if the mud gets any deeper."

Another delay in their journey.

Cobb insisted they move from sunrise to nightfall each day with a nooning only long enough to partially rest the animals. He showed no care for the humans under his guidance, but to give the man credit, he was concerned for the horses and mules. They traveled even on

Sundays. The Quakers chafed at this but had decided from the onset they would abide by it and have their meeting after supper on Sundays.

Perhaps the rain was God's way of choosing the Quakers' side. Gwen smirked at the thought of Cobb being bested by the Lord.

Micah ducked under the makeshift shelter. "'Tis what some would call a real toad strangler." He slapped water from his hat and tried to put it on, but it brushed against the canvas so he took it back off and fidgeted with it in his hands. "I would be happy to milk the goat tonight."

"Thank you." Gwen's face warmed under his steady regard. She handed him the bucket and snatched her hand back when their fingers touched.

"Back in a moment." His one-sided grin pulled at something inside her. She spun around and almost bumped into Betsy.

The older woman's eyes crinkled at the corners. "He is a fine man. So thoughtful."

"Aye." Gwen smoothed her apron. "How will we hold a meeting tomorrow if the rain continues like this?" She blurted out the first thing she could think of to change the subject.

Betsy paused. "I know not. We should ask Thomas when he returns from picketing the horses. Give me a hand cutting these onions, will thee? I will set Owen's porridge to simmer."

Gwen cut the small onions into the pot and listened to Owen babble and coo from his crate. Rain thudded on the canvas and dribbled off in a steady stream from the lowest corner. The spicy scent of onion mingled with the clean smell of freshly washed earth. The sun battled heavy clouds in the western sky, throwing a feeble shadow across her hands.

Micah returned and handed her the milk bucket. "It may be watered down."

"'Tis fine. Mixing it into a pap with the porridge, 'tis plenty thick and filling for Owen."

To Gwen's surprise, Micah scooped the babe out of his crate and held him close. A smile broke the line of his stubbled jaw when Owen's hand tangled in Micah's hair. Strands slipped free of the leather strap tied at the back of his neck and hung loose.

Gwen's cheeks heated when he caught her stare, winked, and tucked the loose hair behind his ear. Her fingers twitched. Did his hair feel as sleek as it looked?

"Worry not, lad." Micah ran a finger over the baby's fair hair. "Thee will have a mane of thy own soon enough. But not dark like your mother's, nor so curly either."

"'Tis hard to know," Betsy said. "Many a babe starts with one hair color only to grow out another in time. I do think his eyes will stay blue though."

Gwen turned back to the cooking pot and gave the vegetables a vigorous stir. Of course Owen didn't look anything like her. He never would. His wispy locks already promised to match his mother's golden tresses.

She almost dropped the spoon.

Not his mother. She was only Constance Whiteford—the woman who didn't want him.

"Who has my boy?" Thomas stooped under the canvas cover and held out his hands to Owen.

The baby waved his arms and babbled, "Gah-gah-gah."

"See here. He said granddad for sure."

"Methinks thee has the ability to hear what perchance thee wishes to hear, husband." Betsy winked at Gwen.

"What is this? Did thee not hear the lad with thy own ears?" Thomas grinned and took the boy from Micah's arms. "Ah, what a fine boy. He must have doubled his weight since thee joined us, Gwen."

"More than. 'Twill take me stitching by the fire each night to keep him in clothing." Gwen stopped stirring and glanced at Thomas. "Not tomorrow, of course, if we will be at meeting."

"Where will we hold meeting if the rain does not cease?" Betsy rested her hand on Thomas's shoulder and held a wooden spoon for Owen to grasp.

"Cobb thinks the storm will break tonight. He may be correct."

"But surely 'tis too wet even now for the larger wagons to move onward," Micah said.

"Indeed. But the day should be fine for meeting."

Owen waved the spoon up and down as if in agreement.

Gwen relaxed, happy to have a day without travel, even if it did slow them down.

"'Twould only be natural." Thomas leaned forward and stirred the dying fire with a thick stick. Smoke drifted in lazy swirls across the humid air.

"I suppose, but sad all the same. If thee had but seen her face—"

"Hush, hush." Thomas tipped his chin at the wagon. Betsy covered her mouth with one hand for a moment. The early evening's torrent had subsided into a gentle patter on the canvas.

"When Micah mentioned the boy's fair hair, she appeared so stricken," Betsy whispered. "If Owen's father did... what thee surmises to have occurred... to be reminded by his countenance in such a way..."

"Our Gwen is made of sterner stuff. She will adjust. Has thee not told me of the great changes she has achieved with us already?"

"Indeed. 'Twas just that—"

"Put that thought to bed, wife." He yawned and stretched, settling an arm across her shoulders. "'Tis about time to put thyself there as well. Off to the wagon with thee."

"I think I should like to join thee here by the fire tonight."

"And what? Cuddle as though a pair of youngsters?"

"If 'twould suit thee?"

Thomas growled low in his throat and wrapped his other arm around her too. He pulled her close and murmured in her ear, "'Twould suit me well, wife."

Gwen jerked awake for the third time since the noon break. Or perhaps the fourth? Her brain refused to think clearly under the oppressive heat of her bonnet. Her one attempt to remove it, however, had resulted in a splitting headache from the sun's fierce rays on her unprotected head. Better to drowse in the heat than suffer that again.

She snapped her head up again and yawned until her jaw cracked. Sassy and Hap plodded along, following the wagon before them. Thankful she held the reins to such a steady team, Gwen wiped a sleeve across her eyes and willed herself to stay awake.

"Don't be fallin' off that seat, missy." Cobb rode toward her on Hap's side. "Those wheels would crush you dead. We ain't got time to be buryin' those who ain't up to the task."

Gwen tightened her lips. She refused to look him in the eye. He hadn't bothered her in days. Why must he single her out now?

A shrill whistle off to her left brought a curse from the shabby scout. From her vantage point on the high seat, she watched a rider on horseback charging down the line of wagons toward them. He whistled again, and Cobb yanked on his reins. His horse pivoted on its back feet, mouth agape. Its front feet hit the ground at a canter. Cobb swerved between her team and the wagon in front of them. Sassy snorted and jumped as Cobb's horse brushed in front of her. Gwen had her hands full for a moment to calm the mare and then the wagon in front of her stopped.

"Whoa!" Gwen pulled Sassy and Hap to a halt.

Thomas strode past her, heading toward where Cobb had intersected with the rider. The rider's wide-brimmed hat and broad shoulders caught Gwen's breath. Micah. What was happening? Too far away to hear anything and unwilling to leave the team unattended, Gwen gathered corner of her bottom lip between her teeth and waited for word.

Thomas and several other men on foot circled the mounted men. Their words were muted by distance, and then Micah wheeled his horse around and rode for the front on the wagon train with Cobb on his heels.

Thomas jogged back and stopped beside Gwen.

"Micah encountered a broad swath of downed trees across the trail ahead. We are to circle the wagons a short distance ahead by a creek. Then we shall have time to assess the damage and figure how to move the wagons through it."

"Downed trees?" Fear spiked through her. Would Indians chop down trees to ambush the train?

"Twister, most likely. He says it looks like they have been down for several weeks at least."

Relief washed over her. She welcomed the early stop and a chance to find both shade and fresh water. When the wagon in front of her moved, she slapped the reins over the broad backs in front of her, "Get up there!" Probably able to smell the water, both horses stepped out briskly.

Before they reached the creek, Micah rode beside the wagon.

"Are thee doing well with the team today?" he asked.

"Aye, they are a steady pair. 'Tis glad I am of it in this heat."

"Indeed." A grin teased the corners of his mouth. "'Tis too easy to nod off in heat like this."

Heat that had nothing to do with the August sun splashed across Gwen's face.

Micah's grin widened. "Behind the seat is a rope. Next time, tie thyself to the seat. Just in case."

She swiveled and reached behind her until her fingers brushed the rough coil of rope. "Aye, I will."

His eyes twinkled in blue mischief before he turned the horse around. "We are almost to the creek now. I shall be back after I return this horse."

He cantered away. She couldn't help but admire the lean strength of him astride the horse. She hadn't seen much of him the past week. He left their fire after supper and returned after she and Owen were abed. It niggled at her conscience that she missed him.

She had no business missing any man.

Betsy stirred a bubbling pot of venison stew. Against Cobb's advice, four of the older boys had left the wagons that morning in search of fresh meat. The remaining men would relish a hearty meal after cutting and moving timbers all day. As would she. The simple meals they'd made on the trail were filling but not savory. Faith and Gwen had found wild herbs growing along the creek. Betsy breathed in the aromatic steam in spite of the humid heat of the day.

Thomas and Micah walked into camp, each shouldering an axe.

"Something smells delightful." Thomas eased his axe down with a sigh. He sat on a crate and worked the leather gloves from his hands.

"Smells like venison stew." Micah lowered his axe and leaned it against the wagon. "I'm hungry enough to lick the pot this evening."

Betsy gestured to the washbasin on the side of the wagon. "Clean water for washing."

"Where are Gwen and Owen?" Micah asked.

"Visiting with Faith and her young ones. She will be along soon, I suspect."

Micah looked around, a sly grin on his face. "I shall return shortly then." He jogged off.

"What is that young man up to?" Betsy asked.

Thomas shrugged. "Seems we shall know soon enough." He winced as his hands hit the water.

"Husband?" Betsy set her spoon aside and took Thomas's hands in hers. She gasped. The angry red flesh oozed. "Why did thee not stop and tend to these blisters before they ruptured?"

"There are so many trees to cut and move. 'Tis such a tangle, the horses cannot pull them out until we get the major branches lopped off."

"'Tis work for the younger men." Betsy pushed his hands back into the water, ignoring the hiss of his breath. "Hold them under for several minutes while I find the balm." She climbed into the wagon to sort through her stash of medicines. Prideful man, working to keep up with the young bucks.

"So that is what has kept you away these evenings past." Thomas's voice reached her as she grabbed the crock of ointment. She scurried from the back of the wagon.

Micah held a cradle in his arms, a wide grin gracing his face.

"Will she like it?" Micah asked.

"How could she not?" Betsy admired the fine grain of the wood and the soft polish. "'Tis beautiful. Set it near the fire where she will see it."

Thomas wiped his hands dry and took a step toward the cradle, but Betsy grabbed hold of his shirt.

"Hold still." She turned his hands over and soothed the ointment into his palms. She wrapped each hand in strips of soft cloth, then she cocked an eyebrow at him. "Thee will do no more work this evening."

"'Tis naught but a few blisters."

"Thee will be no use to anyone if they fester."

Gwen's chatter to Owen as she approached from the other side of the wagon stopped their conversation. Micah moved in front of the cradle, partially shielding it from Gwen's sight.

The young woman walked into view and stopped. Her eyes widened. Everyone's attention was centered on her. Her hand went to her throat as her gaze fell on Thomas's bandages.

"You are hurt."

"Nay, he has been stubborn." Betsy went to Gwen and turned her gently to face the fire. Micah stepped away from the cradle.

Gwen gasped.

Betsy took Owen and gave the young mother a nudge toward the gift. Micah's eyes never left Gwen. That the young man was smitten, there was little doubt.

Gwen sank to her knees beside the cradle. She ran her hand over the curved footboard. It was a large piece, plenty big enough for the boy's first two years.

"How can I thank you?" Gwen tipped her face toward Micah, and Betsy's heart swelled.

If that look meant what she hoped it did, Micah wasn't the only one smitten.

Gwen searched his eyes. Emotions she didn't understand skittered across their blue depths. Her heart responded with a jolt, and she pressed her hand to her chest.

"'Tis the finest gift I have ever received."

"Then it pleases thee?"

"Aye." The wood slipped like satin against her fingertips. "Owen will sleep like a king in so fine a cradle." Her son, who had always slept in a drawer or a crate, would now sleep like the son of a privileged family. As he should have from birth, if Miss Constance hadn't turned her back on him.

"He deserves no less," Micah said.

"Indeed." And yet, she would never be able to give him what his birthright deserved. The meager trio of coins Mr. Whiteford had left for them—his only true inheritance—remained tied in a cloth in her carpetbag.

Micah's voice quieted, for her ears only, even though Betsy and Thomas kept their distance. "Thee deserves no less as well."

She swallowed and met his eyes once more, their fervent blue holding her mute. He esteemed her too much, and panic swelled in her throat. She didn't deserve his regard or his kindness. If he knew the lie she lived...

He would not regard her at all.

Chapter 19

July 1799

G WEN STRUGGLED TO THEIR wagon with a basket full of wet clothing and set it near the clothesline Thomas had strung between the two wagons. Easing Owen out of the sling she used to carry him, she placed the sleeping boy in his cradle in the shade of the wagon, then straightened and pressed her hand to her back.

Cobb had warned them not to spread their clothes over nearby bushes. He said it created cover for curious Indians to sneak close to the wagons. Apparently, Indians were fond of woven cloth and would steal as much as they could carry away, and Indian men would wear women's dresses if they could steal them. Gwen didn't know if she believed him or not, but she hung her clothing on the rope stretched inside their circle of wagons all the same.

It was their fourth day in camp waiting for the men to clear the trail ahead. She appreciated the opportunity to catch up on chores, such as laundry, but worry hung as heavy as the humidity at yet another delay.

"'Tis clear he dotes on her." A high-pitched voice drifted from the other side of the wagon, the speaker blocked from sight by the canvas covering.

"Indeed," a second said.

"He made a cradle for the boy, after all. Surely that is telling in itself."

Gwen paused, a wet petticoat dangling in her hands. The voices grew stronger, accompanied by footfalls and skirts swishing through tall grass.

"And did she not sleep in his wagon those first few nights?"

"Surely Thomas and Betsy would not have condoned such if they suspected."

"Surely they see only what they wish to see."

"But the boy has such fine blond hair, nothing like her curly darkness or his sleek brown hair."

"It could change. The boy's eyes are blue and so like..." The voices trailed off as their footsteps died away.

Gwen clasped her hand to her chest, the damp petticoat soaking the front of her dress. They spoke of her and Micah—speculated that Micah was Owen's father. Her knees trembled, and she sank to the ground. How could they? Embarrassment and outrage battled within her.

Betsy approached from the creek, a bucket banging against her ample hip, concern etched on her face. "Are thee ill?"

Gwen stared at her, mind whirling over the conversation she'd overheard, tongue stuck to the roof of her mouth.

"Gwen?" Betsy set down her bucket and pressed her open palm against Gwen's forehead. "'Tis not fever. What is it?"

Gwen worked moisture back into her mouth for a moment before she could speak. "They think Micah is Owen's father."

"Who?" Betsy straightened and looked around.

"I'm not sure. I heard some women speaking"—she gestured to the other side of the wagon—"but I could not see them."

"Of all the useless things to prattle on about." Hands planted on her hips, Betsy glared around the wagon circle. "I believe I know who needs talking to. Stay here and finish hanging the clothes. Allow me to deal with this."

"No." Gwen scrambled to her feet and grabbed Betsy's hand.

"Nonsense. Gossip is not tolerated among the Friends."

"But if Micah were to hear—"

"He shan't. The women will handle it." She patted Gwen's hand.

"The men need not be acquainted with matters that do not concern them. 'Tis a matter for the women among the Friends to address."

Betsy marched away, her back as straight and step as purposeful as any soldier facing battle.

Gwen wouldn't want to be the gossiping women when Betsy confronted them. Fear climbed in Gwen's throat. How would the women handle it? What if the Quaker women discovered Gwen's secret? Would she be cast out as a liar? Surely the sin of lying was much greater than the sin of gossiping.

What would these women do to her if they learned the truth?

Sweat trickled down Gwen's neck and soaked into the collar of her dress. She'd removed her bonnet, and the ringlets that had escaped her pins and combs clung to her cheeks and forehead. She pressed her face into her sleeve. If Betsy didn't come back soon, she'd melt into a puddle of nerves.

Supper was ready, the laundry almost dry, and Owen entertained himself on a blanket, his belly full for the moment. Gwen should have taken the time to relax and cool down, but how could she, not knowing what the Quaker women were going to do about the gossipers?

And what they might do to her if they discovered her secret.

Deep voices and masculine laughter heralded the return of the men from their day's labor. Gwen had hoped to have a private moment with Betsy before the men returned. Frustrated, she poured water in the washbasin and set it on a crate for the men to clean up, laying a clean towel beside it.

"'Tis a fine sight to behold." Thomas's voice separated from the general chatter. "Was ever a man so blessed than to return to home and hearth and find his family waiting?"

Gwen smiled as Thomas and Micah broke away from the group to join her at their wagon. Zachary waved as he passed, and she returned his greeting. It was good to see the men in high spirits.

"Betsy," Thomas called.

"She is not here."

"Not here?" He scratched his fingers through his beard. "Where else would she be?"

"I'm not sure, exactly."

He cocked an eyebrow in question.

"She said she was meeting with some of the other women." Gwen twisted her apron into a knot. "But I have dinner ready and fresh water poured for you to wash." She pointed at the basin and hoped he didn't notice the tremor in her hand.

Thomas and Micah took turns at the basin and by the time they were finished, Betsy had joined them.

"Where has thee been, wife?"

"Dealing with a bit of women's business."

"Oh?"

"Nothing to concern thee, to be sure." Betsy took a bowl of stew from Gwen's hand and set it on the makeshift table in front of her husband. "How did the clearing go today?"

"Wonderful. We have cleared enough for the wagons to pass."

"Cobb's quite beside himself with the delay, but even he could not fault the work we have done." Micah accepted a bowl with a nod of thanks.

"We move on tomorrow then?" Betsy asked.

"Indeed," Thomas said. "I expect Cobb will push us even harder to make up for the four lost days."

Betsy shot a quick smile toward Gwen. "'Twill be good to be moving again. Keeping busy keeps us out of mischief."

"Eh? What is that?" Thomas's brow furrowed.

"There." Betsy sat the last bowl on the table and gestured for Gwen to be seated. "We shall be sure to thank the Lord for His blessings of both rest and work tonight." She smiled at her husband and bowed her head for the silent prayer.

Thomas shifted on his crate before lowering his head as well.

Gwen closed her eyes, but not before catching the twinkle in Micah's. He'd obviously caught on that Betsy wasn't going to share her activities with Thomas. Gwen stifled the giggle of relief threatening to surface. When Thomas cleared his throat to signal the end of the prayer, she kept her eyes away from Micah.

The men talked about their day clearing trees and repairing the trail ahead. Along with the downed timber, there were also deep ruts that had to be filled and several places where new growth was cut back to widen the original trail. Gwen ate in silence until Owen howled from his spot on the blanket.

Once her son was dry and had slurped a bit of pap from his pewter feeding cup, she handed him over to Thomas.

He launched into an explanation of why it was important to grease the wagon axles to the child in his arms as he walked around the wagon. Micah left to check on the horses and Tiny. Betsy joined Gwen near the fire where the water heated to wash dishes.

Gwen leaned close to whisper even though neither man was near enough to hear. "What happened?"

Betsy grabbed the ladle and added hot water to the bucket she'd piled with dirty dishes. "I had a pretty good idea who the gossipers were, based on whom I had seen walking along the back of the wagons earlier. A couple of the other older women and I visited them. They were most regretful of their hasty words and opinions." She studied the bowl in her hand, then plunged it back into the water. "I believe thee may rest assured that any rumors along the lines they were contemplating have been squashed."

"Who were they?"

"'Tis best thee knows not. I do not believe there was any true malice involved. 'Twas more idle hands wanting for something to do. Nobody will have those tomorrow. And some less than others." Betsy's wink drew forth the giggle Gwen had fought down earlier.

"Are they angry?"

"I should say not. Their extra chores were not harsh, just enough to keep them from the temptation of idle hands and loose tongues."

Gwen heaved a sigh. "'Tis blessed I am to have you watching out for me and Owen.

"Oh, my dear, 'tis I who am blessed to have thee here."

Gwen grabbed the drying rag and checked that the men were still occupied elsewhere. "What could have happened to those women if they'd committed a more grievous sin?"

"Such as?"

Gwen swallowed and plucked a bowl from Betsy's fingers, unable to look her in the eye. "If they had stolen something or... lied."

"Ah." Betsy scrubbed another bowl. "Each offense deserves its own consideration. We have no set consequence for any particular infringement. The Friends believe in being led by the Light of Christ.

We follow that leading in all things as much as we can."

Gwen vigorously dried the bowl in her hands. The words meant little to her. The Light of Christ was a phrase she'd heard during meetings, but she didn't understand it. She'd never seen any light other than the sun during the meetings since she'd attended.

Gwen hunched over her stitching in the shade from the wagon. She tried to ignore her crying son and her cramped muscles. They were two weeks on the trail since the men finished clearing the fallen timbers. Thomas and Micah drove the horses on the narrow mountain trails. Gwen had ridden most of that time in the back of the wagon, crammed into a space too small and too hot for comfort. As Thomas had predicted, Cobb pushed them relentlessly to make up for lost time.

"How will I keep you clothed if you will not settle and let me sew?" Gwen set aside her sewing with a loud sigh and plucked a fussy Owen from his cradle.

Instead of calming, he stiffened his back and wailed.

"What ails you this evening?" Gwen paced beside the wagon with her son against her shoulder. She rubbed his back and hummed an old lullaby that usually soothed him, but he continued to fuss and cry. Why couldn't she comfort him? She moved him to her other shoulder and gritted her teeth when he screamed in her ear. Maybe because she wasn't his real mother—

Her thought was cut short as Betsy and Thomas returned from their evening stroll.

"The poor dear. Let me take him for a while." Betsy held out her arms, and Gwen thankfully deposited Owen into them.

"He has been fussy all day, but now I cannot get him to settle at all."

"The poor boy." Betsy brushed Owen's hair back. "He is so warm. Perhaps we should bathe him and cool him down. Then he will be more comfortable."

"He did not eat well tonight either." Memories of her brothers leaped to mind, and she grasped Betsy's sleeve. "You do not think he is truly ailing, do you?"

"Let us not borrow trouble." The older woman patted Gwen's hand.

"Like as not 'tis but the heat."

"I shall fetch cool water from the creek." Thomas swung a bucket off the side of the wagon and hurried away.

Gwen pulled down the washtub and peeled Owen's sweaty clothes from his back. Her heart slammed to a halt and then galloped out of control. "Betsy!"

Betsy leaned over her shoulder and peered at the rash peppering Owen's belly and under his arms. She ran a finger over the tiny, raised bumps. "'Tis only a heat rash. Look closely. The bumps are dry."

Gwen sagged against the edge of the washtub. That would explain it. Heat rash would make anyone cranky.

Thomas set the bucket of water beside her.

Gwen poured half of it into the washtub before setting Owen inside. His little face scrunched into distressed lines, and his stiff body trembled in her hands.

"He does not like this." She looked at Betsy.

"'Tis likely a shock, that cool water on his heated skin. Give him a moment to adjust."

It took more than a moment, but Owen calmed down. His cries became wobbly hiccups, each one tugged at Gwen's heart. When his body finally relaxed, she wrapped him in a thin piece of cotton sheeting and rocked him until he fell asleep. Thomas had already hoisted the cradle into the wagon. Gwen laid her son down and stretched onto her own thin mattress.

Worry warred with fatigue and doubts. What would she have done if Betsy hadn't been there? Maybe she wasn't meant to be a mother. Surely a woman who had birthed a child would know instinctively what to do. If anything gave her secret away, it might be her own inadequacies.

How long before Betsy and the other women noticed?

The wagon rocked when Betsy crept into the other cot. But sleep eluded Gwen until the only sounds in camp were frog songs and the occasional stomp of a hoof from the picket line.

Gwen tossed and turned, but it was impossible to find comfort between the heat and her inner turmoil.

Shouts woke Gwen well before dawn, but they weren't Owen's cries. She pushed up on one elbow and swiped her hair out of her face.

Betsy rose from the narrow bed opposite her. Their eyes locked as another round of shouts rippled through the canvas.

Owen roused and added his voice to the confusion.

Thomas leaned over the tailgate of the wagon and poked his head inside. A tuft of dry grass clung to his hair.

"Stay inside. I shall return as soon as I learn what has happened."

"Be careful," Betsy called after him.

Gwen lifted her son and gasped. "Betsy, he is burning up." Heat radiated through the sweat-plastered sheet around Owen's body. "Oh, God... help him!" The prayer slipped from her lips. Fuzzy memories of praying for her brothers, when their father wasn't around, scampered around the fear that filled her.

"There now, let me have a look." Betsy took the child and un-wrapped the cloth. Gwen pressed a fist to her mouth. The rash looked no different. Betsy examined every inch of the boy's body while Gwen held her breath.

"'Twould appear to be just a fever." Betsy looked out the back of the wagon. "We shall stay put as Thomas said. When he returns, we will bathe Owen in fresh creek water."

Owen quieted against Betsy's shoulder while Gwen looked over the seat and out the front of the wagon.

"Here comes Thomas now. Zachary is with him... leading Tiny." Gwen's stomach clenched. Neither man smiled or spoke as they ap-proached. The news couldn't be good.

"The early watch caught sight of an Indian, and three of the milk cows are missing." Thomas's voice was strained. "None of the horses are gone, thank the Lord. With half a dozen lame from pushing them so hard, we could not afford to lose even one."

"Your cow, Zachary?" Gwen asked.

"Bossy is too lazy to be driven off quietly." Zachary flashed a grin. "I took the liberty of bringing thy goat along. 'Twould be wise to tether her close until we know 'tis safe."

"Thank you." Gwen jumped down and took Tiny's rope, tying her to the wagon. "I shall milk her after I fetch some creek water."

"Allow me to fetch the water." Zachary shot a glance at Thomas.

A chill crept up Gwen's spine.

"'Twould be best if thee women stay close to the wagon," Thomas said.

Betsy pressed a hand to her chest. "Is there a danger still?"

Thomas and Zachary exchanged another look. Gwen wished they would speak their minds and do so quickly. Owen fussed again. She needed the cool water.

"Cobb thinks not," Thomas said. "He thinks the Indian was but a lad trying to earn respect by stealing from the enemy."

"We are enemies with no one." Betsy drew herself up and gave a sharp nod.

"But the Indians do not know that," Zachary said. "They do not know us."

Owen bawled and flailed his arms.

"The boy is fevered." Betsy's voice was tempered but urgent. "We need the creek water to cool him."

Zachary's brow creased. He grabbed a bucket off the wagon's side. "I shall make haste."

Betsy began preparing a simple breakfast.

Thomas and Micah readied the teams while Gwen bathed Owen. He ate very little of his porridge and goat's milk.

She dreaded the long day ahead.

Gwen flopped to the ground beside Betsy with a groan. Her son slept on the grass in the shade of the wagon during the noon break after a morning of crying and thrashing her in arms.

"I cannot console him," she said to Betsy.

"This heat does not help. But take heart, if it were something mortal, we would know by now. All children get fevers."

Zachary walked along the row of wagons toward them. A bucket swung from his hand.

Gwen sat up and smoothed her dress and apron.

"Good noontide," Betsy greeted him.

"Good noontide." He nodded to Gwen. "I see the boy is sleeping. This is good?" Zachary asked.

"He was fussy all morning. I fear he has worn himself out."

"Ah. I see." Zachary passed his bucket from one hand to the other and back again. "I made a poultice that might provide some relief for him."

"A poultice?" Betsy peered into the bucket.

"A remedy I learned years ago... from an Indian."

"Heathen medicine?" Betsy took a step backward, one hand raised.

"Heathens get sick too." Zachary rubbed his earlobe and looked into the bucket. "They know more about the local plants than we do, how to use them, what they are good for—"

"Thank you." Gwen stood and took the bucket. "Tell me, what do I do with this?" She was eager to try anything that would bring Owen relief. She followed Zachary's instructions as he watched over her shoulder. When Owen was smeared front and back with the earthy-scented concoction, Zachary laid a hand on the boy's back and bowed his head in silent prayer, as was the Quaker way.

Gwen touched Zachary's arm. "I hope the poultice will bring my son relief soon."

"The poultice should help, but thy prayers are a much more potent medicine."

Her prayers? She remembered calling out to God to help Owen, but had she truly prayed? Did she know how? Of course she did. She'd been attending the Friends' meetings for months. She turned her back on the others and placed her hand on Owen's back, where Zachary had touched him.

"God, please, if You're listening, heal my son." She spoke the prayer aloud, prompted by a memory of her mother doing so many years before. Her despair and frustration lessened as love flooded her heart. A fierce and protective love. The love for her son.

Following that came a sensation of peace. Perhaps God had been listening.

Betsy twisted on the wagon seat and leaned over its back. "He has been quiet for some time."

"Aye." Gwen rubbed her eyes and yawned. The poor girl must be exhausted, but she'd refused Betsy's offers to sit with Owen during the day.

"Remove the sheet. Let us have a look at his skin." Betsy held her breath while Gwen untangled the cloth from the sweaty boy. "Thee will need to brush off some of the poultice so we can see."

"Do you think I should?"

"Indeed. 'Twill be dry by now anyway."

The flaky leaves and dried mud crumbled under Gwen's fingertips. She lifted her face, hope shining from her eyes. She stood and lifted Owen so Betsy could see him better. "See here, 'tis almost gone."

"Praise God." The rash had faded. Owen popped a thumb in his mouth and sucked noisily.

"He is cooler too. Zachary's poultice worked."

Betsy muffled her snort. She put much less stock in the heathen remedy than she did in the prayers of a mother's heart. Overhearing Gwen's fervent prayer at the noon break was an answer to prayer for Betsy. But whatever the cause, she breathed a sigh of relief to see the contented baby in his mother's arms. Even though she had not allowed her own fear to rise to the surface, it had lurked deep in the corners of her mind.

"He must be hungry by now. I covered the rest of his porridge in that crock at the back." Betsy pointed to the spot just as the wagon lurched over something in the trail. She grabbed Thomas's arm as Gwen plopped onto her bunk, the babe safe in her lap. Owen's eyes rounded and his little mouth popped open.

And then he giggled.

It was the type of giggle that caused adult hearts to melt.

Gwen's eyes shone.

Thomas chuckled and clicked to the horses.

Betsy turned forward on the seat and tucked her arm through her husband's.

She loved Gwen as much as she'd loved her own daughters. And little Owen, how could she not love him? She patted Thomas's arm and smiled at his answering grunt. Everything was going to be fine.

In God's own time.

Gwen tipped the cup against her son's open mouth. He gurgled and slopped, his little hands grasping at Gwen's sleeves. She pulled the cup away and laughed at the messy face in front of her.

"Thy laugh is like a medicine. 'Tis such a joyous sound." Micah stepped close to her, his hat held upside down in his hands.

"Aye. I have good reason to be joyous." Gwen wiped the thinned porridge from Owen's face before she tipped the cup once again to his eager mouth. "I feared so for Owen these past two days."

"Indeed. So have we all."

"Look at him now." She pulled the cup away and grinned as the pudgy hands tried to grab it back. "He cannot get enough to eat."

"I found some berries near where I picketed Sassy and Hap." Micah held out his hat. "Perchance Owen will like these?"

Gwen peeked into the hat half full of shiny blackberries. "That was very thoughtful of you. I shall mash a few of them into his porridge." She set the cup down, but before she could lay Owen on the grass, Micah set his hat beside the cup and scooped the boy from her lap.

"We shall take a little walk while thee prepares it." Owen's head bobbed over the top of Micah's broad shoulder as they walked away.

A lump solidified at her collarbone, and her eyes misted. If only Owen had a father who would treat him so. A father who loved him and wanted to raise him to be a good man. She swallowed the lump. That wasn't going to happen. Marriage was out of the question for her.

She couldn't keep her secret from a husband. And there was the oath she'd signed.

"I see someone found the berries before me," Thomas said.

Gwen swiped at her eyes with the back of one hand.

Thomas approached Gwen, his hat as full as Micah's.

"Aye." She nodded toward the departing man and boy. "Micah brought some for Owen."

"Only for Owen? Or for Owen's mother as well?" Thomas chuckled as he poured the berries from Micah's hat into his own. "I shall take these to Betsy. She will make something delightful from them, I'm sure."

"I shall help her and mash a few for Owen." Gwen whisked up the cup and followed Thomas to the campfire burning a few yards from the wagon.

Betsy shook the berries into a wooden bowl. Thomas's hat was hanging suspended in her hands when shouts broke from across the wagon circle.

"Indians." The word arose among the shouting.

A woman's scream ripped the air.

"Owen!" She dropped his cup, gathered her skirts, and raced to where she'd last seen Micah and her son.

"Gwen, come back!" Thomas's shout followed her, but she had to reach Owen. Cobb's warning about Indians stealing children rang each time her feet struck the earth.

People milled around inside the circle of wagons with a disorganized sense of panic. Gwen was forced to stop in the crush Friends. She bounced on her toes and stretched to see above the people in front of her. Bodies shifted and through a crease in the crowd, she spied a set of broad shoulders pushing against the tide.

Coming toward her.

"Owen!"

Micah shielded the boy with his hand, the little head pressed against his chest.

"I returned as quickly as I could." Micah reached her and placed Owen in her arms. "I knew thee would be worried."

"What news?" Thomas asked, almost at Gwen's heels, while Betsy caught up with them and grasped her husband's arm.

Gwen clutched Owen to her chest and breathed in his sweet scent.

"More Indians were sighted. It may be those who stole the milk cows, we cannot know for sure," Micah said. "Cobb is saddling his horse to investigate. I volunteered to accompany him."

"Nay." The word escaped Gwen without thought. She looked at Betsy. The same fear she knew must be mirrored in her own eyes stared back at her from the older woman.

"Cobb thinks it best if he goes alone." Micah herded them toward their wagons. "I shall be staying with the wagons. He says we should have our rifles visible and within reach."

Gwen released her breath.

"Cobb knows we will not shoot another human being," Thomas said.

"He knows. But he said the Indians do not, and if we show our rifles, they are less likely to attack us."

Thomas frowned and thrust out his chin. "I shall go and speak with the others. I do not like this. We are a people of peace." He strode off.

"I shall move our cookfire into the circle. Better to put up with smoke than Indians." Betsy grabbed a shovel and hurried off.

Micah took a step toward Gwen. "Thee did not wish me to go with Cobb?"

The intensity of his regard caused Gwen's middle to tighten. "I worried for your safety."

"A man appreciates that." He bent closer, his low voice sending tiny tremors along Gwen's skin. "'Tis a comfort to know someone worries for thee."

"Oh." Gwen's face burned, and she turned away, unable to sort out her emotions. Fear for Owen followed so quickly by fear of Micah riding out with Cobb. How had he come to mean so much to her? She dare not entertain the idea any further. She had a son to raise. An oath to keep. A sister to find. But hadn't Micah pledged to help her find her sister?

Micah cleared his throat. "I shall give Betsy a hand."

Her back still to him, Gwen nodded. She pulled her bonnet ties out of Owen's mouth and sighed when he grabbed them back again.

What was she going to do?

Chapter 20

August 1799

"COBB HAS NOT YET returned?" Betsy asked. They'd been traveling nearly a week without the guide.

"Nay. And he is long overdue." Thomas poked a stick in the fire. Hungry flames popped and crackled along the dry wood. Smoke clung to the night air and blanketed the wagon circle with its fragrance.

Betsy laid her sewing in her lap and stared into the dancing flames. The days were growing shorter. The evening's fire gave them light and a sense of comfort, even though its heat was not necessary.

"What will we do... if?" She didn't like Cobb and wasn't sure she trusted him, but it was said he knew the trails ahead.

"I have spoken with the other men. Cobb told us how to reach Redstone Old Fort in Pennsylvania. We plan to stay on Braddock's Road until it breaks northwest, and then take Burd's Road until it ends at Redstone Old Fort. We will continue on that far as planned."

"And then?"

"'Tis hard to say. Without a guide, we would be foolish to set forth into lands we know not. The roads after the fort will be rough in comparison, little more than trails and likely hard to follow."

"Winter will be upon us before we know it."

"Indeed. We need time to hunt and salt meat for the winter months. There are many mouths to feed among us."

"The women will want to gather what we can from the forest as well. There will be a mercantile at the fort, will there not?"

"I'm told there is a large one in Brownsville. Cobb said it has grown into a good-sized town."

"The fort is close to town?"

"According to Cobb, the town has grown up around the fort."

They were running low on flour, cornmeal, and several other items. Eggs would be a treat. She smiled at the thought of Owen having his first taste of a fluffy scrambled egg.

Micah joined them at the fire and squatted near the flames. "The wind carries the threat of a chill tonight."

"It seems cool for the end of August, to be sure," Betsy said.

"We are farther north than we have ever been before." Thomas hitched his collar higher around his neck. "And at a higher elevation. Back home, 'tis probably much warmer than here."

Betsy hadn't considered that. From the deepening lines on Thomas's face, he hadn't either. Not only were they behind schedule, but they were entering a territory where winter came early. Earlier than they had planned for.

"Where are Gwen and Owen?" Micah looked around the darkening campsite.

Betsy picked up her sewing. "Retired for the evening."

"So soon? Are they well?"

"Indeed. Owen did not nap much today, and poor Gwen was worn out from keeping him entertained. An early night will do them both a world of good."

Thomas chuckled and tugged on the end of his beard. "He is a fine lad, that one. Would make any man proud to call him grandson... or son."

Betsy squinted at her husband, who studiously refused to notice her.

Micah bowed his head, hat brim shading his face.

She feared Thomas's none-too-subtle hint had embarrassed the young man. Her husband had the delicate touch of a lumberjack some-times. And wasn't he the one who had scolded her about letting God put these two together if it was His plan? She blew out a breath—just short of a snort—and returned to her sewing.

Gwen swayed on the seat, the loose reins comfortable and familiar in her gloved hands. The pungent scent of damp leaves carried on the morning breeze. The briskness of the morning invigorated human and beast alike the length of the wagon train. Sassy and Hap clipped along at a good pace, their plate-sized hooves striking the ground in perfect rhythm to the jingle of buckles and chains.

With no new Indian sightings—though still no sign of Cobb—the men had determined it worth the risk to send hunters out again. Fresh meat would refresh the travelers as much as the cooler temperatures.

Micah had joined the hunting expedition at first light. Gwen welcomed the chance to drive his team again. While her love for Owen filled her in ways she couldn't fully describe, she relished a break in her motherly duties. Guilt pinched her. Did real mothers feel this way?

Probably not.

She twisted sideways on the seat, as far as Micah's safety rope would allow, and glimpsed the wagon behind through the openings in the canvas. Thomas had his feet propped up, elbows on his knees, battered hat shading his face. Betsy rode beside him with Owen on her lap. Gwen caught a glimpse of his little hand tangled in Betsy's bonnet ties before her wagon lurched over a rock. She faced forward and tightened her grip on the reins.

Owen was safe and content with Thomas and Betsy. They were his grandparents in everything but blood.

In every way that mattered.

Disloyalty to her parents warred with her love for the Quaker couple. And she did love them. How could she not? She'd never met anyone so gentle, caring, and loving.

But... her heart twisted painfully.

They could not replace Faye as her family. She still needed to find her sister. Surely Thomas and Betsy would accept Faye as they'd accepted her. Had not their attempts to help her locate her sister proven that? But how could Gwen afford to buy her sister's indenture?

Would Martha McClure be willing to let her go even if Gwen could earn the money?

She shifted on the wooden seat and leaned as far as she could over the side. The line of wagons snaked ahead along a gentle curve across the land. A new land. A free land. A place where she and Owen would make a home for themselves with the Baldwins.

And Faye. Somehow. Someday.

What about Micah? Could there be a place for him in her future? The memory of scratching her name across the paper on Mr. White-ford's desk silenced that fragile hope.

At the nooning, Gwen cuddled Owen and fussed over him while feeding his regular porridge mixed with a handful of berries she found growing near their wagon. Betsy had unearthed a small silver spoon from her trunk. Owen gobbled the gooey mixture while trying to grab the spoon away from his mother.

Gwen pulled the spoon back from his sticky hands.

"Is he trying to grab the porridge off the spoon again?" Betsy asked.

"Aye, and making a fine mess of things."

"'Tis the way young ones learn to eat. For so young a babe, he has a good grasp with his hands."

"He does, but 'tis not the time to let him. Nooning is almost finished and there is no time to wash his meal from my face or scrub berry stains from my clothes."

Betsy chuckled. "Indeed." She packed away the remains of their food.

Gwen spooned the last of the porridge into Owen's mouth and then wiped his face and hands. She put him on his belly on the ground and climbed to her feet with a sigh. He rolled over onto his back and grinned at her. Gwen wished the day's drive were over. She wanted to spend the afternoon with her son. As much as she'd relished her driving time that morning, it pained her to watch Betsy scoop him up.

Betsy raised her eyebrows at Gwen. "What has caused this sadness on thy face?"

"'Tis nothing." How could she explain her confusing emotions to

Betsy when she hardly understood them herself?

"I think 'tis indeed something. Will thee not confide in me?"

Tears prickled Gwen's eyelids and tightened her throat. What was wrong with her?

Betsy settled Owen on her hip and held out a hand to Gwen. With a silent sob, Gwen stepped into her embrace.

"'Tis all such a muddle in my mind." The wide white collar of Betsy's dress muffled her speech. "One moment I'm relieved to have some time to myself and the next it fairly breaks my heart to pass Owen off to you." She pulled in a shaky breath. "Sometimes I think, if only I—" She stuffed her fist against her mouth, horrified that she had almost blurted out the truth, almost admitted she wasn't Owen's real mother. She held her breath, afraid to lift her head or look at Betsy.

"There now, all mothers share these feelings. And 'tis only natural thee would wonder about... how things might have been different... if thee had a husband. Someone to share the joys and shoulder a share of the burdens."

Gwen pushed herself upright. She closed her eyes and nodded, thankful beyond words that Betsy hadn't guessed the real end of her unfinished sentence.

"Do not despair. The Lord knows thy every need. If He wishes thee to have a husband, then He will provide the right man."

"I will never marry."

"Thee are much too young to think in terms of never. Do not close a door that has yet to be opened."

Thomas approached, leading both teams of horses. Gwen hurried to take Sassy and Hap. Her raw emotions welcomed something to keep her hands busy.

Four days later, the wagons crested a small rise. Before them sprawled the town of Brownsville. It spread along the wide Monongahela River in a disorderly fashion. Buildings clustered along the river and more wandered out from them in haphazard lines. Most were low wooden affairs, but here and there a brick structure stood tall among them.

"Is that the fort?" Gwen pointed toward a wooden palisade on the outskirts of the town while holding onto the wagon seat with her other hand.

Thomas squinted in that direction. "Indeed. I believe it is."

Gwen turned to Betsy in the wagon bed. "We have arrived."

"Praise the Lord." Betsy came to the back of the seat and craned her neck to peer between the shoulders of Thomas and Gwen.

The wagons rolled into town and headed for the fort. Gwen hung onto the edge of the seat, leaning to peer around Micah's wagon in front of them. They passed the buildings along the river. Up close, they were as diverse a collection as they appeared from afar. Aged and leaning houses marched beside the dull gleam of newly mortared brick buildings rising two and three stories high. The clinging odor of sawdust hung in the air, overpowering the usual river smells of fish and rotting vegetation.

People stopped what they were doing to watch the wagon train pass. Most nodded and a few smiled. Many of those they passed wore plain clothing that marked them as Quakers. Gwen relaxed muscles she hadn't realized were tense. The hostile overtones of Alexandria were nowhere to be seen. Neither were there any dark faces along the street or driving the wagons they passed.

The wooden palisade of the fort came into view, weathered to a dull gray with gaping holes left by broken logs. In front of the palisade, a stagnant moat released its musty odor. The first wagon halted before the bridge. The rest lined up behind.

"Wait here." Thomas handed Gwen the reins. He climbed down and walked off.

Betsy descended from the back of the wagon with Owen and walked around to stand beside Gwen. "It appears ill kept."

"I wonder if we will be granted entrance. There does not seem to be much here." Gwen wrinkled her nose.

"Perhaps with the town grown around it, there is not much need for the fort anymore."

"The town is larger than I thought 'twould be."

"A good thing for us. I expect we shall winter here and set out again come spring."

"Delay our journey again?" If they stopped for the winter, perhaps a letter could be sent—surely someone among the wagons knew how to write well enough to inquire after Faye.

"What choice have we, with no guide and winter already nipping at our heels?"

"Aye." Gwen searched the far side of the river. "Pittsburgh cannot be so far from here, is it?"

"I understand 'tis north, along this same river, but I know not how far." Kindness lined Betsy's face. "It may not be possible to look for thy sister until the spring, if then."

Gwen closed her eyes. To be so close to her sister, closer than she'd been for many years, and not be able to carry on—

"Thomas returns, and Micah is with him," Betsy said.

Gwen opened her eyes and leaned forward.

"They told us to pull our wagons into a field west of here, along the river. We are to make camp there and decide our plan of action." Lines tugged at the corners of Thomas's mouth. Whether from worry or fatigue, it was hard to tell. "Things have changed at the fort since Cobb was last here."

"The size of the town is a welcome surprise," Micah said. "Surely we will be able to purchase all our needs here for the winter as well as for travel in the spring."

"Perhaps." Thomas combed his fingers through his beard. "If all have funds enough to do so."

"Some of us should be able to find employment for the winter." Micah gestured to the town with many buildings in differing states of completion. "It seems there is much to be done. We have many experienced craftsmen among us."

"Indeed." Thomas gave a final tug on his beard. "The Lord provides for all our needs."

They loaded into the wagons again and drove the short distance to their new camp. Gwen jumped from the high seat before the wheels stopped turning.

"Have a care now," Thomas said.

Gwen dusted her hands together and twirled around. "'Tis a fine place to set up camp." She grinned and skipped to the back of the wagon to take Owen from Betsy. "And we do not have to move in the morning. 'Tis the best part of all."

"Indeed." Betsy climbed out of the wagon and joined her. "I'm quite ready for a lengthy stay on one piece of ground."

Gwen twirled again with Owen in her arms. His giggles brought a smile to all of them.

Micah joined her, holding out his arms for Owen. He swung the boy even higher and laughed along with Owen's squeals of delight. The corded muscles of Micah's arms strained against the worn sleeves of his shirt.

Gwen's laughter faded into a tight knot of—was it longing?—at the base of her throat.

Betsy cradled a final cup of coffee, savoring the aroma as well as the warmth in her hands. She had replenished their supply of coffee beans while in town that morning. Their longer-than-expected journey had dwindled their provisions. The other women were restocking as well. Their first trip into Brownsville assured her they could fulfill all their needs. With the town's position on the river, boats brought all manner of goods to sell.

Gwen squinted in the firelight to stitch a new hem in her apron. The poor girl hadn't had time to mend her own clothing in weeks. A break for the winter would benefit them all.

Micah and Thomas strode into camp. The men had gathered at Basil Brashear's tavern to gather information.

"Are we staying, then?" Betsy asked before the men could sit on the crates she had unpacked from the wagon.

"We are." Thomas groaned low in this throat as he dropped to the crate. "The wagon train before us arrived three weeks ago and left just two days after. There is no way to make it through the mountain passes before the snow."

"I thought we were through the mountains now." Gwen paused in her stitching with her hand stretched out and the thread pulled tight.

"Yes and no." Micah grabbed a stick and stirred the fire. "We are through the high mountains of the Allegheny Range, but there are many smaller mountains between us and the new territory."

"And they are not as well traveled," Thomas added. "The roads are little more than tracks, nothing compared to what we have been traveling." He sighed. "The locals are recommending we sell our heavy wagons and buy smaller, lighter wagons for the spring."

"What?" Betsy stiffened, sloshing coffee over the rim of her cup. She looked at their wagon, a comforting shadow in the darkness.

"Truth is, most of the locals advise us to ferry our belongings down the river on their flatboats." The fire's light outlined Thomas's scowl.

"There is logic in what they say." Micah tapped the stick on the ground. "River travel is faster."

"'Tis what they say, but even so, we could not leave until spring. The water levels are unreliable this late in the year. Most of our families would need to sell their wagons to raise the money for the flatboat passage. What good does it do to arrive in our new land without our wagons? Or the money to buy new?"

Micah glanced at his own, its outline visible in the gathering darkness. "Indeed."

"But must we sell our wagon?" Betsy asked. The sturdy vehicle had become home, after all. What else would they live in until they were able to build a house?

"I believe we must." Thomas sagged on his crate, elbows resting on his knees. "What they say makes good sense. I know thee has grown fond of it, but 'twill only slow us down through the passes ahead."

"How will we carry everything?" Betsy asked.

"The spring's journey will be much shorter," Micah said. "We will not need the extra barrels of flour and salted meat. A buckboard would hold enough."

"How much shorter?" Shorter sounded good. As much as Betsy would hate to part with their wagon, she would trade it in a heartbeat for a snug cabin of their own.

"Less than half the distance," Thomas said. "Maybe nearer a third. With good weather and an early start, we can be there by mid-June, in time to plant a garden for the fall."

"But where will we stay the winter if you sell the wagons?" Gwen asked.

"The fort is all but deserted. 'Tis serving only as a land agent's headquarters with all the soldiers moved out. We have made an arrangement with the land agent to rent the empty officers' quarters for the families and the barracks for the single men." Thomas straightened and slapped his hands against his knees. "We move in next week."

Betsy rubbed her thumb along her cup's brim. Brownsville seemed a nice quiet spot to pass the winter months. They had time left before the snow to gather supplies from the surrounding forests and purchase whatever else they needed from the shops in town. Having a house to live in for the winter sounded good too.

"This is home for now, then."

Chapter 21

G WEN FIDGETED WITH HER basket and threw another glance at the closed door of the officer's house that had been their home for more than two weeks. If Micah didn't arrive soon, she was going to the market without him. Her foot tapped against the stained floorboards.

"He will come," Betsy said.

"When?"

"Soon enough."

"Why do I need an escort here in Brownsville? Are we not in the north? There are no slave owners here."

"Indeed, there are." Betsy plopped kneaded dough in a greased wooden bowl. She flipped the dough once, then covered it with a clean cloth and set it near the fire to rise. "Pennsylvania is not a slave-holding state, true, but plenty of slave owners travel through here for this journey or that."

"Surely they would not accost a woman in the market."

"Thy clothing sets thee off as a Friend. Many dislike and distrust us for our faith as well as our stance against the evil institution of slavery. Friends are often targeted for unpleasant words in public."

Betsy washed her hands. "And sometimes more than words."

Gwen ran her fingers over her soft gray dress with its white collar and apron. Anyone would assume her to be a Quaker. There were days when she imagined that herself. Even though she trusted the Quakers themselves above anyone she had ever known, she still didn't understand—or trust—the religious part.

Sapphira's saints-on-earth part.

"There are many Quakers here. We saw them when we arrived. They walked along the street and stood in front of shops. I did not see anyone bothering them."

Betsy dried her hands on the front of her apron. "But that does not mean 'tis a good idea for thee to be on the streets alone. 'Tis always better to be cautious than to be sorry."

Gwen shifted the basket between her hands. "'Twill be a moot point if he does not arrive soon—" A knock at the door made her jump. She hurried to open it.

"Are thee ready?" Micah stepped into the low-ceilinged room, removing his hat when it brushed a timbered beam.

"Aye, and have been." She drew a shawl over her shoulders and secured the basket full of sacks over her arm. She stepped onto the porch when Micah held the door open, and the wind battered her bonnet. Thankful for the warmth of the shawl, she hurried to Micah's wagon. "We could have walked. 'Tis no great distance." She accepted his hand to help her onto the seat.

"'Tis in the field on the other side of town where the farmers meet. Long enough when the wind is like this. We are not used to cool weather this early in the year."

Gwen arranged her skirt and tucked her basket by her feet.

Micah slid onto the seat, his hip brushing against hers.

Her tongue lodged against the roof of her mouth. She inched as far away from him as she could and lifted her chin at the twitch of his lips. And that certain twinkle in his eye. Her cheeks warmed in spite of the wind as he clicked to the team. Gwen held onto the edge of the seat with one hand, and kept her shawl closed with the other.

"I have missed thee since we moved to the fort," he said.

"You have been much occupied in the barracks."

"Indeed. That building had not fared so well as the officer's housing. We have finished the major repairs. The roof no longer leaks onto our table or the bunks." He leaned his shoulder against hers in a brief nudge. "But even if it leaked like a sieve right over my bunk, I would still make time to accompany thee on an errand when thee has need."

"I could have gone by myself, were you too busy."

"Nonsense." He urged the horses into a trot once they cleared the fort's gate. "Did thee not hear me? I will always make time for thee, Gwen."

She squirmed on the hard seat. Her heart battered her ribs until she feared it would raise a bruise. "You should not say such things to me."

"And why not?"

"You know me not that well."

"For months we have traveled across the country together—"

"Not together. I am with Thomas and Betsy. You are—"

"I am falling under thy spell." Micah covered her hand on the seat with his gloved fingers.

Gwen pressed herself against the far edge of the seat. "Please, Micah. We are almost in town. Someone will see or hear."

He straightened on his side of the seat. "Then we shall speak of the weather and no busybody can look at us askance. Notice that pair of old maids across the street? We shall give them nothing to gossip over and leave them sorely disappointed."

Gwen relaxed at the lightheartedness of his tone.

"There will not be many more market days," Micah announced loudly enough for the two women on the side of the street to overhear. "The leaves are turning colors. The farmers will soon sell out of their produce."

"Aye." She answered in a clear voice. "Betsy asked me to buy as many turnips as I can this trip. Thomas enjoys them so, and they keep well in the cellar."

Gwen refused to look at the ladies as they passed. She kept her attention on the shop windows and the people walking along the street, but not at those wide shoulders and teasing blue eyes beside her.

"Tell Betsy I have missed her fine meals." His voice dropped to a whisper. "Zachary is a tolerable cook, but his countenance is considerably less appealing across the table from me."

"I shall tell her you miss her cooking and her face then."

Micah growled low in his throat. "Thee knows that is not what I meant."

Gwen grinned but kept her face turned away. She willed herself to forget the feel of his hip pressed against hers or his fingers over her hand.

Micah maneuvered the large wagon through the main street of town to an open field on the far edge where local farmers gathered on market day. He helped Gwen down and shadowed her as she walked from one farm wagon to the next.

She was bent over a bushel basket filled with winter squash when a cold gust of wind whisked her bonnet off. She grabbed for it and missed, the ties slipping from her fingers. She chased after it for several steps until it slapped into the chest of a man walking toward her.

"Gwen Morgan, as I live and breathe."

Gwen's blood turned to ice.

Jonas Whiteford. Holding her bonnet.

She tried to suck in a lungful of air and failed.

"And all decked out like a simple Quaker, no less." Jonas circled her like a wolf sizing its prey.

Gwen turned with him.

Micah spoke with a Quaker gentleman on a horse several paces away, his back to Gwen.

Her stomach cramped. She wanted to scream for help, but her mouth refused to work. Shock wiped her mind of anything other than the mocking face in front of her.

"Who do you think you are fooling? A little wench like you, making out to be some type of Bible-toter." Jonas stepped closer. His breath, rank with alcohol, brushed her face before she turned her head.

She closed her eyes and whispered, "Please, let me pass."

"Have you no greeting for me, Gwen? Have you not missed me after almost a year? Surely you know I have never stopped thinking of you." His fingers dug into the skin under her chin, forcing her head up. She had no bucket of slops now, but her stomach roiled. She might soil the front of him yet.

"Gwen?" Micah's voice sliced through her misery.

Jonas turned, and Gwen backed away, nearly stumbling in her desire to put distance between them.

A scowl marred Micah's brow as he faced the shorter man. "I do not believe we have met."

"We have not, nor am I inclined to be introduced. My business is with Gwen. Unfinished business and none of your concern. Move on now." Jonas flicked his wrist as if shooing away a pest.

Micah planted his booted feet on the ground beside Gwen and folded his arms over his chest. "I think not."

Gwen slipped her hand around Micah's elbow and tugged. "Come, let us leave here."

"Running away?" Jonas sneered. "Worry not, little Gwen, we will finish our discussion and our... unfinished business... another time. Rest assured."

Micah took a step toward Jonas.

Gwen pulled harder on his arm. "We must go."

Micah's arm tightened like iron beneath her fingers, but he pivoted and led her back to his wagon.

She jogged at his side to keep up. She had no breath left for talk until they were seated. When his hip pressed against hers, she didn't pull away.

She welcomed the security of his touch.

"Who is he?" Micah's voice was low and flat as he flicked the reins and started the team moving.

"Jonas Whiteford, the son of my master." The words left a vile taste on her tongue.

Micah's brows knit together. His jaw firmed to a hard line, and his leather gloves creaked on the reins. "He threatened thee."

"Aye."

"What did he mean about unfinished business between thee?"

Gwen let her chin drop to her chest and clenched the nearly empty basket on her lap. What could she tell Micah about Jonas? How she'd lived in fear of him? How she'd spent her days avoiding him and his advances?

Micah pulled the team to a stop between the marketplace and the town. "Does this have anything to do with Owen?"

Gwen gasped. She searched his face, one hand clasping the collar of her dress. She couldn't interpret the expression in his eyes. Part of her wanted—needed—to tell him the truth. Fear of what it might mean for Owen's future stilled her tongue. The Quakers accepted them as they were, mother and son.

And then there was her oath.

Which was the greater sin, to be a liar or an oath-breaker?

Another thought stirred on top of her already jumbled mind and stopped her breath. Had Constance's secret been found out? Cook's warning about how difficult it would be to keep such a secret rang like a warning bell in her ears. Did Mr. Whiteford think she'd broken her oath? Had he sent Jonas to take Owen from her?

Gwen swayed on the wagon seat.

Micah snapped the reins, and the horses stepped forward smartly. "Pray, forgive me. 'Tis not my place to pry."

How she wished it were.

Gwen burst through the door and flung her almost-empty basket on the table. She rushed past an open-mouthed Betsy to scoop Owen off the floor and into her arms.

"Whatever has happened?" Betsy asked.

"He is here, in Brownsville."

"Who?"

"Jonas Whiteford."

"Whiteford?" Betsy's wrinkled face blanched to the color of her collar. "A relation to your former master?"

"His son." Gwen lifted her face from Owen's downy locks. She shook her head, unable to utter the fear that clawed at her heart.

"Where is Micah?"

"Gone to fetch Thomas."

"Help me bar the door until they return." Betsy wiped her hands on her apron and grabbed a wooden bar that leaned beside the fireplace.

Gwen set Owen on the floor and hurried to help. Together they dropped the heavy crossbar into the brackets on each side of the door. Living in a fort had advantages she hadn't appreciated until then. The only entry to the fort was the gate and bridge. The officer's house was built to protect the family within.

"Thee are shaking. Sit and I will brew a pot of chamomile tea."

While Betsy bustled around the kitchen preparing the hot drink, Gwen sagged into a chair. Owen cooed to her and lifted his arms. His toothless grin tugged at her heart. Once nestled in her lap, she rested her chin on his head.

Betsy had just placed the steaming cup on the table when boots crunched on the front porch. The door rattled against the bar.

"Betsy?" Thomas's voice boomed.

"A moment." Betsy motioned Gwen to remain seated. She shoved the bar up and over the brackets. It crashed to the floor, and Thomas shouldered his way in, Micah a step behind.

"Was he here?" Micah asked. His narrowed eyes swept the room like blue fire.

"Nay, 'twas a precaution only," Betsy said.

Thomas grunted and sat beside Gwen. "Lass, what can thee tell us about this man and his threats against thee?"

"Very little. Micah came upon us before he said much."

"But you fear him?" Thomas asked.

"Aye. I always have."

The grooves above Thomas's beard deepened.

Micah's face might have been chiseled from stone.

Betsy took a step closer to Gwen and gripped her shoulder.

"He will not lay a hand on Gwen or the boy," Micah said between clenched teeth.

Thomas shot him a stern look. "We do not know his intent."

"What else could it be?" Micah's eyes flashed.

"Gwen, if thee would disclose to us the... nature of this man's... interest in thee." Betsy's tentative words broke through Gwen's haze of fear. "Mayhap he has an interest in Owen as well?" The older woman's voice radiated love, but Micah's expression stopped Gwen's heart.

She pulled her gaze away from Micah and read the same compassionate anguish in Betsy's eyes. They thought Jonas was Owen's father. That meant they thought she and Jonas—that they had—bile rose in her throat.

"Nay!"

At her shout, Owen's face scrunched, bottom lip trembling. He twisted in her arms, reaching toward Betsy.

Gwen's heart plummeted. What had she done?

"I'm sorry, Owen. Forgive me." She pulled his stiff little body against her chest and rubbed his back. He cried but did not pull away. She glanced at those watching her, still silent after her outburst. "I need to handle this on my own."

"But he has threatened thee." Micah's voice simmered with suppressed anger.

Was he angry for her sake? Or was he angry with her for not telling them about Jonas? Did it matter?

"I am no longer a servant in his father's house. I am a free woman. What can he do to me now?" She took a deep breath. "Jonas has always frightened me, but he did not actually threaten me today."

"I heard him say—" Micah said.

"He said we have unfinished business." Gwen squared her shoulders. "It frightened me, but I know not what he meant and neither do you." She drew in a deep breath. "There is only one way to find out. I must speak with him again."

Betsy knelt in front of her. "Take Thomas or Micah with thee in case he truly does mean thee harm."

"Quakers do not fight." That much of their religion Gwen understood. "What could they do?"

"No man would harm thee in my presence." Micah's words rang in the room. "Ever."

"Micah is right," Thomas said. "We will not allow anyone to hurt thee or Owen. Quakers are non-violent, but we would gladly stand in harm's way to protect thee."

Gwen's chin wobbled. Such love humbled and shamed her. They would stand in harm's way for her—while she hid the truth from them. Thomas, who was like a father to her and grandfather to Owen. And Micah... Nay, she wouldn't let harm come to them, not for her sake. That was why she must speak with Jonas.

Alone.

She knew beyond a doubt that he would find her again. When he did, she wouldn't hide behind these good men.

Chapter 22

G WEN KEPT HER HEAD high and stared straight ahead, resisting the urge to scurry like a frightened mouse from doorway to doorway of the shops in town. It had been twelve days since her encounter with Jonas, and it was the first chance she'd had to escape the fort's palisade. While she suspected Betsy of manufacturing work to keep her in the house, each task the dear woman assigned was a necessary preparation for the winter. Including the current trip to town.

She must purchase salt to cure the meat Thomas and Micah brought in from the morning's hunt. Game abounded in the nearby forest, but without more salt, they wouldn't be able to preserve it for long. Betsy had argued against her going to the mercantile, but she insisted.

She must know why Jonas was in Brownsville, even while the thought of confronting him threatened to unravel her nerves. And empty her stomach. She couldn't let anyone else overhear what he might say. Even so, she was relieved to reach the mercantile.

As she stepped onto the porch, someone moved from behind a display of shovels and pickaxes and grabbed her by the elbow. She froze, a cry suspended in her throat.

Jonas pulled her against him. "I have been waiting for you." Breath stained with tobacco delivered the menacing words.

"What do you want, Mister Jonas?"

"What I have always wanted from you, dear Gwen."

The smugness of his voice curdled her stomach. She looked him in the eye. She had to know. "And what of Owen?"

His brow furrowed. "The Quaker with you at the market?"

Of course, Jonas wouldn't know the babe's name. She licked her lips and swallowed. "My son." Oh, no. Why had she said that? Why had she admitted to having Owen? Fear and confusion had muddled her thinking.

Jonas dropped her arm and stepped back. Then his slackened mouth firmed into a sneer. "So that stable boy left you with a whelp to remember him by, did he? Well then. . ." He sidled closer, crowding Gwen between his body and the porch's support post. "That being the case, I'm sure you will find me a vast improvement over that poorly bred simpleton."

Relief weakened her knees, and she clutched the sturdy post behind her. He hadn't known about Owen, which meant he wasn't here to fetch the babe back. And now he, too, believed Owen to be her own.

Jonas ran a hand from her ribs to her hip and back.

Her skin crawled, but she stood firm, resisting the urge to look around for help. The owner of the mercantile would hear if she shouted. But first, she needed to find out why Jonas was there.

"What a laugh on my father. He sold you off to keep me away from you. And to Quakers, no less, who doubtless have set you free." He sneered the last word. "Then dear Father sent me here to set up his new business venture." He barked a harsh laugh. "So, little Gwen, we are destined to be together."

"Nay." Relief washed over her even as his disgusting hand moved back to her hip.

Happenstance.

Jonas was there by happenstance. Fear drained away.

Violent pounding on the steps gave her scant warning before she was pulled from between the post and Jonas and thrust behind a broad back clad in dark gray. Micah's shoulders heaved, his breath coming ragged and forceful. He was coatless and his hair tumbled loose over his collar.

"Leave this woman be."

"Or what, Quaker boy?" Jonas slapped his hand against Micah's shoulder and shoved.

Micah didn't budge.

Jonas grunted and swung a fist.

Micah caught it with one hand and stopped the threat.

"I won't fight, Jonas Whiteford, but I will stop thee from accosting this lady."

"Lady?" Jonas barked a laugh.

The muscles in Micah's back bunched under Gwen's hands. Tension rippled through the very air around her. Before she could think of what to say to stop the stare-down in front of her, Thomas appeared on her left and Zachary on her right.

"Be easy, Micah." Thomas stepped forward. "This gentleman was just leaving. Is that not right, Mr. Whiteford?"

"What do you know about it, old man?"

"I am a friend of thy father's."

Jonas pulled back, wrenching his wrist from Micah's hold. He glared at the three men shielding Gwen. "How do you know my father?"

"We have done business for many years. He is an *honorable* man." Thomas stressed the word honorable.

Jonas straightened his coat and scowled.

"Perhaps another day would be more suitable to introduce ourselves. I'm afraid we have rather a lot to accomplish today. Good day to thee." Thomas nodded and turned, his arms spread as he ushered Zachary, Micah, and Gwen down the steps. They crossed the street before Gwen turned to watch Jonas shove his way into the tavern three doors down.

"He is an unpleasant sort, is he not?" Zachary said.

"Indeed," Thomas said.

All three men looked at Gwen. She swallowed and held out her basket. "I still must purchase the salt." She ignored the raised eyebrows and stepped back toward the shop.

"I have need of lamp oil myself," Zachary said.

She looked over her shoulder at Zachary following her and Thomas gripping Micah's arm. Micah's blue eyes gleamed like wet flint.

Gwen shivered at the intensity of them. She lowered her head and hurried into the mercantile.

Once inside, she spun and faced Zachary, who stood relaxed while her emotions tangled and twisted. Part of her was frustrated at the idea that she needed to be watched over. Hadn't she just stood up to Jonas, refused to be cowed by him, even before Micah had barged in? She barely refrained from stamping her foot. "I do not need an escort. I am a free woman now, no longer a servant. I can handle my own purchases."

"And I still need to purchase lamp oil." Zachary's wide smile released the tension in her shoulders.

Gwen whisked her skirt around and marched to the counter and asked for salt. She kept an eye on Zachary who, indeed, purchased lamp oil as well as a packet of hard licorice candies. She thanked the clerk, walked past Zachary and out the door. She paused to glance at the tavern, but the door remained closed against the chill of the fall day. Thomas and Micah were nowhere in sight.

She suppressed a shiver. So much for her fiery burst of independence.

Zachary's steady tread followed her down the wide steps to the street. Relief at his presence filled the part of her that still wanted to cringe at the thought of Jonas nearby. She looked neither to the right nor left but kept her steps measured and calm as she walked to the fort. She appreciated the men and their concern for her safety.

If only she didn't need it. If only being free meant—

Being free didn't mean there was no danger. Hadn't Betsy tried to warn her of that? Could she have stepped away from Jonas if Micah hadn't come running?

Once across the bridge, she drew a deep breath and blew it out before whirling around to face Zachary.

He stopped and shifted his paper-wrapped parcel from one hand to the other, wary eyes focused on her.

Gwen let her shoulders relax, and she cocked her head, her lips softening into a smile. "Thank you."

His eyes widened before a grin tugged at one side of his mouth. "Whatever for?" He hefted his parcel. "I just needed lamp oil."

"When you need lamp oil again, I would be happy to accompany you to the mercantile."

Lines crinkled beside his dark eyes. "'Twould be my pleasure." He tipped his hat and sauntered toward the barracks.

Gwen hurried to the house she shared with Thomas and Betsy. She shut the heavy oak door against a gust of wind that held more than a hint of the winter months to come. After shrugging off her shawl, she faced the fireplace, her arms crossed.

Betsy straightened from a steaming pot near the fire. Wrinkles gathered on her brow.

"There was no need to send the men after me."

Betsy glanced down and combed the edge of her apron through her fingers.

"But I'm glad you did." Warmth flooded Gwen's heart as Betsy's worry lines lifted into her smile. "I suppose Thomas has already told you what happened?"

"He did. I cannot say I'm sorry for sending them."

Gwen walked over and hugged Betsy tightly for a moment. Peace settled over her.

Jonas didn't know the truth about Owen. He could threaten if he liked, but couldn't abduct her in a town full of witnesses, especially with Zachary and Micah close by. Relief played on her heartstrings like a merry fiddle.

"I think I need not worry about Jonas anymore."

"Oh?"

"I'm free, Betsy. I'm not a servant in his father's house any longer. He cannot do anything to me here. Seeing him today—even though he tried to intimidate me until Micah came—it reassured me." Owen was safe. "But I will not go into town by myself again."

Freedom was one thing, prudence was another.

Gwen swung the small milk bucket and resisted the urge to skip her way to the stable that housed Tiny. The north wind blew cold, and when she breathed in through her mouth, Gwen could taste the hint of snow. But she didn't mind. Snow meant winter, winter would lead to spring, and spring would see them on the road to the Ohio Territory.

Away from Jonas.

She hurried on to see her little white friend. She'd missed Tiny more than she'd imagined possible. Thomas had taken over the chore of milking since Jonas arrived. Yet another way he and Betsy watched over and protected her.

She thought of Micah and missed a beat in the swing of the bucket. Her heart missed a beat as well. Micah had also protected her. He'd shown that he cared for her. Dare she let herself think about it? Dream of it?

"Good morning." As if her thoughts had fashioned him in the flesh, Micah leaned against the doorframe of the stable. Sunlight sparkled off the buttons of his gray caped overcoat. The darkness of the stable doorway framed his length.

"Good morning." Her voice came out husky. She turned her head away at the answering spark in his eyes, those eyes that caused her insides to tighten in a disturbing and delightful way.

"I see Thomas has relinquished the bucket once again."

"Aye. He worried about... Jonas."

"As he should. As did we all."

"Aye." She glanced at him from the corner of her eye. "Thank you for your concern."

"'Tis more than concern on my part. Surely thee understands that by now." He stepped toward her, captured her empty hand, and drew her closer until her shawl touched his coat. "Thee brightens my thoughts day and night."

Gwen sucked in a quick breath. Her eyes locked with his.

"And thee?" Micah's question hung in the cold air between them, frosting in the air from his breath.

Something akin to panic fluttered in Gwen's stomach. She longed to confirm her growing feelings for him, but fear kept an icy hold on her tongue. She could not surrender to her emotions lest she risk revealing her secret—and thus breaking her oath. But her expression must have responded even as her tongue could not.

"Thee has the look of a bird caught in a cage, longing to be free."

Gwen's heart thumped until she was sure he would hear it. She was indeed a bird in a cage. A cage not of wood or wire, but of inked words.

A signed oath.

She longed for the freedom to love Micah, but she needed the security her deception afforded herself and Owen. Torn, she pulled her gaze away from his.

Tiny chose that moment to issue a pitiful bleat.

"I must see to Tiny." She slipped past Micah into the stable, thankful for the dark interior that hid her burning cheeks. Fearful he would follow and pursue their conversation, she heaved a sigh of relief when his footsteps faded in the other direction.

"Thank you, Tiny." She hugged the shaggy white neck and let the goat nibble on the edge of her bonnet. "You came to my rescue as much as the men did yesterday. But I shall tell you a secret. Part of me grows weary of being rescued."

"There is nothing so calming as a morning conversation with an animal."

Gwen jumped to her feet and twisted around. Zachary stood with his back to the barn wall, one hand on Bossy's neck.

"You startled me."

"My apologies. 'Twas not my intention." He lifted his chin toward the doorway. "Nor was it my intention to overhear thee speaking with Micah."

Gwen sank to the straw beside Tiny and muffled a groan.

"I would have made my presence known, but there was not time before he spoke out to thee and then..."

At his remorseful expression, Gwen shrugged. "No matter. I'm sure it has not escaped your notice that Micah..." Any ending to that sentence escaped her. That Micah what?

"That Micah is much interested in thee?"

Her cheeks, still warm from Micah's words, flared hotter. "Aye." She stood and kept her face turned while she scooped Tiny's grain into a shallow wooden bowl.

"He has been most concerned for thee."

"Aye."

Zachary chuckled. "And I'm to get no more from thee on that matter this morning, I vow. Still, I cannot help but wonder if thee will be joining us Friends soon."

She spun around, spilling a bit of the grain. "What?"

"Well, 'tis sure that a Friend will only take another Friend for his wife."

She thrust the grain bowl in front of Tiny, who plunged her nose in it. "I'm sure, that is, I do not. . ." Tiny gobbled the grain while Gwen mentally clawed for a way out of the conversation.

Zachary walked around Bossy to Tiny's other side. "Think on it,

Gwen. Even if thee does not take Micah to husband, thee are a part of our group in all ways but one. Have thee not considered it?"

"Aye." She choked out the word. While it was true, she knew she couldn't act on it.

"And?"

"I should speak with Betsy regarding this."

"Thee are right. 'Tis not my place."

"Nay." She reached across Tiny's back and grabbed his wrist before he could turn aside. "That was not my meaning. Betsy told me that women take care of things—things among the women." She didn't know how to explain her hesitation to him.

Zachary's eyebrows rose. "Ah, I see. Thee are worried about having Owen without a husband."

Gwen hadn't thought it possible her cheeks could burn any hotter. She buried her face in her hands.

"Fear not, Gwen. We Friends are not here to judge you. 'Tis not our place to judge those not of our ways. 'Tis true we hold our brothers and sisters accountable, but only other Friends. When thee accepts Christ as thy Savior and puts thy hope and trust in Him, He forgives all thy sins. Can we, as Friends, do any less?" He patted her shoulder before scooping an armful of hay for his cow. "Speak with Betsy. She will explain it better than I." He stuffed Bossy's manger, then grabbed a brimming bucket of milk and strode out of the stable.

Tiny nudged Gwen, and she jumped, one hand pressed to her collar. Gwen tossed another handful of grain in the bowl and knelt to milk the goat. Milk splashed and frothed into the bucket.

She would speak with Betsy. Eventually. When she figured out what to say that would keep her oath and also open the possibility of a future with Micah. Her normal rhythmic motions became jerky.

Tiny stamped a hind foot, almost upsetting the bucket.

"I'm sorry." She scratched the goat under the chin. "Forgive me. I need to keep my mind on what I'm doing and not let Micah distract me so."

But the truth was, it was far too late for that.

Chapter 23

October 1799

G WEN STIRRED THE FIREPLACE coals to life, adding a handful of dried moss to the exposed embers. When flames licked up the sides of the moss, she added kindling. The fragrance of pinesap accompanied the pop and sizzle of the small pieces of wood. In moments, she had enough fire to add the split hardwood logs. Warmth and light spread into the room.

Normally, Betsy was the first to bustle around mornings. But Owen had slept the past three nights through, not rousing Gwen until the first fingers of dawn clawed their way up the morning's curtain of clouds. Gwen yawned and glanced over at her son, who sat on a quilt, gnawing on a wooden spoon. Sitting up already. Soon he'd be crawling, standing, and then walking.

A sigh slipped between Gwen's lips. He was growing too fast. If she were married, would she be thinking about a little brother or sister already? Faye was barely fourteen months younger than she. There had been a gap of three years between Faye and their brothers, who also came just a year apart. Then another gap until the child her mother had died trying to give birth to.

Long-ago bedtime whispers came back to her. She and Faye trying to understand their mother's death. Why had she needed another child anyway? Wasn't she happy enough with their family as it was?

Gwen allowed herself a bittersweet smile.

There was no way their younger selves could have understood the depth of a mother's love. It overwhelmed Gwen sometimes, even though she'd not given birth to Owen. She couldn't imagine loving a child any more than she loved him. But to have another—

"Good morning."

Gwen startled at Betsy's greeting. So deep in thought, she hadn't heard the floorboards squeak or the rusty protest of the bedroom door's hinges.

"Goodness, I did not mean to startle thee."

"'Tis my own fault for being lost in my thoughts."

"And what thoughts so captured thee this morning?"

Gwen pointed at Owen.

He reveled in the attention of both women, showing a wide expanse of pink gums.

"Sitting up all by himself. Such a little man." Betsy stooped and lifted the boy as he babbled a long string of nonsense. "And talkative this morning."

"He slept the night through again. We did not awaken until the dawn."

"He is growing up too fast, much too fast."

"'Tis exactly what I was pondering when you walked in."

Betsy bounced Owen on her hip. "'Twill not be long and thee will start yearning for another one."

Had the older woman read her mind?

Betsy chuckled. "'Tis only what any mother would be thinking on a morning such as this. But thee needs a husband first, I daresay. Perchance thee have someone in mind?"

Gwen turned her face to the fire. Micah's blue eyes and broad shoulders spent more time in her thoughts than she wished to admit.

Betsy settled on a chair with Owen in her lap. "No one with eyes to see has missed Micah's regard for thee. Thy reactions to him hardly seem disinterested. Be there a chance thee might come to return his regard?"

"I cannot." The words all but burst from Gwen. She wished them back as soon as Betsy's eyebrows rose. "He is a Quaker, and I am not. Zachary said Quakers only marry each other."

"That is a matter easily overcome."

"Nay, 'tis not." Gwen wished she could confide everything right then and there. The urge to purge her soul of the secret nearly overwhelmed her, but Owen's trusting face stilled her tongue.

"Have thee no interest in joining us Friends, then?" The fleeting expression of hurt that crossed the dear woman's face was almost Gwen's undoing.

"I am... unsure about the things of God. What you believe and what I was taught as a child, they are very different."

"I see." Betsy stroked Owen's wayward curls off his forehead. "It must be confusing. But I believe that when the time is right, God will speak to thee in thy heart. Indeed, I believe He does frequently with all of us. But it takes us time to learn to listen."

If God had spoken to her, she was pretty sure she'd have heard Him. He must have a large sort of voice to be God. But that was only part of the problem she faced.

"'Tis more than that. I have a child and no husband. You and Thomas have accepted me, and people like Faith, Zachary, and Micah." She closed her eyes and gathered her thoughts before looking at Betsy again. "But there are others who whisper about me. Those who do not speak to me after meeting. Those who pretend not to see me when I pass."

"Indeed, and the shame is on them, not on thee for their actions. But have patience. Now that we are quartered here for the winter, there will be more time for people to get to know thee. Some people, even Quakers, are quick to judge when they know not the circumstances or the character of a person."

Thomas entered the kitchen, pulling up his suspenders as he walked over to take Owen from Betsy. "Good morning, my little man."

"I remember a time, not so long past, when thee greeted me upon rising each morning." Betsy winked at Gwen as she handed the boy to her husband.

"Then I should think thee to have had thy fill of my voice by now." Thomas bounced Owen until he squealed. "This little one is giving thee a well-deserved rest."

Gwen grinned at their loving banter before starting the morning porridge. Love filled the room as surely as heat from the fire. She paused with her hand on the crock full of milled oats. What would mornings be like if she joined the Quakers and married Micah? What would it be like to wake up every morning and prepare porridge for him? To start the day in a room filled with love?

That was a future she longed for. But how would she explain to Micah that she knew nothing about being with a man? Or would he know right away that she'd deceived them all?

The situation was impossible.

She'd stay with Thomas and Betsy. She could care for them in their old age. That would pay them back for their care of her and Owen. That was her future. A good future with people she loved.

A single tear slipped down her cheek all the same.

Betsy shook the kitchen rug with vigor from the end of the porch. Dust billowed and danced in the chilly air, sparkling in the mid-morning sun. How could dust be pretty outside and yet nothing but dirt inside? She'd turned to enter the officer's house when a motion across the parade ground stopped her.

Micah strode from the barracks, heading for the stable. Whatever was he doing around the fort at that hour of the day? She thought he'd gone with Thomas to work in town. The two had hired on at a local sawmill.

Betsy glanced at the kitchen window. Gwen was inside with Owen. They wouldn't miss her for a bit. She laid the rug across the porch rail and hurried down the steps. Her path intersected with his outside the stable door.

"Good morning, Betsy."

"Good morning to thee as well. What keeps thee in the fort this morning? Is all well at the sawmill?"

"Well enough, but not enough work for all of us today. They are expecting another float of logs down the river, but it has yet to arrive."

"Thomas stayed though?"

"They needed another man, but not two. Since Thomas has the care of a family, and I do not, it only made sense that he work."

"Thee are ever a thoughtful one." Betsy glanced toward the house and back. "'Tis a shame thee do not have a family of thy own."

A shadow darkened his eyes to almost gray as he shook his head. "'Twasn't meant to be."

Betsy sucked in a breath and pressed her fingers to her lips for a moment. How could she have forgotten he'd been rebuffed in favor of his older brother? "Pray forgive me. I did not mean to stir up old wounds."

"Nay, 'tis nothing. Not anymore." The twinkle returned to his eyes, and he grinned. "Besides, I have thee taking such good care of me, I could ask for nothing better."

"Nonsense. Thee deserves more, a family to call thy own." She glanced once more at the house. "I daresay there might be one nearby who would suit thee nicely."

A ruddy hue crept across Micah's cheeks. "I'm not so certain of that."

Betsy placed her hands on her hips. "Oh?"

"I only meant..." The color on his cheeks deepened. "She has given me no indication that she would favor..." He removed his hat and plowed his fingers through his hair.

"She is a quiet lass, but thee mustn't mistake quiet for shallow. Our Gwen is special in many ways."

"Even should I wish it, she is not a Friend."

"That, too, can change."

He crammed the hat back on his head. "'Twould have to, as I see it."

"Indeed. And when—I say when—it does, thee should not be caught unprepared."

"These things have a way of working themselves out. I'm in no hurry to take a wife." He shifted his feet and looked to the west. "There will be plenty to do when we reach our new land."

Who was he trying to convince with his well-rehearsed comments? Platitudes she could well imagine her husband having said.

"Indeed, and thee would prosper with a fine wife at thy side."

"Mayhap, if one comes along who is as fine as the one Thomas found." Micah winked and walked into the stable.

Betsy sighed and turned for the house. She had no business meddling in the affairs of others. That was God's place, not hers. Thomas was correct. Not that it had stopped him from meddling either, if she was correct about who had planted those ideas in Micah's head. Irritated with herself, she stomped her way back to the porch, whipped the rug off the railing, and marched into the house.

She would not meddle again.

Gwen bundled Owen until not much more than his nose peeped out before dragging a thick cape around her shoulders. Days of cold rain had kept them inside, and now she craved a walk. She needed to get away from the stuffy confines of the officer's house. It may have been one of the finest houses the crumbling fort had to offer, but it was still cramped with three adults and an increasingly active little boy.

"Do not go too far." Betsy wiped her hands on her apron.

"I shall walk along the river, away from town."

"'Tis a pretty walk, even with most of the leaves down. I believe the next storm will bring us snow instead of rain. Thomas says we can expect it any day, so far north as we are."

"Then Owen and I had best enjoy the sunshine while we have it."

Gwen opened the door and stepped into the blinding light of the early afternoon. The pungent odor of damp leaves rose from the ground and mingled with the sharp tang of wood smoke. The fort buildings, washed clean by the recent rains, sparkled with some of their former glory—if one overlooked the rotting and missing timbers of the stockade and the decided tilt of most of the smaller outbuildings.

Gwen bounced Owen on her hip and then lifted him to look into his eyes.

"Let us have an adventure, shall we?"

His hands escaped the shawl she had bundled around him to pat her cheeks while he babbled.

She laughed and straightened the knit cap on his head before strolling down the steps. Not halfway to the fort's entrance, a door slammed. Gwen turned and scanned the fort's interior.

Micah waved and jogged toward them, stuffing his arm into a coat sleeve as he approached.

"Where are thee destined to this afternoon, Gwen Morgan?"

"Owen and I have planned an adventure."

"Oh?" His eyebrows hiked.

"Just a bit of a walk along the river. But on such a fine day, we are bound to find an adventure."

"I daresay, thee might. Perhaps I should follow along and keep thee safe from harm."

"Harm?"

"Indeed. Thee never knows what pirates might be skulking along the riverbank." He winked and reached for Owen, who had loosened his arms from the shawl and reached back. "At the very least, I can lighten thy load."

"As much as he has grown this past month, 'twill be a pleasure to have someone else tote him along."

They fell into a comfortable silence until they reached the river's edge. Water hurried past them, tumbling and gushing around the rocks near the shore.

"That water will be in Ohio, near where we plan to settle, in a handful of days. And we are stuck here for the winter," Micah said.

"Aye, but I'm glad to be here and not caught in the wagons when the snow comes."

"I suppose 'tis for the best, but I'm anxious to get there. Anxious to get started on my new land. Build my own farm in what is now wilderness."

"Betsy mentioned your family farmed."

"Ever since they arrived from the old country, over one hundred years ago."

His family had lived in America for more than a hundred years? She'd forgotten that people had lived here that long. The country seemed so new, so fresh, so unlike where she'd grown up in Wales. Back there, everything was old, and each family had roots deeper than the silver birch that grew on the village green.

"Did your father farm, back in Wales?" he asked.

"Nay. He was a miner, like most of the men in our village. But he had apprenticed to a cooper in his youth, and he had hoped to find work in a cooper's shop when we landed." She couldn't suppress the sigh that escaped. "But he never made it."

"I'm sorry for all thee has lost. A young lass such as thyself, to have lost so much."

"'Tis why finding Faye is so important to me. She is all I have left."

"Not anymore." Micah shifted Owen to one arm and rested his other hand on Gwen's shoulder. "Thee has this fine young man, a home with the Baldwins, and—perhaps one day—thee will be ready for a husband."

At his earnest expression, Gwen caught her trembling bottom lip between her teeth. The oath hung heavy over her, weighing her down. She couldn't think about a husband. Not a Quaker husband, for sure. But Zachary's words were never far from her thoughts.

She summoned a smile that didn't quiver too much. "The Baldwins are wonderful. I know not what would have become of Owen and me if not for them." She lifted her shoulders in a quick shrug. "But I still need to find my sister. She is out there somewhere. Alone."

Micah's hand dropped to his side. He stared off into the distance for a moment, and then flashed her a crooked grin. "If that is what thee needs, then know that I will help thee all I can."

How could she accept such kindness while repaying it with a lie?

Chapter 24

December 1799

B ETSY HELPED THOMAS SHRUG out of his heavy coat, sprinkling the kitchen floor and the front of her apron with a dusting of snow.

Owen squealed and bounced on his sturdy legs. Both chubby hands clamped onto the seat of a chair that separated him from Gwen and the fireplace.

The young mother stirred a kettle of seasoned stew. The savory steam, hinting of rosemary and thyme, filled the kitchen. Gwen seemed as if in her own little world, staring into the swirling vegetables.

Betsy hung Thomas's coat on a peg. She wished she knew what so occupied her friend's mind.

"There is my boy," Thomas said. He scooped the toddler off the floor and held him high. Owen squealed louder and clapped his hands, and Thomas laughed and lowered himself into the chair. Owen stood on his lap, patted his beard, and babbled in a language only the toddler understood.

"I would warn thee not to spoil the boy, but 'tis far too late for that," Betsy said. "Are Zachary and Micah coming?" She peered out the window. The gray clouds and swirls of snow sent a shiver up her back. She sent a brief prayer of thanksgiving for the roof over their heads and the provisions to see them through the winter.

"Indeed, they will be here shortly." The words no more than left his lips when someone knocked on the door. Micah pushed it open and entered with Zachary on his heels. Cold air flowed across the floor and rustled Betsy's skirt.

"Welcome." Thomas pointed to the mismatched chairs around the kitchen table. "Shed thy coats and join us."

"We bring news from town." Micah looked at Gwen before he dropped onto a chair to the left of Thomas.

"What news?" Thomas asked.

"Cobb rode in this afternoon," Zachary said.

Thomas half rose from his seat, then looked at Owen as if remembering he held the boy. He eased back onto the seat. "Has he explained his absence?"

"Aye, an arrow through his shoulder." Micah shrugged. "To hear him tell it, he managed to ride away from the Indians who shot him but was much weakened from loss of blood and fell from his horse. He broke his leg in the fall. He's gimping badly."

"How did he survive such a thing?" As much as she disapproved of Cobb on a personal level, Betsy's heart went out to anyone is such a dire situation.

"Another Indian found him and took him to their medicine man." Zachary glanced at Betsy. "He surely would have died without their heathen medicine."

"Heathen medicine is fitting for Cobb," Betsy said. He was a heathen after all. Shame flooded her at her judgmental attitude. She must ask forgiveness for that later.

"Will he be fit to lead us west in the spring?" Thomas asked.

"I imagine so," Zachary said. "He was fit enough to drain several tankards of ale during the telling of his adventures."

"Bought and paid for by those who hung on his every word." Micah grimaced.

Betsy plopped a ladle in the stew. The drunken lout. She mentally added that unkind—if accurate—thought to her list of things to ask forgiveness for during her prayers. "Dish out the stew, will thee, Gwen? I shall cut the bread, and we can thank the Lord for Cobb's safe return."

Although, to her way of thinking, it was a mixed blessing at best.

Betsy scooted over on the bed to make room for Thomas. The bed ropes creaked and swayed when he climbed in. She smothered a yawn. His warmth was a welcome addition under the quilt.

"I'm glad thee are still awake," Thomas whispered. "Micah shared some disturbing news."

"What news?"

"He was reluctant to mention it in front of Gwen, and rightly so."

"Tell me." Betsy rose on one elbow and peered through the darkness at Thomas's face.

"Micah listened to Cobb tell his tale in the tavern. Afterward, when the men gathered around had wandered off, Jonas Whiteford joined Cobb at the table."

"Jonas?" Betsy shivered, but the chill had nothing to do with the cold bedroom. "I thought him gone."

"As did I, but he has returned. Micah could not hear what was said, but he witnessed enough to be concerned."

"Does thee worry those two might mean Gwen harm?"

"I can think of no good reason why Jonas would approach a man like Cobb, apart from his position as our scout and Gwen's presence with us."

"'Tis hard to imagine any good can come of it."

"Indeed." Thomas rustled deeper under the quilt.

"All day it seemed as if Gwen wished to speak about something."

"And?"

"I did not press the issue. 'Twas more a feeling I had. Perhaps tomorrow she will be more forthcoming with her thoughts."

"Does thee think she may know of a connection between Cobb and Jonas?"

"Nay. I doubt it. But she has seemed distracted for the past few weeks. Something weighs on her heart."

Thomas grunted and yawned.

Betsy snuggled against her husband's warmth and pulled the quilt around her shoulders. Soon, Thomas's breathing settled into a deep, even pattern. She turned onto her back and stared at the ceiling. The sleep that had almost claimed her earlier now danced out of reach. She rolled onto her side, her back warmed by Thomas, but her eyelids refused to close. She blew out a sigh. Then she prayed. Prayers for Gwen and Owen, for the Friends, for Thomas and Micah, and finally—reluctantly—she prayed for Cobb and Jonas.

Gwen parted from Zachary, who continued along the street to the blacksmith's shop while she hurried up the steps to the mercantile. If Owen hadn't outgrown half his clothing in the past fortnight, she never would have ventured out in such weather. She stamped her boots free of snow and shook her cape on the boardwalk before entering.

Several older men gathered around a checkerboard table by the potbelly stove in the center of the store. Warmth from the fire and the particular smells of dill pickles, lye soap, and gunpowder greeted her.

Gwen walked straight to the sewing notions and picked out the thread she needed. Her fingers lingered over a jar of pewter buttons for a moment before she chose a trio of wooden ones from the next jar. Betsy insisted Gwen charge the material to Thomas's account, and wooden buttons were more than adequate for a toddler's coat. She picked up some fine white muslin and a bolt of soft gray wool. The material warmed beneath her fingers.

Quaker gray.

Why hadn't she approached Betsy yet about joining the church? For the past two weeks, she'd awakened telling herself she'd speak up that day. And for two weeks, she couldn't bring the words to her mouth. While part of her yearned to belong, another part—a fearful part—knew she wasn't worthy.

Zachary's none-too-subtly raised eyebrow that morning niggled at her. How could she hope that Owen would be fully accepted by the Quakers if she didn't join? And what about Micah? Dare she dream?

Not unless she joined the Quakers.

Not unless she accepted God in the same way they had. And she was ready to make that choice.

But would she find the courage to speak when she returned?

She carried the cloth to the counter and waited for the clerk to finish with another customer. The display of festive Christmas ornaments behind the counter caught her attention. Christmas would be nothing like last year. There would be no decorations, no gifts, and no lavish feast like the Whitefords put on. The Quakers did not celebrate the day in any special way. They believed that no one day should be held more holy than any other, lest it demean the remaining days of the year.

While Gwen loved the color and shine of the ornaments and the smell of freshly cut greenery, Christmas had held very little meaning for her. Strange that with people who didn't celebrate the day, she understood far more of what Christmas meant. It wasn't about a babe in a manger. It was about a Savior who came to forgive the sins of His people.

Sins like hers.

One of the Quakers had spoken at length about it last meeting. He'd spoken of freedom in Christ. Her thoughts returned to his words often, and when they did, her fearfulness eased. But there was the oath, the lie...

"What can I do for you today, Mistress Morgan?" the clerk asked.

His words snapped her out of her thoughts. "I need three yards of the muslin and one of the wool."

"Very good. I shall cut those for you." He whisked the bolts to the cutting table in the back.

"Another dowdy outfit to hide behind?"

Jonas's voice grated against her ear. Where had he come from? She refused to look at him and wouldn't let him intimidate her. There were plenty of people in the mercantile, and he wouldn't cause a scene.

She hoped.

"You are getting brave, coming in without your darkie. Although, why you think that slave will deter me, I have no idea."

"Zachary is no slave." Gwen gritted her teeth. She didn't want to speak to Jonas, but she would not let him denigrate her friend.

"He is not my concern, Gwen. You are." His breath burned across her cheek, and she winced. "Does that frighten you?"

"I am not afraid of you."

"Good. Because we are going to be close, you and I. Very, very close."

The clerk returned, and Jonas backed away. Gwen drew in a steadying breath and took the brown paper parcel from the clerk.

"Please put this on Thomas Baldwin's account," she said, "along with the thread and three buttons."

"Very good. Have a pleasant day, miss."

The clerk hurried down the long counter to wait on the next customer. The bell over the door jingled as Jonas left and Zachary entered the store. Zachary scanned the store, spotted her, and strode to her side, deep furrows lining his cheeks.

"Did he say anything to thee?"

"Nothing of importance." Gwen pressed her hands against the wrapped parcel so Zachary wouldn't see them shake. She summoned a smile and nodded to the door. "I'm ready to go if you are."

Zachary looked less than convinced, but he followed close on her heels as she left.

Why had Jonas returned? And what did he mean about them being close? He was no longer a threat to her. She was a free woman, and he didn't know the truth about Owen. So why did her breakfast threaten to leave her? She pressed her hand to her stomach and stepped off the porch, heading toward the fort, thankful for Zachary's shadow on the snow beside her.

"I cannot let that man upset me, Zachary. He has no power over me anymore."

"Thank the good Lord for that."

The good Lord and a steadfast friend like Zachary.

Brilliant sunlight bounced off the newly fallen snow, but it dimmed in comparison to Micah's smile. Gwen's heart squeezed at the sight, and she took a moment to catch her breath.

"'Tis a wonderful afternoon for a sleigh ride." Micah stood with one hand on his horse's broad hip and pointed to the sleigh with the other.

Gwen tugged Owen's cap lower over his little forehead to stall for time and regain her composure. "I cannot believe you found a sleigh." She looked away from Micah to the intricately carved scrollwork along the sleigh's side.

"Indeed. The man from the livery stable said 'tis rarely rented out. 'Tis old, but look at the craftsmanship. 'Twas made by a master carpenter for sure."

Owen squealed and lunged for Micah, slipping from Gwen's grip. "Catch him!"

Micah grabbed the wiggling toddler and secured him against his chest. "Come along, little man. Let us settle your mother in this fine conveyance."

Gwen took Micah's hand and climbed into the sleigh. She arranged her heavy skirt around her legs and retrieved Owen, pulling the squirming youngster onto her lap. They waited while Micah untied Hap and climbed in on the other side. Micah barely sat before Owen crawled onto his lap. Micah smiled and tucked the heavy lap robe around them.

"I guess 'tis time for thy first driving lesson." Micah gripped the reins and let the ends dangle where Owen could grasp them. The sleigh glided on the fresh snow while Owen gnawed on the cold leather.

"What a splendid afternoon," Gwen said. "Look how the snow hangs on the evergreens. I have not seen snow like this since we left Wales. And only rarely then."

"Indeed. 'Tis a perfect Christmas day."

"I thought Quakers did not recognize Christmas." Gwen cocked her head at Micah.

"We do not *celebrate* it as others do, but we are not *ignorant* of the significance of the day." He tossed her a rakish grin. "As Friends, we hold that everyone should treat each day as one the Lord has given them." He nodded at the festive wreaths hung on doors as they slid past the houses on the outskirts of town. "'Twould be a stretch to say, however, that we do not enjoy the sights."

"Mr. Whiteford would bring home the biggest wreath for the door each year. And Mrs. Whiteford would ask why he did not find a larger one." Gwen giggled, and Owen stopped chewing on the reins to giggle with her. "I loved the smell of the freshly cut evergreens we hung around the mantel. I miss that."

Micah nodded.

The runners swished against the snow. Hap's harness jingled a lively tune as the gelding trotted and the miles slipped by. Micah pointed out several beautiful spots he'd come across while hunting. Gwen's cheeks tingled with the cold, but she refused to cover her face with her shawl. The cold air was invigorating and refreshing after several days spent indoors.

They topped a small rise, and a frozen pond lay before them. The sunlight shone off it like a lake of crystal. Owen raised his hands and babbled in a high voice.

"'Tis beautiful," Gwen said.

Micah halted the sleigh.

Gwen leaned forward and squinted. "Look!" She pointed. "Across the way." A deer picked its way to the pond through the deep snow, its slender legs lifted high with each careful step.

Micah leaned close to her, his misty breath stirring the curls of hair that escaped her bonnet. His hand holding the reins wrapped around Owen, and he slid the other one behind her, but he didn't touch her.

Disappointment frosted the edge of her thoughts, but she'd no right to feel that way.

"Beautiful," Micah whispered, his eyes locked on Gwen's.

She forgot about the deer across the pond. She forgot where they were. She swallowed—hard.

Owen let out a piercing squeal and pushed himself back against Micah. His chubby little arms flung out, one smacking each of the adults. A string of excited jabbering followed as the toddler pointed to the deer, bounding away with its white tail waving behind.

Micah laughed, an unsteady sound, while Owen bounced on his lap.

Gwen took a moment to tuck her hair under her bonnet with a hand that trembled.

"He has the makings of a hunter already." Pride reverberated through Micah's voice. "He is a fine lad."

"Aye."

"A lad any man would be proud to call son." Micah's voice grew husky and low.

"Micah."

"I had hoped we might discuss the possibility—"

"—There are so many difficulties—"

They spoke at the same time, and then stopped.

Gwen picked at the hem of the lap rope for a long moment before looking up at him. "It has been on my mind to speak with Betsy."

Micah opened his mouth but didn't speak. His eyes snapped to her right, and his brows drew together. His lips closed in a firm line.

Gwen turned to see what had caught his attention, two men riding toward them. She lifted a hand to shield her eyes against the sun's glare.

It couldn't be. She pressed closer to Micah and pulled Owen onto her lap.

"Jonas. Cobb." Micah's voice carried more frost than the air around them.

"Fancy meetin' you two out here." Cobb stopped his horse, leaned to one side, and spat. "We ain't interruptin' anythin', are we?" His yellow teeth flashed through his beard.

"What do thee want?" Micah asked.

"Just takin' a ride this fine Christmas mornin'," Cobb said.

Owen tugged his hat off and flung it onto the snow between the sleigh and Jonas's horse. The boy's thatch of blond locks gleamed in the sunlight.

Jonas's eyes rounded. Silence hung in the frosty air. Then he pulled his attention from Owen and looked at Gwen with a nasty grin.

Her stomach lurched.

Jonas leaned over in the saddle and studied the toddler's face.

The blood drained from Gwen's head, and she grabbed the edge of the seat.

Jonas dismounted. He picked up the plain knit hat and turned it over in his hands several times. With an evil gleam in his eyes, he handed it to her.

"We will be riding on. Enjoy your day." The smirk on his face was unmistakable. He knew. He had to know. Owen's golden curls and pale blue eyes looked too much like his sister to be mistaken.

The men rode away without a backward glance.

"Take us home," Gwen whispered.

"But—"

"Please."

Micah's expression pleaded with her for an explanation. She turned her face away. As much as she wanted to tell him the truth, all of it, she couldn't. She couldn't risk losing Owen.

Not even for Micah.

The horse pulled the sleigh into motion, and Gwen fought the urge to be sick. Her future, as bright as the sun on the snow moments before, was once again covered with a cloud of dread.

Jonas knew her secret—and he would find a way to use it against her.

The lie she lived snapped around her like a cage.

She wasn't free anymore.

Chapter 25

G WEN WAITED UNTIL THE murmuring in the next room stopped and Thomas's snores reverberated through the wall. She tossed the quilt back and rose, fully dressed, casting one glance at the closed door to the bedroom and another at the boy in his cradle. Thankful that the day's excursion had him sleeping soundly, she tiptoed into the kitchen, where she donned her heavy cloak and stepped into her boots before easing the door open and slipping onto the porch.

The air tingled against her skin. Stars glittered like fairy wings in the blackness above. Her mother had told stories of fairies back in Wales. Gwen struggled to remember her mother, the sheen of her hair, the curve of her face, the lilt of her voice. What would her mother think of the mess Gwen had gotten herself into?

Light from the sliver of moon guided her to the stable. Gwen slid around the door and pushed it shut behind her. The smells of hay, horse, and dust greeted her. One large cow swung its head toward her and moaned a low complaint at the intrusion. Gwen paused until her eyes adjusted to the dim light filtering through two small windows. In the far corner of the stable, a white head popped between the wooden slats of a makeshift stall. Gwen picked her way along the narrow aisle.

"Oh, Tiny." Gwen dropped to her knees on the straw. She buried her fingers in the goat's shaggy winter fur and breathed in the comforting, musky scent. "Jonas knows. I saw it in his eyes. If only Owen did not look so much like Miss Constance." Sobs shook her body and rasped from her throat. Tiny rubbed her forehead on Gwen's shoulder. Gwen wiped her hand across her eyes and drew in a deep breath. "Will the Friends force Thomas and Betsy to turn us out if he exposes the truth? What will I do? Where will we go?"

Tiny's gentle eyes offered no answers, but her steady presence brought a small measure of calm. Gwen stroked the shaggy neck, and a wobbly smile tugged at her lips when Tiny nibbled on her cloak.

"What would I do, dear Tiny, without you to hear my fears?"

The stable door creaked open. Someone thrust a lantern in, spilling light across the straw-littered floor. Gwen raised her hand to shield her eyes and pressed farther into the shadows of the goat's stall.

"Hello?" Zachary's voice sliced through the cold air. "Is anyone here?"

Gwen froze, unwilling to expose herself and her tear-streaked face.

Zachary held the lantern high and looked around the stable. He ambled over to Bossy and scratched the brown cow's hip. His soothing voice blended with the rhythmic munching of the cows.

Tiny pawed at a bit of hay. A mouse jumped from the manger and darted across the hem of Gwen's dress.

With a shriek, Gwen leaped to her feet, batting at her skirt.

"Gwen?"

Hands pressed to her heaving chest, Gwen turned to face Zachary. "Aye."

"Are thee harmed?"

"Nay, 'twas only a mouse. It startled me."

Zachary approached Tiny's stall. The lantern cast a halo of light around him. "What are thee doing here so late?" His brows drew down as the circle of light reached her face. "What has caused thee to weep?"

Gwen's chin quivered. If only she could confide in someone. Someone other than her goat. She laid a hand on Tiny's back and shook her head, unable to meet his gaze. "Pardon me, Zachary." She brushed past him and fled the dark stable. Returning to the house, she crept into her bed.

Tiny's musky smell lingered on her hands, her only comfort in the night.

Betsy slapped the wooden paddle onto the wet clothes and then pressed her hand to her back. She brushed sweat-dampened hair off her forehead, tucking it under her linen head covering. The howling wind outside did little to cool the kitchen with its steaming laundry kettle. She glanced at Gwen, who sat in a rocking chair by the window, needle and thread dormant in her hands.

Betsy didn't need to read minds to know a troubled spirit when she saw one. What had happened on that sleigh ride last Wednesday? All attempts to coax answers from Gwen had failed. Thomas had gotten nothing from Micah on the subject either. And knowing her husband, he'd been blunt in his asking. She pressed on her back again, working out an ache.

"Let me finish the laundry." Gwen rose from the chair and set her sewing aside.

"I'm fine," Betsy said. "Sit and finish that night shirt for Owen. Thee knows my old eyes are hampered sewing in such feeble light."

"And your old back has had enough washing for today." Gwen smiled, the first time in a week. "Owen can sleep in his other shirt a few more nights. Sit." Gwen pulled a chair out from the table and pointed to it.

Betsy lowered herself to the chair with a sigh. "Thee are correct. My back is as old as my eyes. And right fond it is of reminding me."

Gwen dunked heavy work clothes under the steaming water. The pungent scent of wet sawdust filled the kitchen. With the Brownsville area growing at such a rapid pace, many men from the wagon train obtained work at the local sawmills. Betsy and Gwen washed clothes for several of the unmarried ones. The extra coins they earned collected in a jar above the fireplace.

Coins Betsy had hoped would help Gwen and Micah establish a home together.

Owen awoke and babbled from the next room. "I shall fetch him." Betsy waved a hand at Gwen as she climbed to her feet. "I'm rested enough." She lifted the toddler from his cradle and winced at the twinge in her back. He was getting heavier by the day. She changed his wrapping and brought him into the kitchen.

Betsy grabbed a leftover biscuit and plopped the boy on a dry spot on the floor before handing him the snack. He smiled at her, and a glimmer of white caught her eye. "Gwen, I think his first tooth has broken through."

Gwen dropped the paddle with a splash and hurried to kneel in front of Owen. She pushed the biscuit aside and ran a finger over his gums. The youngster bit down.

"Ouch!" Gwen pulled her finger back and laughed. Owen giggled and stuffed the biscuit in his mouth.

At a knock at the door, Betsy looked at Gwen, but the young woman shrugged. Betsy opened the door a few inches and peered through.

Jonas slipped his foot in the opening. The nerve of the man. "I have come to see Gwen."

Gwen scrambled to her feet, positioning herself between Owen and the door.

Betsy leaned on the heavy door, keeping it tight to the man's foot. "What is the nature of thy business with Gwen?"

"Our business is of a personal nature. Grant me entrance."

"'Tis a most inconvenient time." How had the man known when to come? Thomas had yet to return from the mill. That left it to Betsy to turn the man away. "Perhaps thee could return another day."

"I have waited long enough."

How was she to protect Gwen and Owen by herself?

Gwen grabbed Owen and wrapped her arms around him. The boy fastened onto her, his eyes wide.

Betsy clung to the heavy door, her sturdy heels planted on the floorboards, not giving Jonas an inch.

Gwen had to do something. She couldn't run away, no matter how much she wanted to.

No, she didn't want to run. She wanted to fight for the little boy whom she loved above life itself. She squared her shoulders, as much as she could with the toddler clinging to her.

"'Tis fine, Betsy." She nodded as the older woman's eyebrows shot skyward. "Mis—Jonas. Jonas and I have things to discuss." She swallowed and pried Owen's fingers from the collar of her dress. "If you would see to Owen, I shall step outside for a moment with him."

"Nay. Thomas will not be pleased." Betsy's linen head covering slid askew with the vigorous shaking of her head.

"I will not leave the porch." Gwen summoned a quivering smile that did nothing to calm the anguish in Betsy's eyes. "'Twill be fine." She put as much assurance in her words as she could muster, even while her insides twisted like an apron hung on a windy day. "There are men in the barracks who will hear me should I cry out," she said loud enough for Jonas to hear.

"Gwen shall be out in a minute. Thee can wait on the porch." Jonas's boot disappeared from the doorway, and Betsy shoved the door closed. She leaned back against it and faced Gwen. "Are thee certain?"

"Aye. 'Tis best gotten over with."

"But..."

Gwen pushed Owen into Betsy's arms, pulled her cloak from a peg behind the door, and wrapped herself in its folds. If only it were armor as in days of old. After drawing a deep breath, she opened the door. Snow swirled around her ankles as she pulled it shut behind her. Her stomach in knots, she forced her chin up to face the man who could tear her world in two.

Fear that she might spew resurrected the memory of dousing him with the slop bucket. Had it only been a year before? The leer on his face brought it all crashing back. Pressing her hand to her stomach, she fought for control. She could do this. She was a free woman, and Jonas couldn't change that. But her shaking knees named her a liar.

"I have waited a long time for you, Gwen."

"I know not what you mean."

"Do not play coy with me." He moved closer. She refused to retreat but averted her face from his breath.

"I have no business with you, Jonas."

"Jonas, is it? Not Mister Jonas." He dug the tip of his finger into the soft skin beneath her chin, tipping her face toward him.

She gritted her teeth and met him stare for stare. "You do not own me and neither does your father. Not anymore. I'm a free woman."

"Are you? Are you really?" He chuckled, and the skin on the back of her neck writhed. "I think not, little Gwen. What did you call him? Owen, was it? And how can it be that your—son—bears such a striking resemblance to my own dear sister? She who left rather abruptly after Christmas a year ago, only to return home in the spring minus a maid or a child."

Gwen pressed harder on her stomach and sucked the cold air through her nose. Even so, the porch boards tilted beneath her.

Jonas grabbed her by the elbows and gave her a shake. "You are not going to swoon on me. We have business to discuss, you and I."

Gwen pulled out of his grasp and stepped back. She pressed the heel of one hand to her forehead. "What are you talking about?"

"As much as I would enjoy pursuing you for other reasons, you are more valuable to me in another capacity now."

Gwen forced herself to look at him. What was he up to?

"My father sent me to establish our trade with the merchants in this backwater town. But there is too much competition here already. I think he would be most pleased if I were to follow your Quakers into the wilderness and set Whiteford and Son up there. Yes, most pleased." He stroked one hand across his chin. "And you will assist me."

"Nay." Outrage flooded through her.

"I think so, dear little Gwen, for if you do not, my good conscience may force me to reveal to these Bible-toters the truth about you and your... son."

The blood drained from her face, her already cold skin turning to ice. She tightened her hands into fists at her sides.

The twist of his head and the lift of his eyebrows slashed her heart. "Ah, 'tis as I surmised. They know not the truth."

"I swore an oath to your father." Oh, why had she told him that?

"I calculated as much. An oath that will now benefit me. How thoughtful of Father. However unknowingly, he has set things up for you and me to work very well together. Very well indeed."

Gwen leaned over the porch railing, breathing through her nose until the pounding in her ears lessened. The cloak slipped from her shoulders, and the icy wind blasted across her back.

"What is happening here?" Never had Micah's voice been more welcome.

Hope surged through Gwen. The porch shook under her feet. A

moment later, her cloak was draped across her shoulders.

"The lady is not feeling well. I shall return at a more convenient time to discuss my business with Thomas Baldwin."

Gwen didn't turn at Jonas's parting words or at the thump of his boots on the steps. The thought of him returning at all left an oily feeling at the back of her throat.

"What business does he speak of?"

Micah's soft question and his warm hand on her shoulder loosened tears she didn't want to fall.

"Gwen?"

His breath warmed the back of her neck, and she turned into his embrace. She wasn't sure if he'd intended to embrace her, or if her motion had simply propelled her into his arms. Either way, for a moment, a welcome sense of security washed over her.

His chest rose beneath her cheek.

Time slowed. Minutes ticked by. Ghost clouds of their breath mingled around them. He stroked her back. Her trembling stopped. Snowflakes collected on their woolen clothing. Gwen's breathing evened, and she fingered the pewter buttons of his coat.

"Ahem."

Gwen wrenched herself from Micah's arms.

"Good evening, Zachary." Micah's hands disappeared behind his back. The ruddy glow of his cheeks belied his calm voice.

"'Tis peculiar weather to linger on the porch, if thee were to ask me." Zachary looked at the clouds and shook his head. "But I cannot deny there are things to keep a person warm, even in such weather."

Gwen pressed her shaking hands to her cheeks.

"'Twas not—"

"I know, Micah, rest easy." Zachary's eyes sparkled, and he flashed them his wide grin.

"Jonas Whiteford was here," Micah said.

Zachary's smile vanished. He twisted to look behind him. "What did that weasel want?"

"I know not. He mentioned some manner of business. Gwen has not spoken yet."

Gwen stepped back toward the door. "Please, come inside. There is nothing to tell." She yanked the door open and rushed past a startled Betsy at the window. Scooping Owen off the floor, she fled to her bedroom and collapsed onto her pallet, pulling the toddler onto her lap. He squirmed and fussed until she relaxed her hold.

She looked at the ceiling and whispered, "I know not what to do." Was God up there?

Even if He was, why would He listen to her?

Chapter 26

"**S**URELY THEE OVERHEARD SOMETHING?" Thomas's whiskers tickled Betsy's cheek. She smoothed the wiry hairs away from her face and tucked them under the quilt.

"They spoke too softly for me to hear more than a word or two. 'Twas obvious she was distraught, and I was prepared to open the door when Micah appeared. Then Jonas left, and those two were quiet for a long time. I could see only Micah's back from the window."

"I wish we knew Jonas's intent."

"It may be in regard to his father's business."

"Oh?"

"I distinctly heard him mention Whiteford and Son."

Thomas rolled onto his back and tugged the end of his beard free. Betsy nestled closer to his side.

"Perhaps we have judged him wrongly," Thomas said.

"But Gwen fears him so."

"She may have had reason in the past. Thee knows I have my suspicions about his involvement with her... and Owen."

"Indeed. And not thee alone. His hair is as fair as the child's."

"Can thee not ask her?"

Betsy cringed at the thought. The girl had suffered much, from the loss of her family to being sold into servitude and likely abuse as well. How would she react to such an inquiry?

"I will pray about it."

Thomas grunted.

Betsy closed her eyes, and in her heart, beseeched the Lord long into the night for His wisdom and guidance.

The crash of a metal pot lid awoke Gwen the next morning. She rubbed at her grainy eyelids and coughed against the pasty dryness of her mouth. Owen's cradle sat empty at the foot of her pallet. She pushed herself to her knees with a groan. Brilliant sunshine filtered through the patched curtain.

How long had she slept?

Wrapped in one of Betsy's old dressing gowns, she opened the door to the kitchen. Cinnamon from the porridge scented the room. Owen sat on Thomas's lap, slapping at an almost empty bowl with a spoon.

Betsy straightened from the fireplace and shot a look at Thomas, who stood.

"I best be on my way." He handed Owen to Betsy before pulling on his heavy coat.

Gwen remained in the doorway to her room until the outside door shut behind him. No greeting? Not from Betsy either. A cold weight pressed against her chest. She stepped into the kitchen.

"Good morning."

"Good morning. Did thee sleep well?"

"Nay."

"I feared thee were ill. If not in body, at least in spirit." Betsy's wrinkles creased deeper in her cheeks. "'Twas so upsetting for Jonas to come here as he did."

"Aye." Gwen sank onto a chair. Owen wiggled until Betsy put him down and he toddled, holding onto the other chairs until he reached her. His sloppy grin loosened the coldness in her chest.

Betsy pulled another chair near Gwen, poured two cups of tea, and sat facing her. "I would speak of this man, if thee will allow it."

Gwen swallowed. The earnest face in front of her radiated love and worry. She couldn't avoid the subject any longer. It wasn't fair to this woman who cared so much. But how much could she tell her without endangering her oath and losing Owen? Gwen sipped the tea and let the hot brew wash away the last of her sleepiness.

Betsy cleared her throat. "I can think of no delicate way to ask such a question. Pray forgive me if I give offense." She fiddled with the edge of her apron. "Is Jonas the father of our Owen?"

Gwen pressed a hand to her collarbone. She knew they all suspected this, but to hear the words still hurt. Of course they believed it. And why would they not? Owen resembled his uncle enough to raise the question. Her mind clawed for the best way to deny it without revealing too much. Her gaze darted to the door, then to Owen, then back to Betsy before she settled on the truth.

In this, at least, she would not lie.

"He is not. Owen's father is a ship captain in the employ of Mr. Whiteford."

Betsy sagged against the back of her chair. "Then why does thee fear him so?"

"'Twasn't easy to stay out of Jonas's way when I lived with the Whitefords. Cook helped me. She moved me into her own sleeping room. She devised ways for me to avoid him almost from the start. He would corner me in the hall and reach for me." Gwen closed her eyes and rubbed her hands up and down her arms. "Cook protected me from him."

"Bless her."

A hush fell over the kitchen. Owen sat motionless at her feet, starring at her with wide eyes. Gratitude filled her that he couldn't understand what she'd said.

"I do not wish for Owen to know of this."

"Of course. We shall never speak of it again. It pains me that I asked thee now."

"Nay. You have every right to know." Gwen took Betsy's hands and squeezed. "I'm glad I told you. You and Thomas deserve the truth. Always." Her voice broke on the last word as guilt twisted inside her like a writhing serpent.

But she'd given as much truth as she could without breaking her oath.

March 1800

Betsy wiped condensation from the window with a towel. The men filed in through the fort's gate, coming home from the mill after a full day of work. They trudged across the parade ground to the single men's barracks. Micah was not among them. Again. Betsy had hoped, the way he and Gwen had huddled together on the porch after Jonas left, that they'd patched things up between them.

Where had that young man gone?

She studied Gwen, who was hunched over her sewing, stitching yet another shirt for Owen. The boy grew overnight, it seemed. At the first thump of Thomas's boots on the porch, Gwen jerked upright, her eyes fixed on the door. When Thomas entered, Gwen's shoulders drooped and she bent over her stitching again.

Betsy shook her head and patted her husband's shoulder as he walked by. He quirked an eyebrow, and she shrugged. It had been the same for weeks. If Micah didn't return soon, she feared Gwen might wither away.

"'Tis good to be home." Thomas hung his coat and smothered a yawn.

"Thee are late this evening." Betsy knelt beside the hearth and scooted the Dutch oven further from the coals. She lifted the lid to expose golden-brown biscuits wreathed in a buttery scented steam.

Thomas leaned over her shoulder and sniffed. His stomach rumbled. "And hungry as a bear in spring." He patted his belly.

"Gwen?" Betsy swung the stew kettle away from the heat.

The girl didn't answer. She stared out the window, the material limp on her hands, her head tilted to one side.

"Has thee discovered his whereabouts?" Betsy whispered to Thomas.

"If I had, would I have not said as much already?" He tipped his chin toward Gwen.

"Indeed." Betsy patted his arm. "Why did he leave in such a hurry? And without a word to us."

"To be fair, he told Zachary he was leaving."

"But of where or why he gave no clue." Betsy kept her voice low, but Gwen wasn't listening. They could shout and dance around the table, and she would pay them no attention.

Owen babbled from the bedroom, and Gwen headed that direction. For all her melancholy, nobody could accuse Gwen of being neglectful of her child.

She returned to the kitchen with Owen on her hip.

"There's my boy." Thomas held his hands out, and Owen squealed, his pudgy legs pumping.

Gwen handed him over to Thomas. Her wan smile twisted Betsy's heart.

Where was that Micah?

They sat and bowed their heads for the silent prayer. Betsy beseeched the Lord for Micah's swift and safe return.

And then she would give that young man a piece of her mind.

Thomas cleared his throat, and Betsy pushed his bowl of stew across the table. "Mind his hands. 'Tis hot."

"Indeed?" He arched a brow.

Betsy shifted on her chair. "What kept thee out so late this evening, thee and the others from the mill?" She passed him a biscuit before setting the plate within Gwen's reach. Not that the girl even looked at it.

"We stayed to finish the last order we intend to work on."

"What?" Gwen's eyes widened.

"Our time here is almost finished. The roads are dry, and we shall be heading west soon. 'Tis time to ready our wagons, gather our stores, and pack our belongings for the trip. I expect to leave within the week."

Gwen's spoon clattered to the table. "But—"

"Micah knows we will pull out when the weather is right." Thomas paused to chew a mouthful of biscuit. "If he does not arrive before we leave, he should soon catch up."

Gwen pushed her untouched bowl of stew aside.

Betsy clenched her hands beneath the table. Where was that dratted man?

"We shall meet here tomorrow night to discuss a business venture with Jonas Whiteford." Thomas dropped that information like a cannon ball in the room.

At the news, Gwen blanched to the color of finely milled wheat flour.

"What sort of business? Why him? Why here?" The words tripped out before Betsy could think them through.

"He approached us about supplying the new settlement. He says he is expanding his father's business. We always worked well with Daniel Whiteford. He is an honest man and not a slaveholder."

"Yes, but—" Betsy glanced at Gwen and back to her husband.

"Amos's wife has been feeling poorly, and Joseph's house is too crowded with eight of them living there. We could have met at the pub, I suppose." He raked his fingers through his beard.

"'Tis fine. 'Twill bother me not," Gwen said.

But Betsy didn't believe a word of it.

The following evening, Gwen aimed another mouthful of mashed stew into Owen's open mouth. The boy grabbed for the spoon, but Gwen pulled it back. She didn't have time to clean him before the men arrived.

Betsy bustled around the kitchen. She wiped the already clean table one more time and straightened a couple of chairs that didn't need it. She glanced at the door and dabbed her brow.

"What flusters you so about this meeting?" Gwen's own calm surprised herself. If anyone should be anxious, it should be her. And yet, all she felt was numb, as if, with Micah gone, it didn't matter what Jonas might do.

"'Tis the very idea of him in my kitchen." She took another swipe at the dry sink with her rag. "We will stay in the bedroom. Thee need not be in contact with that... that man."

Boots scuffing against the porch brought Gwen to her feet. She set the bowl aside and settled her son on her hip. "I shall retire there with Owen now."

"Hurry. I shall join thee soon." Betsy faced the door, hands at her hips and elbows wide, a mother hen ready to protect her chicks.

Gwen left the door to the bedroom ajar so she could watch through the narrow opening. Thomas entered first, followed by several men she recognized from meetings. When Jonas's boots scuffed across the rough wood floor, Gwen rubbed her free palm down her apron and hugged Owen closer with her other hand.

Was she doing the right thing? What harm would come to the Quakers by trading with Mr. Whiteford? He was known for his honesty. If he weren't, Thomas wouldn't have done business with him in the past.

Jonas's eyes locked on hers through the narrow opening, and the numbness fled. She stepped away from the door, heart galloping, worry building.

What could she tell the Quaker leadership anyway? That Jonas was a scoundrel? That he tried to accost a young girl against her will? He had never succeeded. What was he truly guilty of?

Other than knowing her secret?

Spring had arrived, and the wagons would roll out in three days—with or without Micah—leaving the decaying fort behind. The Quakers would need supplies brought to their new settlement. Whiteford and Son could deliver those supplies. It was as simple as that.

There was no reason to oppose Jonas in a business venture.

She kissed Owen's brow.

And every reason not to.

She cuddled her sleepy son. Jonas wouldn't try to corner her anymore. He wanted the business—the money—more than he wanted her. Any attempt to harm her, and the Quakers would turn their backs on him for good.

Yet if he revealed her secret, they might turn their backs on Owen and her as well.

Betsy slipped through the doorway and left it ajar. She pulled a chair behind the door and sat with her ear next to the opening, out of the men's line of vision.

Owen drifted to sleep, and Gwen placed him in his cradle before kneeling on the floor next to Betsy's chair. Some of the men, probably those facing away from the door, they could not hear clearly. Thomas they heard the best, as he asked many questions about rates, guarantees, and time schedules.

After an hour, Gwen shook her head and settled onto her pallet.

"Business discussions and nothing more." Betsy yawned and stretched her arms in front of her, flexing her shoulders. "The men will do what is best for the whole community."

"'Tis not like they are accepting Jonas as one of them."

"Certainly not. Nor would they. The very idea." Betsy folded her arms and nodded at the door. "Thomas is not taken in by the likes of him."

"But he would do business with him?"

"I believe so. Not because of Jonas, but because of his father. And Thomas knows about…"

"About what?"

"I spoke to Thomas regarding what thee shared with me." Betsy's eyes glimmered in the room grown dark with evening's shadows. "About Owen's father."

"'Tis good that he knows." Gwen swallowed past a lump in her throat. Thomas wouldn't view Jonas as a threat to Owen, knowing that.

"My husband would have no dealings with a man who had… done such a thing."

Jonas hadn't molested her. She'd told the truth about that.

And after all, what harm could come from Jonas trading with the Friends?

Gwen loosened the shawl around her shoulders and drew in a long breath. The damp evening air carried a hint of green waiting to burst forth. The silhouettes of the new wagons bordered the west side of the crumbing palisade.

She pressed her hand against her chest.

Where was Micah? Would the Quakers reconsider and wait for his return?

Nay. Thomas had been very clear on that issue. With roads dry enough to travel, the time to leave was at hand. It would be a shorter trip, and they could arrive at their new home in plenty of time for late spring planting if they got moving. The day had seen a flurry of activity, people packing their belongings and provisions into the smaller wagons. Cobb had been everywhere, his weasel eyes inspecting each barrel and crate. He hounded the Quakers to leave more behind when they had only the basic necessities to begin with. At the thought of his voice, she shivered and pulled the shawl tighter.

She and Betsy planned to load what they could into Micah's wagon. He had to return. She raised her chin and pressed her lips into a firm line. If he didn't, she'd hitch Sassy and Hap herself and drive his wagon. Zachary said Micah had bought a riding horse in Brownsville. He'd follow them.

He had to.

A cow lowed, and Gwen turned toward the stable. Her heart hung as heavy as that cow's sorrowful note. She kept busy with Owen during the day, as well as helping Betsy prepare their wagon, but as the shadows gathered, a comforting visit with Tiny drew her to the stable. The fuzzy white face greeted her over the wooden gate. Gwen climbed into the stall and wrapped her arms around the goat's scrawny neck.

"I miss him, Tiny." The goat nibbled on the tie of her bonnet. "You are the only one I can talk to. I know there can be nothing between Micah and me, but..." The hope she shouldn't harbor refused to let go. She sank onto the straw and scratched Tiny's chest. The goat's eyelids half closed as she leaned into Gwen's shoulder. Gwen let her head rest back against the rough wooden wall. The rhythmic munching of cattle and the comforting smell of the stable lulled Gwen into a semi-doze.

"What took you so long?"

The harsh whisper cut across the peace of the stall. Gwen's eyes flew open, and every muscle in her body tensed. Was that Cobb?

"It would hardly do for me to be spotted entering the fort, now would it?" another man answered.

The hair on the back of her neck prickled to attention. Jonas? What was he doing there? She turned her head, pressing her ear closer to a weathered crack in the board behind her.

"Are those wagons loaded?"

It was Jonas all right. She winced at the arrogance in his voice.

"Almost. These Bible-thumpers will only move so fast." The man hawked and spat. That was Cobb, no doubt about it.

"Keep after them. And get them to toss more of their junk. The more they leave behind, the more we can sell to them later."

Gwen stifled a gasp with her fingers. How dare he?

"I ain't worryin' about that. We can make more money on them darkies than we could ever make sellin' pots and pans."

Darkies?

"You best start worrying about it." A soft grunt followed, like someone had been poked in the chest. "I fully intend to make money on both. I have a particular bone to pick with that darkie they call Zachary. He shall be the first one we capture and haul back to Carolina. Where he belongs."

Gwen bit her hand to stop the protest that leaped to her throat. Jonas wanted to take Zachary away? She held her breath, straining to hear every word, wishing she could see the men through the crack.

"'Twould be real easy to grab him here, before we leave. Shorter trek back to Carolina. There be plenty of other darkies runnin' loose in Ohio. Runaways is flockin' up there like geese in spring." Cobb spat again. "We ain't goin' to be short of cargo for our return trips."

"Don't be an impatient fool. We must establish Whiteford and Son as their sole supplier. The price of slaves will increase when the government stops us from importing them from overseas. 'Tis only a matter of time before they pass that law."

They were planning to take Zachary back to Carolina and sell him as a slave? Gwen's heartbeat roared in her ears.

"They's fetchin' a fine price now."

"You have been paid to see us to Ohio." Jonas's voice dropped to a sneer. "I shall take care of the rest."

"You better. Or I aim to do it myself."

The barn siding thumped against her back; the grunt of whoever had hit the other side was startlingly loud. Gwen dropped flat on the straw, her heart slamming against her ribs.

"Don't mess with me, Cobb." Jonas was so close she could hear his ragged breaths. "After the meeting tomorrow night, I will have a contract in hand. Keep your mouth shut and do exactly what I said."

Fear spiked through Gwen like a living thing.

Chapter 27

G WEN RUBBED HER HAND over her face, then grabbed a bowl off the table. She ladled out the breakfast porridge with a plop and yawned. The steamy tang of cinnamon did little to clear the tangled web of her thoughts that morning. The words of Jonas and Cobb had jumbled and chased themselves around her mind all night, leaving questions she couldn't answer.

What should she do? Could she expose those two without exposing herself? And what about Zachary? He'd done so much for her, like the older brother she'd never had. How could she turn her back on him? But how could she expose Jonas and Cobb while still protecting Owen?

The toddler squealed, and she jumped.

Betsy reached and steadied the bowl in Gwen's hands. "Are thee ill? Thee are so pale this morning."

The back of Betsy's hand pressed against Gwen's brow. Gwen closed her eyes and leaned into its coolness, picking up a faint whiff of lavender.

Was she ill? Was this all some delusion brought on by a sickness? If only it could be. But white hairs clung to her skirt. Tiny's hairs. The goat was shedding her shaggy winter covering, and Gwen's skirt was proof enough last night had been no delusion.

"I did not sleep well."

"Thee were so quiet last evening—" Boot heels scuffed on the porch steps and drew Betsy's attention. "Who could that be?"

"I shall see." Thomas opened the door. "Micah!"

Thomas swung the door wide, and Betsy rushed to his side.

Gwen stood rooted to the floor beside the hearth.

Shadows bruised the skin below Micah's eyes, and no smile eased the firm slash of his mouth. Not even when his eyes locked with hers. He didn't look happy to have returned to them. Had he come to say a final farewell? She swallowed against the pain of that thought.

"Where have thee been?" Betsy reached for his coat and hung it on a peg. "Come, join us. We are just sitting down to eat. Another bowl, Gwen."

"Sit, before thee fall off thy feet." Thomas pressed Micah into a chair. "We will pray, and then hear thy tale."

Gwen grabbed another bowl from the shelf and set maple syrup and butter on the table. The silent prayer was mercifully short. She couldn't gather her thoughts enough to pray, anyway. She had to concentrate to remember to breathe.

"Thee looks worn," Thomas said.

"Indeed. Worn is how I feel." Micah stared at the bowl in front of him for a moment. "I went to Pittsburgh."

Gwen pressed her hands to her cheeks, but she lowered them when Micah's eyes met hers. Her tears welled when he shook his head.

"I'm so sorry, Gwen. Faye was not there."

"Did thee search the whole city, then?" Thomas asked.

"I found the house of Martha McClure the very day I arrived, a stately home and well cared for. The place was vacant except for an elderly couple left to manage it. Their mistress is abroad and has been gone for more than a year and a half. They have no idea when she may return."

"Did they know of Faye?" Betsy grasped Gwen's hand and squeezed.

"Indeed. The couple knew her by name. She is with their mistress abroad."

A single sob worked its way from the depths of Gwen's heart.

Gone.

An ocean separated her from her sister. Faye was lost to her. Again. She wrenched herself from the chair and fled out the door. Cold and damp, the morning air swept the last of her scattered thoughts away.

The clarity jarred her to her soul. Everything was lost to her. Her parents, her brothers, and even Faye. Owen babbled in the kitchen behind her.

He was all she had.

She clenched her hands together and pressed them under her chin. She could not lose him. Not ever.

She could not risk exposing Jonas and Cobb.

Betsy slid a crate under the seat of Micah's wagon. She sat back on her heels as Gwen approached with another. Her pale countenance, slow steps, bowed head, and rounded shoulders all tugged on Betsy's heart.

Micah's return that morning—not his return, but his sorrowful news—had broken something in that girl. Something Betsy feared would be very hard to mend. Gwen had pulled back into herself, starting with Micah's abrupt absence. She was almost the same insecure, silent Gwen who had first come to live with them. Betsy grieved the loss of the more confident, lighthearted Gwen who had begun to emerge.

Betsy closed her eyes and knocked at heaven's door, praying that the Father would mend the broken heart of the girl she loved so much.

As Gwen pushed the last crate onto Micah's new wagon, Betsy offered a tender smile, but Gwen lacked the strength to summon the gesture in return. She pushed the crate as far forward as she could reach. The new wood, still green enough to be sticky, caught at her apron. She tugged to free it.

"Whoa." Micah pulled Sassy and Hap to a halt beside her. "I cannot thank thee enough for readying my wagon." His words were directed at both of them, but his gaze settled on Gwen.

"'Tis the least we could do." Betsy climbed down, and Micah hurried to steady her. "Thee must know how much we appreciate thy journey on Gwen's behalf."

He nodded. "Yet it saddens me to bring such news."

"Sad, indeed. But not hopeless."

Gwen whipped around to face Betsy. What was she saying?

"God has not answered our prayers to reunite Gwen and Faye with a no. He has simply made known that now is not the time." Betsy dusted off her dress and tidied her bonnet. "I have a few things left to pack before tomorrow. I shall leave thee both to finish here."

Gwen's mouth hung open as the older woman walked away.

"She is wise indeed." Micah removed his hat and wiped his forehead.

"A no or a not yet, 'tis much the same. Either way, I have no sister."

"I'm so sorry—"

"Nay, 'tis I who am sorry. I have not thanked you for your trouble on my behalf. It could not have been an easy thing, to travel there and back so quickly." She met his intense stare. "I do thank you, Micah."

He mangled the hat in his hands. "Come to town with me?"

"What?"

"I must go to the mercantile, and I would speak with thee. Please come?"

Gwen glanced toward the officer's house where Betsy shut the door behind her. Owen was well cared for with both her and Thomas. She had no excuse to refuse. She fidgeted with the ends of her shawl. "Aye."

A smile lit Micah's face. He pulled his team around and backed them to the wagon. While he secured the harnesses, Gwen climbed aboard. He slid onto the seat next to her until their shoulders touched. She had no room to move away on the smaller wagon's narrow seat.

He braced his boots against the kickboard and chirped to the horses. Fresh from their winter rest, the animals started out at a lively trot.

Micah cleared his throat and fingered the reins in his hands. "I had a lot of time to think while on my journey."

Each brush of his shoulder against hers left her mouth a bit more dry. Too dry for words, even if she could think of something to say.

"I suppose thee wondered at my leaving as I did."

From the corner of her eye, she caught his glance but didn't turn her head. Her heart tripped over itself in her chest.

"When Jonas came that evening, and I saw how much it upset thee, I knew I had to do something. I am ashamed to admit that my first thought was to go after him and, well, I know not what I would have done. Friends do not fight." He hissed those last words through clenched teeth.

Gwen swallowed and nodded.

"So I thought if I could find thy sister, if I could speak with her and bring thee back news—" He lifted one shoulder and let it drop. "I know not what it would have accomplished. I lack the money to have bought her indenture."

"You would have done that? For me?"

"Indeed. That and more were it within my power." His voice dropped to a velvet murmur. "Gwen—"

She raised her hand, palm toward him, and drew a deep breath. She wasn't ready to hear what she feared he might say next. Better to stay on the subject of her sister. "Knowing she was safe and well... 'twould have been a comfort."

"But the servants said she was."

"A year and a half ago. Who knows where she is or how she fares now?"

"I have the address in Pittsburgh. Thee can write to her."

Gwen turned her face away. Her heart sank until she felt its weight on her stomach. "Nay."

"But surely, when she returns and finds the letter—"

"I cannot write. I never learned." Tears crackled in her voice.

"Then I will write the letter for thee. Whatever thee wishes it to say." The pleading note in his voice drew her gaze to meet his. At the softening of his blue eyes, a tear slipped down her cheek.

"Faye cannot read, either."

"She can find someone to read it to her. If word of her means so much to thee, 'twould surely mean as much to her."

"Aye. I suppose so."

"We can purchase paper at the mercantile and send the letter today, before we leave. It will await her return."

Gwen placed her hand on his gloved fingers holding the reins. "How can I thank you for your kindness?" As the words slipped from her lips, the softness of his eyes sparked into blue fire. She snatched her hand back.

"Thee owes me nothing. As thee will not allow me to state why, suffice it to say that I would see thee happy in any way within my power."

Gwen turned to face forward. She pressed against the wood backrest. Micah would do anything to see her happy, but only because he didn't know the truth.

She harbored not one, but two secrets of which she could not speak.

True to his word, Micah purchased paper and an envelope at the mercantile and borrowed a quill and ink from the clerk. They huddled together at the checkerboard table and labored over exactly what to say. When finished, they walked to the post office, where Micah purchased the required stamp and a bit of wax to seal the envelope. Gwen's hand trembled as she dropped the letter into the slot on the counter.

Restless after their return to the fort, Gwen decided on a last walk to the river. Owen's chubby legs kicked on both sides of Gwen's hip. The toddler stretched his arms toward the water and babbled a steady stream of nonsense. A wan smile was the best Gwen could muster for her son's enthusiasm. She lowered the boy to his feet and matched his chugging gait to the river. At the water's edge, she steadied him. He pulled at her fingers which formed a restraining barrier across his chest.

"Nay, my love. 'Tis too cold splash around. Look." She pointed to the ripples flashing by. "It moves swiftly this time of year. 'Twould wash a wee lad like you away." Her heart twisted at the thought.

Owen scooped up a muddy fistful of pebbles and flung them. He squealed at the splash and pointed before grabbing another fistful and repeating the process. Joy radiated from his face.

"Seems I'm not the only one enjoying a last stroll along the river." Zachary stopped beside them.

Gwen tucked her chin to her chest, unable to look at him. Owen strained toward the man he knew as a friend, and Gwen sucked in a deep breath. She released her son into the strong, dark hands that opened for him.

Hands that had held so much kindness.

She stood and cast a glance at Zachary. His smile widened when their gazes met, his eyes warm with friendship. She pressed her hand to her stomach and turned her face to the river. Of all the Quakers, aside from Thomas and Betsy and Micah, Zachary had been the most steadfast friend to her. Could she turn her back on him now?

Owen squealed and pointed to a branch twirling in the current, and Zachary explained to the boy what it was and what it meant.

If Jonas and Cobb had their way, the gentle man beside her would be kidnapped and sold back into slavery. She squeezed her eyes shut.

To expose those men, she must forfeit her claim to Owen. She must turn her back on her son. No matter who birthed him as a babe, he was now and would forever be her son, just as Evie had told her.

He is your son. You be proud of him!

"He is a fine boy. Thee are blessed to have him." Zachary handed the toddler back to Gwen. "Micah told me about thy sister." He touched her shoulder. "Thee have always a place here, among the Friends. We might not be family by birth, but we would be thy family if thee chooses. And I still hope thee will." With a quick ruffle of Owen's downy locks, he left them there on the banks of the Monongahela.

Not by birth, but by choice. She stared into the wide blue eyes of her son. Just like Owen was hers—also not by birth—Zachary was offering her acceptance into the family of Quakers, into the family of God. Had she missed her opportunity to be truly a part of their world? Did she even have a choice anymore?

Or would Jonas control her forever?

Gwen sank to the ground and ignored the dampness soaking into her knees. Head bowed, she opened her heart in a silent prayer, thankful for the softness of her sweet son as he climbed into her lap. How could she do anything that would endanger him? What would become of him if she were hauled back to fulfill her indenture? Who would raise him? Love him? Provide for his every need? The answer came like a gentle whisper brushed against her heart.

God would.

They weren't words in the spoken sense, but she heard them all the same. Could she trust Him?

She flicked a glance at the sky and rose. Half running and half walking, Owen bouncing on her hip, she made her way to Faith's house. Faith was pinning a towel to a line strung across the porch as Gwen approached.

"Is something wrong?" Faith looked past Gwen and then back at her.

"Aye. I must go to the meeting this evening. Would you watch Owen for me?"

"Indeed." Faith's grin spread. "'Twill please Mary to no end. She will help me watch him. She is anxious about leaving tomorrow and has fair driven me to distraction with her questions. Something to do will suit her."

Gwen set Owen on the porch as little Mary appeared at the front door. With two fingers stuck in his mouth, his other hand held firmly by Mary, he toddled after her into the house. Gwen balled her hands into fists to keep from snatching him back.

"Thank you."

"Anytime. Should I mention that I hope thee has made an important decision?" Faith's eyes glinted with expectation.

"Aye. I have."

But not the one Faith hoped for.

Chapter 28

G WEN STOPPED AT THE bottom step of the large central building inside the fort, the Quaker's makeshift meetinghouse. People milled around the entrance and more filled the benches inside. She tucked errant strands of hair under her bonnet and smoothed her apron.

Maybe they would turn Jonas down, and then her problems would be solved. Without the supply contract, he would have no reason to stay near the Quakers or Zachary, much less her and Owen. She pressed her hand against her stomach. Surely the Quakers knew they couldn't trust a man like Jonas, no matter who his father was. Surely they would turn down his offer.

But why would they? Hadn't she herself been the one to tell Thomas that Jonas was not a threat? Hadn't she spent the past weeks supporting him by her silence?

Gwen slipped into the meetinghouse. A dank mustiness hung strong in the air despite every window open. The crush of bodies, her turbulent emotions, and the smell tormented her queasy stomach. She eased her way to the women's side of the room and sat beside Betsy.

"Gwen." Betsy scooted to make more room. "Thee are joining us for this meeting?"

"Aye."

"Where is Owen?"

"With Faith."

"Why? Are thee...? Has thee decided to...?"

Thomas called the meeting to order, saving Gwen from having to answer Betsy's half-formed questions. She did her best to tamp down the guilt that had assaulted her from the earnest hope on her friend's face. She didn't need the guilt of raising Betsy's hopes that she was here to join the Quakers. She carried more than enough guilt already.

She sat straight on the bench, glad that Faith had Owen. She couldn't have managed the wiggling youngster and her nerves.

Minutes ticked by as those assembled dealt with the mundane issues regarding the start of their journey the following day. Then Thomas asked if anyone wished to address those assembled. His glance touched Gwen before moving on across the room. Gwen kept her face blank and ignored Betsy's throat clearing.

"As thee are already aware, we have a business offer proposed by Jonas Whiteford." Thomas nodded toward the door where Jonas leaned against the wall. "He has made us an offer. He and his father desire a business contract with our new settlement. They would be our exclusive mercantile suppliers for a term of five years. In return, they would guarantee a discount on goods of five percent."

A man in the back row stood. "Will they guarantee safe delivery?"

"Indeed," Thomas said. "They are retaining Cobb as wagonmaster to be sure the goods arrive in a timely fashion. Cobb knows the rivers and trails, and his experience with the natives will be helpful."

Betsy snorted softly.

At least someone wasn't taken in by Jonas and Cobb. Hopefully, there were enough like Betsy seated among those gathered.

Another man stood closer to the front. "Why should we limit ourselves to one company for our goods? How do we know they will not hike the rates to offset that five percent?"

"'Tis a fair question. Jonas can answer that himself." Thomas gestured to Jonas and stepped to the side.

Jonas sauntered to the front. He passed Thomas and puffed out his chest. "My father and I are well-known and our company is well-established. We have nothing to fear from competition." The smirk on his face twisted Gwen's stomach a notch tighter. "But there are risks involved in supplying the frontier. Larger wagon trains with more guards are needed to ensure the safety of both your goods and our employees. To run a smaller train would not be cost-effective. Being your sole supplier means we shall have the volume to fill the larger train and thus keep our costs lower." He waved a hand as if erasing the questioner's worries. "Any honest supplier would tell you the same."

The man in the back stood again. "Five years is a long contract for a country that is growing as fast as this one."

"Indeed, it is," Jonas replied with a tilt of his head toward the speaker. "But my father and I are committed to helping your community grow and thrive for the duration." The smugness of his words grated on Gwen's frazzled nerves.

There was a general murmuring from the crowd, especially on the men's side of the room. A small boy wiggled on the bench beside his father. He couldn't be more than four years old. Would Owen be wiggling on a bench like that in a few years?

Would she be there to witness it if he did?

If she held her silence?

She searched the crowd for Micah and Zachary. Both men wore grim faces. They weren't taken in by Jonas or his scheme. Gwen's fingernails bit into the wood of her bench seat.

Thomas raised both hands over his head. "If there is no other discussion, let us have the vote."

Gwen held her breath. Micah glanced at her from across the room, and her heart sank at the smallest shake of his head. Zachary stared at the floor.

The proposal couldn't pass. They had to vote it down. Every muscle tightened and tingled under her skin.

Hope crashed around her feet as the "ayes" rang out through the room. Micah's and Zachary's voices joined the "nays," but to no avail.

"Well, that settles it then," Betsy muttered beside Gwen.

She told herself to speak but couldn't form the words.

The men stood and shuffled around, some stopping to speak with those close by, others moving toward the door. The women around her chattered about their readiness, or lack of readiness, for the trip ahead.

The Quaker meeting was over. They were leaving the building. She had to speak. It was her last chance.

"Wait!" Gwen's voice rose in a hollow wail. The various responses throughout the room were muted by her thundering heart. She pushed to her feet and took three shaky steps toward the front. "Wait. You cannot do this. You know not..."

The buzz in the room hushed. The people turned to stare at her.

"What is this?" Thomas faced Gwen.

She stumbled on wooden legs to his side and turned to the crowd. The faces before her reflected curiosity, concern, and annoyance.

Jonas stood next to the door. His glare was nothing short of poison. Her knees trembled, and she clutched Thomas's sleeve.

Micah's piercing blue eyes lent her strength from across the room. She gritted her teeth and sucked in a deep breath. She pointed a shaking finger at Jonas. "He offers you a contract too good to be true—because that is exactly what it is. I overheard him speaking with Cobb two nights back." She clamped her hand over her mouth and fought down tears.

"This woman is talking crazy." Jonas stepped forward. "She is obviously out of her head. Cobb stays in town at night, not in the fort." He turned to the crowd and spread his hands wide. "Has anyone seen him?"

There were many in the crowd shaking their heads. Gwen gulped a lungful of air.

"He was here. He was behind the stable. I know because I was there with Tiny. I often visit her in the evenings." She looked at Thomas.

"Indeed," he said. "Gwen tends to her goat most evenings."

"Cobb and Jonas were there behind the stable. I heard them talking."

"This woman lies." Jonas took another step toward her, his face a patchwork of angry red blotches. When Thomas raised a hand in his direction, Jonas stopped moving but continued to speak, his voice rising in tone and volume. "She is a liar and has been from the start. She has lied to every one of you."

Gwen sank until the rough wood of the plank flooring bit into her knees.

"You see? She is guilty. She cannot deny it." Jonas crossed his arms over his chest. "She has lied to you, and now she is lying about me. This woman is not to be trusted."

Betsy, her face gray and drawn, rushed forward and knelt beside Gwen. "What is this he says?"

Gwen's heart cracked and broke. Tears gushed, but she rose and squared her shoulders. Betsy stood alongside her, lending a comforting strength. Gwen lifted her chin and sought out Micah, whose hands were balled into fists at his sides.

Zachary had a hand on his shoulder and, even from the front of the room, it was obvious how deeply those ebony fingers dug into Micah's coat.

"Jonas is right. I have lied to you. I have lied to all of you. But I'm not lying now." She jabbed a finger at Jonas. "I heard that man and Cobb plot not only to supply this community with trade goods, but to also"—she drew in a shuddering breath—"capture and force any free Negroes in the territory back to North Carolina to be sold as slaves."

The collective gasp pulsed through the room.

"She is crazy!" Jonas backed two steps closer to the door.

"She is not!" Micah pushed his way through the crowd toward Jonas, dragging Zachary in his wake.

"I heard him and Cobb." Strength flooded Gwen, and she shouted above the clamor that filled the room. "They said they could make more money selling slaves then they would ever make on the goods. They mentioned Zachary by name. They planned to kidnap him."

Bedlam broke out in the building. Jonas dashed for the door, but Micah got there at the same time and slammed into him. The two men fell through the opening with several others on their heels.

Betsy hugged Gwen, and Thomas clasped a hand on her shoulder.

"I have lied to you. I'm so sorry."

Betsy hugged her tighter. "What is this lie? We do not understand."

"Come." Thomas shepherded them to the front corner of the building farthest from the door, shielding them from the crowd with his body. He looked over his shoulder. "The Friends are departing. Now, tell us what this is all about."

"Owen is not my son." Her whisper ended in a sob.

Thomas grunted as if someone punched him.

"Not thy son?" Betsy's bewildered cry tore another section from Gwen's heart. "How can this be?"

The room grew eerily quiet, the scuffling and voices outside muted as someone closed the door. Gwen swallowed another sob at the shock on Betsy's face, so distressed she feared the older woman may collapse.

"My mistress, Mr. Whiteford's daughter, is Owen's mother. He offered me my freedom in return for an oath that I would claim the boy as my own and never tell another soul the truth. I signed the oath." She bowed her head.

Thomas's arm crushed around her, and she was pulled against his side. "What sort of a man gives away his own grandson? Father in heaven. What sort of a man did I almost sign a contract with?"

"Mr. Whiteford will come after me."

"He will not take thee from us, Gwen Morgan. Thee belong with us now. Not as a servant, but as a daughter. Daniel Whiteford cannot change that." Thomas pressed a kiss on the top of her head.

Oh, how she wanted to believe that. "But I signed an oath. I agreed to keep his secret and if I ever broke the oath, I agreed to fulfill my indenture to Mr. Whiteford with double the years I owed him."

"'Twas an unholy oath, and one the Friends will not recognize."

Gwen shook her head, unable to believe what he said.

"Thomas is telling thee the truth." Betsy cupped Gwen's face between her hands. "We would never turn thee over to such a man as that."

"Thee are safe here with us. Thee and thy son. And mark my words, Owen is thy son." Thomas's words came out in a fierce whisper.

He is your son. You be proud of him!

Thomas's breath half-whistled through his teeth. "That man may have given away his grandson, but he shall not take mine from me."

"So much makes sense." Color had returned to Betsy's cheeks. "Now I understand. Oh, that thee could have trusted us with this secret sooner."

"I know. Now 'tis too late."

"Nonsense." Tears shimmered in Betsy's eyes, but she smiled. "Nothing is too late. God's timing is always perfect."

"There is nothing of God in what I did."

"My darling Gwen. What a man—even Daniel Whiteford—means for evil, God in His loving wisdom can use for good." Betsy's face glowed. "He brought thee to us, and with us, thee will stay."

"But I have deceived you."

"Indeed. Thee will need to confess and ask for forgiveness at the next meeting. And correct me if I'm mistaken, but will that not clear the path for thee to join our group of Friends?"

"You would still have me?"

"Have thee not learned by now that we do not expect perfection this side of heaven? God forgives sins if one repents. Can we do any less?"

The kindness in Betsy's eyes, the love in her voice, and the gentle shake Thomas gave Gwen's shoulder cast a binding net over the brokenness of Gwen's heart. Hope, radiant like an August sun, seeped into the cracks and filled her with joy. More tears flowed until she couldn't see at all. Worry and guilt left with each tear, washing her clean.

Thomas gave her shoulder one last squeeze and then headed toward the door.

Gwen mopped her face with a handkerchief Betsy pressed into her hand. They were alone in the makeshift meetinghouse.

Betsy draped her arm over Gwen's shoulders. "Come, daughter. Let us go home."

Gwen rose when the first wispy fingers of dawn clutched the horizon, thankful for the morning after a night of tossing and turning. Owen slept in his cradle, one hand balled under his cheek. The thumb of his other hand rested between relaxed lips until he gave a wee jerk and latched onto it, suckling quietly. Maternal love surged through her, stirring a sweet ache in her heart with its intensity. There was nothing she wouldn't do for Owen. He was worth whatever price she had to pay.

She tiptoed into the kitchen and stirred the fire to life, then put together a simple breakfast of porridge before waiting for Thomas and Betsy to awaken.

Would the Quakers leave that day as planned? Who would guide them now? Not Cobb, not after last night.

Would they still want to take her with them, or had they changed their minds?

She paced from the door to the hearth and back again. She wiped her hands on her apron. With one more glance at her sleeping son, she grabbed the milk bucket and slipped her shawl over her shoulders. She needed something to do and someone to talk to—even if it was only Tiny.

She backed out the kitchen door and eased it shut, then whirled and almost ran into Zachary. He steadied her for a moment with his hands on her elbows. No smile lit his face, and his eyes were outlined by darker circles and deeper wrinkles then Gwen had seen before. He dragged his hat off and rubbed his fingers through his hair.

How he must despise her for nearly letting him be captured by those men.

She gripped the bucket's handle hard enough to leave its imprint in her palms. She'd known she'd have to face him at some point, but she hadn't thought about what to say. She blurted out what laid so heavy on her heart. "I'm so sorry."

"Sorry? Whatever for?"

"I almost did not... I thought... If I had not..."

He raised his hand, and she stopped babbling. "Thomas told us about the oath."

"He did?"

"That was a wicked thing Daniel Whiteford made thee sign. And yet in spite of that, thee risked all to—" His voice choked off.

"How could I not? You have shown me every kindness. You brought the medicine that soothed Owen when he fell ill. You protected me from Jonas. You even fed Tiny from your own provisions when hay ran low aboard the ship."

"I did only what anyone would have done under the circumstances. But thee, dear Gwen, thee has saved my life."

She dropped her gaze to the bucket and eased her grip. "I almost did not."

"What changed thy mind?"

"I have lived a lie for almost a year now." She raised her chin and looked at him. "I could not let another lie put your life in danger and rule mine as well. Do you not see? 'Twas the lie that kept me from joining the Friends. 'Twas the lie that prevented me from... from being who God made me to be."

White teeth flashed, and a deep chuckle rumbled from Zachary. He tossed his hat in the air and caught it. "Praise God. What man means for evil—"

"God can use for good."

"Thank thee, Gwen Morgan, for what thee has done."

"Thank you, Zachary Brown, for being so gracious." Her gaze drifted toward the men's barracks. "I can only hope others will be half so understanding."

"About that." Zachary cleared his throat. "It may take some people longer than others."

Across the fort's parade ground, Micah exited the barracks. He glanced their way, and then pivoted in the other direction.

Her hopes sank as he stalked off.

Chapter 29

B ETSY SURVEYED THE KITCHEN fire glowing beneath a kettle of simmering water, and a pot of porridge steaming in front of that. Cinnamon teased her nose when she leaned over the pot. The peg that normally held Gwen's shawl was empty, and the milk bucket was gone. The girl was industrious early that morning. Last night's emotional confession and tears were, Betsy hoped, a sign of good things to come.

She yawned and tied her apron over her dress. She'd awoken when Thomas came to bed. He'd kissed her cheek and told her they'd talk in the morning. She touched her cheek. Hopefully he'd wake soon. His snoring, along with her curiosity, had robbed her of much of the night's sleep.

A thump followed by a howl had Betsy dashing for Gwen's bedroom. She stopped at the doorway and clutched the doorpost for support. Owen lay on the floor, his feet tangled in his blanket, which was caught on the side of his cradle. His face scrunched into a red mask at the sight of her, and he let loose another cry.

"What happened? What's going on?" Thomas charged into the bedroom in his nightshirt. His beard and hair fanned from his face like the sails of a windmill.

Owen's eyes rounded at the sight. His mouth opened before a hiccupy giggle replaced his cries.

Betsy smothered a giggle of her own.

"Little scamp." Thomas lifted the boy free from the tangled bedding. "Laugh at me, will thee?" He steadied Owen on his tiny feet.

The boy wobbled and pointed a finger at Thomas. "Pa-pa-pa-pa-pa."

"Grandpapa, that is right." Thomas crouched with his hands on his knees and beamed at the boy.

"He will hurt himself crawling out of that cradle." Betsy shook the kinks from the blanket and folded it before tucking it back in place.

"Nonsense. He will learn how to do it gracefully soon enough. A knot on the head is a good teacher."

Betsy snorted. There were easier ways to learn life's lessons.

Was that what had happened last night? Had Gwen's oath been a spiritual knot on the head? And had she learned the lesson she needed from it?

She scooped Owen into her arms. "Make thyself presentable for breakfast, husband, while I change this boy's wrappings and get him dressed. We slept later than we ought."

"The wagons shan't leave as early as we hoped today." Thomas yawned and stretched. "First, the issue of Jonas is to be dealt with."

"Then thee reached a decision last night?"

"We did. I shall tell thee when I'm *presentable* enough." He gave his beard a tug and returned to the bedroom, pulling the door shut behind him.

Betsy huffed and set about changing Owen's clothing. Infuriating man.

A smile graced her lips.

Gwen pushed the door shut and set the milk pail on the table.

Owen grinned around the wooden spoon he gnawed on, and Betsy turned from the fire. Thomas entered the room, buttoning the front of his waistcoat. All three stopped and stared at her.

"Good morning."

As though released by Gwen's words, Thomas and Betsy returned her greeting and resumed what they had been doing. Betsy ladled out breakfast, Thomas finished buttoning his waistcoat, and Owen banged his spoon on the table.

"Thee were up early and busy this morning," Betsy said.

"Aye. I could not sleep."

"'Twas a common malady last night, to be sure." Thomas tugged on the ends of his beard and shot a glance at Betsy.

"As if thee noticed amidst thy snores."

"I do not snore, wife."

Gwen chuckled. Everything felt normal for the first time since her mother's death. She slipped off her shawl and glanced out the window. She'd speak with Micah at the first opportunity. With Owen on her lap at the table, she bowed her head when Thomas and Betsy did.

Lord, grant me the courage to believe that everything will work out. And the strength to always do the right thing, no matter what.

Thomas cleared his throat to signal the end of their morning silent prayer.

"What was decided about Jonas?" Betsy asked before Thomas could lift his spoon.

Gwen took away the wooden spoon and handed the small feeding spoon to Owen, steadying him while he ate.

"We shall not be entering into any business dealings with him or his father."

"Certainly not." Betsy gave a sharp nod to punctuate her agreement.

"But the truth is that Jonas has broken no law."

"He meant to deceive us, to use us for his own gain." Betsy slapped her spoon on the table and pushed her bowl of porridge to the side. "How can this not be wrong?"

Thomas leaned back and tugged on his beard. He shot a glance at Gwen, and her heart twisted.

"I did the same thing." The words dried Gwen's mouth. She couldn't have swallowed if she'd had to.

She was no better than Jonas.

"Nonsense." Betsy's chin thrust forward. "Thee had Owen's best interest at heart. Thee did what thee felt must be done."

"Not at first." Gwen kept her focus on the table in front of her. She wanted to tell the whole truth, but she couldn't look at them. "At first, I wanted my freedom so that I could find Faye. I was already attached to Owen, that is true. But it was the promise of freedom that enticed me to sign the oath."

Thomas's hand settled over hers on the table. "We understand. 'Twas not something thee could turn down at that point. Thee had not been raised in the teachings of the Lord."

"It didn't occur to me that what I did was wrong, not at the start. I struck a bargain. I exchanged my word to guard Mr. Whiteford's secret in exchange for my freedom. It seemed—a business arrangement at the time."

"But thee soon learned differently," Betsy said.

"Aye. It did not seem right to lie to you, not after you took Owen and me into your home and treated us like family."

"'Twasn't right." Thomas's gruff voice held a trace of censure. "But we understand the position thee were in. And in the end, thee did the right thing. 'Tis what separates thy actions from those of Jonas." He cleared his throat. "Now, there is more thee must do."

Gwen raised her face to his. "I will do whatever it takes to make amends for my deception."

Thomas nodded. "Thee must confess before the Friends and ask forgiveness."

"Aye. This I will do at the next meeting."

"'Twould be best if thee do it this morning. There will be a meeting before the wagons roll."

So soon? No time to prepare, to think about what she'd say. Gwen closed her eyes for a moment and remembered the kindness on many of the faces of those who had assembled the night before. There was no reason to fear her confession. She swallowed. "Aye."

"And is Jonas allowed to walk away then?" Betsy's eyes blazed.

"I never said that, wife. I said he had broken no law."

Betsy looked from Thomas to Gwen and back again. "So what will be done with him?"

"That will be discussed at the meeting. For now, let us put this meal away and pack our remaining trunk into the wagon." Thomas dug into his porridge.

Gwen held her bowl while Owen smacked his lips on the spoon. He'd eaten most of the porridge, but she didn't mind. She wasn't hungry and wasn't sure anything would stay down if she swallowed it. She grabbed a rag and cleaned Owen's face and hands.

Thomas finished his breakfast and left to hitch Lonny and Lad. He'd bring the wagon around for loading while Betsy and Gwen washed and dried the dishes and kettles before stacking them in the trunk.

"Why must I confess before all the people?"

"Why?" Betsy's eyebrows rose.

"When those women gossiped about me..."

"Ah, the gossips. Thee remembers that the women dealt with them."

"Aye."

"'Twas a different situation. Not a smaller sin, as all sins are equal in the sight of God, but one that could be handled quietly. What they did was wrong, but their sin was against thee alone, not against the whole."

That made sense. Nobody but her had heard those women gossiping. And even she didn't know who they were. She'd wronged everyone, but especially Thomas and Betsy.

And Micah.

"I had hoped Owen would never know the truth of his parents."

"Do not fear the truth, Gwen. Owen will know thy love for him long before he understands the rest. He may wonder about the woman who birthed him, the man who fathered him, but he will know thee and love thee."

Gwen sighed. "What should I say, when I confess before the people?"

"Those words must come from thy heart." Betsy laid a hand along Gwen's cheek. "The Lord will give thee the words to say. Do not be anxious."

"I'm not anxious." Her cheeks warmed when Betsy tipped her head. "Not much, anyway. 'Tis odd."

"Not at all. When thee are right with the Lord, thy spirit is at peace. I think 'tis the very peace thee have been lacking for a long time. Am I correct?"

"Aye. And due to my own foolishness."

"We are all foolish before we learn. Thee had no one to teach the ways of a godly life."

"I see now 'twas the Lord who put people in my path to help me. First 'twas Cook who protected me at the Whitefords', then Evie and Sapphira who showed me how to care for Owen." She dried the porridge kettle. "They also told me that I could trust you, the Quakers."

"And thee trusts us now?"

Gwen tucked the kettle in the trunk, and then wrapped her arms around Betsy and squeezed. "Aye. You have shown me love as I have never known before."

Betsy pulled back to arm's length, and her eyes misted over. "'Tis the love God gives us to share."

"I have wished to talk to you for many weeks about joining the Quakers. The Friends." Gwen looked at the toes of her shoes. "But I knew myself unworthy."

"And now?"

"I wish to join. I want to be a true part of the community."

"Do thee believe, in thy heart, that thee have accepted Christ as thy savior?"

Gwen looked Betsy in the eyes. "I do."

"Then thee are ready. But first, the confession."

Gwen nodded.

The jingle and creak of harness outside sent both women into a flurry of activity. They had the wagon loaded in moments. Thomas drove it to the fort's entrance while Betsy and Gwen, with Owen on her hip, walked behind.

Betsy grabbed Gwen's hand and squeezed.

The reassuring action sent a surge of love and acceptance through Gwen that put an added measure of confidence in her stride.

Gwen hung toward the back of the loose circle of Quakers. They gathered beside the wagons waiting for the leaders to start the meeting. Micah stood on the other side of the circle from her, arms laced across his chest. No smile softened the planes of his face. He watched the fort entrance as if he couldn't wait to be gone.

Gone from her? Her heart did a painful flip.

Thomas and several other Quaker men stood together and spoke in low voices. Gwen clung to her earlier peace even while her foot tapped. She wanted to confess and be done with it. The sooner the better.

A man with a tall hat broke through the circle near where Micah stood. The town marshal. What was lawman doing there? Then Zachary and Amos escorted Jonas into the group, each grasping an arm, and a hush fell over the gathering.

Betsy gripped Gwen's elbow.

The sound of birdsong broke the silence until Thomas raised his hands and drew attention his way.

"As we have been made aware of Jonas Whiteford's intention to capture and enslave free Negroes from the Northwest Territory, to which we resume travel yet this very day, it has been decided to cut all ties with the company of Whiteford and Son. Neither shall we be retaining Cobb, our former guide, whose whereabouts is currently unknown, who has also been implicated in this evil scheme.

"Marshall Caldwell has been informed of the intended actions of these men. As Pennsylvania is a free state, he is agreeable to make known to the good men of commerce in this area the unsavory disposition of these men. They have not broken man's law—yet—but most assuredly intended to break the greater law of God."

Jonas, one eye swollen almost shut, scanned the crowd with the other.

Gwen ducked behind a tall woman in front of her and peeked in time to see Marshall Caldwell gesture for Jonas to precede him. The circle parted in silence as the two men left.

"We have acquired the services of David Boehm to act as our guide to the new territory." Thomas nodded to a smooth-faced man slouched atop a gray horse near the fort entrance. "On four previous trips, he has traveled the very trail we shall take and comes highly recommended for the job."

The Quakers murmured around the circle. Surely nobody wanted Cobb back among them, but they needed someone who knew the route that would accommodate their wagons. Relief was palpable in the air.

Thomas raised his hands once again. "We have just one more item to attend to before we pray for the last leg of our journey. Gwen Morgan?"

Gwen handed Owen to Betsy, whose smile held both love and encouragement, and picked her way through the circle. The leaders turned to face her, and she stopped in front of them. She let her chin drop to her chest for a moment, then raised it and faced the people.

Kindness, curiosity, and nods greeted her, but there were a few eyes squinting in suspicion as well.

"I have wronged each of you. I have let you believe something that was not true." She turned until she could see Micah from the corner of her eye. He still faced the gate through which the marshal and Jonas had departed. Even from inside the circle, she could see his white knuckles where he gripped his sleeves.

Would he ever forgive her for her deception?

"Owen was not a son born to me but one given to my care to raise as my own by his grandfather. I swore an oath not to reveal the truth about him or his family in exchange for my freedom from indenture." She looked at Thomas, who nodded for her to continue. "I agreed to this deception willingly, but now I understand how wrong it was to do so. This morning I ask each of you for your forgiveness."

She lowered her chin again until Faith's hug enveloped her. Several other women also came forward, touching her shoulder and whispering, "Bless you." The crowd grew and the noise rose until Thomas raised his hands.

"'Tis time to offer our journey to the Lord, my friends. Let us pray."

The group fell silent. Gwen snuck a peek toward Micah, but he was gone. He hadn't come forward. None of the men had, but she'd seen nods of approval behind the ring of women. She filled her lungs, her heart light and clean with the release of her guilt.

Surely in time, Micah would forgive her as well.

Chapter 30

G WEN MANEUVERED THE TEAM and wagon around rocks that thrust up out of the ground like petite mountains. The trees grew sparsely here compared to the forest they'd traveled through most of the day. David Boehm had led them to an open space amid the wilderness with a grassy meadow to pasture the livestock for the night.

Once the wagons had rolled out of Redstone Old Fort and ferried across the Monongahela River, their new scout pushed them almost as hard as Cobb had. With a dry road, cool weather, low rolling hills, and fresh horses, they made almost ten miles that first day, despite their late start.

Gwen chirped to the horses and guided their wagon into the circle. She set the brake and wrapped the lines around the handle. Thomas had walked ahead to speak to the scout once the wagons started forming their circle, leaving Gwen and Betsy to set up camp.

From her high seat, Gwen searched for a glimpse of Micah's wagon. Unlike on their journey last year, he traveled near the front now, a long way ahead of her and the Baldwins. In the circle, his wagon was straight across from them, though Sassy and Hap were nowhere to be seen. She stretched a little farther but could see neither meadow nor brook through the wall of short, hooped wagons.

If only there had been time to speak to him before they'd left the fort. He was probably keeping his distance until they had a private moment to talk. She wanted to be sure he'd forgive her. He was a Quaker, one of Evie's saints. He had to. Didn't he?

"Are thee planning to stay up there all night?" Betsy called from beside the wagon, Owen in her arms.

"I'm coming. And put him down, Betsy. He's getting too heavy to tote around like that."

"Indeed." She lowered Owen to the grass. "But I wanted to be sure the brake was locked before letting him loose near the wheels, lest he get in the way."

"'Twas easier to travel with him last year, before he could walk." Gwen climbed down and unhitched the team. When Thomas returned and led the horses away for water and grazing, she joined Betsy at the cookfire already crackling near the wagon.

"Ack, keep thee back." Betsy grabbed a stick from Owen's hand and blocked the boy from getting close to the fire. His bottom lip pushed out and his eyes narrowed, his little hands striking his hips.

"Oh, my." Before he could get a good fuss going, Gwen scooped him up. "Perhaps I should take him for a long walk and let him release some of that energy."

"I think 'twould be a most agreeable arrangement." Betsy's eyes twinkled. "I shall have supper together within the hour."

"Until then"—Gwen set Owen back on his feet away from the fire and grasped his hand—"come with me, my little man, and we shall fetch a bucket of water from the stream." She grabbed a bucket off the side of the wagon as they walked past.

Once clear of the wagons and cookfires, she let loose of Owen's hand and dawdled along beside him as he stopped to investigate every rock, root, and stick they passed. Gwen didn't mind the slow pace. She scanned their surrounding until she spied a pair of broad roan backs. Sassy and Hap, Micah's team, grazed on the grassy meadow not far from the stream. A familiar black hat poked up on the other side of Hap. Taking Owen by the hand, she tugged him toward the horses.

And Micah.

Hap's rear hoof nestled between Micah's knees. Head bent over his work, he prodded a blunt pick around the hoof. Muscles rippled under the heavy fabric of his shirt. He pushed his hat back with his knuckles and blew out a sigh as he lowered the hoof to the ground.

Owen, who had been tugging to get closer to the water, saw Micah stand straight. With a squeal, the boy broke Gwen's hold and dashed in his stumbling gait toward the rear of the horse. Micah stepped between the careening youngster and those plate-sized hooves. He scooped the boy off the ground and glared at Gwen.

"Thee should have enough sense to not let the boy run at a horse like that." Micah's brows formed a forbidding line above his eyes. "Even though he's not thy son, thee should be more careful of him."

Gwen opened her mouth and then snapped it shut. Fire crept from under her neckline and blazed across her cheeks. How dare he?

"'Tis best thee does not try to explain thyself." He thrust Owen into her arms. "I should find whatever thee says difficult to believe. If thee were to tell me that grass grows green, I should need to see it for myself."

"I have confessed my deception before all. You were there. You heard me." Gwen raised her hand and let it drop again. "I have asked for forgiveness."

"'Tis the Lord's place to absolve sins, not mine." He crossed his arms over his chest.

She searched his face for some hint, a flicker, of his former regard for her. The burn of anger cooled to a bleakness of despair. "I have felt the Lord's peace—"

"Then let that be enough." The sun glinted off eyes of granite below the brim of his hat.

Gwen closed her eyes a moment and then met his stare. "I have cared for you—"

"Cared for me?" His harsh bark of laughter held no vestige of humor. "Thee did not care enough to tell me the truth. Used me is more like it." Wheeling around, he grasped the lead ropes and jerked the horses behind him.

Gwen clutched a struggling Owen to her breast as she turned and fled. Each step toward the wagon came quicker than the last until she was running over the uneven ground. She tripped and almost dropped Owen, who cried and pushed against her arms. Pain shot through her ankle and straight to her heart. Tears grayed the landscape around her, but she stumbled forward until someone caught her elbow. She flinched and pulled back.

"Easy now, lass." Thomas's voice cut through the fog of her misery, and she fell against his chest. His coat muffled the sobs she could not control.

"Give the lad to me. Come on, turn him loose." Thomas pried her fingers from Owen, and he soothed the boy against his other shoulder. "Let us return to our wagon."

Our wagon. At least Thomas and Betsy had forgiven her. She hadn't lost everything due to her deception.

Just Micah.

Betsy gave supper a quick stir. She swung the pot a little further from the fire and put a lid over the bubbling beans with ham. She pushed a hand against her back. She was ready for a good night's rest. It would take her a few days to acclimate to trail life again.

Thomas cleared his throat behind her, and she turned to face him. He stood at the back of the wagon, his arms loaded with Gwen and Owen, helplessness written on his face.

Betsy hurried to them, away from the eyes of those who camped nearby. "Whatever has happened?"

"I know not, but the lass is in a bad way."

Gwen lifted her head from Thomas's shoulder. Smearing the palm of her hand over one eye, she sniffed.

Betsy's heart lurched. There could be only one explanation for such level of misery.

Micah.

"Come with me, Gwen. Thomas, see to Owen for the moment." She patted her husband's arm. "Mind thee, keep him away from the fire." Betsy took Gwen's limp hand and led her into the wagon, where she helped her onto the cramped single bed before pulling the back canvas shut. Privacy was in short supply on the trail when everyone lived in such close quarters for protection, but she'd do what she could. She sat down beside Gwen. "Micah?"

Fresh tears poured forth like the spring melt off a mountainside.

Betsy cradled Gwen's head against her shoulder. How much emotional upheaval could one heart take in such a short time?

Betsy cleared her throat. "Gwen." She gave a gentle shake to the rounded shoulders leaned against her. "Gwen dear, 'tis enough now."

"Aye." Gwen pushed herself upright and drew in a ragged breath. "'Tis."

Betsy patted her hand. "If thee wishes to speak of it—"

"He will not forgive me for my deception." Gwen shook her head. "And as much as it hurts, I cannot say I blame him."

"Why would you say that?"

"This is the consequence of my own making. I signed an ungodly oath. I deceived—willingly deceived—people I care deeply for."

"Love forgives. Micah knows this. He is hurting now, but he will come around. Give him time." Betsy tilted the tear-streaked face toward her. "Do not give up. I know that man loves thee."

"I thought he'd come to love me." Gwen twisted the apron on her lap. "But I cannot blame him if he has changed his mind."

Betsy pursed her lips and patted Gwen's shoulder. "Thee stay here until thy tears have run their course and thy eyes are dry. I must speak with Thomas and check on Owen." Gwen half-rose but Betsy urged her back onto the cot. "Rest. 'Tis nothing I cannot handle."

Gwen nodded before burying her face in her hands.

Betsy resisted the desire to pull the girl into another motherly embrace. What she needed now was time to pull herself together. Betsy moved the canvas and peered out the back of the wagon. On the outer side of the wagon circle, Thomas and Owen crouched over something on the ground. Betsy climbed down and joined them.

"Gah-ba-ba-pa-pa." Owen pointed at a fat toad.

"Very nice." Betsy grimaced at the warty creature that held Owen's fascination. "Thomas, please speak with Micah."

"The source of our drama, I presume."

"Aye. Seems he refused to extend forgiveness."

"Indeed?" Thomas's eyebrows lifted skyward.

"Indeed."

Thomas tugged on the ends of his beard. "Perhaps he needs some time—"

"And perhaps he needs some wise counsel from an elder who knows a thing or two." Betsy tilted her head toward the opposite side of the circle.

Thomas tugged his beard a little harder. "Perhaps." He heaved to his feet. "If thee would be so good as to watch young Owen and his new pet."

"Pet?" Betsy eyed the bumpy brown lump on the dirt. "I think the goat is pet enough. That creature is not coming into my wagon."

Thomas chuckled as he walked away.

"Come, Owen. Let us see to supper before 'tis scorched. Not that anyone is likely to eat around our fire tonight." She grabbed his sticky hand, stickiness she hoped wasn't toad slime. With a grunt, Owen pulled free and dropped to the ground. He crossed his little arms and poked out his bottom lip.

So much for Betsy's quiet night.

Wiping her face one last time, Gwen stood and picked her way through the crowded wagon. Owen's howls of protest sent her scurrying over the tailgate. She winced as her swollen ankle hit the ground but hobbled to Betsy as quickly as she could.

"Let me take him." Gwen gathered the sobbing boy into her arms. Dirt, tears, and the drippy nose tugged at her heart.

"He is a mess, but unharmed." Betsy wiped her hands on her apron.

"I must fetch some clean clothes and give him a quick wash before supper."

"Thomas is on an errand. I shall keep supper warm." Shaking her head, Betsy walked away.

Gwen had never seen Betsy so disgruntled before. The lack of the woman's usual calm demeanor shook her as she brushed Owen's wispy curls from his streaked face. Her tears, Owen's tears, and Betsy's obvious ill-humor. Was anything worth this much angst? Wiping her own hair out of her way, she glared across the circle at Micah's wagon.

With clean clothes and a towel, Gwen took Owen to the edge of the stream. She shucked him out of his soiled clothing, right down to his skin. She soaked the edge of the towel in the frigid water and sponged her son clean. He squirmed and pulled away, but the worst of the dirt was already removed.

Thoughts of Micah filled her mind's eye. Gone were his ready smile and twinkling blue eyes. What replaced them twisted her heart. Hard eyes. The condemning slash of his mouth. The stiffness of his shoulders all but shouting his desire to be far away from her. She turned to reach the clean clothing when a splash, followed by a spray of cold water, doused her with fear.

"Owen!" She grabbed for the slippery, naked boy who'd plopped into the water, lifting his sobbing, dripping body against her own. "Oh, my darling, I'm so sorry. Momma is so sorry."

Their tears mingled on the front of her dress. She wrapped him in the dry part of the towel and sank to the ground. Her legs shook, her ankle throbbed, and she didn't think she could walk to the wagon if she had to. She rocked Owen back and forth until his sobs reduced to hiccups, and he relaxed in her arms.

What kind of mother was she?

Her mind preoccupied with a man who didn't want her, she'd put her son in danger. Self-loathing wrapped around her like the wings of a sleeping bat. Micah was right. She should be more careful. Owen was her first priority, if anything happened to him...

She wiped her tears on the towel and dressed Owen in his clean clothes. "Come. Betsy will wonder what has kept us." When Owen slipped his hand into hers, she swallowed the lump of conflicting emotions that threatened to choke her.

Betsy banged the ladle against the side of the pot. "I wish I knew."

Zachary rubbed his fingers through his hair. "Micah is not happy, that much is plain."

"He could give a mule lessons on being stubborn."

"Now then, thee knows 'tis more complicated than that. I understand he is on this journey because of a woman who betrayed him, rejected him in favor of his own brother, no less. That he could learn to trust again so soon is a testimony to his good nature. And now another woman he trusted has played him false. Give him time, and he will see that Gwen has sincerely repented."

"Thee are correct." Betsy shook her head. "I'm out of sorts. Please, forgive my sharpness."

"There's nothing to forgive. 'Tis thy love for them—both of them—that spawns thy worry."

"Indeed. But worry is a sign of a lack of trust. Praying does more than worrying ever will."

"Thee are a wise woman, Betsy Baldwin."

"Thee are a gracious man, Zachary Brown." She dipped her head toward him and smiled. "And thee had better plan to stay for supper. I fear thee will be the only one eating what I have prepared."

Thomas arrived with a slouch to his shoulders that boded no good news. He glanced around. "Where are Gwen and Owen?"

"At the stream. Owen needed a bath." Rising on her tiptoes, Betsy looked over his shoulder. "Here they come now. Oh, the poor girl is limping badly."

"Allow me to assist her." Zachary trotted off in Gwen's direction.

"Did thee speak with Micah?"

"Is that not why thee sent me?"

Betsy rested her hands on her hips. "Do not tease me. Gwen will be here shortly. What did he say?"

"He is hurting, wife. We need to give him time. I fear his issue with forgiveness is deeper than we knew. Before he can forgive our Gwen, he needs to forgive the girl who left him for his brother."

"Oh, my." Betsy pressed her hand to her forehead. "I should have thought of that." She looked at her husband. "But thee gave him counsel?"

"Indeed. He is a good lad. Give him time, and he shall do what is right."

"That is what Zachary said."

But if time would make it right, then Micah should have forgiven the girl back in New Jersey by now. Betsy tapped her finger against her chin.

Time could ease a hurt—or permanently fasten it to the soul.

Chapter 31

"**I**F I NEVER SHED another tear, so much the better for me." Gwen slapped the right rein across Lonny's back. Tossing its head, the gelding stepped forward, drawing even with Lad. "There's a boy. Keep up now. Pull your share of the load. Another hour or so, and we shall camp for the night."

Gwen wasn't sure exactly when she'd started speaking to the horses as if they understood. The reins rested in her gloved hands, as at home there as a hen on its nest. She rotated her shoulders and stretched her back. The horses weren't the only ones ready for a break from the day's travel. Twisting on the seat, she checked on Betsy and Owen, asleep on the cot.

Betsy worried her. The woman had been too quiet these past three days, ever since her argument with Micah.

Gwen sighed. She had to learn to think of Micah without the threat of tears. Each night when their wagon pulled into the circle, his wagon was parked across the way, the horses already unhitched and gone.

Micah and several other men were hunting that afternoon, so Thomas was driving Sassy and Hap. Fresh meat would be nice for supper, assuming the new guide would bring them to a halt with enough time to dress and cook it.

Maybe Gwen should offer to cook supper and give Betsy a reprieve. Although that would leave Betsy to watch over a well-rested Owen. Gwen's lips twitched. That wasn't much of a reprieve.

Shouts broke out and thundering hoofbeats approached from behind. Gwen leaned over to look around the canvas hoop just as a gray horse leaped a fallen tree to the left of their wagon. The animal's feet barely touched the ground before it sprinted ahead at the same breakneck pace.

"What is happening?" Betsy stood behind the seat and pressed against Gwen's back to peer out.

"I'm not sure. Our guide is racing to the front of the wagons."

"I fear that cannot be good."

Betsy stepped back and returned with Owen on her hip. More shouts reached them, from in front this time, and the wagons ahead of them lurched, the horses breaking into a canter.

"Hurry up! Move these wagons!" David Boehm's shouts became clear as his lathered horse raced back down the line. "Form the circle up ahead! On top of that hill. Keep close to the wagon in front of you!"

Pushing aside both questions and fear, Gwen gave the reins a firm crack. "Get up there!" The team responded with a jolt, and they careened after the other wagons.

Betsy clung to the back of the seat with one hand.

"Sit down." Gwen tossed the command over her shoulder. "The wagons in front are rocking something fierce. The ground is very rutted here."

Betsy and Owen disappeared behind her. Had she just barked an order to Betsy? She clenched the reins in both hands. Lad took a bad step and almost went to his knees. She drew back on his rein. "Steady on, Lad." Lonny pulled to the left, and she straightened him out. Feet braced against the violent pitching of the wagon, she fought to keep her seat. All her attention on the horses, she ignored the chill of fear that squeezed the base of her neck.

The wagon in front of her lurched to the left. She hauled on the reins and steered Lonny and Lad to follow. They charged past a wagon sprawled on its side, both its horses fighting to regain their feet. Men rushed to control the animals and pull the family free. Gwen clenched the reins even tighter.

They labored up an incline toward an open hilltop. Lonny and Lad leaned their heavy shoulders into their collars. Sweat slicked the leather, and white foam gathered around it. Their hooves scrambled for purchase on the rocky slope. The lead wagons disappeared from her view. As their wagon topped the crest, Gwen shouted behind her, "We made it." Her chest heaved almost as much as Lad and Lonny's.

"Praise God." Betsy appeared beside her again as Gwen maneuvered their wagon into their assigned place in the circle.

From the front of Micah's wagon, Thomas waved his arm at them. Gwen waved back, and he nodded before climbing down.

"Stay here." Gwen jumped down after securing the reins to the brake. She winced at the lingering pain in her ankle as she trotted across the circle, meeting Thomas mid-way.

"Praise God we are all safe." He pointed toward the last wagon—the one that had been lying on its side—as it topped the rise.

"What is happening?"

"Indians. Some of our hunting party have been injured."

"Micah?" Fear oozed through her voice.

"I know not." He clamped his hand on her shoulder. "Be strong. I need thee to unhitch the horses and bring them into the circle to tether while I do the same with Micah's team. Do not let them drink yet, not after that uphill run. Let them cool down first."

"Aye." She scurried back to the wagon, where Tiny stood tied behind the tailgate, her sides heaving. Nudging the goat aside, Gwen poked her head through the canvas opening.

"Some of our hunters are injured," she told Betsy. "I must unhitch and tether the team. Stay inside the circle if you leave the wagon. Thomas said there were Indians involved."

Betsy pressed her hand to her collar. "Owen and I will stay here until Thomas arrives."

"Good thinking." Gwen unhitched the horses, sliding the harness off their sweated flanks. Steam rose from their hides, and the pungent scent of horse permeated the air.

She led them into the circle, where Thomas helped her tether them beside Micah's team. She was patting Lonny on the hip when more shouts heralded the return of the hunters. Micah's black riding horse was not among them.

She grasped Thomas's sleeve.

"Be easy, lass. I think 'tis him riding behind Amos."

Gwen picked out lanky Amos on his bald-faced bay with another man slumped against his shoulder from behind. Lifting her skirts, Gwen ran as best she could. The hunters stopped not far from the Baldwins' wagon, and she rushed to the bay's side.

Micah lifted his hatless head. Drying blood matted his hair to the side of his face. Eyes fogged and dulled with pain met hers.

Thomas arrived and, with Amos's help, eased Micah to the ground and supported his weight.

"Have Betsy prepare the cot for him in our wagon," Thomas said.

"Nay." Micah's voice was a feeble croak.

"Go, lass." Thomas jerked his head at Gwen.

She dashed to the wagon.

"I heard him from here. Take Owen." Betsy thrust the squirming youngster out the back of the wagon. "I shall have the cot ready in a moment."

"I shall fetch some water—"

"Use what is in the barrels." Thomas puffed to the wagon, half-dragging Micah with him. "Nobody leaves the circle tonight. Not for any reason."

"Aye." Gwen tapped the barrel loaded on the side of the wagon toward the circle center. Awkward as it was to juggle the bucket, tap the barrel, and hold Owen, she refused to set the boy down. He fussed. "There now, be patient. I shall take you around the circle once we know Micah is going to be fine."

Please, God. Please let him be fine.

The wagon rocked as Amos and Thomas hoisted Micah aboard. His groan shattered her heart. She plugged the barrel and hefted the bucket to Betsy's waiting hands.

"How is he?"

Betsy shook her head. "I'll start cleaning the wounds and see what is beneath. Find Zachary if thee can. He is not a doctor, but he is knowledgeable about healing."

"I will." Shifting Owen to her other hip, Gwen trotted into the circle. Zachary's wagon was in front of Micah's. Owen babbled and pointed at the horses. "We might pet the horses later. We must find Zachary now." Owen stuffed a finger in his mouth and grinned. "Not to entertain you, my son, but to help Micah."

Zachary's wagon was empty. She hurried around the circle asking if anyone had seen him.

"He helped Joseph off a horse. I'm pretty sure he had an arrow in his arm." Faith pointed to a wagon three down from hers. Her children stood on either side of her, their hands clenched in her skirt. "Is it Micah?"

"Aye. Betsy wants Zachary to come."

"I'm sure he will. I shall be praying."

With a quick squeeze of her hand, Gwen thanked her friend and hurried on. Zachary stepped from the wagon and swiped his sleeve across his brow. He stopped mid-swipe when he saw her.

"Micah?"

Gwen nodded. "Betsy is asking for you. Can you come?"

Zachary's brow wrinkled, and he glanced at the Baldwins' wagon. "As soon as I can. Joseph's arm is broken, and I need to set that first."

"You know how to set a bone?"

"As well as anyone else here, I suppose." He sighed. "Once we are settled, we must recruit a real doctor to join us. I'm more comfortable doctoring cows and horses than humans." He hurried toward his own wagon.

Lowering Owen beside her, Gwen gripped his hand and marched across the circle, dodging horses tethered in her way. Owen's little legs pumped to keep up. They reached the back of their wagon, and Owen grabbed Tiny's collar. The goat stood patiently while the boy babbled at her. Gwen kept a firm hold on his other hand.

Betsy poked her head around the canvas. "Is he coming?"

"Aye, but first he must set Joseph's broken arm. How is Micah?"

"I wish I knew." Betsy pushed a few stray hairs off her forehead. "He is sleeping now. That gash on his head is not as bad as it looked, but I fear he may have broken some ribs and his hand..."

"What happened to his hand?"

"I need Zachary's opinion on that, too." A low moan came from inside the wagon. "If thee would start a fire?" Betsy's words trailed off as she disappeared behind the canvas.

Owen's hand firmly tucked in hers, Gwen laid the kindling. The first tongues of flame were licking the dry twigs when Zachary arrived.

"Give the boy to me," Thomas said. "He and I shall tend the fire and boil water."

With her son in good hands, she followed Zachary to the wagon.

Betsy crawled out and grasped Zachary's hand. "He has a knot on his head, and I'm fairly certain a broken rib or two, but I fear his right hand has been mangled."

Stuffing her knuckles against her teeth, Gwen stifled a gasp. She took a step toward the wagon before Zachary stopped her.

"Let me see him first."

Betsy's arms enfolded Gwen from behind. "Pray."

"Aye."

"I shall help Thomas with Owen. Stay as long as thee wishes."

Gwen stared at the back of the wagon. *Lord, I've been angry with Micah these past three days. Angry and hurt. But I cannot stand the thought of him injured.* She wrung her apron between her hands. *Heal him, Lord. And... give us another chance.*

"Gwen!" Zachary's voice boomed, and she jumped.

"Aye?"

"Come here. I need another set of hands."

"Not her." The thickness of Micah's words did nothing to lessen the scorn in their tone.

"Thee are in no position to argue. Gwen?"

Gwen all but leaped into the wagon. What met her sight knocked her breath out of her. Micah lay on the cot, his long length filling it from end to end. His shirtless chest rose and fell in an unsteady rhythm.

A rhythm that matched Gwen's breathing, but for an entirely different reason.

"I should get Thomas—"

"I need thee with thy gentle touch, not ham-fisted Thomas."

"But—"

"Send her away." Micah's cold eyes pinned her to the wagon's canvas side.

"Perhaps thee would like to bind these broken ribs thyself? And set that thumb while thee are at it?" Zachary's tone brooked no argument. "Gwen?"

"Aye." She took the one step needed to be at the edge of the cot. "Tell me what to do."

"I'm going to set him upright," Zachary said, "and steady him while thee wraps these linen strips firmly, but not too tightly, around his chest. Understand?"

She snatched the cloth from his hands. "Aye."

Micah groaned and swayed as Zachary lifted him to a sitting position and supported his weight. Micah placed both hands on Zachary's shoulders, leaving Gwen just enough room in the narrow space to work. She planted one knee on the cot and put her arms around his chest. Her fingers twitched as they made contact with his warm skin. She bit her bottom lip and flicked a glance at Zachary. He inspected her first wrap and nodded approval.

Gwen relaxed layer by layer as Micah's chest was covered. Zachary inspected each wrap and instructed her where to place the next one. It was clear he'd done such a thing before. When it met his satisfaction, he lowered Micah onto the cot.

"Now his hand." A deep furrow marred Zachary's forehead as he lifted Micah's right hand in both of his. Micah moaned and drew up his knees in protest. "I know it hurts, but we have to set it."

"'Tis broken then?" Gwen stared at the misshapen hand and swallowed.

"I do not believe so. If I'm correct, the thumb has been displaced out of the joint."

"Is that all?" Micah's words rasped between clenched teeth.

"How did this happen?" Zachary's dark brows drew together as his fingers pressed along Micah's injured hand.

"My horse." He gasped when Zachary's fingers probed near the thumb joint. "They shot my horse out from under me."

Gwen cringed at the violent act against such a fine animal.

"I fell hard. If not for Amos..."

"And your horse?" Gwen asked.

"Probably roasting over some Indian's cookfire by now." Micah's good hand balled up the blankets beside him. "He deserved better than that. He was a good horse."

Gwen gritted her teeth against the pain in his voice.

"Steady on, my friend. This has to get worse before it can get better." Compassion filled Zachary's voice. "Gwen, I will need thee to steady his arm. Wrap thy arms around it in this way." Zachary demonstrated the hold.

Gwen sat on the cot and leaned into Micah. With her hip pushed against his shoulder, she steadied his arm across her knees, heartbeat quickening at his closeness.

"Ready?"

She nodded at Zachary and ignored the tremor that rippled across the muscles of Micah's arm.

"Hold him steady. He will not be able to control his reaction."

With those words, Zachary pulled and twisted the misshapen hand. Micah jerked against her hip, his good hand clamping down on her shoulder in a bruising grip before he collapsed. A loud popping noise was followed by Zachary's grunt of satisfaction. Gwen stared at the hand, no longer bent at the wrong angles, and then at Zachary.

"'Twas out of joint, but we have put it back. Thank thee, Gwen."

She scooted off the cot, and Zachary laid Micah's arm on the soft blanket. Micah didn't move.

"Is he...?"

"Passed out cold. 'Tis not unexpected. 'Tis why I wanted to see his ribs wrapped first. He has endured enough pain for today. Now he can rest and begin to heal. Fetch me when he awakens and I shall splint his hand."

"But you said 'twasn't broken."

"'Twill still need a splint for a fortnight or better to allow the joint to stabilize. He shall need at least that long for his ribs to mend as well."

After Zachary left, Gwen eased herself onto the edge of the cot. Micah didn't move, but his chest rose and fell in the regular rhythm of sleep. She smoothed his hair away from his damp forehead, her fingers brushing the bandage there.

Owen's cheerful chatter blended with the voices of Thomas, Betsy, and Zachary on the other side of the canvas. She heard enough to know that no Indians had been sighted near the wagons. The normal camp sounds lulled her into a sense of peace as she sat there.

Stroking the hair of the man she loved.

Chapter 32

“I DO NOT REMEMBER falling in love being so difficult back when we went about it.” Betsy nestled her head against Thomas's shoulder as they sat before the dying fire.

“'Twas easy as pie. How could it be otherwise when thee chose the best?”

She poked him in the ribs. “Thee were the best pickings, but the field was small.”

He clamped his hand over his heart. “I am wounded.”

“Thee are impossible.”

He growled and pulled her closer. “I may be a lot of things, but with thee beside me, nothing is impossible.”

She smiled into the darkness and patted his arm, which was tight around her. Secure. Strong. Loving. “I wish with all my heart that Gwen and Micah could find such joy as we have known.”

“I know. But 'tis not our decision, 'tis theirs.”

“Perhaps, with Micah laid up—”

“Woman, push such a thought from thy mind. 'Tis not our place to interfere.”

"Not our place? Is Gwen now a daughter to us or not?"

Thomas grunted. "Thee knows she is."

"Then surely—"

"Then surely, we shall pray."

Pray. Had she not worn her knees to the nubs over these young people already?

Then why do you not trust Me?

Startled, she looked around at the sleepy camp.

"Did thee hear something?" she asked.

"Nothing out of the ordinary."

An overwhelming sense of peace settled over Betsy. She relaxed deeper into her husband's embrace. "Thee are a wise man, my husband."

"To choose such a wife, I could be no less." His beard tickled her cheek, and she giggled. Giggled. At her age. What would Gwen think if she'd heard?

Gwen hurried across the circle to Betsy, who stirred the morning pot of breakfast porridge over the fire. Bumping against her hip, Owen pointed at the horses and cattle they passed. The circle was full of animals corralled to keep them safe from Indians. Dodging around one grumpy-looking milk cow wearing hobbles, Gwen reached Betsy's side.

"How is he?"

"Good morning to thee as well, Gwen." The twinkle in Betsy's eyes washed any sting from her greeting.

"I'm sorry. Good morning."

"Nay, 'tis I who should not tease thee. He is going to be fine. No fever, praise God."

A weight lifted from Gwen's shoulders. She rubbed her neck, stiff from a poor night's sleep in Micah's wagon. Betsy had insisted that she and Thomas stay near Micah in case he needed Thomas's help in the night, so Gwen and Owen spent the night in Micah's wagon. Owen had slept while Gwen prayed and worried and prayed some more until after she heard the third watch take their shift.

"Thomas is harnessing the horses, both teams. He spoke with our guide. Thee are to pull Micah's wagon in front of ours in the line."

"Will you tend to Owen then, and Micah?"

"I am hopeful that Faith will watch Owen for a few days if thee would ask her."

"Of course, I shall ask her now." Gwen turned to leave.

"A moment. Let us feed the boy first."

"Of course."

Gwen wasn't sure what encouraged her more, Micah without a fever or the return of Betsy's cheerful self. She fed Owen his breakfast while Betsy packed a sack of extra wrappings and a clean shirt. Gwen strained to hear Micah's mumbled responses to Betsy in the wagon. She longed to be the one tending him, but his protest over her helping Zachary the night before gave her pause. Better to wait.

With Owen occupied between Faith's children in their wagon, Gwen hitched Sassy and Hap to Micah's and guided it off to the side. She waited and watched team after team pass by until the Baldwins' wagon came into view. With a snap of the lines and a click of her tongue, Sassy and Hap pulled into line in front of them.

The day was long and warm, spring fast giving way to summer. Was time her enemy or her friend where Micah was concerned? He hated her for lying to him. She couldn't blame him. There were times her stomach crawled, and she wanted to hide her face from everyone, including God, when she thought about what she'd done. But she was forgiven. She remembered that washed-clean feeling after her confession.

How could she make Micah sense it too?

They broke for the nooning beside a shallow creek. Zachary came to tend to Micah while Gwen was still unhitching Sassy and Hap. Her fingers fumbled with the fasteners in her haste.

Thomas walked past, leading his team. "Hand me their ropes, and I shall take them with these fellows."

"Thank you."

Gwen handed over the team and hurried to the back of the Baldwins' wagon. Betsy was nowhere to be seen. As Gwen approached the wagon, Zachary's voice rose.

"Are thee devoid of all sense?"

"I will not stay on this bed while that woman drives my wagon."

"That woman?"

"Thee knows who I mean."

"And thee cannot say her name anymore, is that it? Does it have such a power over thee?"

"Do not be absurd."

"I have no fear of being absurd, myself."

Gwen stood rooted to the ground. The words flew fast and furious between the men in the wagon. She couldn't believe what she was hearing.

"How can thee defend her? She would have seen thee taken back a slave."

"Never."

"She almost did."

"She saved my life. What would those men have done to me had she not spoken up?"

"She lied to us. To all of us."

"Gwen was faced with a difficult decision at a very young age." Zachary's voice lowered, and his words came out in a vehement rush, so different from the tempered rhythm she associated with the calm man. "Who are thee to judge her so harshly? Did thee face such weighty decisions of thy own? Did thee take on such a burden? Or did thee turn tail and run when thy betrothed chose thy brother instead?"

The wind blew Gwen's hair across her cheek. She pushed the tendrils under her bonnet with shaking fingers as tears blurred the canvas in front of her. *Betrothed?*

The wagon rocked and creaked. "Forgive me, Micah. My tongue got ahead of my thoughts. I know thee—"

"I will stay in the wagon another day. Leave me now."

Gwen brushed the tears from her eyes as Zachary pulled the back cover aside and stepped out.

"Gwen." He kept his voice low.

She cleared her throat. "How is he?"

Zachary glanced in the wagon. "In a foul mood. 'Tis not a good time—"

"I know." She patted Zachary on the arm and walked past him. She put her foot on the tailgate and drew a breath between her teeth. Anger dried her tears more effectively than any cotton handkerchief could have. "I heard." She hauled herself up and pushed the canvas flap aside.

"I said leave me." Micah lifted his head off the pillow. The blue ice that slammed into her would have sent her running days before. But not anymore. She hadn't been the only one keeping secrets. She'd see what he had to say about his.

"You were betrothed to someone, and you never told me?" Surprised and emboldened by the quiet calm of her own voice, Gwen stepped to the edge of the bunk.

Micah groaned and covered his eyes with his forearm. "Go away."

"Nay."

He groaned again and pulled his forearm away. "I have nothing more to say to thee."

"'Tis my good fortune, then, that I can speak without interruption."

"How dare thee—?"

"You have judged me harshly, and 'tis true that I deserved it. But now I learn, quite by accident, that you have not been completely honest with me."

"I never lied."

"A lie by omission is not the truth."

"There was no reason to tell thee—"

"No reason? How can you say that? You knew I was falling in love with you." Gwen slapped her hand over her mouth. She turned her head away and wished those words back. But they were gone. Out and heard. There was nowhere to go but forward. She lowered her hand. "Now to learn that all that time, your heart belonged to another."

"Nay." The word was low and hoarse. Micah struggled to sit up.

She wanted to help him, but her feet wouldn't move. Her breath came in shallow pants.

Sweat beaded Micah's face by the time he braced himself against the back of the wagon seat into a sitting position. He blinked, and his eyes lost their icy hardness. His face, drawn and pale, made him look years older.

He lifted a hand toward her.

Gwen's heart stopped, started, and then galloped. She stepped toward him and laid her fingers in his palm. His hand wrapped around hers, and he drew her closer until her knees brushed against the bunk's frame. She could drown in the liquid sadness of his eyes.

"Nay. My heart did not belong to another. From the moment I met thee, I knew Elizabeth had made the right choice. She wounded my pride, to be sure, but not my heart. Not for long." He rubbed his hand across his bandaged forehead. "If she had, I could not have given it to thee."

Gwen sank into the edge of the mattress. "Is there a chance for us?"

"I know not."

"If only you could forgive me, as the others have."

He pulled his hand free from hers and plowed his fingers through his hair. "I forgive thee, Gwen. I do. But forgiving and forgetting are not the same."

"'Tis a start."

"What is love without trust?" He bit out each word.

She bowed her head. He was right. She pressed her hand against the pain in her chest. "Betsy needs help preparing the noon meal."

He said nothing as she climbed out of the wagon without a backward glance. He'd forgiven her for her deception.

Could she ever win his trust again?

The next morning, Gwen awoke to the coo of a mourning dove. Light illuminated the canvas above her. Had she overslept? She sat up before remembering... it was Sunday. And the new guide wasn't against them holding their meetings.

She grinned and peeked into Owen's cradle. He rested on his side, his little hands folded under this chin, his knees drawn up to his belly.

She stood and stretched, feeling alive in the faint tingling of her fingers and toes. An excited tingling. It was the day she would officially join the Quakers—the Friends.

Someone was moving around below the wagon. She bit the corner of her lip. If only she could convince Thomas that it was safe for her and Owen to sleep on the ground. Ever since the Indian incident, he'd ordered her into the wagon every night. He claimed no Indian in his right mind would steal away a couple of old people, but a young woman and child were tempting game. Even knowing he was right, she hated the thought of them sleeping on the ground.

After hurrying to dress, she left the wagon.

"Good morning." Betsy poked at the fire with a stick.

"Good morning. I fear I slept too long."

"Nonsense, 'tis the day the Good Lord set aside for rest."

"Had I rested any longer, I would have missed the meeting." She bounced on her toes.

"I cannot tell thee how much this pleases Thomas and me." Betsy wrapped her arms around Gwen and squeezed. The scents of woodsmoke and cinnamon clung to her clothing.

Gwen returned the hug. "Where is Thomas?"

"He and Zachary are helping Micah get ready." They'd moved Zachary's wagon in front of Micah's in the line last evening, so either he or Thomas could hear if Micah—who'd been moved to his own wagon—called out in the night.

"I should roust Owen then."

Gwen slipped back into the wagon and lifted the sleeping toddler, who stretched and yawned and laid his head against her shoulder.

"Enough of that now. Time to wake. We need to get you dressed and changed. Today you will watch your momma become a Friend." She hummed an old hymn, the parts she remembered her mother singing to her. Would Mother be proud of her today? Father surely wouldn't, with his distrust of the church and all things related to it. But maybe, buried beneath all the hurt and anger, maybe her father really had believed.

She hoped so.

They shared their morning meal with Zachary and Micah. Zachary's smile rivaled the sun for its brightness and width. Micah rested on a wooden chair they'd unpacked to help support his healing ribs. Pale and silent, his face never turned Gwen's way. He worked his spoon with his good hand and gripped his bowl with his knees. Gwen's heartbeat dropped every time he grimaced, whether in pain or frustration.

She changed into her best dress and apron and then fussed with her hair, trying to capture it under her bonnet. She stood in front of Betsy for inspection, since the only looking glass was packed away, nestled in straw to protect it on the trip. Betsy smoothed Gwen's collar and patted her cheek.

"We are not to boast on the external, but I must say, thee are a sight to behold."

"Thank you." Gwen gave her a hug.

"'Tis as if thee were my own."

With both a grin and a tear, Gwen nodded. "I feel the same."

"There shall be tears for sure if we do not start walking now." Thomas, with Owen in his arms, raised an eyebrow at the women.

"Oh, never mind that old curmudgeon. He is only ready to pop three buttons himself."

"Are thee calling me prideful, wife?"

"I shall call thee late for meeting if thee does not get a move on." Betsy linked arms with Gwen and sailed right past Thomas, leaving him sputtering about an impudent woman.

Gwen chuckled, her heart light, although it dipped when they passed Micah, silent upon the chair Zachary had set up for him.

Most of the Friends sat on the ground, some on barrels or up-ended buckets. The usual hush fell over the group, but it carried an undercurrent of expectation. Several Friends, mostly women, stood and spoke the words the Lord had laid on their hearts. Gwen did her best to concentrate on each one, her hands gripped in her lap, her eyes lowered so she wouldn't sneak glimpses of Micah.

After what seemed like a full day, although it couldn't have been more than two hours by the sun, one of the leaders rose and raised his hands. "Is there any other who would come before us today to share what the Lord has put on their hearts?"

Her moment had arrived. Gwen rose and smoothed her skirt. "I would."

He nodded and sat back down.

Gwen let her gaze travel over the crowd. If it lingered an extra moment on Micah, she couldn't help it. He didn't look up, and disappointment pinched her heart. Others smiled their encouragement—the number of which surprised her. She spread her hands in front of her and said, "'Tis my wish to be joined with this meeting." She let her hands drop to her sides and waited.

The leader once again rose. "Has thee experienced the Inward Light of Christ in thy life?"

"I believe I have."

"Will thee agree to live simply and in harmony with the rest of the Society of Friends in this meeting?"

"I will."

"Then we welcome thee, Sister Gwen Morgan."

The crowd rose and each one, from the oldest man to the youngest child, came before her. Each woman touched her and most offered a welcome and a smile. The men nodded and many blessed her. Thomas and Betsy, with Owen, stayed by her side. Her heart nearly burst with the simple, heartfelt words of welcome and encouragement.

She belonged. She truly belonged.

Zachary came last. "I took Micah back to his wagon. He was in no shape to stand in line."

"I understand." Micah hadn't wanted to greet her. She pushed that one dark cloud from her thoughts.

"I'm glad thee are fully a part of us now."

"'Twas easier than I thought 'twould be." Gwen shrugged. "I thought accepting God would be more difficult. But in truth, 'twas almost too easy."

"I think that baffles many people who do not believe."

"I would not have accepted this faith in Christ if 'twere not for you."

His dark eyebrows lifted skyward. "Me?"

"Aye. 'Twas you more than any who prodded me toward this decision."

"But thee believes?"

"Oh, aye. God's hand has been guiding me my whole life. But it took everything I have been through to show it to me. And you, Betsy, and Thomas. The sorrows were plenty, but He never left me truly alone, even if at the time I could not see that. I have no more doubts."

Not about God and His love.

But what about Micah and his?

Chapter 33

G WEN FUMBLED THE LID on the stew pot she was drying, and it slid toward the fire. She grabbed it, but the end of the towel touched the flame and ignited. Sliding the lid back on the pot, she threw the towel to the ground and stomped out the flames. She couldn't do anything right. Palm pressed against her forehead, she stamped her foot and turned on her heel, right into Micah's chest.

"Oh!" She stepped back.

He caught her by the elbows before she tumbled into the fire. "Steady."

Irritation and hope warred within her. Had he been watching her again? She glanced at his face. No smile. No dancing blue eyes that teased and promised. Nothing but the brooding stare that had her nerves screaming from the time she arose to the time she sank onto the bunk at night. It even haunted her dreams.

A week ago, she'd been on the mountaintop. Accepted into the Society of Friends, she'd thought her problems were over. The ups and downs of the week that followed had little to do with the steep hills of the terrain they crossed.

At first, she was thrilled that Micah had started to look at her again, that he'd stopped avoiding her. But it was always brooding, distant. His wrapped ribs made his movements slow and stiff. His new demeanor rattled her and ate away at her confidence. They hadn't spoken more than a word or two since he'd admitted he loved her... but could no longer trust her.

"Thank you." She stepped sideways, away from him, and stalked to where Betsy sat on a crate mending one of Thomas's socks and telling Owen a story.

"I shall take Owen for a walk to the creek."

"Thee should not go alone."

Gwen shaded her eyes from the sun and rose onto her toes to peer into the distance. "There are other women already there, and some of the men as well."

"Ah, fine then. A bit of exercise will do thee both good. Thee are a touch pale today."

Gwen summoned a ghost of a smile. "I'm fine."

Owen's hand firmly in hers, she started for the creek. Their guide always found water for them to camp near, but the evening prior, he'd set the wagons on a hill a quarter mile away from the creek. Even though they kept a full guard each night to watch for Indians, he preferred them to camp on a hill or in an open place not too close to trees. The creek was lined with trees, except for the shallow widening that formed the natural ford where they'd crossed before forming their circle. That was where a group of Friends gathered.

At Owen's pace, Gwen had plenty of time to think about Micah. Truly, she thought of little else. He loved her, and she loved him. Why wasn't that enough? He hadn't told her about his betrothal, so they had both kept secrets. She shook her head. Hers wasn't just a secret, it was a lie. She rubbed her hands over her arms and hurried after Owen, who had broken into a run.

He waded into the creek and squealed at the cold water on his toes. Gwen leaned over, clasping his hands while keeping her shoes dry. His stamping and splashing brought a grin to her face.

Then a heart-stopping scream ripped the air.

Indians mounted on small horses pounded toward them, brandishing spears.

Gwen leaped into the water beside Owen and scooped him up.

She scrambled onto land, her shoes sliding on grass trampled into a slippery mess by those running to escape. Children cried, a woman screamed, and men shouted.

With Owen held against her belly, Gwen ran, keeping her body between him and the Indians. A line of men—unarmed as the Friends always were—formed around the women and children. Up ahead, several of the large work horses jumped over wagon tongues with riders clinging to their bare backs.

A shot rang out. David Boehm charged from the tree line, shooting his rifle into the air. The Indians veered their horses in one fluid movement away from the creek.

The men in the circle cheered.

"Don't be fools! They will be back. Be ready." David's voice carried across the open meadow.

One of the horsemen galloped close to her. Gwen caught a glimpse of red roan hide before it half-reared to a halt.

Micah!

He slid to the ground and coughed, grabbing his side.

"Get on!" He pushed Gwen onto the horse's broad back.

She scrambled up with Owen still clutched to her front, his little hands digging into the fabric of her dress. Micah shoved the lead rope into her hand.

"Go!" He pointed to the wagons with the rifle in his hand.

"Come with us." She stretched her hand out toward him.

"No."

"Please, Micah. You cannot fight them. Quakers do not fight." She leaned down and Hap, upset by the noise, danced sideways. She struggled to stay on his back.

"Go, Gwen. I do what I must." His eyes blazed with their old fire. For a moment, the chaos around them blurred out of focus. She read the words on his lips. "I love thee."

The words he couldn't hear hammered against her heart. *I love you too.*

He cracked his hand on Hap's rump, and the nervous horse jumped toward the wagons before she could say the words out loud. Clutching the lead rope with both hands, Owen pinned tightly against her body with her forearms, she urged the horse on.

More men streamed by her toward the Indians, including some

brandishing rifles.

"Do not abandon those wagons!" David's voice whipped across the meadow, sharp enough to cut across the pounding of hooves.

Men near the wagons stopped and turned back.

Hap jumped a wagon's tongue, and Gwen squeezed her knees and shut her eyes. Her teeth jarred when he struck the earth inside the circle. She slid half-way onto his neck but kept her hold on Owen.

Hands reached to help before others pulled the horse to a full stop. Thomas took Owen and handed him to Betsy before grabbing onto Gwen as she slid from the horse.

"Micah—" she said.

Betsy grabbed her hand. "I know. Come with me." Barrels and crates had been piled to make an inner circle. Women and children huddled inside. Thomas pushed Owen into Gwen's arms. The crying boy clung to her neck, his tears soaking her collar.

"Get in." Betsy herded them toward the others. Within minutes, the circle was quiet, the sobbing children muffled against their mothers.

"We must pray."

Gwen didn't recognize who said it, but the rightness of that command filled her being.

Father God, protect Micah and all the men out there.

She repeated those words in her heart, knowing her silent prayer joined those offered by the women around her to reach the ears of God. Even the children quieted.

Hoofbeats set off a rustle of clothing as women pulled their young ones closer.

"'Tis our men." Betsy's voice, filled with hope, unleashed the collectively held breath.

The women climbed out of the shelter. Some rushed to hug their husbands, some to their fathers, and some to sons or other relatives. Betsy went to Thomas. Gwen searched frantically for Micah.

David rode in on his horse, and Micah walked beside him. Both men held rifles by their sides.

When David raised his free hand and whistled, the crowd quieted. As he walked his horse into the center of the circle, people backed up and gave him room.

"They were a bunch of young bucks, Delaware Indians, too young to have guns of their own. We were lucky this time. They were out for mischief, to gain a little respect from their fellows. Most Delawares are fairly peaceful, but that Shawnee chieftain to the west is getting some of the younger ones riled up."

"Will they be back?"

"These are probably the same bunch that jumped our hunters. I'm guessing they are done harassing us for now." David rested the butt of his rifle on his thigh.

"Are we safe?"

"As safe as you ever were. This is the frontier. Indians are part of it, but you knew that before you left your homes in North Carolina." David's relaxed slouch in the saddle reassured Gwen more than his words as he answered questions thrown at him.

She scanned the crowd for Micah.

He leaned against his wagon, bent over, arms wrapped around his middle.

Gwen moved toward Betsy.

"Please, take Owen."

"Is something wrong?" Betsy drew her eyebrows together as she took the boy.

"'Tis Micah. He is hurting."

"I should go too—"

"Nay." Gwen cleared her throat and put her hand on Betsy's arm. "I will fetch you if he needs more help."

A slow smile graced Betsy's face, and the corners of her eyes crinkled. "Go then, and God bless."

It took Gwen far too long to weave her way through the crowd. They had started to disperse by the time she reached the edge. Micah watched her approach, and she couldn't look away. The brooding look she so dreaded was gone. She stopped in front of him.

"Your ribs?"

"They pain me, but not nearly as much as my actions these past weeks."

Hope fluttered like a basketful of fireflies in her chest.

He took a step toward her and winced.

"Let me see—"

"'Tis nothing."

His eyes burned with that blue light she had missed for so long. Surly he could hear her heart racing. He took her hand and pulled her into the shadow of his wagon, away from the circle of milling people.

"If anything had happened to thee, or to Owen, I could not have forgiven myself."

"Micah, I'm so sorry—"

He pressed his fingers against her lips.

"'Tis my turn to be sorry, Gwen. Thee are already forgiven. Now, 'tis my time to ask."

"There is nothing to forgive."

"I need to ask forgiveness of the others." His gaze turned to the wagon, where his rifle rested against the wheel.

"You took the gun."

"Indeed."

"But—"

"Quakers do not fight," he finished for her.

"Would you have shot one of the Indians?" She remembered David's rifle, pointed in the air. She only remembered hearing the shots he fired.

"I know not." He raked his hair back with a quick scrub of his fingers. "If they had touched thee or Owen... I know not." He hung his head.

Gwen closed the remaining gap between them and laid her hand against his cheek. "Let us pray we never have to find out."

He leaned into her palm and nodded. "There will be no more secrets between us."

"None."

"Who is Owen's father?"

Gwen didn't hesitate. "A ship's captain in Mr. Whiteford's employ. I believe he has no knowledge of the child."

"It worries me, somewhat, to think that a man out there"—he waved his arm toward the east—"has a son he knows nothing about."

"If I may be so bold, from what Cook said about him, there may be more than one child he has left behind." Gwen's face warmed, and she pushed a stray lock of hair back under her bonnet.

"But if 'twere me—"

"You are not the kind of man to have a child with a woman not your wife."

Micah's face flushed a ruddy hue. He shuffled his feet, staring at them as if he needed to count the movements.

Gwen pressed her hand to her heart, as if to contain the love she felt for this man.

"I thank thee for that," he said.

"'Tis only the truth."

"Indeed." He took her hand again. "Between us there will be truth only from this day forth."

"Can you trust me, then?"

"Trust—like faith—is something we choose. I see that now. I choose to trust thee, and I know 'tis the right decision. Gwen Morgan, I love thee with all my heart." He drew her into his arms and grunted.

"Your ribs—"

"Hang my ribs."

Gwen giggled and pressed her knuckles to her mouth before another could escape.

"Thee would laugh at a man in pain who is trying to propose to thee?" Micah's lips twitched, and those amazing eyes danced.

Gwen hardly dared to believe his words. That she, an orphaned waif left on a foreign shore, sold like an animal at auction, who had willfully engaged in an unholy oath, would have such a man trying to propose to her.

Lowering his head until their foreheads touched, he whispered, "Marry me."

She raised her face until their noses touched. "I will."

He pressed his lips against hers, a warmth so full of promise, and love.

She pulled back and framed his face between her hands. "I love—thee."

"Thee?" His smile filled her vision.

She nodded. "Aye. Thee. And only thee."

"Together we shall build a good life in this new territory. The three of us. And together, I promise we will somehow find thy sister."

Gwen Morgan's heart soared to the heavens, where surely, somewhere, an angel smiled.

THE END

Author's Historical Notes

THE QUAKERS—WHO CALLED THEMSELVES Friends—didn't hold with the institution of slavery. While some individuals may have owned slaves during the early settlement of the American colonies—a practice brought over from Europe—it was soon condemned by the leaders of the American Quaker movement as a whole.

It was not uncommon for wealthy Quakers to purchase slaves and give them their freedom. This practice, as well as their religious views allowing black members to join their meetings, made the Quakers particularly unpopular in the Southern states.

When it became against the law to free slaves, many meetings—which is how the Quakers referred to their churches—packed up their entire communities and moved to the Northwest Territory, the future states of Ohio, Indiana, and Illinois, which were brought into the United States as free territories.

While the journey of Gwen, the Baldwins, and their community of Friends is fictional, the account mirrors an actual migration—one of many—that took place beginning in the late 1700s and continuing well into the 1800s.

Reviews are Golden

R EVIEWS ARE THE LIFEBLOOD of authors. Leaving a review on **Amazon**, **Goodreads**, and/or **BookBub** means that more readers will find our books! Reviews can be long or short - your honest opinion of the book. Shout-outs on any social media platforms also help!

Pegg Thomas lives on a hobby farm in Ossineke with Michael, her husband of *mumble* years. She is published in six Barbour historical romance collections and has indie-published six historical romance novels. Pegg won the 2019 FHL Readers' Choice Award for novellas, was a double-finalist for the 2019 ACFW Carol Award for novellas, and a finalist for the 2019 ACFW Editor of the Year. She was a finalist in the 2021 FHL Readers' Choice Award for novellas. Pegg won the 2022 Selah Award for historical romance and placed 2nd with her second entry. She was also a finalist for the 2023 FHL Selah Award. Pegg spent 3 ½ years as the managing editor of Smitten Historical Romance. When not writing or editing, Pegg can be found in her garden, her kitchen, or sitting at one of her spinning wheels creating yarn to turn into her signature wool shawls.

PeggThomas.com

Facebook

Goodreads

BookBub

Amazon

Newsletter signup